T0009503

FIND
HER
ALIVE

ALSO BY
D. S. BUTLER

Lost Child
Her Missing Daughter

DS Karen Hart Series:

Bring Them Home
Where Secrets Lie
Don't Turn Back
House of Lies
On Cold Ground
What She Said

DS Jack Mackinnon Crime Series:

Deadly Obsession
Deadly Motive
Deadly Revenge
Deadly Justice
Deadly Ritual
Deadly Payback
Deadly Game
Deadly Intent

East End Series:

Harper Grant Mystery Series:

FIND HER ALIVE

DETECTIVE KAREN HART SERIES

D.S. BUTLER

THOMAS & MERCER

Text copyright © 2023 by D. S. Butler
All rights reserved.

Published by Thomas & Mercer, Seattle

www.apub.com

Amazon, the Amazon logo, and Thomas & Mercer are trademarks of Amazon.com, Inc., or its affiliates.

ISBN-13: 9781542036276
ISBN-10: 1542036275

Cover design by @blacksheep-uk.com

Printed in the United States of America

For Chris & Matt

PROLOGUE

Will Horsley stood shoulder to shoulder with his new workmates, clutching a bottle of beer and feeling thoroughly miserable. It was Friday night, and they were all crammed into Imporium, the new bar in the centre of Lincoln.

He looked around, noticing the other customers, and couldn't help feeling out of place. Most of them were barely out of their teens. The lads wore jeans in various shades, slim-fit shirts and dark shoes. Trainers weren't allowed. There was slightly more variation in the young women's outfits, though most of them involved plunging necklines and incredibly short skirts. Not that Will was complaining about *that*. The eye candy was the one thing making the evening tolerable.

Will had been pressured into coming out by the rest of the lads in his new department. Most of them hadn't seemed that bad at work, especially the other fitters. They'd been down-to-earth, friendly. But now that they'd had a few drinks, their personalities had changed considerably. On the way to the bar, they'd whistled and called out to a couple of women walking ahead of them. And one of them had already been sick in the gutter outside a dress shop.

Will appreciated a laugh as much as the next bloke. He just didn't find this sort of evening fun. Especially not now that he was nearly thirty. He hadn't been out on a lads-only night for years. Now he remembered why.

'All right, *William*?' Todd asked with a massive grin. His face was flushed, eyes glassy. Another one who couldn't hold his drink. At first, Will hadn't known why Todd was insisting on calling him William. He'd corrected him multiple times, until he'd realised it wasn't a mistake. Todd was doing it on purpose to wind him up.

Though Will had known him for less than a week, he'd quickly worked out that Todd had a mean streak. He enjoyed lording it over the fitters. Todd had an admin role at the council and seemed to think this made him superior to the others. Will guessed it was because Todd had a white-collar job, even though it was common knowledge that a fitter's base salary was more than Todd got paid.

People like Todd were best ignored. But since Todd was currently staring at him, swaying slightly and pointing his beer bottle in Will's direction, ignoring him wasn't an option.

'Yeah, grand,' Will said, forcing a smile.

'Told you this place was banging on a Friday night, didn't I?' Todd had to shout to be heard over the noise.

'You did,' Will agreed, wondering how much longer he'd have to stay until he could sneak off without causing offence.

He looked around the room, keeping a smile fixed on his face and attempting to look like he was enjoying himself, and took in his surroundings.

Will's discomfort wasn't helped by the imp illustrations that were plastered all over the walls. Two of the beer taps were shaped like imps as well. The place had got its name – Imporium, rather than Emporium – due to the Lincoln Imp. Apparently, it was a big deal here.

He stared at one of the pictures now as though it were the most fascinating thing he'd ever seen. The imp seemed to be looking directly at him, grimacing, showing its oddly shaped teeth and taking delight in Will's discomfort. It had one leg crossed over the other, in a position that looked extremely uncomfortable. In his peripheral vision Will could sense Todd waving, trying to get his attention. But he studiously ignored the other man. Surely he'd get the message and just leave Will alone?

The music was loud and the chatter around the bar even louder. Will lifted the beer bottle to his lips and swallowed. After a moment or two, he dared to glance back and saw, to his relief, that Todd had turned his attention to one of the other fitters, prodding the chap firmly in the chest and shouting in his ear.

Will really wanted to go home, sprawl on his new sofa and watch mindless TV. But he didn't want to seem like an anti-social loner to his new workmates. This was only his first week, and first impressions were important. In his last job, nicknames had been doled out after just a few days. Will had been christened Mouse by his old team – not the worst nickname in the world. One of the other men had been known as Bubbalicious, because he liked to chew bubblegum. It was a ridiculous nickname for a fifty-year-old man, but no one had asked for Will's input.

Todd's nickname was Toddster, which was unimaginative. The first time Will had heard someone say it, he'd misheard and assumed the guy had called Todd 'Toaster'. At least that was a nickname that sounded like it might have an interesting story behind it.

It was probably too much to hope that Will wouldn't get lumbered with a nickname from the Lincoln team. He just hoped it was something a little more interesting than Mouse.

He needed to fit in here, make new friends, build a new life. He'd moved all his stuff to Lincoln and had said his goodbyes to family and friends. He didn't want to go back now with his tail between his legs, particularly as his ex-girlfriend had already moved in with her new fella.

Will sighed and stepped out of the way of a huge group of people who'd just entered the bar. He needed a fresh start. Besides, the Lincoln lads weren't too bad. Sure, they were a bit rowdy, but who wasn't on a Friday evening after a few drinks? He just needed to relax and get to know them and then everything would be fine. At least the money was good, and his new flat was nice enough. He had a studio near the Brayford Wharf with a great view of the water.

He heard a burst of laughter from the blokes around him and saw that the group had turned to gawp at something or someone. Will shuffled to the side to get a look. Todd was leering at a young woman with long, dark hair who was wearing a tight skirt and the sort of shoes that looked expensive. She was unsteady on her feet and staggered as she approached them.

Todd took the opportunity to grab her elbow, pretending to be concerned. 'Watch out, love,' he said. 'I think you've had a few too many.'

All the lads laughed, Todd the loudest of all. He then smirked at the woman when she tried to wrench her arm free.

'I'm fine,' she said. But the effort of trying to remove her arm from Todd's grasp made her stagger again, and Will thought she was going to fall. She knocked into a neighbouring table, jolting the drinks on it before righting herself.

Will glanced around the bar, wondering who the woman was with. Where were her friends? Her boyfriend? But there didn't seem to be anyone with her.

'All right, love,' Todd said. 'Calm down.'

She managed to take a step back from Todd, and then staggered forward before wobbling again and grabbing on to Will's shoulder.

'Sorry,' she muttered, brushing her hair back from her face. Her eyes were half closed as she looked up at Will.

She put her hand to her throat and swallowed. Her skin looked clammy, and Will wondered if she was about to throw up.

'Where are your friends?' he asked. 'Do you want me to get someone for you?'

She shook her head and looked around the bar as if surprised to see all the other people. 'I don't know. I think they went home,' she said. 'I think I've been . . .' The final words of her sentence were too quiet for Will to hear over the noise.

Had she said she thought she'd been drugged?

'Do you want me to call you a taxi?' Will asked. 'Or I can ask the staff to do it.' He nodded towards the bar and then realised that would be a tall ask. It would take ages to make it through the crush of people trying to order drinks.

She didn't reply, so Will lowered his head, made eye contact and gave her a smile, which he hoped was reassuring.

Suddenly her expression turned hard. She dropped her hand from his shoulder. 'Do I know you?' she snapped, her voice cold.

Will was suddenly aware that the lads around him were watching this encounter closely, with smirks on their faces. And then Todd let out a whoop. 'Will's found himself a girlfriend,' he shouted in a childish, singsong voice.

To his annoyance, Will could feel his cheeks burning.

'I'm just trying to help,' he said gruffly.

'Do I know you?' the girl repeated.

'No.'

'Then why are you talking to me?'

Will took a step back, smarting at the unfairness of the situation. He was just trying to help, and hadn't she put *her* hand on *his* shoulder? He studiously ignored the group of men he was with, turning his back on them.

'You don't know me. I'm just offering to call you a taxi. You seem really . . . drunk. I want to make sure you get home safely. That's all.'

She pulled a face, screwing up her nose, and tilted her head back so she could look down at him. 'I'm not drunk. I've only had a couple of drinks, and I don't need your help.'

She took another couple of wobbly steps, heading for the exit.

Will watched her for a few moments and then glanced back towards the bar. What should he do? The lads were all smirking at him now.

'Oh, did she turn you down, Will?' one of them squealed, which earned a burst of laughter from the rest of them.

'I was worried about her,' Will shouted back. 'You hear about bad stuff happening to women all the time. I just wanted to make sure she got home okay.' He shrugged, took a long swig from his bottle of beer and pretended not to care.

Not much reward for trying to be a good Samaritan, he thought. But despite her dismissal, he felt a niggle of guilt. It wasn't right to let her walk away. It really had sounded like she said she'd been drugged . . . What if something bad happened to her? And he'd let her walk off in that state . . .

He turned abruptly. 'Wait a minute!' he called after her and weaved through the small crowd of people separating them. 'You've got a lift home arranged, haven't you? You're not just going to walk around the city centre? You said you've only had a couple of drinks, but you're clearly wrecked. What if someone put something in your drink?'

She turned around and stared at him. Then she shouted, 'Leave me alone!'

He drew back as though she'd slapped him.

The people all around them turned to look, staring at him like he'd done something wrong. As though he were harassing her.

Embarrassed, he lifted his hands, pointing the bottle of beer at her. 'I was trying to help.'

'You were following me, you weirdo!' she spat.

'Have we got a problem here?' a bloke to Will's right asked.

Will turned and took him in. He was a well-built kid, had to be at least ten years Will's junior. Acne lined his jaw.

'No. There's no problem,' Will said, shaking his head and walking back to his group.

'You've really got to learn to take no for an answer, Will,' Todd said with a cackle.

Will put his beer bottle down on the nearest table. 'I was trying to make sure she was all right,' he said again.

'Yeah, yeah,' Todd said, smirking. 'You were just trying to see if you could get lucky more like. Think we'll start calling you Desperado!'

The others snorted and laughed in agreement, and Will fumed and tried to let their comments wash over him. 'Yeah, good one, Toddster. Will Desperado Horsley!' 'It suits him!' 'Desperado – it's perfect.'

Will felt the tension build between his shoulders. He'd had enough. There was no point trying to bond with this crowd; he didn't need the hassle. It was too loud in the bar. People were drunk. And now he had a nickname far worse than Mouse. He'd been humiliated when he'd been trying to do the right thing.

He stared at the floor angrily. He could still feel eyes on him, judging him. They all believed he was the type of bloke to hassle a woman in a bar.

He took a deep breath. He needed to forget about her. She'd likely be fine. He didn't know why he was so bothered.

He bit down on the inside of his cheek.

There'd been stories in the news recently about women being drugged, assaulted . . . murdered.

He turned back towards the exit and noticed that she'd gone. An uneasy feeling crept into his stomach.

All right, so she'd knocked him back, made him feel like a bit of an idiot, but maybe that was because she was scared. He should have at least told someone at the bar, tried to get her some help, but he'd been angry at her reaction so he'd shrugged her off.

Later, he'd regret that. Later, he'd see her picture in the news – her face bright, young, hopeful, vulnerable – and he'd realise he should have done something.

He should have persisted.

He should have helped.

CHAPTER ONE

Karen stretched her arms over her head and sighed. For the past hour, she'd been comfortably sprawled on the sofa after eating a huge Sunday roast that she and Mike had cooked together that afternoon.

Mike was currently elbow-deep in suds in the kitchen. They'd put the plates and cutlery in the dishwasher but Mike was scrubbing the pans. He'd told her he *liked* it. He'd said he found it relaxing. Karen had never heard anything so shocking. Imagine *liking* washing up! She'd teased him, told him she had an ironing pile if he needed to do any more relaxing later.

Karen reached for her wine glass and smiled at Sandy, Mike's spaniel and ex-police dog, who was curled up in the middle of the rug in front of the fireplace. It was her favourite spot even when the fire wasn't on, and it certainly didn't need to be on that evening. It was mid-July, and after a few days of intense sunshine the house had held on to the heat.

Karen felt her eyelids droop. All that food, plus a liberal helping of wine, had made her sleepy and content. Well, almost content. If she could just put work completely out of her mind, she'd be happy. The day would have been perfect if it hadn't been for those dark worries intruding. Even now, half asleep with a belly full of food and slightly tipsy, she couldn't get her latest investigation out of her head.

It had been a tough week. They'd finally got together enough evidence to make an arrest on a case they'd been working for months. A highly organised group of criminals had been targeting the elderly population in the villages surrounding Lincoln. After casing properties, they would identify vulnerable individuals and break into their houses late at night, often seriously injuring their victims if they resisted or tried to stop the burglary.

The CPS had agreed they had enough to go forward with a prosecution, and Karen had been there when they'd brought in the ringleader. She'd had the satisfaction of reading him his rights. Gratifying moments like that didn't come along as often as she'd like, but it had reminded her why she'd joined the police. When a case came together and resulted in a big arrest, taking dangerous criminals off the streets, it made her feel like she was still making a difference.

Suddenly, Sandy barked, and Karen, on the verge of dozing off, jerked upright, causing the small amount of wine left in her glass to slosh around. Sandy stood, tense, quivering.

Karen placed her glass on the coffee table. She got up, glancing through the living room window to look out on to the drive, but she couldn't see what had caused Sandy to bark. She glanced at her watch. It was nine thirty already.

She expected to hear the doorbell at any moment. Sandy was a very reliable early warning for people walking up the drive. But the bell didn't ring, and Karen's phone didn't make its usual shrill beep to inform her the security camera had detected movement.

She followed Sandy, who padded out into the hall and barked again.

Mike appeared in the doorway to the kitchen, frowning. 'What's all the noise?' he said, looking at the dog.

'Probably nothing,' Karen said. 'I didn't get an alert on my phone.' She peered through the window by the front door but only saw her own car parked next to Mike's.

'No, Sandy doesn't get it wrong. There'll be something out there,' Mike said.

Karen turned to look at him, concerned.

Mike gave her a bemused smile. 'I just meant she'll be reacting to something. Probably wildlife. There's nothing to worry about. I'll go and check if you like,' he said, drying his hands with a tea towel and looking around for his shoes.

'No, it's fine. I'll go,' Karen said. 'You're in the middle of washing up.' She slipped on her shoes, which were by the front door, and stepped outside.

Despite the warm evening, Karen shivered.

She could smell the honesty blooming close to the front door, mixed with the green scent of cut grass. She took a deep breath of soft night air and pulled the door shut behind her. She didn't want Sandy getting out and deciding to chase the wildlife. Not that that was typical Sandy behaviour. Karen had never known such an obe dient animal. Mike had trained her himself; he had once worked with police dogs, and it was essential the dogs obeyed commands and were under control at all times.

Stepping off the driveway on to the small lawn in her front garden, she peered around. There were plenty of shrubs and small trees casting shadows, making good hiding places, but she didn't see anything unexpected. Would she be this concerned if they hadn't just arrested the head of a gang of vicious criminals?

She made a slow loop of the front garden. By the road, a bat swooped manically around the streetlight, chasing moths drawn to the brightness. After Sandy's reaction, Karen had expected to see *something*, maybe a fox snuffling by the bins. She rubbed her arms and shivered again as she walked towards the beech hedge, trying and failing to stop thinking about work. Arresting those responsible for the OAP break-ins had been a real coup for the team. DCI Churchill was still on cloud nine and couldn't stop smiling. And the superintendent had even come downstairs to congratulate them and thank them all for their hard work.

But the case had shaken Karen. When the top man had been in cuffs, being led towards a marked police car, he'd stopped, leaned in close and said, 'You don't know who you're messing with.' He'd growled the words, his breath sour against her face. 'I have friends in high places.'

Karen had known it was an empty threat. She'd heard plenty of them in her time, but recent events had made her vulnerable and his words had struck deep, sending her mind into a spiral of what-ifs, worrying how any fallout might affect those close to her.

But she had stood her ground as DC Rick Cooper yanked him back.

'Is that a threat?' she'd said coolly. 'Bigger men than you have tried.'

'Keep your mouth shut,' Rick said, pulling him along.

'No, keep him talking. We might get him on a few more charges if we're lucky.' Karen had forced a smile.

'You little—' he'd snarled, but Rick had pushed him against the side of the car, winding him and stealing the rest of his words.

But after he'd been deposited into the back seat of the marked car and driven away, Karen hadn't been able to stop her hands trembling. She might have played it cool, but she didn't feel calm, at all. Her mind kept returning to what had happened to Josh and Tilly. Her husband and daughter had been killed after being run off the road by a criminal who'd been intending to target Karen. Her job was the reason they'd died.

She could handle the threats when they were directed at her personally. It was part of her role as a police officer. But when it came to her family, any risk was unacceptable. And now that Mike was practically living with her, she worried about him too. Could she be putting him in danger by dismissing this threat?

Their relationship had developed into something she cherished. They'd met during one of Karen's cases and hadn't clicked immediately. But now she loved spending time with him, and they had a closeness she hadn't shared with anyone since Josh had died. She was, without a doubt, happier than she'd been for years, and yet . . . Could she ever forgive herself if something happened to him?

There was a movement beside the hedge. Karen held her breath as the leaves rustled.

From the darkness, a cat – pale orange, slim and elegant – emerged. It didn't run but moved slowly, staring at Karen with a haughty expression.

She smiled. 'Oh, so you're the cause of the ruckus tonight, are you? Good job I didn't bring Sandy out here. If I had, I don't think you'd be moving so slowly.' The cat meowed, coming nearer to Karen and winding itself around her legs.

Karen reached down to stroke it. 'You know, you should be careful this close to the main road. Where do you live?' she asked softly as it rubbed its cheek against her hand.

The cat soon got tired of being fussed over and stretched before walking back through the hedge.

She turned back to the house and saw Mike standing in the living room window, his face etched with concern as he watched her. The light around him was bright and warm, and for a moment she thought her life really would be perfect if she didn't have all this worry. Was it worth it? Maybe she should get a job away from all the stress and danger.

She could have a fresh start with Mike. Though he still had a flat in the city centre, he spent most of his free time with Karen now, living in her house. They'd fallen into a routine that suited them both, although Karen's job rudely interrupted their domestic bliss at times.

Maybe it *was* time to move on. She loved her job and her team. A team didn't work together for so long without forming a tight bond; they were like a second family to her. But could she really cope with the constant worry that something might happen to the people she loved for a second time?

She smiled at Mike, lifted a hand in acknowledgement and then headed back inside.

'Everything okay?' he asked as she closed the door. 'I was just about to come out.'

'Just a cat,' Karen said. 'Quite a sweet little thing.'

'Don't let Sandy hear you say that,' Mike said. 'She gets jealous.'

Karen glanced at Sandy, who was sniffing her legs with suspicion. The spaniel looked up with such a comical expression, Karen couldn't help laughing. 'It's all right. I still love you best.'

She felt her tension melt away as she ruffled the dog's fur.

CHAPTER TWO

Karen had spent Monday morning going through the paperwork with a fine-tooth comb. They couldn't afford to put a foot wrong. Not if they wanted convictions.

At lunchtime, Karen's stomach was grumbling, protesting the fact she'd skipped breakfast. She had pushed back from her desk, intending to go to the canteen and grab a sandwich, when her mobile rang. She glanced at the screen. It was Erica Bright.

She hesitated before answering. Erica was a woman Karen had met at her counselling group. They'd visited a local coffee shop together a few times after the sessions. Although coffee was provided in the counselling room, it was weak and flavourless, and rather than satisfy, it seemed to only intensify Karen's craving for good, strong coffee. They'd exchanged numbers a couple of weeks ago, but this was the first time Erica had called.

She answered. 'Hello, Erica. How are you?'

'I'm sorry to disturb you, Karen. I know you're probably at work.'

'Yes, I am, but I was just about to take a break for lunch. I'm fine to talk.'

'Right.' Erica paused, then continued. 'If you're about to have lunch, why don't you come to mine and have lunch here? I really wanted to talk to you about something.' Erica sounded nervous, and that was unlike her.

Although the counselling group were an eclectic bunch, Erica seemed as though she didn't quite fit in with the rest of them. She was always impeccably groomed, stylish, confident. She looked like the last person who'd need counselling. But Erica was the perfect example of why you couldn't always rely on first impressions.

Her mother had died six months ago, and shortly after that, her husband had, rather heartlessly in Karen's opinion, announced he was having an affair with his secretary and demanded a divorce. The combination of the two traumatic events had caused Erica to spiral into a deep depression, unable to leave her apartment for weeks. She was making excellent progress in working through her problems, and was now back at work. She had an important job – registrar at the local hospital. Her voice was normally calm, soft and slow, but today she was talking quickly, sounding brittle and nervous.

Something was definitely wrong.

Karen thought through her options. A sandwich at her desk or lunch at Erica's? She couldn't afford much time away from her desk today, but it didn't sound like Erica wanted to chat about whatever was bothering her over the phone.

She stood up, grabbing her bag. 'I'll head over to you now. Can you text me your address?'

'Oh, thank you. Yes, of course, I'll send it,' Erica said with a rush of relief.

'What did you need to talk about?' Karen asked.

'Oh, I'd prefer to discuss it in person if that's all right?'

'Of course, no problem. I'll see you soon.' Karen hung up and then headed over to Sophie's desk.

Sophie was engrossed in a replay of CCTV footage. Over the past two weeks, there had been an increased number of women having their drinks spiked in bars. Sadly, it wasn't an uncommon occurrence, and Karen suspected it was vastly underreported. The sudden jump in cases was extremely concerning, especially as the women targeted told very similar stories about how they'd been assaulted.

Sophie was on CCTV surveillance, assisting DCI Simpson, who was head of the investigation known as Operation Starling. Various teams were pooling resources, and undercover officers had been deployed to bars around the city centre, but so far the investigation hadn't yielded results.

Sophie was working strategically. She was concentrating on two areas: a club where the two prior incidents had occurred, and a bar in the city centre called Imporium. There had been recent talk on social media implicating Imporium, but the staff denied any incidents and no one had officially reported women being targeted there. Sophie was hoping she might spot something on the CCTV that would give them more to go on.

'Sophie?'

Sophie paused the playback and rubbed her eyes. 'Are you going to the canteen? I think I'll come, too. I'm getting square eyes.'

'Actually, I need to go out for lunch today. I'll be back in about an hour. If anybody needs me, you can reach me on my mobile.'

'Meeting Mike?' Sophie grinned.

'No, just a friend. She's making me lunch.'

'Oh, lucky you,' Sophie said. 'The highlight of my day is going to be choosing between a ham or cheese filling for my sandwich.'

Erica's flat was not far from the Cathedral Quarter. It was a wide block set in lush, green, well-maintained grounds, and every flat had a large balcony. The building was only four storeys tall, and

Karen guessed the flats must have been built in the sixties when land wasn't at so much of a premium. The new, modern flats springing up around Lincoln were tiny.

Erica buzzed her in, and when Karen walked into the flat she was greeted by the delicious smell and sizzling sound of chicken frying.

Erica walked ahead of her into the open-plan space. She gestured to the kitchen. 'It's just chicken and salad. I hope that's okay.'

'Sounds great,' Karen said.

'You can put your stuff there,' Erica said, pointing at a bright turquoise armchair.

Karen put her bag down and looked around. Erica's home was just as Karen had expected – stylish and modern. It was the sort of interior that would be photographed for a magazine. The walls were white, the floor pale wood, but the splashes of colour from the wall art, houseplants and furniture made it feel unique and fresh.

Huge windows flooded the room with light. The room was elegant and beautiful, and suited Erica perfectly.

'You have a gorgeous home,' Karen said.

'Thank you,' Erica said as she removed the pan from the heat.

Even wearing an apron, Erica looked stylish. She wore dark jeans, an ivory jumper and gold earrings. She had her black hair cut short, which suited her. Karen caught a glance of her own reflection and frowned at her hair, which she thought could do with a trim.

Erica scooped the chicken out of the pan, put it on plates and handed them to Karen. 'Can you take them over to the table?'

The table was next to a window with a view over the grounds. Karen put the plates on the blue placemats. A large wooden bowl filled with salad sat in the centre of the table. Even the forks looked expensive. Karen thought of her own mismatched cutlery drawer at home.

Erica came in carrying a jug of orange juice and a basket of bread rolls.

'Thanks for coming,' she said, taking a seat and reaching for a roll.

Karen did the same, and after breaking the roll in half, she realised they were fresh from the oven and smelled delicious. 'Thanks for making me lunch. This certainly beats a sandwich from the canteen.' As she spoke, a tabby cat appeared in the hallway. 'I didn't know you had a cat.'

'Well, actually, that's part of what I wanted to talk to you about,' Erica said.

'I'm intrigued.'

But rather than launch into what was bothering her, Erica purposely changed the subject. 'So, how have things been with you?'

'Oh, not too bad. Work is keeping me busy.'

'Mike?'

'Yeah, he's great.'

'And how are you finding the anxiety?'

Karen stopped chewing and swallowed a mouthful of bread that now felt like a stone as it travelled down to her stomach.

'Not good?' Erica said, reading Karen's expression with a sympathetic smile.

It felt odd talking like this outside the counselling room. That room was a safe space, somewhere Karen could open up. But here, in Erica's fresh, stylish apartment – far away from the smell of stale coffee, the sound of creaking pipes and the baking-hot radiators that always seemed to be on in the counselling room, even in the middle of summer – it was harder to confide in Erica.

'I'm struggling a bit, to be honest,' Karen said, stabbing a piece of chicken with her fork. 'Sometimes my cases remind me how vulnerable my family are because of my job.'

'Mike especially?'

'Yes, because he practically lives with me now, so that makes him a target. But also my parents, my sister and her little girl.' Karen stared down at her plate. 'I've been thinking about giving it all up.'

She glanced at Erica, who looked almost as surprised as Karen felt. She hadn't intended to admit that. She'd just blurted it out.

'You're thinking of leaving the police?'

'Oh, I don't know. Sometimes I think a life without stress would be nice.'

'I know what it's like to have a stressful career. But my job doesn't tend to put me in the line of fire, unless you count A&E on a Friday night.' Erica smiled. 'So, have you thought what you might like to do instead?'

'No, not yet. I've been thinking about it, but I'd find it hard to leave. I love my job and the people I work with.' Karen shrugged. 'I keep hoping I'll find a way to deal with it, a way to make sure everyone is safe and keep my job as well. The best of both worlds.'

'Couldn't you make a sideways move? Perhaps carry on working for the police in a less public-facing role?'

'Sitting behind a desk, you mean?' Karen asked.

Erica shrugged. 'It might give you everything you need.'

'It's worth thinking about,' Karen admitted, although the thought of being buried under mounds of paperwork while her colleagues went out and did the real police work didn't sound particularly appealing.

The tabby cat, seemingly annoyed at being ignored, jumped on to the chair beside Erica. With a tut, she shooed him off. 'You're not allowed up here when we're eating. You know that.'

'So, when did you get the cat?' Karen asked.

Erica sighed as the cat completely ignored her, jumped back on to the chair and began scratching at its collar.

20

When Erica didn't answer, Karen added, 'It doesn't seem to like its collar much.'

It was bright red with a silver bell.

Erica frowned. 'No, he doesn't. Because he's a serial killer and doesn't like to forewarn his victims.' She chuckled. 'He's an accomplished hunter. This way he can stalk birds but they can hear him coming.'

'What's his name?'

'Tommy,' Erica said.

'And he's not yours?'

Erica put her knife and fork together and shook her head. 'No, he belongs to my friend. Phoebe. Phoebe Woodrow. We were at university together and both moved to Lincoln after we graduated. We haven't seen that much of each other recently, but she called me, asking me to look after her cat overnight. She was going out and wouldn't be back until late, and as Tommy had recently had an operation she didn't want to leave him alone.' Erica shrugged. 'She gave me some of his special food. But she didn't come on Saturday to pick him up. I've tried to call, but I can't get hold of her. It's like she's disappeared off the face of the earth.'

'Disappeared?' Karen repeated.

'Yes, I'm really worried.'

Karen leaned back in her chair. 'Don't take this the wrong way, Erica, but if you're worried, why didn't you tell me over the phone? Why wait until we'd finished lunch?'

Erica rested her elbows on the table and put her face in her hands. 'Because I sound neurotic.'

'It's not neurotic to worry about a friend who's missing.'

Erica looked up. 'But that's just it. According to everyone else, she isn't missing.'

'Everyone else?' Karen frowned. 'You've lost me.'

21

'I reported her missing. Called the police and they took me seriously, or at least they did until they spoke to her family. Her family told the officer that Phoebe wasn't missing. They made it sound like I was making the whole thing up for attention. I really didn't want to get you involved but . . . I really am worried about her, Karen.'

'When was the last time you saw her?'

'Friday morning when she dropped Tommy off. She said she'd be back on Saturday morning to pick him up.'

'And you haven't heard from her since Friday?'

'No.'

'Have you spoken to her family and friends?'

'No, I don't have contact details for them.'

'What can you tell me about Phoebe? Does she have a partner? Has she been upset about anything recently?'

'I don't think she has a boyfriend now. She split up with her long-term partner a few months ago.'

'Was it a bad break-up?'

'I think it was mostly amicable. They just grew apart.'

Karen nodded. 'Okay. What else can you tell me about her?'

'She's doing well career-wise. She's always been a high-flyer, very ambitious. In fact, that was why she was going out on Friday night – to celebrate a new business deal she'd landed.'

Erica poured a glass of orange juice, and Karen noticed her hands were shaking. 'I know this probably sounds awful, but I need to be honest. Phoebe isn't the most considerate person on the planet. I wouldn't have been surprised if Phoebe had asked me to keep the cat for a bit longer so she could keep partying. She's always been a bit like that.

'She doesn't always take the time to think through how other people will feel. When we stayed in halls in our first year at uni, she met a man in a bar and I didn't hear from her for a week. She's

22

always been that way, but the thing is, this time feels different. She's not even answering her mobile, and that's not normal. She's never without her phone. She's not updated her social media, and she's usually always on Instagram. There's something about this situation that worries me.' Erica used her phone to access one of Phoebe's social media accounts. The profile image showed a young woman with dark hair styled in a chin-length bob. She was attractive, and was smiling confidently in the picture.

'What happened when you reported her missing? Who did you speak to?'

'PC Naylor. I called on Saturday evening, and he called back. He said he would file a report. At first, I thought he was taking me seriously. But later he called back to say he'd spoken with Phoebe's family and, according to them, she was absolutely fine and they'd seen her that very day.' Erica shrugged. 'Then I started to think I was overreacting. Maybe I was thinking the worst, when she'd just been having a good time and stayed away, expecting me to take care of Tommy. I'd just feel terrible if something *had* happened to her and I hadn't tried to report it.'

'Do you have her address?' Karen asked.

'I don't. I think she might have moved recently. Things are going so well for her at work, she's bought a property.'

Karen nodded, thinking things through. She understood why Erica was feeling uneasy. It could be that Phoebe was a little self-centred and hadn't bothered to tell Erica about her change of plans. But the fact that she hadn't been answering the phone was odd. Her family telling PC Naylor that Phoebe wasn't missing also struck Karen as unusual. Why would she ignore Erica in particular? Had Phoebe's family really seen her, or were they covering up her disappearance?

If it was a cover-up, what were they hiding? Had something happened to Phoebe? Were the family trying to protect someone?

'How old is Phoebe?' Karen asked.

'Same age as me, twenty-eight,' Erica said.

'Still quite young. Perhaps she decided you could be relied on to look after Tommy while she enjoyed herself?'

Erica took a deep breath. 'I hope that's all it is.'

'What else can you tell me about her?'

'She studied biochemistry at Nottingham when I was doing medicine. We took some classes together and used to hang out a lot. She was fun, always lively, always up for a good time. But as I said, she's also very ambitious. She works hard. After we graduated, she did a master's at Lincoln. I'm not sure what subject, but after that she set up her own company with a fellow graduate, a guy called Cary. The company has something to do with medical diagnostics. She was always vague on the details, but they'd designed a type of scanner that could operate on a minimal budget. Pretty much the Holy Grail of medicine. Now a major company is interesting in buying them out.'

'So Phoebe's about to come into a lot of money?'

'Yes, I think so.'

'Have you met Cary? Have you got his contact details? As it's Monday, perhaps she's called into work.'

'I haven't met him. I don't even know his last name. And I can't remember the name of their company.' Erica shook her head. 'I've been wracking my brain, trying to remember it.'

The cat tiptoed on to Erica's lap and curled up, purring contentedly. 'Do you think I'm being paranoid, Karen?'

'No, I don't. I think you're being a good friend. From what you've said, it sounds possible that she's just carried on celebrating for a couple of days and figured that you'd continue looking after the cat. If her family have seen her, that's reassuring.'

Erica nodded slowly. 'Yes, I suppose.' She looked down at the tabby cat. 'On Friday, she texted me three times to ask how Tommy was doing, checking he was eating and was settled. But since then, I've heard nothing. Phoebe may not be the most considerate person, but she absolutely adores this cat. He used to belong to her grandmother, who had to move into a care home a year ago. I don't think she would dump him like this. I've just got a feeling something bad has happened.'

Karen nodded. As a police officer, she was used to dealing in facts and ruling out the most obvious explanations first. But she couldn't deny that on occasions a feeling had given her a lead she wouldn't have found with logic and facts. Call it intuition, a police officer's gut, whatever you wanted, but Karen had learned only a fool would ignore it.

After leaving Erica's, Karen headed back to Nettleham. She turned on the radio as a presenter reeled through the news and weather, but she wasn't listening. She was trying to work out a way to investigate Phoebe Woodrow while keeping DCI Churchill onside.

She'd be able to take a quick look at the report as soon as she got back to the station, and could try to gauge if there was anything suspicious going on.

She decided not to mention it to DCI Churchill immediately, not until she knew more. He wouldn't be happy about her taking time away from her other cases. He was results-oriented, and liked the superintendent to see those results. He didn't like his officers finding extra work if they wouldn't get credit for it.

No, he certainly wouldn't be keen on Karen interfering, especially if the missing person's report had already been dismissed by another officer.

She'd keep it to herself for now, and quietly investigate it for Erica. She'd need to tread carefully. It was a delicate situation. No police officer liked a colleague wading through their work. It implied they couldn't be trusted to do their job properly. So, she'd need to be diplomatic.

There was a good chance it would only take a few minutes of her time. All Karen needed to do was check PC Naylor had seen Phoebe Woodrow and spoken to her. If he had, she'd be able to reassure Erica nothing nefarious was going on.

As she pulled into Nettleham station, she made up her mind. It really wouldn't take that long to glance through the report, and it would set Erica's mind at rest. She could work late tonight to make up for her long lunch. What Churchill didn't know wouldn't hurt him.

CHAPTER THREE

Karen entered the open-plan office, intending to go directly to her computer and look up the report on Phoebe Woodrow, but Sophie had other ideas.

'Perfect timing, Sarge. We're off to Imporium.'

Karen stopped walking. 'We are?'

'Yes, if that's okay with you. We've had an email, reporting the possible drugging of a woman at Imporium on Friday night. Not much to go on. The email was brief, but perhaps we'll get more from the staff.'

'Do we know who sent the email?' Karen asked.

'Not yet. Harinder's working on it.'

'Does Churchill know about this? We aren't the ones leading the investigation. We're only supposed to be doing auxiliary work to help out, aren't we?'

Sophie nodded. 'Yes, but . . .' She looked around the office to make sure no one was listening. 'You didn't hear it from me, but apparently the super's been praising Churchill for being such a good team player – lending out his staff, but still meeting his own targets.' She lowered her voice. 'You know he's a sucker for praise.'

'So he's volunteered us for more work?'

Sophie shrugged. 'I can't say I mind. Visiting Imporium is going to be more interesting than viewing endless CCTV footage. Ready to go?'

Karen looked towards her computer. She'd have to follow up on Phoebe Woodrow later. 'Yes. Let's go.'

◆ ◆ ◆

Karen and Sophie left the car in the car park near the library and walked along Free School Lane to St Swithin's Square.

When they reached Saltergate, Sophie paused and nodded to a narrow alley between the Waterside Centre and the old Liberal Club. Despite the sunshine, it was completely in the shade. There was no sign to indicate a street name.

Halfway along the alley was a square two-storey building with sixties-style architecture.

'That's Imporium?' Karen queried.

Sophie nodded. 'Yes. Looks ugly, doesn't it?'

'Have you been here before?' Karen asked.

'No, it's only been open for six months. It used to be a snooker hall before that.'

Karen was surprised she hadn't noticed it before, but it was tucked out of the way, and she did vaguely remember the old snooker hall.

'Are the staff expecting us?'

'Yes, although the manager, Dom Whitehead, didn't sound too enthusiastic on the phone.'

'Right,' Karen said, looking up as they reached the front of the building. The large windows were tinted, which made it hard to see inside. The word 'Imporium' was scrawled above the black door in bright pink lettering, with a cartoon-style imp sitting on top of the I.

Sophie pushed open the door and they walked into a large seating area. Booths lined the side walls and smaller tables were scattered between them, but the central area was free so people could easily make their way to and from the bar, which was at the back of the large room.

The seats were covered with a black faux-leather, and the tables were hot pink. Drinks menus decorated with imps sat in the centres of the tables. Large chandeliers hung from the ceiling, and there were even more imps in the artwork hung on the walls.

A man called out, 'Ladies! Over here!'

They both turned to see a tall, slim man with slicked-back blond hair approaching them. He wore a tight white shirt with the top button done up, but no tie. Even before he reached them, Karen could smell his aftershave.

His wide mouth stretched in a smile that didn't quite reach his eyes. 'Dom Whitehead at your service,' he said, giving a small bow. His gaze lingered on Sophie, looking her up and down. Sophie folded her arms over her chest.

Smarmy was Karen's first impression.

He held out his hand to shake theirs in turn.

'We're here about—' Sophie began.

'Oh, I know. It's awful. Those poor women being drugged,' he said, cutting her off. 'You must be DC Jones. I spoke to you on the phone, right?'

Sophie nodded and handed him her card. 'Yes, that's right. And this is DS Hart.'

Dom's eyes flickered over to Karen and then back to Sophie. 'Of course, I'll help as much as I can, but fortunately we've had no problems here at Imporium.'

'Glad to hear it,' Karen said, 'but there's been some chatter on social media.'

Dom waved a hand dismissively. 'Rubbish. I'd know if any-thing had happened at *my* bar. Tell you what, why don't you come and sit over here?' He gestured to a booth.

A young woman with pink hair was wiping the table. She lifted her head and stared at them. She wore heavy eyeliner and had a velvet choker around her neck. A swirling pattern of tattoos ran up her right arm. She didn't smile or say anything, and when they approached the booth, she scooped up her cloth, turned her back and walked off.

'That's Cassidy,' Dom said. 'Friendly, isn't she?' He grinned, as though sharing a joke with friends. 'Cassidy, be a love. Make us all a coffee, would you?' he called.

Cassidy turned and glared at him with such intensity Karen half expected to see steam rising from her ears. She was impressed with the young woman's self-control. It couldn't be easy, working for a lecherous creep. Cassidy didn't reply but stomped behind the bar and stopped beside a large chrome coffee machine.

'I take it you could do with an afternoon pick-me-up?' He lifted his eyebrows. 'I assumed coffee would be your drink of choice because you're on duty.' He winked.

'Coffee will be great, thanks,' Karen said.

Sophie rummaged in her bag and pulled out a wedge of A5-sized leaflets. 'I hoped you could put some of these up and keep them by the bar,' she said. 'We want women to be aware.'

Dom shuffled up close to Sophie. Too close.

'You don't need to sit in her lap to look at the leaflet,' Karen snapped.

Dom huffed. 'Touchy,' he said as he moved back to his original spot. Then he picked up a leaflet and stared at it before shaking his head. 'Oh, you're kidding. I can't put this up, it'll scare people away. Look, I told you, we've not had any problems with that sort of thing here.'

'We're asking all the bars to put them up. You're not being sin-gled out. We're trying to make people aware that this is happening in Lincoln. It's about keeping women safe,' Sophie said, nudging the leaflets towards him. 'At least put a couple up.'

'All right. I'll do it for you, darling. Never could say no to a pretty face.' He put the leaflet back on the pile then pushed them to the side of the table.

Cassidy came over with a tray, put it down on the table with a thump and then handed them all black coffees.

'What, no milk?' Dom muttered to her retreating back.

'I don't mind my coffee black,' Karen said.

'Same,' Sophie quickly added.

There was another member of staff at the bar now, a young lad. He wore a tight black T-shirt and black jeans. He had long wavy hair that fell forward over one eye, and he kept pushing it back from his forehead.

Karen took a sip of her coffee. 'We've been told a woman may have been drugged here on Friday night.'

After dropping the bombshell, she waited for Dom's response.

'What? No way,' he spluttered. 'I was here Friday. Nothing like that happened.'

'How can you be so sure?'

'Because I'd have noticed.'

'Would you? Would you have noticed a woman getting helped out of the bar? Maybe you just thought she'd had too much to drink?' Sophie asked.

Dom stared at her. 'Look, all this is bloody horrible, and there are some nasty folks out there. I'm not denying it happens. But there was no one who even seemed that drunk on Friday.'

'How many people were here on Friday night?' Karen asked.

'Hard to say.'

'Your best guess?'

'Well, fire regs mean we're allowed one hundred and fifty.'

Karen waited for him to give a proper answer.

He exhaled, puffing out his cheeks. 'I'd say we had close to one hundred people Friday night, give or take a few.'

'And you were able to watch all of them closely?'

'Well, no, of course not, but if something had . . .' He trailed off, hesitating, then asked, 'What happened to her?'

'We don't know. The report is unsubstantiated. Do you have security cameras inside?'

He nodded. 'I suppose you want a copy of the footage?'

'Yes, please.'

He shifted across the seat to get out of the booth.

'We'd like to talk to the rest of your staff as well,' Karen said as he stood up.

'They won't tell you anything more than I have,' Dom said, looking affronted.

'Maybe not, but we'd like a word with them anyway.'

'Suit yourself, but only Cassidy and Tom are working this afternoon,' Dom said with a shrug.

He picked up his coffee and called to the young man behind the bar, 'Tom, come and have a word with these ladies, would you? Remember, we'll get busy soon, so don't take too long.' He sat in the next booth along and started scrolling on his mobile, clearly intending to listen in.

'It won't take long,' Karen said as Tom slid into the booth. 'You know why we're here?'

'Yeah, some weird guy is spiking drinks,' he said.

'That's right. Is there anything you can tell us?'

'Like what?'

'Have you seen anything suspicious? Noticed anyone acting unusually?'

He shook his head. 'No.'

'When do you normally work?'

'Up to five evenings a week – usually weekends and then a few days in the week as well,' he said. 'Things are a bit tight money-wise. I'm a student at the university.'

'Right. Does it get busy here?'

'It does on weekends. On weeknights we get the after-work crowd. Then it gets quiet until around eight o'clock. Then we get a few more in, students mainly, but it's not usually busy in the week.'

Sophie took down Tom's contact details, and Karen asked a few more general questions then pushed the pile of the leaflets towards him.

Dom butted in. 'Look, I've already told you I'll keep some behind the bar, but we don't need to shove them in people's faces. We'll scare them away. They're our customers. We can't run a bar without customers. And it's not fair. We haven't had any trouble here at Imporium despite your *unsubstantiated report.*'

'We need women to be on their guard,' Sophie said.

'What we *need* is for men not to go around drugging people. Why is it always women who have to change their behaviour?' Cassidy snapped, glaring at them all.

Karen hadn't noticed that she'd come back to clean the other tables. Without waiting for a response, Cassidy stormed off.

Dom rolled his eyes. 'Sorry about that. She's new. Still in training.'

'She's not wrong though, is she?' Karen said.

Dom shrugged. 'Are we finished now?'

'No, I'd like a chat with Cassidy,' Karen said.

'Do you have to?' Dom asked.

'Yes.'

He threw his hands up in the air. 'Fine.'

Karen and Sophie took their coffee cups back to the bar, where Cassidy was unloading the dishwasher. Dom followed them.

Cassidy didn't pause when she saw them but started to put the clean glasses on a shelf.

'Can you please be careful, Cassidy? The glasses are *fragile*,' Dom said.

Cassidy ignored him and continued putting the glasses down heavily.

'Can we have a word?' Karen asked.

Cassidy shrugged. 'It's a free country.'

'Have you noticed any trouble while you've been working here? Anything or anyone strike you as suspicious?'

Cassidy paused and looked at Karen through narrowed eyes. 'That's just it though, isn't it? You can't tell. Whoever's doing this could be any one of the blokes that come in here.'

'Could be a woman even?' Dom piped up.

Cassidy gave him a scathing look.

'I thought you might have noticed someone here on their own, perhaps standing back from the crowd, watching.'

'It's not always the awkward loner though, is it?' Cassidy said. 'It can be the boy next door, the popular kid at uni, the successful businessman.' She tucked her pink hair behind her ears, revealing a line of silver earrings. 'Then, when something happens, it's always the woman's behaviour everyone focuses on. People asking why she was out so late, why she was on her own, why did she dress like that? Instead of asking why some men are so sick they want to drug women and hurt them.'

'I know it's not fair,' Karen agreed.

'But nothing ever changes,' Cassidy said, slapping her hand on the bar. 'Nothing. The only thing that's different is women altering the way they live their lives. They have to go to the bathroom in pairs. They can't walk home on their own. It's just wrong.' She pointed at the leaflets in Sophie's hands. 'We're always warning the women. Why don't you warn the men?'

Sophie glanced down at her leaflets, crestfallen. 'It's about trying to keep women safe.'

'But why should we put the responsibility on to women? Why don't you hand out leaflets telling men not to drug or attack women?' Cassidy folded her arms and stared angrily at Sophie.

'Because that wouldn't help,' Karen said. 'Most men don't want to hurt women, but the ones that do aren't going to stop just because a leaflet tells them to.'

'So you're saying men just can't control themselves?' Cassidy said, shaking her head. 'Hardly fair, is it?'

'You're right. It isn't. It's not fair that women worry about their safety more than men, but right now it's important to highlight the risk and try to catch whoever is doing this.'

'Yes,' Sophie said, nodding. 'Forewarned is forearmed.'

Cassidy rolled her eyes and turned back to the glasses.

'Look, do me a favour. Keep an eye out when you're working.' Karen pushed her contact card over the bar towards Cassidy. 'You can call me, even if it's late, okay?'

Cassidy stared at the card before picking it up and sticking it in the back pocket of her trousers. 'All right,' she said.

'You can't let it get to you like this, Cassidy,' Dom said, leaning on the bar. 'It's not all men, you know. It's just a few bad apples.'

'Even one bad apple is too many,' Karen snapped, and then clenched her teeth. Great. Now she was talking in clichéd phrases like Dom.

'Whoa, don't bite my head off. I was just *saying*.'

'Then don't dismiss her,' Karen said. 'Cassidy has good reason to be troubled by this. We should all be concerned.' She glanced up at the camera behind the bar. 'Did you make a copy of the security footage?'

Dom nodded. 'Yeah. From the one up there.' He pointed to the camera. 'And the one at the front door. I've sent the access link to the email on your card. You should be able to view it online or download it.'

'All right. Thanks for your time,' Karen said.

'He made my skin crawl,' Sophie said as they left the bar. She stuffed the rest of the leaflets in her bag. 'Cassidy had a good point. I don't know why I bothered with these.'

'You bothered because you're trying to help.'

'But am I making a difference?'

'Of course you are,' Karen said.

'But she's right, isn't she? We do just accept that it happens and then try to pick up the pieces afterwards.' Sophie put her hands in her pockets and shook her head. 'There's some sicko stalking the bars in Lincoln, and women who want to go out and enjoy themselves have to worry that they might be drugged, raped or murdered by the end of the evening.' She looked at Karen and sighed. 'Sometimes this job is really depressing.'

CHAPTER FOUR

As they left the shaded alleyway and stepped out into the bright sunshine on Saltergate, Karen squinted, wishing she'd remembered to bring her sunglasses.

Sophie's mobile rang, and she rooted around in her bag to find it.

'It's Harinder,' she said to Karen before answering the call. She listened for a moment and then said, 'That's fantastic. Thank you. We're in the city centre, so we can speak to him now. Can you send me the details?'

When Sophie finished the call, Karen asked, 'Harinder has managed to track down our anonymous tipster?'

Harinder headed up the tech team at Nettlcham. He was talented and intelligent, and Karen admired his abilities. There had been many occasions when his work had led to breakthroughs on cases. He and Sophie had been dating for a few months now, and Karen thought they made a good match.

Sophie nodded. 'Yes. He's sending across details for the man who sent the email.'

They'd just entered the pedestrian zone and were passing the Stonebow Centre when Harinder's text arrived.

'Will Horsley, twenty-eight. He works for the County Council. Newland office.' She put her phone back in her bag. 'That's not far from here. Shall we leave the car where it is and walk?'

Karen agreed, and they crossed on to the High Street and walked by the Stonebow. People passed beneath the arches, scurrying along, heads down, more likely to be looking at their phones than at the historic architecture. A group of tourists were paying closer attention, listening to a guide describe the history of the Guildhall.

Karen glanced at the carvings – the Virgin Mary, patron saint of Lincoln, on one side of the arch, and the Angel Gabriel on the other. The famous Lincoln structure was surrounded by modern shops. The shiny glass front of an Ann Summers shop on Karen's left was quite a contrast to the elegant arches to her right.

Karen was grateful to be back in the shade as they passed into Guildhall Street. There were people sitting outside small cafés enjoying the warm weather.

When they reached Newland, the sound of traffic grew louder. Vehicles were the priority here, and the lights seemed to take forever to change.

Sophie rolled her eyes and jabbed the button beside the pedestrian crossing again. 'Must be something wrong with it.'

Eventually the lights changed. The cars stopped and they could cross the road.

The shops grew fewer and far between. The buildings here were mostly offices, with the occasional optician or convenience store. Karen glanced in the window of All Smiles, her dentist, as they passed, which reminded her that it was almost time for another check-up. Next door to the dental surgery was a fantastic little Greek deli, which along with delicious traditional olives, tapenade and stuffed vine leaves, sold the most fabulous pain au chocolat

Karen had ever eaten, and she liked to consider herself a connoisseur of pastries.

The County Council headquarters was a substantial red-brick building with large, rectangular sash windows that had stone surrounds. A portico with white stone columns was in the centre of the ground floor. They climbed the steps leading up to the wooden double doors, which were open. They entered a foyer and spoke to a smartly dressed woman behind the desk.

After asking to speak to Will Horsley, they sat down beside a low table scattered with magazines and waited. Karen scrolled through the messages on her phone, intending to use the wait time to reply to emails, but it wasn't long before a young man with short, dark hair appeared in reception. He wore navy-blue trousers and a short-sleeved light blue shirt with a white and green logo on the breast pocket.

Karen stood up and held out her hand. 'Will Horsley?'

He nodded but didn't smile. He seemed nervous.

Karen showed her ID. 'I'm DS Hart and this is DC Jones. Can we have a quick chat?'

'Uh, yeah. Okay,' Will said, looking over his shoulder at the receptionist, his cheeks turning pink. 'What's it about?'

'Nothing to worry about. You're not in trouble,' Karen said quickly, smiling. 'Is there somewhere we can talk here, or do you want to go out and get some coffee?'

'Um, well, technically I'm still on the clock,' Will said, and then he shrugged. 'Oh, never mind. There's nowhere private here. Let's go outside.'

'What's your job at the council?' Karen asked as Will led them out of the council building.

'Gas engineer. Well, any kind of heating maintenance really. I spend most of my time fixing or installing boilers.'

'Interesting job?'

Will shrugged. 'It's all right.'

'How long have you worked there?'

'Not long at all. I only moved to Lincoln ten days ago.'

'Oh? Where were you before that?'

'Nottingham. Look, I don't mean to be rude, but what's with all the questions?'

'I think you know the answer to that, Will.'

He paled, but Karen didn't immediately put him out of his misery.

They got takeaway coffees from the Greek deli, and Karen showed great restraint by resisting the pain au chocolat.

They sat on chairs outside the deli. The sun was hot on Karen's back, and she wished she'd worn a short-sleeved shirt.

'What's this all about then?' Will chuckled nervously. 'Unpaid parking ticket, is it?'

'Let's not play games. You know what it's about,' Karen said.

The smile dropped from Will's face. 'It's about the email, isn't it?'

Karen nodded. 'Yes, about Imporium.'

'I should have known you would be able to track me down. You are the police, after all. It's your job.' He took a deep breath and then sighed. 'I don't even know if she was drugged. She was just acting out of it.'

'And this was on Friday night?' Sophie asked.

He nodded. 'Yeah, that's right. I'd gone out with some of the lads from work. Like I told you, I'm new to the area, so I thought I'd make the effort and go out with the team. The bar was busy. A woman walked past us and seemed . . . Well, at first I thought she'd had too much to drink, but then I thought it might be more than that.'

'What made you think that?' Karen asked.

He frowned and stared at his coffee cup. 'She staggered into me and grabbed hold of my shoulder to stop herself from falling. She acted odd. A bit like she wasn't sure what was going on. I *thought* she said she'd been drugged, but I couldn't hear her properly over the noise in the bar. Her eyes were wide, but she kept blinking like she couldn't focus. I tried to help, I really did, but she was quite . . .' He blew out a breath and shook his head and then looked at Karen. 'She was defensive. I mean, I can understand why. She didn't know me. I was just some bloke approaching her, asking if she wanted a taxi, but I really was trying to help.'

'And was she with anyone else?'

'No one that I noticed,' Will said. 'I did ask where her friends were, and she said she thought they'd gone home. I'd heard two women had their drinks spiked on nights out in the city centre recently, and seeing her like that . . .' He ran a hand through his hair. 'I don't know why I bothered to send the email. I can't really help. Maybe she just had a few too many Proseccos, you know?'

'Do you remember what time this happened?'

'Um.' Will hesitated as he thought back. 'I guess it would have been about nine thirty when I noticed her.'

'Whereabouts in the bar were you? A booth?'

'No, we were standing in the main section, midway between the entrance and the bar. All the tables were full, so we were just standing there in a group when she walked past. I'm not sure where she was before. I didn't notice her until she walked up to us.'

'What did she look like?'

'Pretty. About my age. Long, dark hair. Average height, I'd say. She was wearing a tight skirt, but it wasn't short. High heels . . .' He trailed off and glanced at Karen before quickly lowering his gaze, perhaps embarrassed when he realised how he sounded. 'That's all I can remember.'

'She walked up to you to start a conversation?'

'No, no. Nothing like that. She was walking past, and she was a bit wobbly, so she kind of . . . bumped into us.' He shrugged. 'Sorry, I can't remember exactly. I wish I could be more help.'

'You're being very helpful,' Karen said. 'So, this was about nine thirty, and did you see her leave? Was anyone with her?'

Will rubbed the side of his nose. 'Well, that's the thing. I should tell you everything, even though it's a bit embarrassing. She walked off towards the exit, and I followed her. I swear, I just wanted to make sure she was okay. But she shouted at me and called me a weirdo. A few people noticed.' His cheeks turned even pinker. 'I was trying to help, but I guess she thought I was trying to follow her or something.'

Karen nodded and waited for him to continue.

'Well, then she went outside, and I'm ashamed to say I was a bit annoyed, you know, because I felt like I'd been trying to do the right thing, and she just threw it back in my face. So I thought, fine, I won't bother. But then I realised I was being stupid. She was probably scared. It's hardly surprising she called me weird when I'd followed her. So I decided to check outside to see if she was still there.'

'And was she?'

He nodded. 'Yeah, I saw her walk up to a bloke. At first I was concerned, you know, because after everything that's been in the local news, I wondered if she'd been roofied. I thought he might have spiked her drink. But she said, "Oh, it's you. I'm so glad to see you." And then she hugged him. So, I thought everything was okay.' He ran a hand through his hair again and then looked at Karen. 'I did the right thing, didn't I? She's not hurt, is she?'

Karen shook her head. 'We're not aware of a woman being hurt on Friday evening. What did the man she walked up to look like?'

'He was a tall white guy. He had black hair, like her, and was wearing a dark jacket and jeans.'

He paused to drink some of his coffee, and Karen took the opportunity to study him. His cheeks and the tips of his ears were still pink. It was a hot day, which explained the sheen of sweat on his forehead, but the way his glance kept darting between Karen and Sophie and then back to the table, along with the tense way he perched on the edge of his chair, told Karen he was nervous.

She didn't think he was lying to them. He really seemed to believe the woman at Imporium on Friday night might have been drugged, and sending an anonymous email wasn't so unusual. A lot of people didn't want to play the role of witness. They didn't want to get dragged into a police investigation.

He fiddled with the lid of his coffee cup. Perhaps it wasn't nerves. He looked uncomfortable. Why was he looking so forlorn? Trouble with the police before, maybe?

'Are you all right, Will?'

He blinked and ran a hand through his hair yet again. 'Yeah. Just worried I suppose.'

'About the woman you saw?'

'Well, yes, and I don't want to get in trouble for wasting police time.'

'What do you mean?'

He shifted back in his seat. 'I didn't send the email until today because I told myself she was probably just drunk.'

'We appreciate you sending it,' Sophie said. 'Even if it turns out to be unrelated to the investigation. We want to be thorough, and the public coming forward with information is always helpful.'

Karen wasn't so sure about that. She had enough experience of working on tip lines during investigations to know that irrelevant information was sometimes a curse.

Will smiled at Sophie, seeming to relax a bit.

Karen handed him her card. 'If you remember anything else, get in touch, okay?'

He pushed back his chair so it scraped on the paving, stood up and said, 'Yeah, of course. Thanks for the coffee.'

'No problem.'

Karen and Sophie watched Will walk back towards the County Council offices.

'What did you think, Sarge?'

'I think he probably was trying to help. He was on edge. But some people get that way when talking to the police. He wanted to leave an anonymous tip. Us turning up was probably a bit of a shock. That could explain his hesitation and nervousness.'

'And do you reckon she was drugged or just had too much to drink?'

Karen shrugged. 'Your guess is as good as mine. But we've got a date and a time, so I think we should look at the security footage from Imporium from Friday night around nine thirty.'

Sophie groaned. 'More recorded footage. Lucky me. I suppose it's nice to have a narrow time frame for once.' She drained her coffee. 'Ready to head back to the station?'

Karen stood up. 'Give me a minute.'

It was no good. Her willpower had a limit. She headed back into the deli and ordered two pains au chocolat. Outside, she handed a bag to Sophie.

'Ooh, what's this?'

'The most delicious pain au chocolat you'll ever eat,' Karen said with a grin.

CHAPTER FIVE

It was late afternoon by the time Karen got back to the station and logged on to her computer. She quickly located the report on Phoebe Woodrow, but the system wouldn't cooperate. She couldn't download or open the report. Every time she tried, an error flashed up on the screen.

Rather than spend precious time trying to work out what was wrong with the needlessly complicated and convoluted electronic filing system, she spoke to PC Naylor's sergeant, who confirmed that he would be able to talk to her before the start of his evening shift, in an hour.

It would be a quick chat. She just needed to confirm that Phoebe was safe and well, so she could pass on the news to Erica.

An hour later, when she got downstairs, uniformed officers were filing out of the large briefing room.

'DS Hart?' A tall, bald man with a beard stopped in the doorway and gave her a businesslike smile.

'Yes,' she confirmed.

He nodded and shook her hand. 'I'm Sergeant Thompson. We spoke on the phone. You can call me Brian. Come in.'

She walked into the room, skirted around the rows of chairs, and saw another uniformed officer sitting down, staring glumly at his boots. He glanced up at her and then his gaze returned to his boots.

'This is PC Naylor,' Sergeant Thompson said.

It didn't look like the sergeant was about to leave Karen to chat to Naylor alone.

'I hope there isn't a problem,' PC Naylor said, licking his lips nervously.

Karen decided to come clean. This wasn't official business, and she didn't want to give them the impression it was. 'There's no problem at all. I just wanted an informal chat, really.'

'Okay, go ahead,' Sergeant Thompson said. He was still standing behind them. Karen had been right. He wasn't going to leave them alone. She didn't blame him though. He was looking out for a member of his squad.

'Right. It's about Phoebe Woodrow. A friend of hers reported her missing on Saturday. I couldn't download your report. The system was playing up on my computer.'

'Oh, that's no problem. We can print you a copy of the report,' Thompson said, walking over to a computer that was sitting on a small desk in the corner of the room. He began tapping on the keyboard.

'Yes, I remember. A missing persons case that had a happy ending for once. I contacted her next of kin. Her family had seen her that very day,' PC Naylor said. 'It seems it was a false alarm. I'm not sure what happened with the report. I'm positive I filed it correctly.'

'Oh, I'm sure you did. The system often plays up for me. Usually it's a matter of time, patience and constantly refreshing the database. But I was short on time today so thought I'd come and ask you directly.'

'Ah, I see.' He relaxed a little, uncrossing his arms and smiling. 'Thought I'd messed up and you were on the warpath.'

'Not at all. I did wonder though . . . You say the family had contact with Phoebe on Saturday. Did they see her in person? Was it texts or emails? Messages could be faked.'

There was a chuckle from behind them. 'PC Naylor is not wet behind the ears, DS Hart,' Sergeant Thompson said, his tone chastising.

'Sorry, I didn't mean to imply that,' Karen said quickly. 'Look, I'm not digging for dirt here or trying to catch you out. Phoebe's a friend of a friend, so I want to make one hundred per cent certain she is safe. I don't want to tread on your toes, and nothing makes me think there was anything wrong with how you handled the case.'

'I should hope not,' Sergeant Thompson said as the printer whirred in the background. His tone was definitely not friendly now.

'I just wanted to speak with you for reassurance more than anything else.'

PC Naylor leaned back in his seat and seemed far more relaxed than Thompson, who was still stern-faced.

'Oh, well, I'm happy to give you the reassurance you need. So many of the cases we see in this job end badly, so it was nice to have a positive result for a change.' He smiled. 'Her grandmother saw her in person on Saturday. It's all in the report,' he added as Sergeant Thompson handed it to Karen.

'Thanks. I appreciate it.' She skimmed the pages. There was a headshot of Phoebe on the first page, likely taken from the DVLA records. Her hair was tied back, and she wore a serious expression. 'Did you speak to her grandmother yourself?' she asked PC Naylor.

'No, I spoke to Phoebe's sister. Lisa Woodrow.' He stood up, walked over to Karen, and pointed to the section of the report that mentioned Lisa. 'She told me her grandmother had seen Phoebe just a few hours earlier.'

'Was there anything to suggest she might have been lying?'

He frowned. 'No, not at all. She seemed very helpful, friendly.'

'But you didn't see or speak to Phoebe yourself,' Karen clarified.

Naylor's frown deepened and he shuffled back to his seat. He didn't answer straightaway and tugged at his collar. 'Well, no, I didn't. But her family said she wasn't missing, so I didn't think I needed to take it further. I had plenty of other work to be getting on with on that shift.' He glanced at Sergeant Thompson. He was getting defensive. 'Anyway, if anyone was acting strangely, it was the woman who reported it. She set alarm bells ringing for me.'

'Erica?' Karen queried.

Naylor looked up to the ceiling, thinking. 'Yeah, Erica. That was her name. It's in the report. She was going on and on about a cat. She was anxious. Overwrought.'

'Well, she believed her friend was missing,' Karen said. 'That was understandable.'

'Maybe, but she seemed strung out to me. Thought she had a bit of a problem.' He tapped his temple.

Karen tried not to react, but it wasn't easy. She'd seen female victims and witnesses dismissed in this way before. A woman's reaction waved away as too emotional, unreliable. It wasn't so explicit these days, but you could still sense it if you knew what you were looking for.

'I looked into it,' Naylor continued. 'And when I found out Phoebe had been seen by her family, I called to let her know.'

'How did she respond?'

'She didn't sound convinced. But she thanked me for the update. She sounded a bit calmer by then. She'd worried me earlier. Thought I might have to call the paramedics.'

'Why?'

'She was really over the top. Agitated. She had a full-on anxiety attack. I'm not surprised Phoebe didn't respond to her messages, to be honest. A friend like that must be hard work.'

'And your connection with the case, DS Hart?' Sergeant Thompson queried. 'Erica is your friend?'

Naylor grimaced. 'Oh, sorry. I didn't think. I'm sure she's normally very nice.'

Karen nodded. 'Yes, and she's still concerned. I hoped I could tell her you'd seen Phoebe in person to stop her worrying. Perhaps I should go and visit Phoebe, just to make sure she's okay.'

'Oh, so this is an *official* enquiry then?' Sergeant Thompson said, with a coldness to his tone that made it clear he knew it wasn't official.

Karen gave him a tight smile. 'Not official, no.'

'Does your senior officer know you're looking into this?'

'No, not yet, but I'll tell him of course.'

'Very good. Is that all? PC Naylor has a shift to get started.'

Karen nodded. 'Yes, thanks very much for your time. I appreciate your help,' she said as PC Naylor scurried past her, glad to get out of the room.

She nodded to Sergeant Thompson and left.

Great.

Now she would have to tell Churchill, because if she didn't, Karen was sure Sergeant Thompson would.

When she got back upstairs, she poked her head around the door of Morgan's office. 'Got a minute?' she asked.

He nodded, gesturing for her to come inside. 'How are you doing with all the paperwork?' he asked. 'It's the worst part, isn't it? I swear I've read this page three times already.'

'I'm a bit behind, to be honest,' Karen said. 'Sophie and I were roped into doing some of the groundwork on Operation Starling.

We visited Imporium, a bar in the city centre, and spoke to a potential witness.'

'Did you get anything from it?'

'Too early to say. Sophie's looking through some security footage, as there was a potential incident on Friday evening. The manager of Imporium is a bit of a smarmy so-and-so, but the staff say they didn't see anything out of the ordinary.'

'It's not proving to be an easy case, is it?' Morgan said.

'No, it really isn't,' Karen replied. 'Can I ask your opinion on something?'

'Sure, go ahead.' Morgan pushed the papers in front of him into a pile.

'Someone from my counselling group, Erica Bright, thought her friend was missing over the weekend. She'd agreed to look after her friend's cat for one night. But her friend didn't show up to collect it the next day.'

'Has she reported her missing?'

'She tried, but apparently her family says her grandmother has seen her and she's fine. I really shouldn't be sticking my nose in. She probably *is* fine, but . . .' Karen shrugged.

'You don't sound convinced,' Morgan said.

'No, there's something weird about it. I've just spoken to the officer who filed the report, and he didn't see her in person.'

Morgan smiled. 'So it's a potential mystery?'

'Maybe. I just want to make sure. I think I've managed to annoy Sergeant Thompson though. Pretty sure he'll be having a word with Churchill tomorrow.'

'What did you do?'

Karen gave him a hurt look. 'I didn't do anything! Just asked a few questions.'

'And implied they didn't perform their duties correctly?' Morgan asked drily, raising his eyebrows.

'No . . . Well, I suppose they could have interpreted it that way.' Karen sighed. 'I'd better get ahead of the problem. I'll speak to Churchill now, ask him if I can take a couple of official hours to look into it.'

'You won't be able to this evening.'

'Why?'

'He's just left. He's off to his kid's parents evening tonight. He told me no interruptions on pain of death.'

'Great. I'll have to get to him first thing tomorrow.' She thought for a moment then added, 'I could go to Phoebe's address tonight. Just to make sure.'

Morgan frowned. 'It's not a good idea.'

Karen knew he had a point. Using police resources to investigate something for a friend was, at best, frowned upon. And she had no reason to think Phoebe Woodrow had come to harm. If PC Naylor's instincts were right, perhaps Phoebe was avoiding Erica's calls. His description of Erica had irritated Karen. But Erica did suffer from anxiety and depression, and perhaps this had caused a setback.

'Maybe you're right,' Karen said. 'I'll leave it until after I've spoken to Churchill. I can check in with Erica tonight, hopefully reassure her a bit.'

Morgan picked up a pen and twirled it in his fingers. 'I think that's the wisest plan of action. Especially if you're going to try to make inspector soon.'

Karen grimaced. 'I still haven't made my mind up about that.'

'Why not? You'd be a great DI.'

'You think so?' Karen smiled. Morgan wasn't the type to heap praise, so this was a compliment to be remembered. 'Maybe I'll give it some more thought.'

As she reached the door, he said, 'You need to make sure your senior officer is on board if you go digging.'

'You sound like you say that from experience?'

Morgan grunted. 'You could say that.'

Karen waited for him to elaborate, but annoyingly he didn't. Morgan wasn't exactly chatty. At times, it was like getting blood from a stone. 'Technically, you're my senior officer, and I've told you.'

'Doesn't count. Churchill now allocates resources. You need to talk to him if you want to investigate.'

'Okay, that's what I'll do. I don't like leaving it overnight, but you're right. And there's nothing to suggest she's in danger.'

Nothing except Erica's concern, Karen thought. She didn't feel comfortable discussing it with Morgan now, but what PC Naylor had said had worried her. She didn't want to see Erica relapse when she'd been doing so well.

Karen felt protective. She knew what it was like to worry and have others refuse to take your concerns seriously. She understood why Erica was troubled, and she didn't want anything to derail her recovery.

'I'm supposed to be going to dinner with Mike tonight, but I'll pop in to see Erica on my way home.'

'How are things going with you and Mike?'

Mike and Morgan hadn't exactly been the best of friends, but on the odd occasion they now met socially, they tolerated each other well enough. 'Good. At least . . .'

Morgan glanced up again after shuffling his papers. 'What?'

Karen leaned on the back of the chair. 'Do you ever worry about your relatives? About the job putting them at risk?'

She was still preoccupied with the threat the ringleader of the burglary gang had made. Logically, she knew it was a bluff intended to intimidate. Police officers got menacing threats all the time, which mostly came to nothing. But after everything that had happened over the last few years, it seemed reason had deserted her. Her mind refused to stop dwelling on the worst-possible outcomes.

Morgan paused before answering, and then said, 'Yes, occasionally. If I'm involved in a particularly nasty case.'

'Do you sometimes get that weird sense, that prickle on the back of your neck, and think someone's been watching you?'

Morgan frowned, and Karen suspected that perhaps that paranoia was all hers, but then he said, 'Sometimes. Do you take a seat with your back to the wall, so you can see who's coming into the restaurant or pub?'

Karen laughed. 'It's not just me then?'

He shook his head. 'No, I always like to keep an eye on the door.'

'Are we paranoid?'

'I think we're just being careful.'

'Mike is practically living with me now, and you know how nasty the recent aggravated burglary cases were. I worry that being involved with me is going to get him dragged into something he didn't sign up for. I'm scared it's going to put him in danger.' Karen hadn't meant to share so much. She hated the way her voice sounded small and scared. Conversations with Morgan might often be monosyllabic on his part, but right now Karen felt like she was a Catholic in the confessional. She'd blurted out feelings she'd skirted around even during her counselling sessions.

Morgan leaned forward in his chair. 'Mike's a big lad. And he understands the pressure of the job. Lightning is unlikely to strike twice, Karen,' he added softly.

Karen swallowed the lump in her throat. 'Yes, you're right. I know. I'm sure everything is going to turn out fine.' She spoke in a rush. 'All right. I'm going to give Erica a ring, let her know I've checked out the report and that Phoebe saw her grandmother on Saturday, so it looks like she's fine. And then I'll speak to Churchill tomorrow. I'd like to speak to Phoebe myself, to make sure she's okay and to give her a nudge about picking up her cat. Erica has been through a tough time over the last few months. It's not on to treat her like an unpaid cat-sitter.'

Morgan absorbed the cascade of words and said simply, 'It will all work out.'

I hope he's right, Karen thought as she left his office. *I really do.*

CHAPTER SIX

An hour later, Morgan shut down his computer and began to gather his things. He glanced out of his office window into the open-plan area.

DC Farzana Shah was helping Sophie go through the security footage. Karen was at her desk, typing furiously, no doubt trying to catch up on her reports. Churchill had stretched them thin over the past few weeks. They still needed time to wrap up the aggravated burglary case, but protecting women in Lincoln from whoever was stalking the bars and clubs, spiking their drinks with Rohypnol, was the superintendent's first concern. And rightly so.

Morgan wasn't involved in Operation Starling. His responsibility was to make sure the burglary cases were airtight. It was hard to prioritise the paperwork over the nitty-gritty, but it was the details, the form-filling, that could often determine if a case was won or lost in the courts – whether the result was a criminal behind bars or one free to roam the streets again.

In some ways, it felt like he'd worked with this team forever. His years at Thames Valley were a distant memory.

He couldn't help worrying about them. Sophie was enthusiastic and hard-working, but at times she was still naive. She tended to believe things were clear-cut, when often they weren't.

His gaze shifted to Karen again. She was strong. There weren't many who could cope with what life had thrown at her. And yet she was still here, working the job she loved. It was only natural for her to be worried about the possibility that other members of her family could be harmed, especially after her husband and daughter had been killed by criminals who had been targeting her. And the recent aggravated burglary cases had really shaken her, because the ringleader's threat had reminded her of what she'd lost, and also what she stood to lose now if she was targeted again. He'd noticed how affected she had been by the arrest once she got back to the station. He wasn't surprised. The gang members were brutal. Their ringleader in particular was a nasty piece of work.

Morgan wasn't keen on Mike but had to admit the relationship had been good for Karen. Even he could see that. She smiled more, walked into a room with a new sense of lightness. He had enough self-awareness to accept his reticence over Mike had probably been influenced by jealousy. Not that there had ever been anything romantic between him and Karen. She was a friend, a good one, and they'd spent a lot of time together. Less time now that she was with Mike, and that had caused a small amount of resentment.

Morgan enjoyed spending time in her company. He talked to her openly, in a way he couldn't with others. He smiled at that thought. Karen would disagree. She was always commenting on his lack of conversational skills. He'd never been one to go in for chatter for the sake of it, but he felt comfortable sharing things with Karen. And he was glad that she felt able to confide in him.

And then there was Rick. Morgan frowned as he focused on Rick's empty desk. He was worried about him. Rick had changed. Since he'd joined Lincolnshire Police, Morgan had witnessed the young man turn from a cheerful – and at times even boisterous – lad to a man with a heavy load on his shoulders. He'd caught Rick falling asleep at his desk earlier, head lolling forward, and ordered him to go home. He'd offered him a chance to talk about it, but Rick had shrugged it off and said he was fine, just a bit tired, which is what he always said.

Morgan had spoken with Churchill and had also had a word with the superintendent, and they'd all agreed that another few weeks' compassionate leave should be arranged.

Although Rick didn't confide in him as Sophie and Karen did, he knew the young officer was caught between a rock and a hard place. He needed to work to earn enough money to pay for a carer for his mother. Yes, he could have some time off, but that wasn't a long-term solution. If he took more time off without pay, he wouldn't be able to afford the assistance at home. And he couldn't cope with it all himself. That much was clear.

Morgan reached for his jacket but didn't put it on. It was still light out and would be warm. After sitting in the sun all day, his car would be absolutely boiling. Morgan decided to talk to Rick again tomorrow. Things couldn't go on as they were. Perhaps a few weeks off would give him time to catch up on some rest. He needed it.

Morgan left his office, closed the door behind him, and said goodbye to the rest of the staff as he left the station. For once, he was going home at a sensible hour. He couldn't very well lecture Rick on making time for himself when he was usually first in and last to leave.

◆ ◆ ◆

Rick had just ordered a pizza. Cooking was the last thing he wanted to do tonight. He was exhausted. He'd sent Priya, his mother's carer, home. She had a date, and her excitement and enthusiasm had almost rubbed off on Rick. Nowadays, all he wanted to do when he finished work was get changed, have something to eat and then go to bed.

His sister, Lauren, had gone on holiday to Cornwall. That had caused a bit of bad feeling between them. Rick had suggested, he thought very tactfully, that Lauren should spend more time with their mother, maybe a Saturday or Sunday each week, so Rick could take some time for himself. But that hadn't gone down well.

It wasn't as though he was planning a fortnight abroad. He was only asking for one day a week.

It wasn't an easy situation, and Rick understood that. The simple fact was that their mother felt safe with Rick. She felt secure at home in her own surroundings with people she was familiar with. She didn't like change.

Of course, Lauren was her daughter, but over the past few months Lauren had been visiting less and less and only saw their mother infrequently. Which meant when she did pay them a visit, their mother's reaction was unpredictable.

Sometimes she'd remember. Sometimes she'd even want to give Lauren a hug. But there were occasions when she would deny knowing her daughter at all and would look at her as though she were a stranger.

It was heartbreaking. Lauren would then seethe with resentment, hating the fact that their mother always seemed to recognise Rick. But it wasn't anything to do with favouritism, and Rick had tried to explain that. It was just because he was constantly there. Well, apart from when he was at work, of course. But it was him and Priya looking after his mum. So she was comfortable with them.

There were days – bad days – when she even got confused around Rick. She'd become muddled and think Rick was his father. Once she'd even thought he was his grandfather, who Rick had never met. But that was the course of this awful disease.

They'd known it was coming for a long time, but that didn't make it any easier. It seemed to Rick that she was getting worse, going downhill very quickly, and it terrified him. His mum had had a choking fit a couple of weeks ago and had to be admitted to the hospital. It was a horrible disease. He'd thought dementia was all to do with memories, where the person suffering slowly lost who they were. But the brain forgot other things. It forgot how to perform normal bodily functions. Rick shuddered as he recalled his latest conversation with her doctor.

The doctor had explained how the disease would progress. And Rick had wanted to stick his hands over his ears and hum, like a child, to try to block it out. But of course, he couldn't.

He had to face up to reality, and he had to look after his mum. That was all there was to it.

But it would help if Lauren stepped up occasionally. When he'd pointed that out, they'd had a big row, and Lauren had put her hands on her hips, just like she used to do when they were children and she was bossing him about.

'It's not my fault, Rick,' she had said. 'If you'd agreed to put her in a specialist home where they could care for her properly, you wouldn't be so tired.'

It was hard to explain. Rick had tried to talk to her, to get her to see things from his point of view. He'd even told her about the incident that had occurred when their mother was in hospital a few weeks ago.

All the staff there had been amazing. They'd worked so hard and tried to accommodate his mum and Rick as best they could. But there'd been one awful woman. He didn't even know what she did. She could have been admin staff, for all he knew.

It had happened one evening after Rick had finished work and driven straight to the hospital. His mum had been for a scan, and he'd gone too, waiting outside the X-ray department and then walking back to the ward alongside the porter who was pushing his mother in a wheelchair.

She'd had an upset stomach and had asked the porter to get her back to the ward quickly so she could use the toilet.

When they'd reached the double doors to the ward, there had been a woman standing in front of them, chatting to another porter.

Rick's mum, who by then was desperate, had said, 'Can you get out of the way!'

Rick knew his mother. He could hear the stress and panic, the absolute terror in her voice that she would lose her dignity and soil herself there in the corridor. It was one of his mother's lucid moments, and he almost wished it wasn't.

Instead of moving out of the way, the woman had raised herself up to her full height and looked down at his mum. 'We're not pieces of meat, you know,' she'd said in an imperious voice.

Rick considered himself a level-headed bloke, but at that moment he could have cheerfully grabbed hold of the wheelchair and rammed it into the horrible old cow's legs.

Instead, he'd snapped at her, told her they needed to urgently get into the ward, and if she didn't move of her own accord he would physically move her out of the way. Of course, faced with someone healthy who was a lot bigger than her, and an aggressive tone, she'd quickly moved.

And Rick hated it. He hated himself for getting angry. He hated the way he'd shouted. He hated the woman for not caring enough to notice how distressed his mum was, and not understanding she wasn't being rude. She was just scared. And most of all, he hated the disease that had brought his mum to the hospital.

He'd tried to explain to Lauren. He'd asked her: how could they trust their mum to be safe around people like that? People who didn't understand, who couldn't hear the vulnerability and panic in their mother's voice.

He really hoped that woman wasn't in a patient-facing role. Everyone else was so kind, so compassionate, but it had taken just that one woman to make Rick swear he wouldn't leave his mum with people he didn't trust if he could help it.

The doorbell rang, and Rick got up with a groan, stretching his back. Why did he feel a hundred years old when he wasn't far past thirty? He made his way to the front door and paid for the pizza. Double pepperoni with a stuffed crust. Well, if he was going to eat junk, he might as well eat tasty junk.

He'd taken the pizza through to the kitchen and put a couple of slices on a plate when his mother called out. She'd gone to bed early. She'd been spending more and more time in her bed recently. Everyday tasks wore her out for hours.

'Coming, Mum!' he shouted.

She was sitting up in bed and looked so much smaller than she used to, surrounded by the plumped-up pillows.

'What's wrong, Mum? Can't you sleep?'

She shook her head. 'It's the books, Rick. I need to take my books back to the library.'

Not this again, Rick thought. It was a fixation she'd developed over the last few months. She believed she had overdue books and was going to get in trouble. But she hadn't been to the library for years.

He sat on the edge of the bed and took her hand in his. 'It's fine, Mum. I called them. We'll take them back tomorrow.'

She looked at him, blinking. He could see she was trying so hard to understand.

'Everything's fine.'

After a moment, she nodded, but he wasn't sure she was convinced.

'Do you want some water?' he asked.

She nodded, and he passed her the glass from the nightstand.

She took one sip and then coughed. The jolt through her body made her drop the glass, so the contents splashed across the duvet, darkening the light blue cotton.

She let out a cry of dismay, put her hands against her cheeks. 'Oh no. Oh no.'

'It's fine, Mum. It's just water. Don't worry about it,' Rick said, taking the glass and peeling the duvet back to make sure none of it had soaked through to his mum's nightdress. 'See, it's all fine. I'll strip it off and put a new one on, and you'll be right as rain.'

Her lip wobbled.

'Don't cry, Mum. Honestly, it's just a duvet. It doesn't matter.'

But she couldn't hold back the tears. He flung the duvet to the floor and walked around to give her a hug.

She buried her face against his chest as he patted her shoulder and kept telling her everything was going to be fine, when he knew that it wouldn't be – and there was nothing he could do about it.

After ten minutes, he managed to get his mum settled again and got the duvet from the spare room. She was asleep within moments.

Rick left the bedroom and headed back to the kitchen, where he found his pizza, cold and congealing, sitting on the counter.

After selecting a beer from the fridge, he carried the plate into the living room. That was the good thing about pizza, he thought. It didn't matter if you had to eat it cold.

He set the house alarm, so the ringing would alert Rick in the night if his mother woke and tried to go outside. Then he switched on the TV, turned the volume down low and ate, wondering how Priya was enjoying her date.

It had been ages since he'd been out on the town. So long since he'd gone out for the evening with only himself to worry about. He used to be a party animal, surviving on little sleep and nursing a hangover every weekend. He didn't miss the hangovers, but he missed going out with his mates. He barely spoke to them now. They'd stopped inviting him out. There were only so many times people asked before they gave up.

He'd love a free weekend. A Friday and Saturday to spend as he pleased. A night at a bar with nothing to worry about except the resulting sore head the next day. But a free weekend wasn't likely anytime soon. He envied Priya her freedom. Her busy social life.

With a sigh, Rick settled back to eat the cold pizza.

CHAPTER SEVEN

Karen called Erica's mobile as she left the station. Despite the late hour, it was still warm as she crossed the car park. The sky was blue, but pink-tinged clouds were scattered over the horizon.

Karen opened the car door and was greeted with a rush of hot air. She stood back, leaving the door open for the car to cool as Erica's voicemail kicked in.

'Erica, it's Karen. I just wanted to follow up on our conversation about your friend Phoebe. I don't think there's anything to worry about. Everything seems to check out. I spoke with PC Naylor and he confirmed that Phoebe was seen by her family on Saturday. Anyway, give me a call back when you get this message.'

Karen got into the car and tossed her bag and phone on to the passenger seat. But before shutting the door, she thought for a moment. She had two options. She could go straight home, get changed and get ready to go out with Mike. They'd booked the restaurant for eight thirty. Or she could cancel the dinner and visit Erica, perhaps stay with her for a little while to make sure she was okay.

She picked up her phone again, and this time dialled Mike. He wasn't too upset when she told him she needed to miss dinner. They'd planned to go out with an old friend of his to an Italian restaurant in Lincoln. He could still go, so Karen didn't feel *too* guilty.

She'd met the friend before. In fact, she'd met a few of his friends now, though she hadn't met any of his family. He didn't seem to be as close to his family as she was to hers.

After hanging up, she reversed out of her parking spot, her mind back on Erica. She'd been doing so well recently. But after talking to PC Naylor, Karen was worried.

There were several vehicles parked outside the apartment block when Karen got there. It was a peaceful area, set back from the main road and surrounded by mature beech trees.

After she parked, she scanned the area for Erica's silver BMW. There was no sign of it.

She glanced up and saw a murmuration of starlings. They moved together across the sky, the flock twisting and turning like an ominous black cloud. Dusk was an odd time. The shadows deepened and seemed to shift, and the deep greens of the trees and shrubs enclosing the parking area were dense and dark.

Karen thought she may as well try the buzzer, since she was here, even though it looked as though Erica was probably out.

She put her phone in her back pocket and walked towards the entrance, lifting her gaze to look at the balcony at the front of Erica's apartment. There were no lights on, but it was still just light enough not to need them.

Karen stopped suddenly as a small shape flitted across the inside of the balcony doors. A split second later, she exhaled, realising it had to be the cat. Those burglary cases really had left her hyper-alert for danger.

The breeze sounded like a whisper as it rustled through the leaves on the trees. Dusk was witching hour, Karen thought. The time of day when your eyes could play tricks on you.

She pressed the buzzer, but as expected got no response. It was a good sign. Perhaps Erica had gone out to see a friend. Or maybe she was at work. If she was going about her everyday life, perhaps she wasn't having a setback, after all.

She wouldn't be so concerned if PC Naylor hadn't implied Erica had been needlessly overwrought on Saturday. But it wouldn't be the first time a woman's reaction to an incident had been dismissed as hysteria. Erica was usually so cool and calm. Karen couldn't imagine her in the way PC Naylor had described. And she had seemed fine to Karen when she'd seen her. Concerned? Yes, but not hysterical.

She turned away from the entrance and headed back to her car. She wouldn't make it back home in time to go out with Mike, but she was tired anyway. She could make something quick and easy for dinner, and then spend the evening sitting on the sofa, watching TV or reading a book.

She was just about to start the engine when her mobile rang. It was Erica. She answered.

'I'm sorry, Karen,' Erica said. 'I only just got your message.'

'Not a problem. I'm outside your place now. Are you on the way home?'

'No. Sorry. I'm at work, at the hospital. Is it about Phoebe?'

Karen heard the tension in Erica's voice and was quick to reassure her. 'Yes, but I haven't found anything worrying. I spoke to PC Naylor, and he confirmed he spoke with Phoebe's family. They saw her on Saturday, and she's fine.'

There was a pause, and then Erica said, 'Right. I see.'

'Look, I know you're still concerned, so I'm going to speak to my boss tomorrow, and with his approval I'll be able to pay her a visit myself. I'll remind her she needs to pick up her cat. All right?'

'Thanks, Karen. I appreciate it. I know you've probably got a million other things to work on. I feel guilty roping you into this.'

'It's fine,' Karen said. 'I'd do it tonight, but we're not supposed to use police resources for checking up on the public without authorisation.'

'I understand,' Erica said. 'And I really do appreciate you trying to help.'

'No problem. I'll let you get back to work. I'll call again tomorrow,' Karen said, and then hung up.

Erica had sounded fine. It wasn't always easy to judge someone's mood on the phone, but she hadn't seemed any more anxious or stressed than expected for the situation.

Karen felt a niggle of annoyance that PC Naylor had put the worry that Erica might be unravelling again into her mind.

◆ ◆ ◆

'Do you not have enough work to do?'

Karen should have expected that. She was sitting opposite Churchill, in his office.

She had come straight here at eight a.m. Churchill was a creature of habit. He always arrived at the same time every day.

Fortunately, Karen had got to him first. There was no sign that Sergeant Thompson had been telling tales yet.

'I do have a lot of work to do. We're very busy at the moment,' Karen said. 'But—'

'But what?' Churchill interrupted. 'Look, Karen, as cases come in, they're allocated to teams according to protocol. This procedure is very important. Otherwise we'd all just pick and choose which cases we wanted to work on, wouldn't we?'

'Yes, but—'

He continued: 'You must respect the system. Or you'll get overwhelmed, overworked *and* your successes won't get any acknowledgement. If you want to climb the career ladder, that's something you need to think about.'

Karen was starting to feel like a scolded child in the headmaster's office. She'd already endured a ten-minute lecture on the allocation of resources.

Churchill rested his hands on his desk and interlinked his fingers. As usual, he wore a crisp white shirt free of creases, and his tie was perfectly straight. His hair was carefully styled, and Karen was very tempted to lean forwards and ruffle it.

'Do you think I like spending most of my time behind a desk, working out budgets and making staffing decisions?'

Karen hadn't given it much thought. 'I suppose not,' she said.

'You see!' Churchill said, as though he'd proved his point. 'But somebody's got to do it. Because we need the system to run smoothly.'

'Right, but I'd only need a couple of hours, tops.'

He sighed heavily. 'Why is it you're so interested in this particular case?'

'Well, as I mentioned, Phoebe Woodrow is a friend of a friend.'

'And is there any reason to think she's in danger? From what you've just told me, she's fine. Her family has seen her. She's no longer missing, so why are you so desperate to get involved?'

'I'm not *desperate*,' Karen said. 'I just want to check on her. I'll pay her a visit and make sure she's okay. That's all.'

'But I thought that had already been done?' Churchill said with another sigh.

'Not exactly. PC Naylor spoke to her sister, who said she'd been seen by their grandmother on Saturday.'

'Right. Well, that's it then. She's not a missing person.'

That's what PC Naylor had thought, and technically there wasn't any need to dig further. But the fact Phoebe hadn't collected her cat – and that Erica was still concerned about this – troubled Karen. 'It can't do any harm to double-check, sir.'

'Well, why can't you send uniform around? That should have been your first thought,' Churchill said sharply. 'I don't expect my detective sergeants to be wasting their time on trivial house calls, and I certainly wouldn't expect it if you made inspector rank.'

Karen gritted her teeth and took a deep breath before replying. 'I could have directed a uniformed team to do so, but that's allocating resources – and as you pointed out, I haven't been assigned to this case, so technically I don't have the authority to send uniform anywhere.'

'I suppose that's true.' He tapped his fingers on the desk. 'You just want to check on her?'

'Yes, it really won't take long.'

'All right. But you can do it on your own time,' he said. 'I hope you've got the paperwork for those aggravated burglary cases in hand?'

She nodded. 'I have. There's plenty of it to keep me busy.'

'Any leads on the Rohypnol case?' Churchill asked.

'Sophie's been looking at the CCTV for Operation Starling. There's a potential new victim, a woman who was at the Imporium bar on Friday night, but she hasn't come forward, so we just have a witness who states he saw a woman who seemed as though she might have been drugged.'

'Well, if we do get something concrete, make sure *we* get the credit and not Simpson's team.'

'Yes, sir.'

'All right.' He returned his attention to the computer. 'But like I said, we've got targets to meet and I'm still an officer short, so you investigate this friend of a friend on your own time. After work.'

Karen nodded. 'Okay.' She left Churchill's office and headed back downstairs. She supposed it could have gone worse. At least he'd agreed to let her use the resources. Now she'd be able to access the report again and get Phoebe Woodrow's home address and place of work, so she'd be able to track her down. It was annoying that she couldn't do it now and put it to bed once and for all, but she didn't want to push her luck with Churchill.

When she entered the open-plan office, she saw Rick, who had just arrived. He dumped his bag at his feet then rubbed a hand over his face and smothered a yawn. He hadn't even noticed Karen.

'Coffee?' she offered. 'You look like you could do with it. Tough night?'

He shrugged. 'Thanks, Sarge. It wasn't too bad. Coffee would be great.'

She was standing beside the coffee machine when DS Arnie Hobson strolled in.

He grinned at her. 'A little dicky bird's been telling me you're looking into a personal case, Karen.'

'And which little dicky bird would that be?' Karen asked, annoyed. 'PC Naylor?'

He chuckled. 'You know how fast gossip travels in a police station, but I can't reveal my sources! Anyway, why are you trying to get yourself extra work? Are you mad?'

'Quite possibly,' Karen said. 'Coffee?'

Arnie gave her a broad smile. 'Don't mind if I do, thanks.'

After giving Arnie his drink, she carried a mug over to Rick's desk. 'Here you go, matey,' she said. 'You know, I'm worried about you,' she added quietly, pulling over a chair. It was still early, and most of the desks were unoccupied. 'Is there anything I can do?'

Rick attempted to smile then shook his head. 'No thanks, Sarge, but I appreciate the offer.'

'How are you getting on with the case reports?'

'Fine,' Rick said. 'I'm liaising with the evidence manager today. Double- and triple-checking to make sure everything is spot on.'

'Good. Well done,' Karen said.

She left him to drink his coffee and approached Sophie, who was sitting at her desk, scrolling through CCTV images frame by frame.

'Do you want a coffee?' Karen didn't usually make it a habit to make morning coffee for the whole team, but since she'd already made drinks for Rick and Arnie, she didn't want to leave Sophie out.

'Oh, it's fine. I've already got one,' she said, pointing to a mug decorated with pink swirls.

'Is this footage from Friday night at Imporium?' Karen asked.

'Yes.'

'Was Will Horsley right? Do you think another female victim was drugged?'

Sophie shrugged. 'It's hard to say for sure, but take a look at this. It's footage from outside the front of Imporium.'

Karen squinted at the screen. It wasn't great quality. A slim woman with long, dark hair had her back to the camera and appeared to be talking to a tall, broad-shouldered man with short, spiky dark hair.

'You think this is the woman Will was referring to?'

'Yes, there's footage of her inside the bar too.' Sophie switched to a different window, opening up the CCTV recording from the interior. 'At nine twenty-eight, she walks into the camera's view and she seems under the influence of something. Could be drink *or* drugs. Look at this.' She scrolled back so Karen could see the woman approach.

The camera was too high. And most of the screen was filled with the tops of people's heads. Sophie pointed out the woman of interest. Petite, with long dark hair, she walked unsteadily from the bar and along the wide aisle between the booths, squeezing by groups of drinkers until she stopped beside some lads. There were six of them. The footage was black-and-white and the angle of the

71

camera wasn't great, but Karen thought she spotted Will Horsley. The woman was harder to identify as her face wasn't visible. She had long, dark hair just as Will had described, but it obscured her face. She was slim, very slightly built, and as she walked towards the front of the bar, it looked like her legs might give way at any moment.

Before she reached Will, though, something else happened. A curly-haired man standing in the group grabbed her elbow. It didn't look like a gentle grip.

'Did you see that?' Karen said.

'Yes,' Sophie replied. 'That's what I wanted you to see. The Operation Starling team have all seen the footage and agree we need to identify the man she was talking to outside *and* this guy who grabbed her arm.'

Karen peered closer at the man gripping the woman's arm. 'Who is he?'

She shook her head. 'I don't know. But he's in the group with Will. He probably knows him.'

Karen folded her arms. 'Then I think it's time we had another chat with Will Horsley.'

CHAPTER EIGHT

Within half an hour, Karen and Sophie were outside the council offices.

Sophie paused by the steps at the entrance and pointed across the road. 'Hang on, isn't that DS Rawlings and DC Fraser, from Simpson's team?'

Karen turned and saw the two officers hurrying towards them. They didn't look happy.

'What are you doing here?' DS Rawlings asked when he reached them.

'We're going to speak to Will Horsley again and ask him if he recognises—' Karen started to say.

Rawlings cut her off. 'That's what we're here for. DCI Simpson specifically said *we* had to talk to him.'

'But we're here now,' Sophie said. 'I added the task to the database.'

'So did DC Fraser.' Rawlings turned to look at his colleague, who was staring down at her shoes.

'Well, I was *going* to, but we were in a rush.' DC Fraser hunched her shoulders and withered under Rawlings's glare. 'I didn't expect them to be doubling up. They're supposed to be *helping*, not leading the enquiry. How could I know they'd decide to come and talk to Will Horsley without telling anyone?'

'I added it to the database!' Sophie raised her voice. She valued the importance of admin tasks and didn't like anyone implying she'd been less than comprehensive.

Fraser sulkily stared down at her shoes again while Rawlings glowered at Karen and Sophie.

'It doesn't need all four of us,' Karen said.

Rawlings began to climb the steps to the building's entrance. 'No, it doesn't. We'll speak to him, and you can go back to the station.'

After Rawlings and Fraser entered the council offices, Sophie turned to Karen. 'That's ridiculous. They wouldn't have had the lead if I hadn't entered it into the case file. If they saw that, then why didn't they see my task allocation? What's the point in having an organisation system if people don't use it correctly?'

'It's annoying,' Karen said. 'But there's nothing we can do about it now.'

They started walking back towards the city centre.

'Since we're here,' Karen said. 'Let's go to Imporium. We can ask the staff if they recognise the curly-haired man on the CCTV.'

'I hope they do. I hope *we* get a lead, and *they* get nothing from talking to Will Horsley,' Sophie said indignantly.

'I hope we both get leads. The sooner we can identify this man, the better.'

Imporium was quiet. A few patrons sat in booths, sipping coffee and eating the breakfast that was on special offer. The cheerful upbeat music was at a volume where you could still hear yourself think.

Cassidy was behind the bar, her bright pink hair in a scruffy bun on top of her head. She spotted them as soon as they came in. She didn't smile.

Karen stopped by the bar. 'Hello, Cassidy.'

'Are you here for work, or are you wanting a drink?'

'Both,' Karen said. 'Coffee for me, please.' She turned to Sophie, who said, 'Same for me, please.'

Cassidy plucked two cups from the rack beside the coffee machine. 'Have you managed to catch the creep yet?'

'We're still working on it,' Karen said. 'We've got some photos we'd like you to look at.'

Sophie pulled the A4 prints out of her folio bag. She slid them across the bar. Cassidy turned away from the coffee machine as it began hissing and dribbling a thin stream of coffee into one of the cups.

She glanced at the images. 'This is from the CCTV?'

'Yes. Friday night. We're interested in identifying this man with the curly hair, and this man who was outside the bar.' Karen pointed them out.

'Are these the best shots you have?' Cassidy sneered. 'You can't see their faces well at all.'

Karen pointed to the camera in the corner of the bar. 'It's the angle. You might want to suggest to your manager that he get the cameras adjusted.'

Cassidy stared at the pictures for a moment, then looked up and shook her head. 'Can't help you. Could be anyone.'

Karen thanked her as Cassidy put the first coffee on the bar in front of them. 'You'll keep an eye out? Let me know if you spot anything suspicious.'

She nodded. 'I've been handing out those leaflets. Dom doesn't like it.' She gave a sly smile. 'But I don't care.'

'That's great,' Sophie said brightly as Cassidy passed her a coffee. 'I know they don't solve the fundamental problem, but I hope they'll put women on their guard until we catch whoever is doing this.'

Sophie continued to talk to Cassidy while Karen took in the bar. No curly-haired men were in here now. That would be too easy. A couple of women sat in a booth near the entrance, chatting and both tucking into a full English. A lone man sat at the table opposite, watching them intently, his fingers slowly tracing the length of his glass.

Karen watched as he picked up his pint and crossed to their table. It was ten a.m. – very early in the day for alcohol. She couldn't hear what he was saying. Probably some worn-out chat-up line.

Though the conversation was inaudible, it was easy to follow proceedings by watching their body language. The women shook their heads and shifted positions, so they had their backs to him. But he wasn't deterred. With an arrogant smirk, he placed his glass on their table and spoke again. The women tensed, reaching for their bags, ready to make a quick getaway despite the fact their plates were still half full.

'Just popping to the ladies, Sarge,' Sophie said.

'Okay.' Karen drained her coffee. 'Thanks, Cassidy.' She walked towards the exit and paused beside the women's table, fixing the arrogant man with a glare. 'Everything all right here?'

'What's it to do with you?' he asked, puffing out his chest and giving her a nasty smile.

Karen flashed her warrant card and saw the smile slide from his face.

'I've done nothing!' he said. 'Just being sociable. Talking to these ladies.'

'We were about to leave anyway,' the woman closest to Karen said.

'You don't have to.'

'It's fine. We don't want any trouble.' Of course they didn't. Self-preservation, head down, don't make a fuss. They weren't going to draw attention to themselves when there was a chance he'd follow them after they left the bar.

'Killjoy,' the man muttered as he carried his drink back to his own table as the women settled their bill.

'Couldn't you see they didn't want to be bothered by you?'

'We were just having a nice chat.'

'They turned their backs on you. Can't you take a hint?'

'They were just playing hard to get. I was about to offer them a drink. It's all a game. Women pretend not to be interested until the bloke puts his hand in his pocket. That's just how it works.'

'No, that is not how it works. It really isn't.'

He sat down with a thump. 'What would you know?'

'Clearly more than you. If a woman says she's not interested, believe her.'

He scowled into his pint as Sophie came over.

'What did I miss, Sarge?'

Will Horsley watched the two officers leave the council buildings from an upstairs window. When he'd sent that email, he'd been trying to help, but this was now getting too close for comfort. He was sure the police were eyeing him up as a suspect. No wonder witnesses were reluctant to come forward. Their questions had felt like an interrogation.

And they'd asked him to identify the other people in the CCTV from Imporium. How was that fair? Expecting him to name his new workmates? He wasn't exactly Mr Popular now, but giving their names to the police would make him *persona non grata* around here. Besides, they were all nice enough lads. It's not like one of them could be the nasty bloke spiking women's drinks in bars.

'All right, *William*?'

Will started at the sound of Todd's voice.

'You're so jumpy,' Todd said with a sly smile. 'What have you done?'

'Nothing,' Will said indignantly.

'Sure, because the police always visit people who've done nothing wrong.'

Will sighed. Why did the police have to visit him at work? They could have phoned and asked him to come to the station. That way he wouldn't have been gossiped about. Everyone would be talking about it now.

'So, what did you do?' Todd asked with a grin, perching his backside on the edge of an empty desk.

'Nothing. I'm just helping them with enquiries.'

'Uh-huh, course you are, *William.*' Todd laughed.

Will clenched his teeth. He really didn't like Todd. Maybe he should have given *his* name to the police. He'd been there, after all. He could see how *he* liked being interrogated.

Todd walked away laughing, and Will swore at him under his breath.

He really was obnoxious. But Will was sure that even Todd, as unpleasant as he was, wouldn't drug and sexually assault a woman. Only a very depraved, sick individual would do that. Todd was annoying and had a mean streak, but he wasn't that bad.

When she was back in the office, Karen called Phoebe Woodrow's home phone and mobile again, but got no answer. She rummaged through the active paperwork on her desk and located PC Naylor's original file.

She skimmed the notes from Naylor. He'd included the sister's name and address. Lisa Woodrow, 110 Coronation Road,

Woodhall Spa. It would take Karen a good forty minutes to get there from Nettleham after work, but if she was able to get more from the sister than Naylor had, it would make the journey worthwhile. She called ahead and asked permission to drop in that evening. Lisa Woodrow sounded guarded on the phone but agreed to Karen's request.

For the rest of the day, Karen focused on the aggravated burglary cases, making sure her paperwork was in order. It was detail-oriented and tiring work.

As the officers around her began to pack up and leave for the day, Karen yawned and stretched her arms over her head. She'd heard nothing back yet from Rawlings and Fraser. Had Will Horsley identified the curly-haired man in the club?

She turned her attention back to the paperwork littering her desk and groaned. She didn't feel up to checking more documents. Instead, she put her copy of PC Naylor's report into her bag and switched off the computer. It was too early to go to Lisa Woodrow's house, but if she was quick she could fit in a trip to Phoebe's apartment first.

There was a slim possibility both Phoebe's phones weren't working, and she was safe at home. She hadn't been home, or at least hadn't opened the door, when PC Naylor had called round on Saturday, so it was unlikely Karen would find her there, but it wouldn't hurt to check again.

'I'm off out,' Karen said, stopping by Sophie's desk. 'You can reach me on my mobile if you need anything.'

'All right, Sarge. Did you hear back from Rawlings and Fraser? Do we have an ID?'

Karen shook her head. 'I've not heard.'

Sophie sighed and refreshed her computer screen. 'They've not updated the case report or task database either.'

'I'm sure they will soon. I probably won't be back to the office tonight, so I'll see you tomorrow,' Karen said, leaving Sophie to stare forlornly at the database.

◆ ◆ ◆

Phoebe Woodrow lived on a quiet, tree-lined street. Her apartment block was a modern red-brick construction with sandstone accents. It was four storeys high, and the apartments on the upper floors had Juliet balconies, reminding Karen of her first flat. She'd had a Juliet balcony off the master bedroom, and on hot nights, desperate for cool air, she'd leave the door open. Though it had made her uneasy. It felt very different to leaving a window ajar.

Across the road, there was a long row of Victorian townhouses, and beside a postbox, on a yellowing patch of grass, was a wooden bench.

Unlike Erica's block, Phoebe's building had no pretty grounds. No flowers, no shrubs, no grass. Instead, the front was covered with tarmac and used as a car park.

Karen wasn't really surprised when she rang the doorbell to apartment 3B and got no reply. It had been worth a shot, she figured, and she scribbled a note and pushed it under the front door along with her contact card in case Phoebe came back.

Straightening up, she sensed she wasn't alone. The skin on the back of her neck prickled.

Karen turned slowly.

A woman, who looked to be in her late twenties, was watching Karen with suspicion.

'She's not home,' the woman said. She wore a black sleep mask shoved up on to her forehead, which made her fringe stick up.

'Sorry, did I wake you?' Karen asked.

The woman nodded. 'I was having a nap. I'm going out later, and it's been a long day. What do you want with Phoebe, anyway?'

Karen felt a spark of hope when the neighbour mentioned Phoebe by name. Too often, when canvassing for witnesses, Karen found that people didn't get to know their neighbours. Perhaps they'd only nod as they passed them in the hall. But she was roughly the same age as Phoebe. Perhaps they'd been friends. She might be a good source of information.

Karen pulled out her warrant card and walked towards the neighbour, holding it out. 'DS Karen Hart.'

The woman looked shocked. 'What's Phoebe done? Is she in trouble? Is she hurt?'

Karen shook her head. 'I don't know. I'm just looking for her. One of her friends hasn't seen her for a few days and is concerned. When was the last time you saw her?'

The woman appeared to think back. 'I'm not sure. Maybe Friday? Yes, it was Friday. She was about to go out celebrating.'

'What's your name?' Karen asked.

'Trisha. Trisha Naylor,' she said.

'And how long have you known Phoebe?'

'Since she moved in. Two, maybe three years now.'

'Are you close?'

Trisha smiled. 'Phoebe's a laugh. We've had drinks a few times, usually at my place, not hers. And we go out sometimes. I like her. She's fun. We got to know each other when my fridge-freezer broke. It was full of food about to spoil. Phoebe saved the day by letting me use hers until mine was repaired.'

'Do you mind if we have a quick chat? You might be able to tell me something that would help track her down.'

'All right,' Trisha said warily, 'but I don't want to get her in any kind of trouble.'

'She's not in trouble,' Karen said. 'We're just concerned. We want to make sure she's okay.'

Trisha seemed to accept that. She nodded and gestured for Karen to come inside. 'Do you want a drink?' she offered. She led Karen into the kitchen and opened the fridge, pulling out a half-finished bottle of white wine. Held it up. 'One of these?'

Karen shook her head. 'I'd better not.'

'Oh, still on duty, I suppose,' Trisha said. 'What about coffee, tea?'

'Coffee would be great,' Karen said.

Trisha switched on the kettle and leaned against the kitchen counter. She poured herself a large glass of wine, sipped it, pulled a face. 'It's a bit sour,' she said. 'Never mind.' And then took another gulp. She pulled off the sleep mask and put it on the windowsill.

The kitchen was small and narrow. There was a large fridge-freezer which took up quite a lot of the space. And at the other end of the kitchen was a narrow window that looked out on to the street. Karen guessed Phoebe's apartment would have a similar layout. Her kitchen likely looked out on to the same street.

She had Erica's description, but Erica had known Phoebe for years. People changed. Trisha had got to know her recently and she might give a fresh perspective.

'I know you said Phoebe was a laugh, but I was wondering . . . is there anything else about her that you could tell me? Small details – even seemingly insignificant ones – can often prove useful in an investigation.'

'She's fun. She likes going out, having a drink. Doesn't take herself too seriously. She's close to her family. Well, I say that, but it's just her grandma really. Her mum and dad died a few years ago. She goes to see her gran at least once a week. Oh, that's a point.' She ran a hand through her hair. 'She's looking after her gran's cat, Tommy, because they don't take animals in the care home.' She paused for breath. 'I should check on the cat if she's not home. It's weird, though, because she could have asked me to feed him. I wonder why she didn't.'

'Do you have a spare key?' Karen asked.

Trisha nodded.

'We could go and take a look now.'

But Trisha narrowed her eyes. 'I don't think that's such a good idea. Phoebe might not want you poking around in her flat. No offence.'

'None taken,' Karen said drily. 'You could go and check. I'll stay here.' She knew very well that Tommy was safe and sound with Erica, but this was a way of making sure Phoebe wasn't lying injured, or worse, in her apartment.

Trisha narrowed her eyes again, assessing Karen. After a moment, she nodded. 'Yeah, all right. I hate to think of anything happening to Tommy.' She got a key from a kitchen drawer and said, 'Coffee's in that cupboard up there. Cups are in the one next to it. Help yourself. I'll be back in a minute.'

She left Karen alone in the kitchen.

Karen was tempted to go out into the central hallway and try to get a glimpse into Phoebe's apartment while Trisha was in there. But she wanted to earn Trisha's trust, so she busied herself making the coffee.

A couple of minutes later, Trisha returned. 'Well, there's no sign of the cat,' she said. 'I looked in the cupboards and under the bed.' She shrugged. 'I've left out a bowl of food and refreshed the water, so if he is there, then at least he's got something to eat and drink. I know cats tend to hide.' She chewed on her lower lip. 'Although the litter tray was empty, so that suggests he isn't there. Wherever she's gone, she must have taken the cat.'

It was time for Karen to come clean. 'Actually, I think a friend is looking after Tommy.'

'Oh, right. Well, that's okay then,' Trisha said.

Karen felt a tinge of guilt, but this way, if anything had happened to Phoebe and there were obvious signs in the flat, then Trisha would have noticed them.

Karen sipped her coffee, and Trisha pulled her phone out of her pocket and flicked through some of the photographs. 'This is me and Phoebe.' She showed Karen a photograph of the two of them clutching narrow champagne glasses and beaming at whoever was taking the photograph.

Karen zoomed in. 'Has Phoebe still got long hair now?' she said.

'Yeah.'

She was beautiful, Karen thought. Dark eyes lined with thick lashes, and long, dark hair framing a fine-boned face. She looked happy.

Where is she now?

'Has there been anything bothering Phoebe recently?' Karen asked, handing Trisha back her phone.

'Bothering her? She isn't really the type to let things bother her. She's quite brisk and businesslike about life. She isn't emotional about things. She wants to be successful and happy. And I think she is.'

'Has she been worried about anything? Anyone in her life, ex-boyfriend maybe?'

Trisha raised her eyebrows. 'Actually, there is one really creepy guy. Phoebe doesn't take it seriously at all. She laughs at him. She says he's a harmless saddo.'

'Who?' Karen asked.

'Some weird guy. He sometimes sits outside.' Trisha moved closer to the window and beckoned for Karen to do the same. 'He sits outside on that bench, see?' She pointed at the bench by the postbox and gave Karen a direct look. 'That's odd, right?'

Karen felt a heightening concern. Perhaps something really had happened to Phoebe. Something bad.

'He's not there today,' she said, 'but he is most days.'

'How long has he been doing it?'

'A few weeks,' she said. 'I think Phoebe knows him, but she doesn't really talk about it. When I asked her, she just laughed it off, said he was a creep and that it was a free world. That she wasn't bothered if he wanted to sit on a bench.' Trisha shrugged. 'I thought it was bravado at first, but I don't know. I think she really isn't bothered by him. She doesn't seem to think he's a threat. I asked her why she hasn't reported him to the police. It would creep me right out if I had some bloke spying on me.'

Karen nodded. 'I think most people would be disturbed by that.'

Trisha shrugged. 'She hasn't told me anything about him. She sometimes waves at him when she leaves the apartment, and laughs.'

'I can look into that. See if I can get him on any local cameras.'

'Good.' Trisha leaned on the kitchen worktop. 'Also, she works with a weird old guy sometimes.'

'Cary?' Karen queried.

'No, that's the younger guy. The good-looking one. Always smiling. I quite like him. This one is older, and he picks her up in a black Range Rover with tinted windows. He has two other men with him all the time. Massive blokes, built like the proverbial . . . well, you know, ginormous blokes. I think they're bodyguards. When she first moved in and I saw him picking her up, I thought she might be a high-class escort. I told her that, and she nearly died laughing.'

Trisha grinned at the memory. 'No airs or graces. Phoebe's fun. She's probably out now having a good time somewhere.'

'Is she often away?'

'Yeah, quite a bit. She does usually tell me, but not always. So I've not really been concerned that I haven't seen her for a few days.'

'Has she been stressed lately?'

'Well, a little bit, but that's understandable. She's buying her own place. She just rents her apartment, like me, but this new place she's bought is gorgeous. It's huge, with a massive garden. On the outskirts of Lincoln, I think she said Burton Waters. She's definitely on the up. Like I said, Phoebe is determined to be successful.'

Karen thanked Trisha for her time, then swallowed the last mouthful of coffee. 'You've been a lot of help. If you do see Phoebe, give me a ring.' She put her contact card down on the windowsill next to Trisha's sleep mask. 'And let her know how worried people have been. Ask her to get in touch with me directly.'

Trisha nodded. 'Sure.'

'And give me a call if you see that man lurking outside again.'

She nodded. 'I will do.'

'And what about ex-partners?' Karen remembered to ask as she walked along the hallway to the front door.

'She dated one man on and off for a couple of years. I can't remember his name, but he seemed nice enough. I never heard any rows or anything like that. I think they broke up about six months ago, maybe a bit less.' She shrugged. 'But I don't think there was any bad feelings between them.'

'That's helpful, Trisha. Thanks.'

Karen walked down the stairs deep in thought. Trisha hadn't seem overly concerned, and as Phoebe often went away without telling anyone, it gave Karen hope she would be fine. But the man who had been sitting outside Phoebe's apartment filled Karen with foreboding. She'd worked on cases involving stalkers before, and they had rarely ended well.

CHAPTER NINE

Karen walked back to her car thinking through everything Trisha Naylor had said.

She'd been surprised at the photographs Trisha had shown her, too. In them, Phoebe had long, dark hair, which she hadn't in the other photographs Karen had seen.

The long, sleek hair had made Karen recall the woman caught on CCTV at Imporium. Was her mind looking for connections that didn't exist, or had Phoebe also been at Imporium on Friday night?

If Phoebe had been at Imporium, that was an extremely worrying development.

Her phone beeped with an incoming message. It was Mike texting to say he was heading up a training course and would need to be away for one, or possibly two, nights soon. She smiled, pleased that things were picking up for him. He'd been a police dog handler for years, but after the death of his son, he'd given up. When Karen had met him, he'd been working as an estate manager for an awful man. But he'd now decided to take on a new challenge and was training dog handlers, and so far it was going well.

Karen noted the time and realised she'd better get a move on. She needed to get to Woodhall Spa and speak with Phoebe's sister.

She put through a call to Mike. It went straight to voicemail, so she left a message telling him she'd be working late. One of the good things about being with someone who knew the job was that he wasn't surprised by Karen's long hours. He knew exactly what it was like.

The drive to Woodhall Spa took forty minutes. It was an interesting town with historical ties to the RAF and the bouncing bomb. It was the sort of place you could go to for Sunday lunch and then spend time wandering around the small eclectic shops. There was an old-fashioned butcher and a lovely deli.

There was also a golf course nearby, and Petwood Hotel, which had the bouncing bomb memorial in its grounds. It was somewhere she could imagine living when she retired. She had a sudden thought of sharing a bungalow in one of these quiet streets with Mike. She smiled. She wouldn't mention retirement plans to Mike just yet. She didn't want to scare him off with that level of commitment. Karen was surprised he hadn't been scared off already. Her job wasn't without risk.

Lisa Woodrow lived on Coronation Road, not far from the Tea House in the Woods, a tea room and restaurant that Karen had visited a few times with Mike.

Karen frowned as she drove along slowly. The road shifted into shadows after she passed the Kinema in the Woods. The road was lined with tall trees, and she could have sworn there were no more houses this far along, but just as she was starting to think she must have missed it, she spotted a tiny, narrow bungalow half hidden by the trees. She parked at the side of the road.

Despite not being far from town, the area still felt isolated. She got out of the car. It was cooler out of the sun, and Karen shivered. The stillness was unnerving. Tense, she turned in a tight circle, half expecting to see someone lurking behind the trees watching her. But there was nothing.

The bungalow had a large driveway covered with seed pods from the surrounding trees. Phoebe's sister took a while to come to the door, and when she did, she was dressed in a blue smock smeared with a variety of paint colours. Her black hair was piled on top of her head and there was a paintbrush behind her ear.

'Lisa Woodrow?'

'That's right.'

'I'm DS Hart,' Karen said and showed her ID. 'Thank you for taking the time to see me.'

'Not at all,' Lisa said, standing back and letting her in. 'I'm starting to get concerned. You know I spoke to the police on Saturday?'

'Yes. Have you heard from your sister since then?'

Lisa shook her head, dislodging the paintbrush but catching it just in time. 'No, I've left lots of messages, but she hasn't got back to me.'

'Does she often go away without letting you know?' Karen asked, as Lisa led her into a sitting room with large bay windows. There were stacks of paintings in one corner and a worn-out sofa, along with a wing-backed armchair and a small table and chairs that looked antique. Karen had once seen pictures of Jane Austen's writing table, and Lisa's table looked very similar. Karen thought it might collapse if she looked at it the wrong way.

'Yes, that's why I wasn't worried at first,' Lisa said, putting her hands at the small of her back and stretching. 'But since I spoke to the police, I've been trying to get in touch with her, and she hasn't responded.' Lisa shrugged. 'She can have tunnel vision when she's busy at work. She's very focused, which sometimes means other things, like her social life or her family, can fall by the wayside. Not that she's selfish,' Lisa added hurriedly. 'But she can be single-minded. And at the moment, she's preparing for a really big deal at work.' Lisa smiled. 'We couldn't be more different. She's the business-minded one and I'm the arty, creative one.' She looked around the room as if noticing it for the first time. 'Sorry about the paintings. I do have a studio in the garden, but I'm always running out of space.'

'I like it,' Karen said, nodding at the top painting on the pile. It was an eye-catching work of colourful lilies in a basket.

'Thanks,' Lisa said. 'I mainly paint flowers. They sell well. Do you want to sit down?'

Karen was relieved that Lisa gestured to the sofa rather than the spindly table and chairs. She sat down gratefully. 'You told PC Naylor that your grandmother saw Phoebe on Saturday.'

'Yes, that's right.'

'Is there any reason she might have got the day wrong?'

Lisa thought for a moment and then shook her head. 'I suppose it's possible. She's getting on in years. She did say to me once that, after retirement, all the days of the week seem the same. She doesn't get confused with times or dates generally. That's not why she had to move to the care home. It was because she's physically frail, not mentally. Everyday tasks wear her out. She's had problems with her heart.'

'Can you think of anyone Phoebe might be staying with?'

Lisa tilted her head thoughtfully. 'She was seeing someone for a while, but that's been over for months. Maybe a friend . . . but I don't really know that much about her social life.'

'You mentioned she's been working on a big deal. Who does she work for?'

'Well, it's her own company,' Lisa said. 'CaP Diagnostics.'

'What do they do?'

Lisa pulled a face. 'I'm going to sound like an awful sister, but I don't pay as much attention as I should. They do something with medical equipment, I think. Her business partner's a man named Cary. They also have an investor. He's ridiculously rich.

Came on board a couple of years ago. What was his name? Quentin Chapman. Yes, that was it.'

Quentin Chapman. The name sounded familiar to Karen. She couldn't place it. She would look him up when she got back to the station.

'When did you last see Phoebe?' Karen asked.

Lisa looked up at the ceiling, trying to recall. 'I think it was Easter.' She glanced at Karen. 'Yes, I know. Quite a while ago. I should make more of an effort. I bought Easter eggs and took them to her apartment. It's something we used to do as kids. Eat our Easter eggs in the space of minutes.' She smiled. 'It's silly. I think Phoebe thought I was mad, but I do feel a bit melancholy for the old days sometimes. She doesn't. She's very matter-of-fact. We're not very alike, but I am proud of her.'

'PC Naylor said you weren't concerned when he spoke to you. Was that because your grandmother had seen her?'

'Well, yes,' Lisa said. 'And Phoebe does ignore my messages on a regular basis. It's not that she's being nasty. It's because she's busy. Like I said, she's very focused on business. I know that she probably *is* fine . . . but I am worried. Now. Will you let me know when you manage to contact her?'

'Of course,' Karen said. 'Was Phoebe worried about anything when you saw her at Easter?'

'No, I don't think so. We didn't talk much about our current lives. I wanted to reminisce about when we were kids, and Phoebe indulged me.'

'Is there anything else that might help me find her?'

'She's quite close to her neighbour. I can't remember her name. I think it's Trish or Tracy, something like that.'

'I've spoken to her,' Karen said. 'She hasn't seen Phoebe for a few days.'

Lisa frowned. 'Have you checked her passport? She might have gone on holiday. She does tend to do things on the spur of the moment.'

'That's not something we've looked into yet,' Karen said, 'but of course, we can. If Phoebe's grandmother saw her on Saturday, she might know more. With your permission, I'd like to visit her, if that's okay?'

'I'll get you the address.' She left the room, and Karen took a moment to study the painting of the lily. It was very lifelike, almost like a photograph.

'It's realism,' Lisa said, as she came back in and saw Karen looking at the artwork. 'My favourite style. I like it when people aren't sure if it's a photograph and lean in for a closer look.'

Karen nodded. 'I like the little ladybird on the stem.'

Lisa beamed. 'Not many people notice that. You must have a good eye.'

Karen smiled. It wasn't so much that she had a good eye for art, more that her job required an attention to detail.

Lisa handed her a scrap of paper. 'Here you go. It's Pineview Care Home, Branston.'

'Great,' Karen said. 'It's not far from where I live, so I can pop in on the way home. Thanks very much for your help, Lisa.'

Lisa led Karen to the front door. 'You'll let me know when you hear anything?'

'I promise.'

CHAPTER TEN

The care home was within walking distance of Karen's house, so she decided to leave her car at home.

Pineview was a single-storey, relatively new building. There was parking out the front and around the side, but a lot of the spaces were taken, so Karen was glad she'd left her car at home. At the door, she pressed the button and waited for a few moments until the speaker crackled. She had to repeat her name a few times before the door release clicked.

Inside, the air was warm and stifling. It felt stale, and Karen would have liked to open a few windows.

She stopped by the reception desk and showed her ID to the woman sitting there.

'I hope you can help me. I'm looking for a woman called Phoebe Woodrow. She's the granddaughter of one of your residents, Barbara Moore. We've been told that Phoebe was here on Saturday.'

The woman behind the desk was dressed in a lilac tunic and navy trousers. Her name tag identified her as Maeve. Her cheeks were flushed, and she fanned herself with a hand. 'I'll check the book for you, duck,' she said. 'When did you say? Saturday?' She ran her finger along a page in the sign-in book.

'Yes, Saturday,' Karen said. 'Morning.'

After barely glancing at the book, the woman looked up and shook her head. 'Sorry, she isn't in the book.'

'Is there a chance she came in without signing the book?'

'No,' the woman said. 'If her name's not down here, she hasn't been in. We're strict about it. Not only to protect the residents, it's the fire regulations. We must know who's in the building when there's a fire alarm.'

'Of course. I just wondered if she could have slipped in unnoticed.'

Again the woman shook her head. 'I think that's unlikely. The door is always locked. You've got to be buzzed in by someone. And the door release is under this desk.'

'There's another one over there, though, isn't there?' Karen asked, pointing to a large green button on the wall, by the door.

'Yes,' the woman said, grudgingly. 'There is, but someone would still have had to let her in.'

'Perhaps someone leaving opened the door and Phoebe slipped in?'

'I really think that's unlikely,' the woman said, seemingly irritated now.

'Could you double-check?' Karen asked, nodding at the list.

The woman huffed. She probably had a lot of work to do. Karen sympathised, but she really needed to know if Phoebe had been here on Saturday.

She studied the list, more carefully this time, then looked up. 'No. She wasn't here on Saturday.'

'Would you be able to check the lists to see when she last signed in?' It was a long shot, but Karen thought Phoebe might have signed for the wrong day. 'It's Phoebe Woodrow,' Karen said again.

'Yes, I know. I haven't forgotten,' the woman said with impatience. She flipped the pages. 'Ten days ago,' she said finally. 'She's not been here since then.'

That was very odd.

'Could I speak to Phoebe's grandmother? I have permission from her other granddaughter, Lisa Woodrow. Her name's Barbara Moore.'

'Barbara? Well, I'm not sure. Can you come back tomorrow? We like to get the residents settled by this time in the evening. That's why we have visiting hours.' She slammed the book shut.

'It is important,' Karen said. 'Her granddaughter could be missing.'

'I understand that, but—'

'I don't think you do understand,' Karen said. 'Phoebe could be at risk.'

'Of what?'

'I don't know yet, and I don't know where she is, which is why I need to speak to her grandmother.'

After a few moments, the woman sighed. 'All right. I'll get Tara. She's her carer tonight.'

A good ten minutes passed before Tara appeared. She was shorter and had a more cheerful face than the woman who had greeted Karen at reception. Her hair was neatly pinned back and she wore the same lilac tunic with navy-blue trousers and sensible black shoes.

'Hello,' she said cheerfully. 'I'm Tara. You wanted to speak to Barbara?'

'Yes, that's right,' Karen said. She held out her ID. 'I'm DS Hart. I want to have a quick word with her about her granddaughter, Phoebe Woodrow. I hope she's not sleeping.'

'Oh no,' Tara said. She pulled open the heavy fire doors and led Karen into a corridor. 'She's in her chair reading. She gets through so many books. I'm a bit envious. I wish I had more time to read, don't you?'

'Yes,' Karen said. 'It would be nice.'

'It'll be no bother. She'll be glad to see you, I'm sure.'

'Has she been worrying about her granddaughter?'

'She hasn't mentioned it. Not to me. I've been looking after her this afternoon. Gave her dinner and her afternoon tea.' She shrugged. 'She hasn't mentioned her granddaughter at all.'

'Could Mrs Moore have misremembered a visit from Phoebe? Perhaps she gets her times or dates mixed up?'

'It's possible,' Tara said. 'She doesn't usually get muddled, though. She noticed I forgot to bring her custard creams last week, and I haven't heard the end of it since.' She smiled. 'I'm kidding. She's a sweet old thing really.'

Tara led the way along the corridor and then stopped beside a light blue door. Each of the doors had a label with the name of the resident in the central panel.

'It's more personal,' Tara said, 'having names, rather than numbers. And when someone's new, it helps them. Instead of saying *dearie* or *duck*, they can use the patient's name. It's nicer.'

Tara rapped on the door, waited until a reedy voice told them to enter and then opened the door.

Karen followed her inside.

'Hello, Barbara. You've got a visitor. A police officer.'

'A police officer?' Barbara sat in an armchair beside a set of patio doors. She was tiny. Her grey hair was carefully styled back from her face in waves, and her dark, bright eyes looked at Karen inquisitively.

'Yes, I'm DS Karen Hart. I hoped you could spare me a few minutes for a quick chat.'

'Of course,' Barbara said. 'Have a seat.'

Karen took the chair opposite her.

'I'll leave you to it,' Tara said. 'Barbara, if you press the call button when you're done, I'll come and show DS Hart out.'

'All right, dear.'

Tara left them alone.

'I don't want to worry you unnecessarily,' Karen said, 'but we're looking for your granddaughter. We want to make sure she's okay.'

'Is she in any trouble?'

'She's not in trouble with the police,' Karen was quick to reassure her. 'But one of Phoebe's friends reported her missing, and we haven't been able to track her down. So I'm following up with you today to see if you know anything that might help me find her.'

Barbara nodded.

'When did you last see Phoebe?'

'On Saturday.'

'Definitely Saturday? You're sure?'

'Yes,' she said firmly, but then frowned and hesitated. 'At least, I *think* it was Saturday.'

'What time?'

'About half past ten, I think. I was sitting in my chair. I'd drifted off to sleep after breakfast. I do that quite a lot these days. I woke up from my nap, and there she was, sitting in that seat you're in now.' She smiled. 'It was a nice surprise. She normally comes on Sundays, and occasionally during the week if she can get away from work. She works very hard.'

'The receptionist I spoke to told me Phoebe didn't sign in on Saturday morning,' Karen said cautiously. She didn't want to insult Barbara Moore, but Karen wondered if the elderly lady had dreamed the visit.

'Well, she might have forgotten,' Barbara said, lifting a hand and then letting it drop.

It was possible. Had Phoebe slipped through the door when somebody else was leaving? Or had she entered the building through a different entrance? Could Phoebe have walked around the back of the care home and entered her grandmother's room through the patio doors?

'Do you ever have these doors open?' Karen asked.

'Yes. Quite often. It gets ever so hot in here. They're terrified of the residents catching a chill. But I think fresh air is good for you.'

'So do I,' Karen said. 'Do you want me to open them now?' she asked.

Barbara smiled. 'Yes, that would be lovely.'

The key was in the door. It turned easily, and Karen slid the door open a couple of inches. The cool evening air entered the room.

'That's better,' Barbara said, taking in a deep breath.

'Do you know anything about your granddaughter's life?'

'Of course I do,' Barbara Moore said. 'She works very hard. She's got her own apartment, and she's buying a new house.'

'I heard that,' Karen said. 'You must be very proud of her.'

'I am proud of both my granddaughters, and my grandson.'

'Does Phoebe have a brother?'

'No, just a sister, Lisa, and a cousin, Simon.' Then Barbara asked, 'Do you know where Tommy is?'

'Your cat? Phoebe asked a friend to look after him on Friday evening. She's still looking after him. He's well cared for.'

'Oh, that's good,' Barbara said. 'I should have known Phoebe wouldn't have abandoned him. Surely that means she planned to go away, doesn't it? If she thought to leave Tommy with a friend.'

Karen nodded. 'That's very possible. Do you have any thoughts on where she might be or who she might be with?'

Barbara thought for a moment. 'Not really. She doesn't go out with friends often. Occasionally she goes to a work event. I worry about her sometimes. I tell her she works too hard. She's such a good girl. So hard-working. The perfect granddaughter.'

Karen thought how odd it was that everyone who knew Phoebe gave a slightly different description of her. Was it their own interpretation, or did Phoebe deliberately show different sides to the people she was close to?

'How were things going for Phoebe at work?'

'I'm so proud of her. She was about to do a big deal. That was why I was surprised to see her on Saturday. I wasn't expecting to see her last weekend.'

'When Phoebe comes to visit, does she ever enter through these patio doors?' Karen asked, looking out at the shady gardens.

'No, she comes in the front, like everybody else. That's what you're supposed to do.'

'Is it possible to walk around the side of the building?'

'I think there's a gate,' Barbara said, frowning. 'But I'm not sure. I've been in the garden, but I haven't seen around the side.'

'What about boyfriends?' Karen said. 'Has she been seeing anyone lately?'

'No, she doesn't have any time for romance. She ended a relationship a few months ago. Rohan. He was a nice chap. She told me she needed to give work all her attention.'

'Was there any bad feeling between them?'

'No, I don't think so. Phoebe didn't mention it if there was.'

'What about someone else? Had anyone been bothering Phoebe?'

Barbara's hand fluttered up to her cheek. 'You're worrying me now, Detective. Do you think somebody's hurt Phoebe?'

'I just want to make sure she's safe,' Karen said. 'It's my job to look at all possibilities.'

Barbara nodded thoughtfully. 'She's been working quite closely with a man called Cary. They usually get along, but I think he's been getting on Phoebe's nerves recently.'

'Really?' Karen asked, leaning forward. 'What has he been doing?'

'I don't know exactly. I don't think it's anything serious. She's just getting fed up with him. Phoebe likes to do things her own way.'

Karen returned Barbara's smile. 'That would be Cary who works at CaP Diagnostics?'

'Yes, that's right. That's the name of Phoebe's company. I remember now.'

Karen would need to pay them a visit. She needed to talk to this Cary chap, but it was too late tonight. Perhaps she could fit a visit in tomorrow, before work. Life would be a lot simpler if Churchill would give Karen official time to investigate Phoebe's apparent disappearance.

She thanked Barbara and tried to reassure her that, though Karen wanted to locate Phoebe, it was unlikely her granddaughter had come to any harm.

Outside, in the fresh air, Karen pulled out her mobile as she strolled back to her house. She gave Erica a call and updated her. Though there wasn't much news, Karen tried her best to be reassuring.

She paused beside a large beech tree and scrolled through Phoebe's social media profiles. They weren't private, and they hadn't been updated since Friday. Karen clicked on a couple of the photographs and was reminded again of how similar Phoebe was to the woman in the CCTV footage from Imporium. The woman in the bar's face wasn't visible in the recording, but everything else – hair colour, build – was very similar.

Karen decided that, when she got back to her laptop, she would log onto the system and add it as a note to Operation Starling.

It would be helpful if she could look into Phoebe's financials and phone records, but that wouldn't be possible without the go-ahead from Churchill.

She put her phone back in her pocket and looked towards her house.

She froze.

There was a shadowy figure, lingering beside the entrance to her driveway.

A moment later she saw a tiny Jack Russell beside the ominous shadow. She released the breath she'd been holding. It was just a dog walker.

Karen gave herself a mental shake. It didn't hurt to be cautious, but she couldn't keep expecting danger around every corner. If she wanted to keep her job *and* her sanity, then she needed to brush off empty threats from the criminals she encountered daily. She couldn't allow their menacing words to cause her to live in fear.

She crossed the road just as Mike came around the side of the house with a bag of rubbish to put in the wheelie bin.

'Ah, you're back,' he said. 'I thought we'd have a stir-fry for dinner. Quick and easy. What do you think?'

'Sounds great to me,' Karen said. 'How's your day been?' She stepped inside and was greeted by a very affectionate Sandy. Karen fussed over her as Mike told her about his day and his plans for the new training course. When he'd finished, he asked, 'And what had you working late?'

Karen poured herself a glass of water. 'A bit of a mystery,' she said. 'There's a woman who may or may not be missing.'

Mike frowned.

'Well, a friend says she went missing on Friday night,' Karen explained. 'Her grandmother says she saw her on Saturday.'

'That sounds like a tricky case,' Mike said.

'It's not even a real case yet. I said I'd look into it as a favour for a woman in my counselling group. Churchill took a bit of persuading.' She didn't mention the fact that she was only allowed to investigate it outside working hours.

'What do you think? Is she missing?'

'I honestly don't know, but I've left a message and asked her to get in touch, and she hasn't yet. She's not answering the door of her apartment, and no one seems to have seen her since Saturday.'

'So, something's going on,' Mike said.

Karen sipped her water. 'Yes. The trouble is, I'm not sure what.'

CHAPTER ELEVEN

DC Rick Cooper woke with a start. It was dark, and his neck hurt. It took him a moment to remember where he was. He rubbed the back of his head as he reoriented himself.

He'd fallen asleep on the sofa. Again. His neck was sore because his head had lolled forward as he slept. With a groan, he straightened, trying to ease the crick in his neck.

What he *wanted* to do now was stagger off to bed. But what he *needed* to do was take his dirty dishes to the kitchen and clear up after dinner, because Priya would be here in the morning and he didn't want her to think he was a slob.

He stood up, switched on the lights, and grabbed his plate and glass. The plate was smeared with the remnants of a chicken tikka masala ready meal.

Rick carried his plates towards the kitchen but paused in the hall.

It was quiet.

The light was off in the hallway, but there was a glow coming from his mother's room. It seemed brighter than usual. They left the side lamp on all the time now, so she wouldn't be scared by the dark when she woke up. She found the darkness disorienting, and that, on top of her memory issues and confusion, was too much for her to deal with.

But the level of light suggested the *main* light was on, rather than just the bedside lamp.

A stab of fear jolted his stomach.

Had he remembered to set the alarm before he fell asleep?

No, he hadn't.

He walked quickly to his mum's room, still holding the plate and glass, and his worst fears were confirmed when he saw she wasn't there.

The room was empty. The duvet cover had been thrown back. Where was she?

'Mum!' he called out.

He dumped the plate and glass on the telephone table and rushed to the downstairs toilet. There was a commode in her room now. She was too weak to make it to the bathroom under her own steam, but she wasn't in her room . . . She had to be somewhere. Maybe she'd forgotten about the commode and had tried to make it to the bathroom.

The door was shut. He rapped on it. 'Mum. Mum, are you in there?'

There was no answer, so he yanked open the door. *Empty.*

She was so weak now. Surely she wouldn't have tried to tackle the stairs on her own. He'd thought about installing one of those stairgates designed for toddlers, but he'd never followed through with it, and his mum had *never* tried to get upstairs on her own before.

He raced up the stairs, taking them two at a time, but she wasn't there. He looked in every bedroom, the main bathroom, then even checked the cupboards.

She was gone.

A wave of nausea crashed over him. He stood at the top of the stairs, swaying slightly, light-headed, unable to think straight.

He pressed his hands to his head to stop the racing panic.

Think. Just think.

He flew back down to her bedroom and checked her wardrobe. Her coat was missing, the red one. Her shoes? They were all still there. Had she gone out in her slippers?

Rick grabbed his keys and wrenched open the front door, running along the path to the street. He looked all around, but there was no sign of her. He called out multiple times.

The security lights came on next door. The front door opened, and the neighbour came out. Rick stared at him blankly, momentarily unable to remember his name. He couldn't think of anything but his mum.

Then it came to him. *Jeffrey.* That was his name.

'Have you seen my mum?' Rick said. 'She's gone.'

Jeff and Deidre had lived next door for years. They knew Rick's mother from the old days, before the disease had ravaged her.

He gave Rick a sympathetic grimace. 'No, we've not seen her.'

'I fell asleep,' Rick said, and guilt slammed into his chest like a visceral pain.

'We'll help you look, mate. I'll find a torch and get the missus out as well.'

'Thanks,' Rick said.

He reached in his pocket for his mobile. He should call his sister. She'd want to know, but what could she do? She was in Cornwall. He imagined her reaction. She'd be frantic and angry with Rick for letting this happen.

He decided not to call her.

Instead, he dialled the number of someone he could always rely on.

She answered on the third ring.

'Sorry, Karen. I know it's late, but I didn't know what else to do.'

Karen and Mike got to Hykeham in record time. Mike had brought Sandy.

Karen stood with Rick as he explained what had happened, and Mike got Sandy out of the back of the car.

'I've reported it,' Rick said, 'so local units will keep a lookout. I don't know where she's gone. She can't have walked far. She's really weak.'

'We'll find her,' Karen said, putting a hand on Rick's arm. 'If we split up, we can cover more ground.'

He nodded. 'I've been up and down our road and checked the cul-de-sacs either side, but she's not there. The neighbours are looking, too. Three sets of them.'

'That's good.' Karen squeezed Rick's arm. 'It's going to be okay.'

He shook his head. 'It's my fault.'

She had never seen Rick so pale. 'No, it isn't. Come on, you need to hold it together. We'll find her.'

Mike joined them and said, 'Have you got something of your mum's, something that will have her scent?'

'Do you think Sandy will be able to track her?' Karen asked.

'It's a little out of her wheelhouse, but a scent is a scent. I reckon she can handle it,' Mike said.

Rick nodded eagerly, darted inside and came back out holding his mother's dressing gown.

Mike took it from him and held it close to Sandy's nose. 'Can't promise anything, but we'll give it a go.'

Rick nodded. 'I'll try anything. We just have to find her.'

Before long, Sandy gave a single bark. The dog trotted along, nose to the pavement, but Mike kept her on the lead. Karen and Rick followed them.

Sandy stopped suddenly, going forward then circling back, then finally edging out to sniff the tarmac.

'She likely crossed here,' Mike said.

'Do you think it's working?' Karen asked, jogging after Mike.

'I think so. It looks like she's picked up a scent.'

'You don't think we should spread out?'

Mike shook his head. 'I think we should follow Sandy.'

Karen nodded in agreement, and they carried on, faster now as Sandy picked up speed. Though Mike kept up with her quite easily, it wasn't long before Karen was feeling out of breath and wishing she took the time to exercise.

As the minutes passed, Karen grew wary. Could Rick's mum really have travelled this far? Sandy was a scent dog, but she wasn't used to tracking *people*. What if she was leading them – quite literally – up the wrong path.

But then suddenly Rick said, 'I know where she's gone! The library.' He pointed ahead. 'She keeps talking about it.' He smiled in relief. 'Of course, I should have guessed. It'll be shut, so she's probably sitting outside.'

Sirens sounded in the distance, and Rick's gaze met Karen's.

His expression turned from happy relief to absolute terror in a second.

Rick raced ahead.

When Karen turned the corner, she was greeted by a sight that made her stomach clench. A group of people were gathered in the road. Karen heard them talking.

'A little old lady,' one of them said. 'She just stepped right out in front of the car. I saw her. There was nothing the driver could do. No way they could stop in time.'

'A tragedy,' another voice said. 'Absolute tragedy. Poor thing.'

Karen walked forward. Her legs felt numb. Rick was kneeling on the ground beside the frail form of his mother. There was blood. A definite head injury, and her left leg was crooked.

The sirens ceased as the ambulance pulled up.

Karen moved back so she wouldn't get in the way. The paramedics spent time working on Rick's mother, trying to stabilise her.

That was good. It meant she hadn't been killed on impact, but she looked in a bad way.

Karen rubbed the back of her neck, pacing backwards and forwards as Rick spoke to the paramedics.

When he took a step back and the paramedics moved Mrs Cooper to the ambulance, Karen put her hand on his shoulder. 'Are you going with her?'

'Yes,' he said.

'We'll come straight to the hospital. Do you need me to contact anyone for you?'

Rick looked stunned. 'Um, my sister, but I'll do it when I learn more about Mum's condition.'

'You might want to do it soon, Rick,' Karen said gently. 'Just in case she needs to get here.'

He flinched at the implication. 'You're right. I'll do it as soon as we get to the hospital.'

CHAPTER TWELVE

The next morning, Karen was up early, thinking of Rick. She'd called but he hadn't answered, which was understandable if he was still at the hospital. When she and Mike had left the hospital in the early hours, Mrs Cooper had still been hanging on, but things hadn't looked good.

By seven thirty, Karen was in her car and heading to Lincoln. She intended to visit CaP Diagnostics before work. She parked in Lucy Tower Street and walked along the Brayford Wharf, watching the swans glide along in the calm water.

CaP Diagnostics was in a tall glass building halfway along the Wharf. They didn't own the whole building. Other businesses operated out of there, too – accountants, a small telecommunications company and graphic design firm.

Karen had bought a coffee, expecting to have to wait until the building opened for the day, but as she got closer she saw the doors were already open even though it wasn't quite eight a.m. Clutching her takeaway coffee, she stepped inside and spoke to the man behind the reception desk. 'I need to speak to Cary Swann, please.' She showed her ID.

The man looked at it, blinked and then nodded. 'Take a seat. I think he's upstairs.'

Karen sat beside the large windows. The city was just getting busy. It was going to be another sweltering day. She took a sip of the strong, hot coffee and wondered again how Rick was doing. Had they managed to save his mother?

'Hello?'

Karen turned to see a tall man in grey trousers and a white shirt with the sleeves rolled up. He held himself confidently, but not arrogantly. He looked young. Even younger than Phoebe, though Karen knew from a cursory background check he was the same age, twenty-eight.

He gave her a warm smile and held out his hand. 'Cary Swann. How can I help?'

Karen switched her coffee to the other hand so she could pull out her warrant card. 'DS Karen Hart. I'd like to ask you some questions about your business partner, Phoebe Woodrow.'

If he was surprised, he didn't show it. 'Why don't you come up to my office?'

They went through the door behind reception, and he jabbed a button to call the lift.

'It's a bit hectic today,' he said, delivering that warm smile again as they both entered the lift. 'We're moving our offices upstairs to the penthouse.'

'Oh, I see.'

'I was wondering where Phoebe had got to. I thought she'd left all the moving to me.' He watched Karen as he spoke, taking cues from her reaction. His smile lessened. 'I hope Phoebe's all right?'

'Have you seen her recently?'

'I've not seen her since Friday.'

'Is that unusual?'

'Not really. She doesn't keep typical office hours. I thought her celebrations had extended past the weekend. We've had a bit of success with the business recently. A lot of hard work, but it's paying off now.'

'I'm glad,' Karen said as the lift doors opened and they stepped out. There were boxes everywhere, but not many people moving them.

'How many employees do you have here?'

He chuckled. 'Unfortunately, not many. It's me and Phoebe and our assistant – who's not in yet.' He nodded at several boxes of files. 'I suppose I won't have to go to the gym tonight.'

The lights flickered on in the corridor as they walked. The walls were white, decorated with splashes of colour from abstract art prints. 'Come in here,' Cary said, leading the way into an open-plan office filled with cubicles. Odd when there were only three staff, Karen thought.

'Planning to expand?' Karen asked, nodding at the empty desks.

'Possibly. If all goes well.'

He stopped beside an office with glass walls. What was the point in offices like that? There was no privacy.

There were even more boxes stacked inside. Cary offered Karen a seat, and moved some clutter off the chair behind his desk so he could sit down.

'So, when you saw Phoebe on Friday, how was she?' Karen asked.

'How was she?' Cary repeated the question. 'Fine, I think. Just normal.' He shrugged.

'What time was that?'

'Oh, let me think. We'd gone to a bar in the city centre for drinks to celebrate. I didn't stay long, left about nine p.m.'

'Was she still there?'

'Yes.'

'And what was the bar called?'

'Imporium.'

Karen felt her stomach sink. She pulled out her phone. 'Sorry, won't keep you a moment.'

Phoebe looked like the woman captured on the cameras at Imporium, and now Cary had confirmed she'd been there on Friday night. Had the man who'd been drugging women and assaulting them escalated his crimes?

She typed a message to Sophie, asking her to send over the still images of the woman at Imporium. She had a sickening sense that something awful had happened to Erica's friend.

Sophie, as efficient as ever, sent the pictures back within seconds.

'Is this Phoebe?'

Cary took Karen's phone, studied it for a moment and then pursed his lips. 'Could be. It's hard to tell, though. I can't see her face.'

'What about her clothes?'

'Yes, she was wearing something similar, I think.'

'Was she drunk?'

'Probably,' he said with an uneasy smile. 'We were celebrating.'

'Who else was there with you?'

'Our assistant, Lou. It was just the three of us.'

'Did you notice anything odd at the bar? Was anyone watching Phoebe or offering to buy her drinks?' Karen asked.

Cary's expression grew serious. 'You really think something's happened to her, don't you?'

'I'm concerned,' Karen said. 'I need to contact her urgently. Could you try to call her for me?'

Cary nodded and patted down his pockets, looking for his phone. Then he spotted it on the desk.

He dialled, but the call rang out. 'No answer,' he said. 'That's weird.'

If Phoebe had gone away for a few days, which was looking increasingly unlikely, Karen had hoped she would answer his call. If there was a big deal on the horizon, then Phoebe would care about that. Surely she'd answer Cary's call if she could.

'Does she have any personal problems? Ex-boyfriends, that sort of thing?'

'No, I don't think so,' Cary said. 'She's on pretty good terms with Rohan Peck. That was her last relationship. They split a few months back, but there was no animosity between them.'

'Can you think of anyone who might want to harm Phoebe?'

Cary's eyes widened. 'Harm her? No, I can't think of anyone who'd want to do that.'

'Who would benefit from Phoebe's death?'

'Financially, you mean?'

'Yes, who would inherit her assets?'

Cary paled. 'I . . . er . . . I don't know.'

'I'm sorry. I know these questions are difficult.'

'Yes, they are.' He looked down at his desk. 'I suppose you'll have to locate her will to identify her beneficiaries.'

Karen reeled through the questions she had to ask when dealing with a missing person.

She needed full authorisation from Churchill. Phoebe's life could be in danger. That's if it wasn't already too late. There was no way Churchill would be able to turn down her request for an official investigation. Phoebe had been at Imporium, and Karen thought there was a strong possibility that Phoebe might be an Operation Starling victim.

'I understand Phoebe is in the process of purchasing a house?'

'Yes. I don't think it's gone through yet.'

'You're both coming into a lot of money?'

Cary smiled, but without the same warmth as before. 'That's the plan.'

'What does your company do?'

'Phoebe and I designed and built a prototype medical scanner, and we're hoping to sell CaP Diagnostics to a large pharmaceutical company.'

'That's impressive. You and Phoebe managed to do that on your own?'

'Not completely on our own. We needed funding. We have an investor. A chap called Quentin Chapman. And now we're going to sell the IP, the intellectual property, along with the prototype,' Cary elaborated.

'I spoke with Phoebe's neighbour. She mentioned a man who's been sitting on a bench outside Phoebe's apartment and watching her.'

Cary blinked. 'Really? She's never mentioned it to me.'

'The neighbour said Phoebe didn't take it too seriously, laughed it off.'

His frown deepened. 'That doesn't sound like Phoebe. She's not stupid. She'd report something like that.'

'Do you have any idea who the man is?'

'I'm sorry. I can't think of anyone who'd do that.'

'The neighbour also said there's an older gentleman who's called around a few times. He had a black Range Rover and was with a couple of other men who looked like bodyguards.'

Cary said, 'That sounds like Quentin Chapman. He never goes anywhere without them. It's just for appearances' sake. He believes in our project. He's a great guy.'

Karen wondered if Cary was trying to convince her or himself. She'd wait to meet this man and form her own opinion. 'Could you give me Quentin Chapman's contact details?'

After Karen left Cary, she called Sophie straightaway. 'Sophie, I think I might have a potential ID on the woman at Imporium. Phoebe Woodrow. A friend of mine reported her missing and I haven't been able to locate her. You need to let Simpson's team know about the potential ID.'

'Right,' Sophie said. 'I'll add it to the system and then go and speak to DCI Simpson. Have you heard from Rick?'

'No,' Karen said. 'I haven't heard anything yet. I've left him a message, but I suppose he'll get back to me in his own time.'

'Yes,' Sophie said. 'I suppose he will.'

Karen hung up and looked out over the wharf.

Surely Phoebe's presence at Imporium on Friday night couldn't be a coincidence. Had the man who'd been drugging and assaulting women imprisoned Phoebe? Had he killed her? Or was she traumatised after the attack and had retreated somewhere safe?

In previous cases, the victims had been taken back to their own flats or houses and assaulted. The fact that Phoebe was still missing was a serious concern.

Karen's mobile rang. It was Rick.

'Rick, how's your mum?'

He didn't speak straightaway, but Karen could hear him breathing. Eventually he said, 'She didn't make it.'

'Oh, Rick. I'm so, so sorry. Is there anything I can do?'

'Could you let everyone know? I don't feel up to contacting everyone individually.'

'Of course I will,' Karen said. 'And I'll tell Churchill you're taking compassionate leave. Are you still at the hospital? Do you need a ride home?'

'No, there's no need. I've got a taxi booked.'

'Is your sister coming home?'

'Yes,' Rick said. 'But she's in Cornwall, so it's quite a trek.'

'It is a long journey.'

'Thanks for last night,' Rick said.

'Don't mention it,' Karen said. 'I just wish things had turned out differently.'

'So do I,' Rick said. 'So do I.'

Karen took a deep breath after Rick hung up. She shoved her phone in her pocket and looked out over the water. It was a gorgeous morning, and the sunlight glittered over the rippled surface.

People bustled by, on their way to work. The world was going on as usual, and it seemed so unfair on Rick.

CHAPTER THIRTEEN

When Karen got to the station, she headed straight to Churchill's office. She rapped on the open door.

'DC Jones has updated me,' he said as Karen sat down. 'It seems we have a link between Operation Starling and your missing friend.'

She wasn't *Karen's* missing friend, more a friend of a friend, but Karen went along with it. As long as Churchill was doing *something*. 'Yes, that's right. Phoebe Woodrow has got long, dark hair and a similar build, *and* she was at Imporium on Friday night.'

'Promising lead,' Churchill said.

'I take it I'll be able to look into her disappearance full-time now?'

'Well,' Churchill said, 'you'll be able to spend more time on it, but don't forget the paperwork on those burglaries.'

'Of course not, sir,' Karen said.

'It will be a nice bit of kudos for our team. Well done.' Churchill treated her to a smile as he brushed a speck of fluff from the top of his desk and then straightened his tie. 'Was there anything else?'

'Yes, some sad news. Rick's mother died.'

Churchill leaned back in his chair with a sombre expression. 'She's been ill for a while, hasn't she?'

'Yes.' Karen didn't want to get into the gritty details, but she knew she should say enough to save Rick from having to repeat the details to everyone. 'She had dementia. She left the house when Rick was asleep and was knocked down by a car. She was taken to the hospital, but she didn't make it.'

'That's awful,' Churchill said, pausing for a moment and looking down at his desk. 'He must be feeling terrible. I'll get on to HR. He'll obviously need compassionate leave.'

◆ ◆ ◆

Back downstairs, there was a feeling of sadness over the whole office. Karen's gaze kept drifting to Rick's empty seat. She busied herself, grabbing a cup of coffee and then looking into Quentin Chapman.

He was certainly an interesting figure. No criminal record, but there were some very thought-provoking articles about him by Cindy Connor, a journalist who'd previously given Karen a hard time.

From the articles, Karen gleaned that Chapman had been associated with shady business dealings for several years. He always seemed to be in the right place at the right time to get in early.

One of the articles included a photograph of him wearing a long navy coat with a mustard yellow scarf, probably cashmere.

He stood with his hands in his pockets, aware of the camera as he smiled smugly. The picture had been taken as he'd left court, where he'd won a claim against him. He'd been accused of buying a company for an undervalued price after leaning on its customers and spreading rumours about the company's bad performance – false rumours, if Cindy Connor was to be believed.

He was certainly someone to follow up on, but he wasn't their top priority now. It looked as though Phoebe was a likely victim of the drink spiker haunting Lincoln's bars. Quentin Chapman appeared to be a dodgy character, but that didn't mean he had anything to do with Phoebe's disappearance. Still, Karen made some quick notes, determined to find out more about him later.

Sophie arrived back in the office, clutching an A4 folder.

'How did the Operation Starling briefing go?' Karen called.

She set the folder down on Karen's desk. 'It went okay. They're keen to follow up on Phoebe Woodrow.'

'Good,' Karen said.

'They were surprised you didn't attend the briefing.'

'I had a couple of things to look into,' Karen said. 'There's a lot of people involved in Operation Starling. Standing room only. You can give me the highlights, can't you?'

'Sure,' Sophie agreed. 'But first, more coffee.'

She made two steaming mugs and brought them back to Karen's desk.

'Everyone agreed to operate on the assumption that the woman in the CCTV is Phoebe Woodrow,' Sophie said. 'We need to identify the two men of interest who were at Imporium on Friday night. The man grabbing Phoebe's arm and the man she was talking to outside the bar. Members of Simpson's team are tracking all the CCTV in the area to pinpoint them arriving and leaving the bar, and which routes they took. My job is updating the database.' She smiled. To anyone else it would be a punishment, but Sophie looked positively thrilled at being assigned the task.

'Okay, good,' Karen said. 'I've sent you my notes from my meetings with Erica Bright and Phoebe's sister and grandmother. If you need anything else, let me know.'

'Will do.' Sophie picked up her coffee and blew across the top before taking a tentative sip.

'I'm going to pick up lunch in a bit,' Karen said, 'and take it around to Rick.'

She wanted to make sure he was coping, and find a way to offer help if he wasn't. He'd had a brutal shock. Karen had found grief lonely and isolating. She wanted Rick to know he had people he could rely on.

'Oh, that's a nice idea,' Sophie said. 'Tell him . . . Well, tell him we're all thinking about him.'

'I will,' Karen said.

◆　◆　◆

Outside, the sun was now blazing hot. Karen fanned her blouse, trying to keep cool as she headed to her car.

Then she stopped.

To her left was a black Range Rover with tinted back windows. She frowned as the driver's door opened and a huge man stepped out. He had long, dark hair tied back in a ponytail and was wearing a navy suit and tie. He looked directly at her.

Karen strode towards the car.

The big man smirked. 'Mr Chapman would like to speak to you.' He jerked a thumb at the back passenger door.

Seriously? Karen looked the goon up and down. She glanced into the back, but it was impossible to see through the tinted glass.

The big man opened the door for her.

Inside, sitting in the back seat, was Quentin Chapman. He looked older than the photograph in the article Karen had read and wore a suit and tie despite the heat. The air conditioning was on full blast, and Karen felt a rush of cold air leaving the vehicle.

'Mr Chapman,' Karen said. 'What an unexpected pleasure. Why don't we go and speak in the station? It'll be more comfortable.'

Chapman chuckled. 'No thanks,' he said. 'Police stations aren't my cup of tea.'

In the front passenger seat was another huge man whose shoulders bulged out past the sides of the seat. He was wearing a suit jacket too, but his strained across his back. His head was shaved, his neck thick, and even when Karen got in the back seat he didn't turn around.

When the ponytailed henchman went to shut the door, Karen held out her hand, pushing back on it. 'The door stays open.'

'You won't feel the benefit of the air conditioning that way,' Chapman said.

'That doesn't bother me,' Karen said. She wanted to be able to make a quick getaway if she needed to, and that meant the door stayed open.

After a slight hesitation, he smiled. He might have been a good-looking man once, but there was something cruel about his eyes. He had a strong jawline and salt-and-pepper hair that had been brushed back from his forehead and carefully styled. 'You've done your research, DS Hart. You know who I am.'

'Yes, and I see you did your research, too.'

He smiled, wider this time, showing a mouthful of veneers. 'I heard you wanted to talk to me.'

'I do. About Phoebe Woodrow.'

He nodded and arranged his features into a concerned expression. 'What a wonderful young woman. Full of promise,' he said. 'Smart as a whip. Incredibly impressive for someone her age.'

'When did you last see her?'

'Oh, let me see.' He seemed to consider it. 'Over a week ago now. So, I'm sorry, I won't be much help to you.'

'Do you know if Phoebe has been worried about anything?'

'I don't, no. But then she didn't confide in me about things like that. We had a strictly professional relationship.'

'Who persuaded you to invest in CaP Diagnostics and the scanner?'

'I didn't need much persuading, to be honest, DS Hart. You see, my wife passed away from metastatic cancer five years ago. If it had been detected earlier, her life could have been saved, or at least prolonged. So I suppose I have a selfish reason for investing. I was determined to finance the company, hoping that the scanner would someday help people like my wife.'

He looked genuine enough. And it was a compelling reason. Even people who had no morals when it came to business could love their families.

'I read some articles in the press . . .' Karen said, letting the words hang to see if he took the bait.

She'd expected denials, perhaps angry recriminations, but Chapman simply smiled and waved a dismissive hand.

'You don't want to believe what you read in the papers,' he said amiably.

'So you're completely on the straight and narrow?'

'I can't comment on that.' His smile widened to a grin.

'You seem to be very *lucky* in business,' Karen said. 'Swooping in, buying up businesses that are down on their luck.'

'I take on projects I believe in,' he said. 'Money is just a fortunate side effect.'

'Interesting. Have you always been interested in science and technology?'

'Not especially.'

'How long have you known Phoebe Woodrow?'

'Two, maybe three years.'

'And Cary?'

'The same.'

'Are you aware of anyone else who might know Phoebe's whereabouts?'

He shook his head.

'You're a man of few words, Mr Chapman.'

He narrowed his eyes. He was sizing her up, not revealing too much. Wanting to see how much she knew first. 'Are you familiar with Stoic philosophy, DS Hart?'

Karen shook her head.

'There's an Epictetus quote: *We have two ears and one mouth so that we can listen twice as much as we speak.* It's a good code to live by, I find.'

'Could you call her for me?' Karen asked.

'Phoebe?'

'Yes.'

'Now?'

'Yes, please. I want to see if she answers you.'

'All right.' He pulled out his mobile phone and squinted at the screen but didn't put on any reading specs. Was he too vain to use them?

He dialled the number and waited. Karen heard the ringing go on and on until Phoebe's voicemail kicked in.

Operation Starling would soon access Phoebe's phone records and attempt to trace her phone. As well as helping to find out if Phoebe was screening calls, asking Cary and Quentin Chapman to call her meant the team would have their numbers. Phone calls between business partners and investors weren't a crime, but it would be useful to eliminate them.

'She didn't answer,' Quentin Chapman said, tapping the end button on his phone and then spreading his hands. 'I'm sorry I couldn't be more help,' he said. 'It's been a pleasure, DS Hart.'

Karen nodded and exited the vehicle.

When she was outside, the ponytailed heavy moved to shut the door before she was clear, catching her arm.

The man smirked. 'Sorry.'

Karen rubbed her elbow. He didn't look like he was sorry at all.

She moved away, heading for her own car. She'd bet her pension on Quentin Chapman having his fingers in a lot of pies, most of them illegal.

'Take care, Detective,' Ponytail said as Karen walked away.

It was a normal enough thing to say, but the way he said it made it sound like a threat. And compared with the intimidating words directed at Karen from the ringleader of the burglary gang, this threat felt far more menacing.

CHAPTER FOURTEEN

When Karen pulled up outside Rick's house, she spotted Priya walking along the garden path towards her. She'd only met Priya a couple of times, but Karen knew how much she'd helped Rick while caring for his mum.

She got out of the car and waved to attract Priya's attention. 'How's he doing?' Karen asked.

'Okay,' Priya said, hitching her bag up on to her shoulder. 'Under the circumstances. But he's not got any sleep yet.'

'I brought him lunch. Has he already eaten?'

'No. I offered to heat him up some soup, but he said he wasn't hungry.' She checked her watch. 'I'm sorry to rush off, Karen, but the agency's found me another job . . . That must sound heartless.'

'No, not at all. You need to make a living. It must be a hard time for you, too. You spent a lot of time with Mrs Cooper.'

'I spent a lot of time with them both. He's such a nice guy. My heart breaks for him. It was such an awful way for it to happen.'

'Do you need a lift?' Karen asked.

'My car's parked around the corner. Thanks, though.'

Rick answered the door dressed in a crumpled T-shirt and tracksuit bottoms. His hair looked like he'd been running his hands through it for hours. He had circles under his eyes and dark stubble around his chin. 'Sarge?' he said. 'I didn't expect to see you. Is everything okay at work?'

'Everything's fine,' Karen said. 'Nothing for you to worry about. I brought you lunch. A baguette with chili chicken, mayonnaise, lettuce, tomato and extra jalapeños. Just how you like it.'

'You didn't have to do that, boss.'

'Are you going to let me in? I even got you a cookie.'

There was a hint of a smile around Rick's lips. 'Sure. Sorry.'

Inside it was dim. The curtains were still drawn. There were plates on the telephone table by the hallway.

'Sorry about that,' Rick said. 'I dumped them there last night. I was holding them when I noticed she'd gone.' He scooped them up and carried them to the kitchen. 'Do you want a cup of tea?'

'I'll do it,' Karen said. 'You sit down and eat. You need food – then sleep, I should think.'

'Yeah.' He unwrapped the baguette and took a bite. 'Mmm, really good,' he said between mouthfuls.

Karen made the tea and carried it to the kitchen table, sitting down opposite Rick. 'Do you want to talk about it?'

He shook his head, lips pursed.

'Fair enough. If you change your mind, I'm just a phone call away.'

'All right.'

'What about your sister? Is she back?'

'I spoke to her again this morning. We decided she may as well stay in Cornwall. There's not much she can do here right now, and the kids . . . well, you know, it's their holiday.'

'Sure.'

'I feel caught in limbo, to be honest. There's a lot to organise. I don't know where to start.'

'You don't need to do any of that stuff straightaway, do you?'

'I don't think so. I need to get the death certificate from the hospital at some point.'

'Right. Can I do that for you?'

'I think it needs to be me. Sophie's offered to help with the rest of it. You know how much she loves filling in forms.'

Karen smiled. 'I do.'

She was gratified to see that Rick managed to eat the baguette *and* the cookie. She'd brought his favourite lunch on purpose, knowing he wouldn't have much appetite.

They spent some time talking, skirting around topics that had anything to do with his mother's death or the future. Then Karen noticed him rubbing his eyes and yawning.

'You really need to get some sleep,' she said.

'I tried this morning, but I can't.'

'You might be able to now. Sometimes food helps.' She nodded at the crumbs left from the cookie.

'Sugar coma?' He grinned, then stopped suddenly as though remembering he wasn't supposed to be joking around; he was meant to be grieving.

'I'd better get back to work,' Karen said reluctantly. 'You'll be okay?'

He nodded and they both stood up. They hugged, and Karen felt the tension in his shoulders. He was only just holding it together.

'If you need anything, Rick, food, company, *anything*, just call, okay? I'm only a drive away.'

He nodded again, and they walked to the door. As Karen left, she turned back and caught a glimpse of his drawn face before he closed the door.

She got back into her car feeling emotional. Life was so fragile. She was lucky to have her own parents still with her. She thought fondly of her mother and father, and then of how she expected them to always be around. But in the blink of an eye, they could be gone.

It had been a couple of weeks since she'd seen her parents. She decided that this weekend, she'd drive over to visit. They didn't live far away, and she missed them. She'd ask Mike if he wanted to come, too. He got on well with her parents, which was why it struck Karen as odd that she hadn't yet been invited to meet his folks. He didn't talk about them much.

She'd just put the key in the ignition when her mobile rang. She checked the screen and saw a number she didn't recognise. 'Hello. DS Hart,' she said.

'DS Hart, this is Cassidy. You gave me your card. Cassidy from the Imporium.'

Karen sat up straight. 'How can I help you, Cassidy?'

'There was a girl at the bar last night. She was drugged. Her memory is hazy but she's at my flat now, in Lincoln. Can you come?'

'Yes, of course. It happened last night at Imporium?'

'Yeah.'

'Did she report it to anyone?'

'No, just to me. I brought her back here, where she'd be safe.'

'All right. Give me your address.' Karen took it down, promising Cassidy she'd be there within minutes.

Karen then called Sophie, asking her to inform Simpson's team and update the Operation Starling database.

Should she wait and see what Simpson wanted to do? He was the lead on this case. But it was Karen who Cassidy had reached out to. Cassidy had trusted her enough to call, and Karen wasn't about to let her down.

Cassidy lived in a small one-bedroom apartment in the city centre. The lounge, dining and kitchen areas were all open-plan. She had posters on the wall for bands Karen had never heard of.

There was a sofa bed, which had been pulled out and was covered by a crumpled duvet. A young woman sat on the edge of the fold-out bed. She was wearing an oversized hoodie and black-and-white checked pyjama bottoms. Her hair was long and tangled, and her eyes were red from crying.

'I told her we could trust you,' Cassidy said, eyeing Karen suspiciously, suggesting she didn't trust Karen at all.

'Thanks, Cassidy,' Karen said. 'I appreciate you calling.'

'Do you want a cup of coffee? We were just about to have one.'

Karen nodded and Cassidy retreated to the kitchen area.

Karen took a seat beside the young woman. 'What's your name?' she said.

'Vicky,' she said. 'Vicky Cutler.'

'Okay, Vicky. Can you tell me what happened last night?'

'It's all very hazy. I just remember a man trying to take me outside. He was pulling my arm, but I managed to get free and ran to the bar for help.'

'Did you call the police?'

'No.' She shook her head firmly. 'I didn't want to.'

'Don't get heavy-handed,' Cassidy said, carrying two mugs of coffee. She set them down on the small table. 'I spent the whole night trying to convince her we could trust you.'

'No one's getting heavy-handed,' Karen said. 'I just need you to talk me through it. Through the whole evening, from when you entered the bar.'

'Right. Okay,' Vicky said, taking a deep breath and rubbing her face. 'I went out after work and didn't go home first, so I wasn't dressed provocatively or anything like that. I was wearing my work gear: trousers, white shirt and my boots. I was with the girls from my office. We work for an insurance company, and we'd had a bad day. We've got a new boss and he's just changed everything around, and no one knows what they're doing . . .' She trailed off. 'I didn't have *that* much to drink,' she added.

Karen experienced a flash of anger. It made her sick to hear Vicky feel she had to defend her clothing choice as *not provocative* and take care to highlight the fact she was not inebriated. It was hard to listen to Vicky pointing out that it wasn't her fault – when it was never the victim's fault, no matter what they were wearing or how much they'd had to drink. But she needed to hear everything Vicky could tell her about last night.

'Don't go blaming Vicky for drinking too much,' Cassidy said.

Karen shot Cassidy a look, and she seemed to get the idea and stayed quiet.

'He seemed really nice at first,' Vicky said.

'What did he look like?'

'He was young, white and tall. He was dressed in a way that made me think he'd just come to the bar from work – shirt, trousers. No tie, though.'

'Was he with anyone else?'

'Not that I noticed. Do you mind if I smoke?' she asked.

Karen shook her head.

Vicky rummaged through a handbag beneath the fold-out sofa, found her cigarettes and lit one. Her hands were shaking. 'It could have been so much worse. He could have . . .'

'And this happened at Imporium?' Karen clarified.

'Yes.'

'About what time?'

'It was about ten o'clock,' Cassidy said.

'And you brought her back here afterwards?' Karen directed the question to Cassidy.

She nodded. 'Yeah. We got a taxi back to mine.'

'He got really nasty all of a sudden,' Vicky said. 'He was nice at first. Offering to buy my drinks, telling me how nice I looked. But then everything changed. He was practically dragging me out of the bar, saying I was playing hard to get. But I wasn't. I thought we were having fun. It wasn't my fault.'

'No, this wasn't your fault,' Karen said as Vicky started to cry. 'Do you think you could identify him?'

She sniffed. 'I'm not sure. My mind is so muddled up.'

'Would you consent to having a blood sample taken?' Karen asked.

'Why?'

'It could provide proof that you were drugged.'

'Don't you believe me?' Vicky asked.

'I do, but this isn't about whether I believe you or not. It's about gathering enough evidence to make sure we put this man away for a very long time.'

Vicky nodded. 'All right then. Where do I have to go?'

'To the police station. I'll arrange it,' Karen said. 'You don't have to worry. It'll be stress-free, I promise. Were you injured at all when he was trying to pull you out of the bar?'

Vicky shook her head. 'No . . . He didn't hit me or anything like that. He just had such a tight hold on my arm. I really thought he was going to drag me out to the street, and nobody was going to help, and . . . I should have screamed, or shouted, or done something, but I couldn't. I panicked. I froze up.'

'Did you see him doing this?' Karen asked Cassidy.

'No.'

'So you didn't get a good look at him?'

'Not really,' Cassidy said.

'Okay. Let's see if we can get a few more details,' Karen said. 'You said he was young, white and relatively tall.'

Vicky nodded.

'Do you remember anything about his hair?'

'It was light-brownish, I think. And curly.'

'Clean-shaven?'

She nodded.

'What about his build?'

'Slim.'

'Do you remember his eye colour?'

Vicky shook her head. 'Sorry, no. I don't remember. I wish I could remember more, but I just feel so confused. My head feels like it's filled ¡with cotton wool.'

'It's all right, Vicky. You're doing great. It's probably the after-effects of whatever he put in your drink.'

She nodded.

'It will wear off,' Karen said. 'But I think we should probably get you checked out at the hospital. They can take the blood sample there if that's all right with you?'

Vicky nodded again.

Karen looked at Cassidy. 'Are you able to go with Vicky?'

'Sure.'

'When do you have to be back at work?'

Cassidy shrugged.

If it was in Karen's power, she'd have shut Imporium down. But, of course, that would mean whoever was drugging these women would move to another venue. It wouldn't solve the problem long-term.

Karen watched Cassidy hand Vicky a tissue and wished there was more she could do. The next few days, weeks and months would be traumatic for the young woman. It wasn't something she'd be able to put behind her. Every time she went out from now on, she'd remember.

CHAPTER FIFTEEN

Back at the station, Karen raced along the corridor towards the main office area. She'd called ahead and asked Sophie to access Imporium's CCTV again. Surely they'd get a better image this time. They needed a break if they were going to have a chance of catching this evil man.

She was lost in thought and almost collided with DS Rawlings as he stepped out of the Operation Starling incident room.

'Oh, Karen. I thought you'd gone home,' he said.

Karen frowned. 'Why did you think that?'

'You took such a long time on your lunch break. I thought you were on a half-day.'

Karen clenched her teeth. It really wasn't his business. She was accountable to DCI Churchill and to Morgan, not DS Rawlings.

Karen stepped around him and carried on walking, but unfortunately Rawlings decided to match her stride. 'So, where did you get to? You missed the briefing, you know?'

'Briefing?'

'Yes, Operation Starling. We had another briefing at one o'clock. You were supposed to be there. Even DCI Churchill came down.'

'Well, nobody told me.'

'It's on the system,' Rawlings said. He smirked. 'I thought you lot were very keen on logging everything in the system. I'm surprised you missed it.'

Karen wondered why some people made it their life's work to be annoying. Rawlings certainly seemed an expert at it. He could win awards.

'I didn't know there was a briefing,' Karen said. 'I went to visit a friend at lunchtime, and then I got a call. There was an incident at Imporium last night. A young woman called Vicky Cutler said that a man spiked her drink and tried to drag her out of the bar. Fortunately, she managed to get away and got help from the woman behind the bar.'

'Why am I only learning about this now?' Rawlings demanded petulantly. 'It should have been in the briefing. This is completely unprofessional, Karen. You can't just go off and do things on your own. It's *our* investigation. *You* are just support.'

'I know that,' Karen said, taking a deep breath before responding so she didn't bite back. 'I'd given Cassidy, who works at Imporium, my contact details on a previous occasion. She called me about an hour ago, and I went straight to her flat to speak to them both. DC Jones is arranging a hospital visit for the young woman to have blood samples taken.'

'I'm glad you at least managed to cover that,' Rawlings said sarcastically with a shake of his head.

'Have you shown Lisa Woodrow the CCTV images yet?' Karen asked. 'Does she think it's Phoebe? Could she identify either of the men we're looking for?'

'No, she says she can't be sure.'

Karen frowned. 'Did you speak to her in person?'

'DC Fraser did.'

'Maybe—'

'We've got it under control, thank you very much, DS Hart.'

'The system will be updated, and I'm sorry I missed the briefing,' Karen said. 'It won't happen again.'

She walked off, leaving Rawlings fuming behind her. He could fume all he liked. She had a job to do.

Karen pulled up a chair at Sophie's desk and looked at the younger officer hopefully. 'Tell me you've got something.'

Sophie smiled. 'Yes, I contacted Dom. The link he gave us is still active. Take a look at this.' She played the video. It was very reminiscent of Friday night. A man with curly hair gripped Vicky's elbow, just as he had on Friday night with the other woman. Karen was now very concerned about Phoebe. Vicky had managed to escape, but had Phoebe been as lucky?

After letting the footage run for a few moments, Karen said, 'Did you know there was a briefing about Operation Starling?'

Sophie nodded. 'Only just in time. It pinged up on my computer while I was inputting data. I thought about calling you but then I knew you'd gone to see Rick, so . . .' She shrugged. 'I was there anyway, so I took plenty of notes.'

'Churchill was there?' Karen asked.

Sophie nodded. 'Yes, he's quite involved now.'

'Typical. It's because he thinks there's a result for us in there somewhere – a bit of kudos.'

Sophie smiled. 'Simpson's team have been trawling CCTV in the local area from Friday. But they haven't yet managed to identify this curly-haired man, or the man outside the club on Friday night.'

Karen studied the images. The man inside the bar had light, curly hair. Whereas the man outside, the one Will had seen, had shorter, dark hair. Definitely two different individuals.

'We *must* identify these two men,' Karen said. 'That's the most important thing right now. Are they any closer to confirming that the woman in the club on Friday was Phoebe Woodrow?'

Sophie shook her head. 'Nothing definitive yet.'

'Right.'

'But the DCI thinks we have enough to get a warrant to search Phoebe's flat.'

'Great,' Karen said.

She left Sophie puzzling away over the footage and headed to see Morgan. He was squinting at his computer screen as she rapped on his open door.

'Karen, how was Rick?'

'As well as could be expected, I think,' Karen said. 'Pretty fragile at the moment.'

'Understandable,' Morgan said.

'Did you go to the Operation Starling briefing?'

'No, I don't want to step on DCI Simpson's toes.'

'DCI Churchill seems keen for us to be involved now. I'm going to pay Rohan Peck a visit. He's Phoebe's ex-boyfriend. I've done a bit of research and found out he works as a photographer. Do you fancy coming with me?'

Morgan glanced at his computer and then said, 'Yes, I need to get away from all this admin. You know, the higher up you go, the more time you spend behind a desk.'

Karen filed that knowledge away. It was something she'd noticed, and in her opinion it was a good reason not to go for an inspector's position.

◆　◆　◆

'I haven't got a clue where she is,' Rohan Peck said, preparing to shut the door in their faces.

'Hang on,' Morgan said, putting a firm hand against the door. 'We'd like a chat.'

'What for?' Rohan said. 'I told you I can't help.'

'You might know something useful, even if you think you don't,' Karen said. 'Can we come in, or do you want to give your neighbours something to talk about?'

He looked over their shoulders, his eyes scanning the street. Then he rolled his eyes and opened the door wide. 'Fine, come in.'

It looked very much like a normal terraced house from the outside, but the inside was a different story. Every wall was covered in framed prints and photographs, all of them black-and-white.

Rohan wore a blue bandana, which made it hard to see his hairstyle, but it was on the long side. Karen thought it looked a little bit like a mullet, although that could have been due to the bandana.

As he led them past the front room, Karen glanced inside. There were photographs pinned with small pegs on lengths of string hanging from the ceiling.

He noticed her looking. 'I'm working up a scheme for a gallery. I'm planning an exhibition.'

'You're certainly prolific,' Karen said as they entered the kitchen. Every spare bit of space on the walls was covered with photographs.

'Deciding what to include is difficult,' he said. He pointed to the opposite wall. 'This one is a series.'

Karen looked closely. The first photograph was an apple with a bite taken out. Then there was a series of photographs showing the apple slowly decaying and shrivelling up.

'Interesting,' she said.

'It's my study on death,' he said, nodding as he looked at his work.

Morgan lifted his eyebrows, but in typical Morgan fashion made no comment.

'I see,' Karen said. 'It's very . . . detailed.'

'Do you want a drink?' he asked, leaning on the kitchen counter and crossing his arms, clearly not in the mood to make one.

'I'm fine,' Karen said, and Morgan said the same.

'What can you tell us about Phoebe Woodrow?' Morgan asked.

'Not much.'

'When was the last time you saw her?'

Rohan shrugged. 'Months ago.'

'And that's when you broke up.'

'Yeah.'

'Exactly when did you break up?' Morgan asked.

'Well, I can't remember to the nearest minute,' Rohan said.

'I'm not asking you to, but I would like an approximate date.'

He screwed up his face. 'It was winter. January. The most depressing time of year. Phoebe really does pick her moments.'

'So, she ended things?' Morgan asked.

Rohan shot him a hot look of anger, and then glanced at Karen. 'Is he always this diplomatic?'

Clearly a rhetorical question. Karen didn't answer.

'She finished things then?' Morgan prompted.

Rohan nodded. 'Yeah. Said she was too young to settle down. I said at twenty-eight she was past her biological best anyway, and she didn't appreciate that.'

'I can't imagine why,' Karen muttered.

He smirked. 'Anyway, all water under the bridge. I don't care.'

'Really?'

'Yes, really. I'm seeing someone else now. Life's great.'

'Good for you,' Morgan said.

'Does Phoebe often go off on her own without telling anyone?' Karen asked.

Rohan thought for a moment, running a finger along the kitchen counter. 'She did it a couple of times when we were together. It's not malicious. She just doesn't think about how things affect other people. Once she drove up to Scotland and I didn't hear from her for four days. Her sister didn't know where she was either.

I thought something bad must have happened to her. Her sister said she was probably fine, but I was convinced she wouldn't just leave without sending me a message. You know, it only takes a few seconds to send a text, doesn't it? And I left her loads of voicemails and messages, and she didn't reply to any of them.'

Karen listened, thinking Rohan sounded like a man who *was* bothered by the way Phoebe had treated him.

'I mean, who does that?' he said. 'Anyway, she turned up eventually, saying she'd needed a social media break and had turned off her phone. I was annoyed, but I suppose I got over it. Phoebe had a way of laughing things off even when I was upset. She was able to turn it around and make it seem like I was being unreasonable.' He lifted his head, suddenly aware that he was revealing more about their relationship than he'd intended. 'Anyway, none of that matters anymore.' He shrugged.

'What about her work?' Karen asked.

'What about it?'

'You knew where she was working?'

'Yeah. CaP Diagnostics with Cary Swann.'

'How does she get on with Cary?'

'Fine, I think. He thinks she's wonderful. She walks all over him, just like every other person in her life. And now they're both about to make millions. Lucky them.' He looked around at his small kitchen, scowling.

'Things are going well for her,' Morgan said.

'Yes, I suppose they are.'

'What was your relationship like?' Morgan asked.

Rohan gave a mirthless chuckle. 'I fell hook, line and sinker for her. But it wasn't meant to be,' he said.

'How long were you together?'

'A couple of years, on and off.'

'Phoebe is about to come into a lot of money,' Morgan said. 'If you two had still been together that would have meant quite a lifestyle upgrade for you.'

'What are you implying?' Rohan said. 'I can make my own way, thanks. I don't need a woman to keep me.'

'But the extra money would have been nice,' Karen said. 'If you had stayed together, you'd have been very well-off.'

He shrugged. 'It wouldn't be my money. It was never mine.'

'It must have annoyed you, though, to miss out. You were with her through leaner days when she was starting the company, and just when she's about to see success . . .' Karen trailed off.

Rohan scowled. 'I know what you're trying to do. You're trying to give me motive for doing something to her, but you're wasting your time. I bet she turns up after being on a yoga retreat without taking her phone, or something equally daft.'

'If anything happened to Phoebe, what would happen to her newfound wealth?' Karen asked.

'I don't know,' he said, his scowl deepening. 'It would probably go to her sister, or maybe her grandma.' He adjusted his bandana and then paused. 'Actually, that's not true. Any money associated with her shares in the business would go to Cary.'

'The chap she works with?' Karen asked.

'Yeah, so perhaps you should be talking to him and not me. That's a nice little motive for you, isn't it? I haven't seen her for months. It's him you want to talk to.'

That was very interesting, Karen thought. During her conversation with Cary, he hadn't mentioned Phoebe's interest in the company going to him in the event of her death.

'Would you mind having a look at these two photographs?' Karen asked, pulling out her phone and showing him the stills of the CCTV from Friday night, showing the woman they thought might be Phoebe Woodrow.

'Do you think that's Phoebe?' Rohan asked, frowning.

'Don't you?'

He puffed out his cheeks. 'It could be, I suppose. It's not a very detailed picture of her, though, is it. You can't even see her face properly.'

She showed him the image from outside Imporium. 'What about this one?'

'It's hard to say. It looks a lot like her, I'll give you that, but I couldn't say for certain.'

'And what about this man?' She pointed to the dark-haired man standing outside with Phoebe.

He squinted, then zoomed in. 'I don't know. He looks familiar. I can't place him though.' He stared at the screen for some time and Karen really thought he might be able to identify the man. But then he shrugged and handed her back the phone. 'Sorry, no idea.'

'What were you doing on Friday night?' Morgan asked.

Rohan's eyes narrowed. 'I need an alibi, do I?'

'It would help with our enquiry.'

'I was at a party held in a gallery and loads of people saw me.' He reached into a kitchen drawer and pulled out a small printed card. 'I was there, and then I stayed at the owner's house and helped with the clean-up on Saturday. I was there all day, in fact, planning the next exhibition.'

'All right. Thanks for your help,' Karen said. 'Can we get your mobile number, please?'

'What for?' he asked.

'Just to update you if—'

'*When* she turns up, you mean. Then you'll all look like fools, just like I did eighteen months ago.'

'I hope she does turn up,' Karen said. 'That's the best-case scenario.'

Rohan frowned. 'Do you *really* think something's happened to her?'

'We're looking into it,' Morgan said in a tone that ended the conversation.

◆ ◆ ◆

Morgan and Karen walked back to the car.

'Now we've got Rohan's number,' Karen said, 'we'll be able to check Phoebe's phone records and see if he's telling the truth when he says he hasn't been in touch with her.'

'Yes, and we need to check out his alibi. All that study-of-death stuff was weird. Do you want me to drive back?' Morgan asked. 'You can call Sophie with an update.'

Before Karen could answer, her mobile rang. She expected it to be Sophie, but it was an unrecognised number.

She answered it.

'Detective?' a female voice said. 'Can you get here? Can you get here now? He's here. He's right outside.'

Karen couldn't place the voice. But the woman sounded scared and was talking very fast.

'Who is this?'

'It's Trisha, Phoebe's neighbour. It's the bloke I told you about. The one that sits outside and watches her apartment. He's back.'

CHAPTER SIXTEEN

Trisha was waiting for them in the downstairs lobby. 'Did you find him?' she asked as soon as they came through the double doors.

'No, he wasn't sitting on the bench. We had a quick look around the perimeter of the building but found nothing.'

Trisha bit her bottom lip and looked at the floor, worrying a piece of fluff on the carpet with her shoe. 'I think you'd better come upstairs.'

Karen and Morgan exchanged a quizzical look before following Trisha up the stairs.

'I think it might be my fault,' she said as she opened the door to her flat.

'What do you mean?' Karen asked.

But Trisha had retreated inside.

They followed her. 'This is my colleague, DI Morgan,' Karen said, but Trisha didn't respond. She walked off to the kitchen, then stopped by the window and looked down at the empty bench.

'What happened, Trisha?' Karen asked.

She held out her phone. 'I took a photo of him. Well, I *tried* to take a photo. I'm sorry. It's blurred. Probably not very helpful.'

Blurred was an understatement. Karen's hopes plummeted as she looked at the image. There was no chance they'd be able to identify anyone from this. An average-height white male wearing dark trousers and a white shirt. But they already knew that much from Trisha's description; there was nothing new that could help identify him further.

'I think I spooked him,' Trisha said. 'He might have spotted me when I was trying to take the photograph.'

'Marvellous,' Morgan muttered.

She put her hands on her hips. 'Hey, I was trying to help. A little gratitude wouldn't go amiss.'

'It's a blurred photograph that could be a picture of any white man of average height in Lincoln,' Morgan said bluntly and handed the phone back to Karen. He had a point. The photograph wasn't going to be much help at all.

Trisha, still standing with her hands on her hips, scowled. 'I don't know why I bothered,' she said.

'I'm glad you called,' Karen said. 'If you see him again, then give me a ring straightaway, and try to keep your distance.'

'Right,' Trisha said and put her mobile on the kitchen counter with a sigh. 'So, you've not found Phoebe yet then?'

'No, not yet,' Karen said, not wanting to go into detail. 'Have you seen anyone else around? Anyone knocking on Phoebe's door, or heard anything from her flat?'

Trisha shook her head.

'You've still got the spare key, though, right?' Karen asked.

'Yeah, but I don't think I should give it to you. What if she comes back and she's just been on holiday or something? She'd be furious.'

'We're getting a warrant,' Karen explained. 'So, one way or another we're going to get inside the flat. If you've got a key that means we don't need to break down the door.'

Trisha nodded. 'Well, when you've got the warrant let me know, and I'll give you the key.'

'Thanks.'

Trisha wrapped her arms around her midsection, hugging herself. 'You know, I really was trying to help. It's just that my hands were shaking. It was really stressful.'

Karen was surprised to see the change in Trisha. When Karen had called around previously, Trisha had been confident that Phoebe was fine and would eventually turn up. She'd seemed to think disappearing for a few days every so often was something Phoebe tended to do. Now, she seemed upset, and maybe a little scared.

'I know you were trying to help,' Karen said. 'And if you hadn't called, we wouldn't have even known he was there. We've now got a photograph. Even if it is a bit blurry, it's a start.'

Karen couldn't help wishing the photograph was clearer. Being stalked was terrifying for victims. It wasn't a one-off crime and could leave people desperate, feeling like there was nowhere secure they could go to be free of their tormentor. This man's presence outside Phoebe's flat was a repeated reminder that a potential threat was lurking close to her home; a place she was supposed to feel safe.

'It's creepy, isn't it? Him just sitting out there . . . watching.' Trisha shuddered.

'Yes,' Karen said. 'It is.'

◆ ◆ ◆

When they got back to the car, Morgan said, 'What do you want to do? Hang around? See if he comes back?'

Karen shook her head. 'It's unlikely he'll be back this afternoon. Why don't we go and talk to Cary again? I'd like to know why he didn't tell me that the money from their business all went to him if anything happened to Phoebe.'

Morgan raised an eyebrow. 'So you don't think her disappearance is related to Imporium? You don't think she was drugged?'

145

Karen wasn't sure what she thought at this stage, but she knew they needed to investigate every possibility. 'I don't even know if it's Phoebe on the CCTV from Imporium. It certainly looks like her, and we know she was there on Friday night. So, that can't be ignored, but I want to cover all possibilities. And the fact Cary wasn't forthcoming with that information sets off alarm bells, don't you think?'

Morgan nodded. 'Agreed. Shall I drive?'

◆ ◆ ◆

They were in Lincoln, approaching Lucy Tower Street car park, when Morgan's phone rang.

'Can you get that?' he asked.

Karen answered. It was the superintendent.

'Is Morgan not available to talk?' Superintendent Michelle Murray asked.

'He's driving, ma'am. Can I take a message?'

'Get him to call me back. I need to speak to him about the aggravated burglary cases.'

Karen mouthed, *She needs to talk to you.*

Morgan grimaced. Instead of driving into the car park entrance, he pulled up to the kerb just outside.

Karen handed him the phone.

While he spoke to Superintendent Murray, Karen got out of the car, glad to be in the fresh air. It was so hot that her trousers were sticking to the backs of her legs. The sun was blazing, but the tall buildings on either side of the street offered some shade.

After a moment, Morgan got out of the car. 'Sorry, Karen, I'm going to have to go back to the station. The super wants to see a case report. Apparently, the CPS aren't happy about something.'

'That doesn't sound good,' Karen said.

'It's just a routine check. It should be fine. I'll sort it,' he said. 'Do you want me to arrange somebody to come and pick you up?'

'No, don't worry, I'll do it,' Karen said. She waved him off and then walked back down to Brayford Wharf and towards CaP Diagnostics.

As before, she asked for Cary Swann at reception, and a few minutes later was greeted by a harassed-looking Cary. He was flushed and had loosened his tie. He ran a hand through his normally neat hair. 'Detective, I didn't realise you were coming. Did we have an appointment?'

'No, we didn't,' Karen said. 'I thought I'd call in on the off-chance you were here.'

'Well, here I am,' Cary said, spreading his hands. His smile was a bit too wide, his manner a touch too congenial.

He seemed nervous. Why?

'Is everything okay?'

He looked over his shoulder, his back towards reception, but the woman behind the desk wasn't paying any attention to them. 'Let's go upstairs. We're moving the last of our stuff into the penthouse offices today, but it's sweltering and the air conditioning is playing up,' he said, pressing the button to call the lift. 'Have you had any news about Phoebe?'

Karen shook her head. 'No. We haven't located her yet,' she said. At least that was truthful. She wouldn't reveal anything about the investigation until they had something concrete.

They took the lift to the top floor.

'Penthouse,' Cary said, forcing a smile that quickly disappeared. 'We're going up in the world.'

Despite his bluster, he didn't look particularly happy. The offices were still in disarray, with moving boxes everywhere.

A young woman with short brown hair, wearing a brightly coloured outfit – a flared purple skirt, green top and bright yellow cardigan – watched them from a distance.

'That's Lou,' Cary said. 'Our assistant. Do you want to talk to her? She was with us at Imporium on Friday night.'

Lou looked horrified at the idea. 'I . . . uh . . . well, I'm very busy.'

'It won't take long,' Karen said. 'I just want to know if you noticed anyone acting suspiciously on Friday evening?'

Lou shook her head. 'No, everything seemed normal to me.'

Karen asked a few more questions and noticed that, before every reply, Lou would glance at Cary before answering.

Finally, Karen fished in her bag and pulled out a folder containing enlarged prints from the CCTV footage recorded inside and outside the bar.

She passed the prints to Lou first. 'We think this is Phoebe. Do you recognise either of the men she's with?'

Lou looked at the images only briefly before shaking her head and handing them back to Karen. 'Sorry, I don't. It looks a bit like Phoebe, but I couldn't say for sure, and I don't know either of the men.'

Karen gave them to Cary. 'I'd like you to look at these images again. They've been enlarged and enhanced. What do you think?'

'What do I think?' Cary repeated.

'Yes, do you think it's Phoebe, and do you recognise either of the men?'

'It looks like her,' Cary said, nodding slowly. 'It really does. But like I said before, you can't see her face, so it's impossible to say for sure.'

'And the men?'

He studied the prints closely for a moment or two, and then shook his head. 'I'm sorry, I don't know them.'

Karen returned the prints to the folder as Cary looked around at the mess and sighed. 'I really need a cigarette.' He turned to Karen. 'Do you want to go up to the roof? It's cooler up there.'

Karen agreed, and Lou looked visibly relieved that the questioning was over.

Karen and Cary picked their way around boxes to the end of the corridor, and Cary pushed open a door that said *Maintenance Access*. They climbed a set of stairs and then Karen blinked in the bright sunlight as they exited the maintenance area and stepped on to the roof.

Cary took a deep breath, relishing the fresh air. But Karen didn't find it that much cooler. There was a bit of a breeze, but they were standing in the direct glare of the sun. Cary fished out a cigarette and offered one to Karen.

She shook her head. 'No thanks.'

'So, you're not here with news?' Cary prompted.

'No, just a few more questions. One in particular, actually,' Karen said, watching him carefully. 'I've recently learned that, if Phoebe died, you would inherit all her shares in the business. All the money. All the intellectual property. Everything.'

Cary seemed unbothered by the question. He nodded and exhaled a mouthful of smoke. 'Yeah, it's stipulated in her will. It's in mine, too. If anything happened to either of us, all the money and interests in the company would go to the other partner. It's to prevent complications. It's not uncommon in businesses like ours. Think of it this way: if our family inherited our business, they wouldn't understand some of the more complex, intricate stuff that we do. Everything would get held up, tied up in red tape. It's a fast-moving business, and any intellectual property we have would become worthless in the wrong hands. So, we both agreed if anything should happen to either one of us, the business would go to the other partner in full.' He took a drag on his cigarette, and a moment later a frown appeared on his brow. 'You don't think I've done anything to hurt Phoebe, do you?'

He had to know that the police would view him as a suspect if anything had happened to Phoebe, but he still looked incredulous. He was convincing. Maybe he was just a good actor.

'I don't know,' Karen said.

His frown deepened. 'I wouldn't hurt her.'

'You get on well, do you?'

'Like I said before, we get on fine. We occasionally have disagreements about the business, but Phoebe would never have anything to fear from me.'

'That's good to know,' Karen said.

He took another puff on his cigarette and then walked to the edge of the roof. There was a guard rail around the perimeter that reached Cary's waist and was about level with Karen's ribs. He leaned over, resting his hands on the railing. Then, suddenly, he lifted himself to sit on the rail.

It made Karen feel dizzy. 'I don't think that's safe.'

'It's fine,' he said, looking amused. 'I sit here all the time. Look at that view.' He swiped a hand towards the glittering water on the Brayford Wharf.

Karen had to admit it was very picturesque. Small white boats bobbed up and down, and two elegant swans drifted by.

She looked over the edge of the rail. There was a big drop to the pavement. She stepped back, swallowing hard.

'All right. It might not be a London skyscraper, but the penthouse here isn't too bad,' Cary said with a smile. 'Onwards and upwards,' he said again, and then rubbed his forehead with the back of his hand. 'She'd better turn up soon. We're supposed to complete our deal in the next week or so.'

'So you're worried?'

'Well, I wasn't until the police came calling,' Cary said with a mirthless chuckle. 'But I must admit, after all these CCTV images you've been showing me . . . I am concerned.'

'It seems strange that no one was concerned about her earlier,' Karen said.

He shrugged. 'She's a free spirit. Doesn't like to be tied down. Doesn't like to be told what to do. Unfortunately, that often means that a lot of the work for the business falls on my shoulders.'

'That must be difficult,' Karen said. 'Does that cause disagreements between you?'

He shrugged. 'Not really. The business side of things isn't her strong point, and I don't mind doing it. We all have different strengths.'

'What strengths do you have?'

'My main one is planning,' Cary said. 'And a solid work ethic, working out what steps we need to take to achieve what we want. Phoebe's strengths . . . I'd say primarily ambition, followed by vision. She's good on the ideas, less good on the planning. She comes up with the big concepts.'

'And Quentin Chapman?'

Cary's head lifted. 'Oh, did you speak to him?'

Karen nodded. 'I did.'

'Well, he's the investor. The money man.'

'Is he involved in any other way? Does he have input in the technical side?'

'No. He's interested. We give him reports every so often, but no. He's purely investing in the company and hoping to make a handsome profit from us eventually.'

'You should be careful with him,' Karen said.

Cary frowned. 'Why?'

But Karen wasn't willing to get into it now. 'Just be on your guard,' she said. 'You should always know who you're getting into business with.'

Cary laughed. 'Quentin's fine. I know he has a reputation, but most of that is just bluster.'

'He earned that reputation.'

Cary smiled, but when he spoke again, he didn't sound as confident. 'He's always treated us well . . . so far.'

CHAPTER SEVENTEEN

Sophie played the role of chauffeur, picking Karen up from Brayford Wharf.

'DCI Simpson has arranged for a warrant to search Phoebe Woodrow's flat,' Sophie said as soon as Karen got in the car. 'Hopefully that will give us something to go on.'

'Great,' Karen said. 'Her neighbour Trisha has a spare key, so there's no need to force entry.'

'I'll let him know,' Sophie said. 'Are you going to attend the search?'

Karen pulled at the fabric of her blouse to fan herself. 'I'd like to, but I think there'll be enough officers in attendance. I take it they've assigned a search team?'

'Yes. I don't suppose they'd mind us showing our faces, though,' Sophie said with a touch of optimism.

But Karen had better things to do than butt heads with Simpson's team. 'I was thinking of going back to Woodhall Spa, to speak to Phoebe's sister again. DC Fraser asked her if she recognised Phoebe or the men from the CCTV footage, and she said no. I tried calling, but she didn't answer the phone.'

'She's the artist? The one that has a studio in her garden?'

'Yes, so if I do go, and she's in the studio, she might not hear the doorbell, and it's a wasted hour to get there and back if she doesn't answer.'

'Why do you want to speak to her again if Fraser has already asked her?'

'I don't know.' Karen thought for a moment. 'I suppose because if anyone should recognise Phoebe it should be her sister, and . . .'

'And you don't trust Fraser?'

'It's not that. I think nuance can be missed if you do things over the phone.'

'Why don't you try the grandmother again?' Sophie suggested. 'She's closer. Very close to your house, in fact.'

She was. It would be an easier journey, but Karen didn't want to worry the old woman any more than they needed to.

'I don't like to bother her,' Karen said. 'She's genuinely worried about Phoebe. Almost everyone else assumed Phoebe was fine, that this is just how she behaves – going off for days at a time without telling anyone. The others hinted at Phoebe's selfishness, her lack of concern for others. But I got none of that from her grandmother. She just wants her granddaughter found safe and well.'

'Maybe your visit would be a reassurance rather than a worry,' Sophie said. 'It might comfort her to know the police are still trying to locate Phoebe, that she's a priority.'

Karen glanced at her younger colleague and smiled. 'You're right. I hadn't thought of it like that. I've been really impressed with your work recently. Operation Starling has given you a chance to show your worth.'

Sophie's cheeks turned pink. 'Well, I'm only the support. I'm not part of the official team.'

'There's no such thing as *only the support*,' Karen said. 'And you've really excelled yourself.'

Sophie beamed. 'Thanks, Sarge. So where to? Pineview Care Home?'

Karen nodded.

Just as Sophie was pulling away from the kerb, Karen leaned forward sharply, causing the seat belt to catch, and stared out of the window. She thought she'd spotted the skinhead who worked for Quentin Chapman.

But the big man ducked into a side street, and they travelled onwards, leaving him behind.

'What's wrong?' Sophie asked.

'I thought I saw someone I recognised,' Karen said, keeping her voice calm, though her heart was pounding.

Had it been one of Quentin Chapman's men? Had he been watching her? Her mouth grew dry at the thought, and suddenly the car seemed hot and stuffy.

'Mind if I open the window?'

'Of course not.'

As they drove past a flower shop, the sweet, heady scent of lilies mixed with the smell of diesel and hot tarmac from the road. Not exactly fresh air, but it would do. Karen took a few deep breaths, taking in the smell of the summer in Lincoln.

That really had looked like one of Chapman's henchmen. If so, why was he there? Was it simply a coincidence? Did he just happen to be in the vicinity?

Or had she been mistaken? She'd only caught a quick glimpse as the car passed at speed. Maybe it was a man with a similar build who shaved his head.

Karen rubbed the back of her neck. He was a ginormous man. There couldn't be many people who looked like him.

The idea of him watching her made her distinctly uneasy. As usual, her thoughts went straight to Mike and her family. If

Chapman had singled her out, ordered his henchman to follow her, what else might he do?

'You know Rick's back?' Sophie said, interrupting Karen's thoughts.

'What?'

'He turned up at the station while you were out. No one knows what to say to him. He said he doesn't want to stay at home anymore. He needs to work.'

'But I've told Churchill he's taking compassionate leave. He can't possibly be okay to work today,' Karen said.

'You can tell him that,' Sophie said. 'He won't listen to me.'

'Right. I will,' Karen said. 'He didn't get any sleep last night. I don't know what he's thinking.'

'I suppose he's not really thinking straight, is he?' Sophie said.

'No, I suppose not.'

Instead of going straight to the care home to speak to Phoebe's grandmother, they went back to the station to find Rick sitting at his desk, staring blankly at his computer screen.

'See what I mean?' Sophie nodded in his direction. 'He needs to go home, but you know he never listens to me.'

'I'll talk to him,' Karen said. 'What are you doing here?' she asked Rick, pulling up a chair and sitting beside him.

'Keeping myself busy, Sarge. It's doing my head in at home.'

'But you need to sleep.'

He shook his head. 'I can't sleep. Not there. I'm just surrounded by memories. I thought about booking into a hotel just to . . .' He broke off.

'Why don't you stay at my place for a couple of days?'

He shook his head, ready to refuse, but Karen cut him off. 'I'm going to stay at Mike's, so my house will be empty. You'll be doing me a favour.'

He was silent for a moment, then sniffed. 'Thanks, Sarge,' he said. 'I think that will probably help.'

She nodded, taking in the dark circles under Rick's eyes and the paleness of his usually tanned complexion. 'Do you want to go to my place now?'

He shook his head. 'If it's all right, Sarge, I'd like to work. Keep my mind off things, you know?'

'Okay, I can understand that. I'm going to go and visit Phoebe's grandmother again.'

He looked up. 'I'll come with you.'

Karen hesitated. 'I'm not sure that's a good idea, Rick.'

'I'm fine. It'll do me good to get out.' He smiled. 'Please?'

'If you're sure you're feeling up to it?'

'Of course,' Rick said, logging off from the system. 'Helps to keep busy.'

Karen updated Rick on the drive to Branston, and just as before, Phoebe's grandmother was sitting in a chair beside the patio doors when they entered her room.

She looked at them both wide-eyed when they walked in, and dropped the paperback she'd been holding.

'What's happened?' she asked with urgency as Rick scooped up the Agatha Christie book.

'I'm afraid I don't have any news,' Karen said quickly, and some of the panic left the woman's expression. 'We have another question for you.'

'Oh, I see,' she said.

Rick handed the thin paperback back to her.

'Thank you.'

'This is my colleague, DC Rick Cooper,' Karen said as Rick stepped back and stood by the patio doors.

'Lovely view,' he said.

The woman smiled. 'Yes, I'm lucky to have a room on the ground floor.'

'Do you manage to get outside much?' he asked.

'Sometimes. I need a wheelchair for long distances these days.'

Karen noticed there wasn't one in the room.

'But I've got a walking frame, and I can just about get out there on my own, though they don't like me to do it without one of the staff present, and they're all so busy. I don't like to make extra work for them.' She turned to Karen. 'Is there no news on Phoebe at all?'

'We're still trying to locate her,' Karen said. 'In fact, we think you might be able to help. Could you look at these images for us? We think it might be Phoebe. They were taken on Friday night and she's with two men. We wondered if you could identify them for us.'

'Well, I can certainly try,' she said, pushing her reading glasses further up her nose.

Karen showed her the stills from the CCTV.

Mrs Moore's lower lip wobbled. She pressed a hand to her cheek.

'What's wrong? Do you recognise them?'

'I . . . This looks like something you might see on *Crimewatch*. These images . . .'

Rick was quick to reassure her. 'It's just what all the CCTV footage looks like these days. We're looking for anyone who might have seen Phoebe recently. That's why we'd like to identify these men.'

'Is she in trouble?' Mrs Moore asked.

'We don't know, but we're going to find her, make sure she's safe.'

She put her thin hand over Rick's. 'You'll find her?' she asked earnestly.

'We'll do our best. You have my word.'

Karen was starting to regret bringing Rick with her. Not because she didn't think he could cope, but because she had underestimated what emotions this situation might generate in him. He'd just lost his mother, and for years he'd struggled with the idea of putting her in a care home.

Unlike Rick's mother, Mrs Moore didn't seem to have any cognitive problems, but maybe this visit was too much for Rick. Too much, too soon. Outwardly, he appeared to be coping, but this had to be hard for him.

Mrs Moore looked at one of the images again, pulling it closer and hunching over, so it was only inches from her face. 'Oh, I think I know . . . Yes, I think I know who this is.'

'Who?'

'Well, it looks like Phoebe,' she said, 'but I can't see her face, so I can't say for sure. But this . . .' She pointed to the dark-haired man outside the bar and smiled. 'Yes, I'm sure I know him.'

'Who is it?' Rick asked.

'It's Simon.'

'And who's Simon?' Karen asked.

'Phoebe's cousin, my grandson. I can call him if you like.'

'Yes, please,' Karen said.

She pointed at the chest of drawers. 'Would you mind opening the top drawer on the left and passing me my mobile phone.'

Rick did as she asked, and handed her what looked to be an ancient mobile.

She switched it on, and it took some time to start up. 'Sorry, I don't use it much, but it's handy now and again.'

'Do you always leave it turned off?' Rick asked.

'Well, yes, of course,' she said. 'I don't want the battery to run down.'

'Do you have a charger?' Rick asked.

'Yes, but it's a waste of electricity to keep charging it every day.'

'I see.' Rick glanced at Karen, who smiled.

'If anyone needs to contact me, they can telephone the care home.' She leaned closer to Rick and lowered her voice. 'Of course, I can use the telephone here for outgoing calls as well, but it costs more. This is pay-as-you-go,' she said proudly, holding up the mobile. 'Much cheaper.'

'Very useful,' Rick said.

When the phone was finally operational, she dialled a number with a shaky hand. 'Simon, darling,' she said, when the person on the other end answered. 'I'm fine . . . No, honestly, everything's fine. I've got the police here . . . Yes . . . No, don't panic. It's about Phoebe . . . Yes. Did you see her recently? . . . Ah, yes. I see.'

Karen gestured to the phone. 'Would you mind if I spoke to him?'

'Of course,' Mrs Moore said. 'Simon, I'm just passing you over to the detective now . . . Okay, darling. Bye.' She handed Karen the phone.

'Simon. This is DS Hart of the Lincolnshire Police. I understand you're Phoebe Woodrow's cousin.'

'Yeah, that's right. What's happening? What's going on?'

'We're trying to locate Phoebe. Can you tell me when you last saw her?'

'The weekend.'

'When?'

'Uh, Saturday morning.'

'Right. And you saw her the night before as well?'

'Yeah, that's right. I met her in the city centre. She was a bit out of it, so I brought her back to mine. She told me she thought someone had spiked her drink. Is that what this is about? She stayed the night at mine and then left in the morning. She seemed okay then. What's happened?'

'We don't know if anything's happened yet,' Karen said. 'We're just trying to locate her.'

'Right.'

'Do you think we could come and have a chat?'

'Um, I'm at work now, but I get off in about an hour.'

'Okay, where do you live?'

'Waddington. Near the airfield.' He reeled off an address.

'Okay, we can be there in about an hour and a half. Does that suit you?'

'Yeah. Okay, see you then.' He hung up.

'Thank you,' Karen said, turning to Mrs Moore. 'You've been a great help. You're the first person who has been able to identify Simon for us.'

'Oh, it's such a relief. If Phoebe was with Simon, she's safe,' she said, smiling.

I hope so, Karen thought. But she didn't feel the same sense of relief as Mrs Moore. It was an interesting development. Karen had assumed Phoebe had been missing from Friday evening, likely drugged and assaulted. But now that her cousin claimed she'd been with him until Saturday morning, it seemed increasingly credible that Phoebe had visited the care home on Saturday too. Perhaps Barbara Moore hadn't muddled her dates after all.

It was a step forward, but not by much. They still had no idea where Phoebe was. If she hadn't been drugged and assaulted on Friday night, where was she now? Why couldn't they find her?

CHAPTER EIGHTEEN

The village of Waddington was only a few miles from Lincoln. Well known for its association with RAF Waddington, the older part of the village was filled with buildings constructed from local limestone, though new developments had been added as the village grew and stretched out towards Bracebridge.

Waddington had once been home to the famous Vulcan aircraft. Now, a squadron that operated remotely piloted vehicles used the airfield as their base. But the Vulcan hadn't been forgotten. Every time Karen drove by Waddington on the A15, she passed the imposing gate-guardian Vulcan.

Simon Moore lived on Black's Close, just off the High Street, in a semi-detached house. It wasn't easy to find parking outside and they ended up parking halfway down the street and walking back.

As they got out of the car, Rick smothered a yawn.

'Rick, are you sure you're all right? You could just stay in the car if you want,' Karen offered.

'I'm all right, Sarge. Besides, it's too hot in the car.'

He had a point. The day was getting hotter.

Simon Moore answered the door before they knocked.

His hair was damp from a recent shower. He wore a white T-shirt, long navy-blue shorts and was barefoot.

Karen and Rick introduced themselves at the door, and Simon let them in. He led them to the kitchen, which was at the rear of the house. It had been extended, with a small orangery added on the back. Most of the windows were open, but with so much glass it was incredibly hot.

'Can I get you a drink? A cup of tea? Or something cold maybe,' Simon said, pointing at his own can of Coke sitting on the kitchen counter.

'No, I'm fine thanks,' Karen said, and Rick said the same.

'I can't really tell you much more than I said on the phone. I last saw her on Saturday morning.'

'We'd like you to tell us everything you can remember about Friday night.'

He nodded. 'Okay.' He gestured to the small kitchen table and they all sat down. 'I was just about to go into Imporium when Phoebe walked out. We hadn't arranged to meet, but when she saw me she said she didn't feel well and asked me to take her home. Very unlike Phoebe. Normally she's quite a party animal.'

'Do you go out together a lot?' Rick asked.

'Not really. We see each other from time to time, usually for family things. We used to see each other more before Gran went into the care home. We used to go to Gran's house for Sunday lunch most weeks.' He shrugged. 'But anyway, Phoebe said she'd been in Imporium and that she suspected someone might have put something in her drink. I wanted to report it, but she was adamant she didn't want that, so I decided to bring her to my house, and she agreed. So, we came back here.' He scratched at the table with a fingernail absent-mindedly. 'I didn't think it was a good idea to take her back to her flat if she'd been drugged, and she didn't want to go to the hospital, which I thought was *crazy*.'

'Did she tell you why she didn't want to report it or go to the hospital?' Karen asked.

'Not really. But she didn't seem too bad. She was tired and was slurring her words a bit. About an hour after we got back here, she was violently sick. I was frantic at that point. I was about to phone an ambulance, but she talked me out of it. Said she was feeling better after throwing up. But I wouldn't let her go straight to bed. I was worried that she wouldn't wake up, so we stayed up talking. We didn't go to bed until three a.m., and she was feeling a lot better then – more with it, I suppose.'

'And how was she in the morning?'

'All right. She said she had a headache but otherwise was okay. She seemed more worried in the morning, though. She kept looking out the window. I don't know what she was looking for. I got the feeling she was scared the man who'd drugged her was still after her. I told her she was safe with me, but she was still very nervous.'

'Do you have a car?' Karen said.

'Yes, but Phoebe borrowed it on Saturday morning and I haven't seen it since.'

'Did you report it missing?'

'Of course not. She's my cousin. I don't want to get her in trouble.'

'I take it you've been trying to call her.'

'Yes, but she hasn't answered. I thought that was down to her feeling guilty because she hadn't brought the car back yet. Do you think something has happened to her?'

'Did she tell you about the man who's been sitting outside her apartment?' Karen asked.

'What? No. Who is he?'

'We don't know yet. A neighbour told us that a man's been sitting on a bench, staring up at Phoebe's apartment and watching her come and go. She said Phoebe laughed it off.'

Simon shook his head. 'That's awful. Do you think this man might have done something to Phoebe?'

'We really don't know. All we know is that we haven't been able to locate her yet. Could you give me your car details?'

'Sure, but like I said, I don't want to get her in trouble.'

'You won't. This is so we can trace the vehicle. It might help us to track her down.'

'Right. Hang on a minute.'

It took him a few seconds to recall the licence plate number correctly, but he managed to write it down eventually.

'Everything's been going so well for her recently,' he said. 'She's been really happy. She's about to buy her own house, you know?'

Karen nodded. 'Yes, we heard.'

'She told me she's about to become a millionaire.'

'Did she say where she was going on Saturday when she left?'

'No, but she did say she might not be around for a few days. I asked her to have the car back by Monday because I needed it for work, and she said that was fine, but she didn't bring it back.'

'Why didn't you report it?' Rick asked. 'Weren't you worried?'

Simon stared down at the table for a moment and then looked up. 'Maybe I should have, but the thing about Phoebe is . . . Well, let's just say this isn't out of character. I was annoyed about the car, but I chalked it up to Phoebe being Phoebe.'

They finished up with a few more questions for Simon and then thanked him for his time and left.

'What did you think?' Karen asked as they walked back to the car.

'He seemed pretty genuine to me,' Rick said. 'Worried about his cousin.'

She nodded. 'Now he is. But he's yet another person who thought her disappearing for a few days isn't unusual.'

'I suppose it's a bit like a twist on the boy who cried wolf,' Rick said. 'In the past she's ignored calls, disappeared for days at a time without telling anyone where she was going, so this time when she really has disappeared . . . nobody thinks this occasion is any different from the others. No one reports it. No one is worried.'

Karen nodded thoughtfully. 'This heat is getting to be unbearable.'

'We'll be moaning about rain next week,' Rick teased. 'Enjoy it while it lasts.'

'Fancy an ice lolly? There's a shop just around the corner.'

Rick grinned. 'A Solero would go down a treat.'

Karen sighed with relief to be out of the sun as they entered the air-conditioned shop. The freezer cabinet was running low after the recent run of hot days. But she managed to grab two Soleros. As they headed to the till, Karen asked, 'Simon didn't set any alarm bells ringing for you?'

'No, I thought he seemed straight-up,' Rick said. 'Why? Did you pick up on something?'

'No, I got the same impression as you,' Karen said, and then handed over money to the cashier.

But even though he had seemed to be a concerned cousin, Simon Moore was currently one of the last people known to have seen Phoebe.

◆　◆　◆

Karen decided it would be a good idea to at least show their faces at the search. Phoebe only had a small two-bedroom flat. Karen didn't want to get in the search team's way, but she thought there might be something useful she could do if the search unearthed new leads.

Two police vans and other vehicles were parked at the front of the building when Karen and Rick arrived. An officer was doling out white overalls and shoe covers from the back of one of the vans, and they duly put them on before entering the building.

At the door to Phoebe's flat, Karen paused and watched the search team at work. The front door opened on to the living room. Several officers were avidly combing through Phoebe's possessions – opening drawers, removing items from shelves and flicking through books. She quickly spotted the crime scene officer Tim Farthing and DS Rawlings standing at opposite ends of the living room. Two of her least favourite people in one place. Tim was the *senior* crime scene officer, and liked to make sure everyone knew it. He spotted Karen first.

He gave a stiff nod and trudged over to them. 'Didn't think you were on this case, DS Hart.'

'We're offering support,' Karen replied.

'It's a bit of a squeeze in here.'

'We came along to see if we could do anything to help. We don't want to get in the way.'

'If you came inside, you would be getting in the way,' Tim said bluntly.

'Fair enough. We won't crowd you. Have you found anything promising?'

'Give us a chance,' he said. 'We've only just started.'

'The search has been underway for an hour.'

'An hour is nothing when it's a thorough search. And if I didn't have to answer your questions, I'd be done a lot faster.'

Karen bit the inside of her cheek to stop herself snapping back. He could behave like a petulant, annoying creep, but she was more professional than that, and she needed his help. If she had to walk on eggshells and butter him up, she would.

'I've worked with you before, Tim. As one of the best in the business, I thought you might have uncovered something quickly.'

His eyes crinkled as he smiled beneath his mask. Flattery had proved to be an effective tool when dealing with Tim Farthing.

'Well, you know me, I've got a good eye. I spot things before other people do. We've found some promising items already. Her laptop's here, so that might give you something. Her mobile is here, too.'

'She didn't have the mobile with her? That's odd.'

'Yeah, and it's turned off. Maybe she was surprised here at her flat.'

'Any signs of a struggle?'

'Not as far as I could tell.'

'And there's nothing on CCTV?' Karen asked.

'That's not my job,' Farthing said, wagging his finger. 'You'll have to talk to somebody else about that.'

'There are a lot of boxes around. Is that the crime scene team boxing evidence or—'

'No,' Tim said. 'It was like that when we found it. She was moving to a new place apparently.'

Karen nodded. 'Her neighbour mentioned that.'

Rawlings zeroed in on them. 'DS Hart, DC Cooper, what are you doing here?'

'Just came along to see if we could help.'

'Well, as you can see, it's a very crowded scene. I think you'd be more use back at the station.'

It took a huge effort, but Karen managed to hold back the response that was on the tip of her tongue. The nerve of the man. Who did he think he was, ordering her about like that? Rawlings was of equal rank, and though she understood his point – it was a small flat and quite a large search team – she didn't appreciate him telling her to go back to the station and acting like her boss.

Karen rose above his suggestion by ignoring it. 'Phoebe was planning on moving. Have you looked into that?'

Rawlings frowned. 'Not yet. We found some letters from the estate agent. In fact, why don't you go and investigate that. I'll get you the contact details of the estate agent, and you can talk to them. Maybe even check out the property she's moving to.'

'All right.'

'Wait there,' Rawlings said, leaving Karen and Rick standing at the threshold.

Rick rolled his eyes. 'Nothing like a warm welcome, is there, Sarge?'

Rawlings was back after taking a photograph of the letter. 'I've emailed it to you,' he said. 'You should have all the details you need on the letter.'

'Thank you,' Karen said, but he was already walking away.

They headed back downstairs and peeled off the overalls gratefully. The extra layer was unwelcome in this heat.

Rick looked back up at the apartment building and shook his head. 'Is it just me, boss, or is Rawlings a real pain in the backside?'

Karen grinned. 'It's Simpson's case. He's marking his territory. We're only meant to be helping out with support.'

'Maybe so, but he could be more gracious about it.'

'Yes,' Karen agreed. 'He could.'

They opened the car doors but didn't get inside. They waited for some of the heat to dissipate while Karen made the call to the estate agent. It was too hot to be sitting in a car on a day like today, especially as their parking spot was in direct sunlight.

Karen gave her credentials over the phone to Little & Stone but was told she couldn't get the required information unless she went to the estate agency in person with her ID. She offered them the opportunity to phone the Lincolnshire Police station directly and ask to be transferred to Karen as proof she was really a police officer, but apparently that wasn't good enough.

She sighed and hung up. 'Looks like we're going to Little & Stone. It's on Silver Street.'

'That's where they all are,' Rick said. 'All in a row. A bit weird really. They're all concentrated together.'

'Well, I suppose it makes it easier for people looking to buy houses. Lots of options all together.'

Rich shrugged. 'Everyone uses Rightmove or Zoopla these days.' He rubbed his eyes as they got into the car. 'I suppose I'll have to look at putting Mum's house on the market.' He squinted and lowered the sun visor. 'There so much stuff to do. So much legal stuff and paperwork. And the funeral . . .'

'I can help you,' Karen said. 'Whatever you need. Just tell me.'

'Thanks, Sarge. I'm going to wait until my sister gets back from Cornwall. I'm sure we'll muddle through together.'

Inside Little & Stone on Silver Street, Karen and Rick sat opposite a very young and flustered male estate agent, who crouched behind his oversized computer monitor. The sun was blazing through the floor-to-ceiling windows at the front of the shop, making it almost unbearably hot. A small fan whirred on his desk, directing air to his face and making his hair dance around. 'Phoebe Woodrow . . . Oh yes, I see. She's purchasing a house at Burton Waters. It's not gone through yet. They were planning to exchange this week. That's if all the solicitors get their ducks in a row.'

'Where is this house exactly?' Karen asked.

The estate agent gave her an address.

'Are the owners still living there?'

'No. It's an estate property. The owner died and his children are selling it.'

'So the property is currently empty,' Karen clarified.

'Yeah, that's right.'

Karen sat back in her chair and thought for a moment. Could Phoebe be hiding out there? It was possible. Perhaps the drugging incident on Friday night had traumatised her so much that she'd gone into hiding.

'Do you think we could have a look at the property?'

'Um, well, I suppose that wouldn't do any harm. Let me check if we still have the keys.'

When he disappeared out the back, Rick turned to Karen. 'What are you thinking, Sarge? Do you think Phoebe might be there?'

'I don't know. It's a possibility. She was drugged on Friday night. Her cousin said she was scared. We don't know for sure where she went after she left his house on Saturday. Perhaps she did go to her grandmother's care home but didn't sign in because she was keeping a low profile. Maybe she thought whoever drugged her was still a threat. Maybe she wanted somewhere to hide. With the reports of a stalker sitting outside her apartment, I don't blame Phoebe for not wanting to go home.'

Rick nodded thoughtfully. 'Makes sense. But she doesn't own this place yet.'

Karen leaned forward and directed the tiny desk fan so that it blew some air their way. 'If it's empty, she could have thought there was no harm in it.'

'But why not stay with her cousin Simon? She'd be safer with him than hiding out in an empty house on her own, wouldn't she?'

'Maybe she thought staying with him would put him at risk.'

Karen knew her theory was influenced by her own fears. She worried that her family might be targeted by someone who wanted to get to her.

She looked at Rick's sceptical expression. He wasn't convinced.

'It's worth checking anyway,' she said. 'It might even get Rawlings onside.'

Even as she said the words, Karen knew this was wishful thinking on her part. Rawlings was protective of his case. In his eyes, Karen and Rick were encroaching on his turf. Some officers were more territorial than others, and Rawlings didn't like them treading on his toes. But despite the tension between them, they needed to work together to find Phoebe.

'I doubt it,' Rick said. 'I think it'll take more than that to get Rawlings onside.'

CHAPTER NINETEEN

It took Karen and Rick about ten minutes to get to Burton Waters. The property was a large detached two-storey house in a cul-de-sac. It had a pretty, well-maintained front garden, with rose bushes crowding the flowerbeds, a long sweeping driveway that went up the side of the house, and a free-standing double garage.

'Must have cost quite a bit,' Karen commented as they walked up the driveway.

There was no sign of life inside.

'The curtains are all shut,' Rick commented. 'Suspicious?'

'I don't know. Maybe they shut them to keep the heat out.'

They rang the doorbell, but there was no answer.

'I'm going to have a look around the back before we go in,' Karen said, walking up the drive.

There was a shingle path leading to the patio. The back garden was wide, but not very long. A rotary washing line stood in the middle of the lawn, but no washing hung on it. The patio was slightly uneven, and ants had pushed up earth between the slabs. The grass had been cut recently but was very dry.

The patio doors had a vertical blind, making it impossible to see inside. But the kitchen blind was raised. Karen went up on her tiptoes and peered in the window, trying to avoid getting dirt from the window box on her blouse.

The kitchen was empty. The countertops were devoid of anything like a kettle or a microwave. There was no sign that anyone had been living there.

She stepped back and brushed down her blouse, before noticing something odd about the next window.

'Uh, Sarge,' Rick called from the front of the house before she could take a closer look at the window.

Karen heard the screech of brakes and jogged back along the shingle path just in time to see a large silver BMW come to an abrupt halt on the drive. A balding, middle-aged man with a short beard sat behind the wheel. He reached for something in the back seat – a golf club – and then flung the door open. He jumped out of the car, held the golf club over his head and ran towards Rick.

'What the . . .' Rick said, raising his hands to defend himself.

But the man stopped short, and instead of using the golf club he was brandishing, he let out a string of curse words.

Karen approached him cautiously. 'What exactly do you intend to do with that, sir?' she asked, pointing at the golf club and then holding up her ID. 'I'm DS Karen Hart of the Lincolnshire Police, and this is my colleague DC Rick Cooper. Who are you?'

He looked slightly taken aback but soon remembered his anger. 'I'm the *owner* of this house,' he said. His face was flushed and sweaty. 'You can't just turn up here and walk around the back. It's trespassing.'

'We were intending to go inside. The estate agent gave us the keys.'

'Without asking my permission? That's disgraceful.'

'You're right. They should have asked your permission. I'm very sorry. It must have been disconcerting for two people to turn up on your property unannounced.'

'Yes. Yes, it was,' he said, finally lowering the golf club. 'It's not the first time. They let the person doing the survey just waltz in.

They didn't bother to accompany them. And they didn't tell *me* they were coming. I just saw them on the video camera.' He pointed to a tiny camera in a plant pot beside the front door.

'That's a very ingenious spot to put a camera,' Karen said.

'Yes, well, you can't be too careful with empty houses.'

'We actually need your help,' Karen said, attempting to get him onside. 'We're trying to locate a missing woman, Phoebe Woodrow.'

'Phoebe Woodrow,' the man repeated thoughtfully, then his eyes widened. 'The woman who's supposed to be buying this house?'

'Yes, that's right. We haven't been able to find her, and it occurred to me that she might have come here.'

'But she doesn't own the house yet,' he said. 'We haven't even exchanged contracts.'

'Do you think we could just have a look inside anyway? Just in case?'

He propped the golf club by the front door. 'All right.'

He unlocked the door and they stepped inside. The air was warm, but still cooler than outside.

They walked around the living room and into the kitchen, but there was no sign anyone had been staying there recently.

'Does anything look different to you, sir?' Karen asked. 'Anything out of place?'

He shrugged. 'No, I don't think so. It looks normal.'

'How often do you check on the property?'

'I have to check weekly,' he said. 'It's a condition of the insurance because it's an empty property.'

Karen nodded. 'And the camera at the front door didn't pick up anything unusual this week?'

'No, apart from the estate agent handing the keys out willynilly, to the surveyor and *you*.'

Karen was about to turn and leave the room when she noticed a spot of colour just under the hem of a curtain.

It was the corner of a bright blue crisp packet. She leaned down, studying it, and then put on a glove and picked it up. The house looked as though it had been cleaned recently in preparation for the move. Had this been missed?

Karen turned to the owner.

'Well, that's very odd,' he said, staring at the empty packet with a puzzled frown.

'It's not yours?'

He shook his head. 'It could have been from when one of the grandchildren visited, I suppose. It's my late father's house, and he didn't eat things like that. He wouldn't touch processed foods. And I could have sworn I moved all the furniture and vacuumed underneath those curtains.' He shrugged. 'I don't know how I could have missed that.'

'Okay,' Karen said, putting it in a plastic evidence bag and sliding it into her pocket. 'It's probably nothing, but we'll take it just in case.'

The owner nodded. 'I don't suppose . . .' He broke off, rubbing the back of his neck. 'That is to say, if she's missing, does that mean the sale has fallen through?'

'I'm sorry, sir. I don't know. You'll have to get in touch with the estate agent.'

He sighed. 'Right. It'll be ever such a pain if I have to put it back on the market.' He shot them a sheepish look. 'Sorry, that sounds selfish. I hope she's all right. She seemed like a very nice young woman.'

'Did you meet her?'

'Yes, I showed her around the house. She wanted to do an evening viewing, and the estate agent said they couldn't do evenings, and asked me if I'd mind doing it.' He rolled his eyes. 'So, I did their job for them. But Phoebe seemed nice. She told me work was going well and she'd decided now was the right time to buy herself a house.' He smiled. 'She loved the garden.'

'Could we take a look at the other rooms?'

He nodded and led them along the hall.

'I noticed one of your windows at the back of the house looked damaged,' Karen said.

'What?' He spun round so quickly Karen almost walked into him.

'Shall we take a look?'

He hurried along, turning left into what looked to be a dining room, though there was no dining table or chairs. As Karen suspected from her brief glimpse in the garden, it looked like it had been forced. The window was ajar, and the frame was damaged.

Rick said, 'It looks like someone's used a crowbar on this and forced their way in.'

The owner's face fell. 'Utter scumbags!' he said, his face tight with anger. He looked ready to punch something, but then shook his head. 'I don't understand it. Why didn't the camera pick them up? It alerted me when you turned up.'

'Perhaps they avoided going near the front door?' Rick suggested. 'When were you last in this room?'

'Five days ago. I cleaned the windows. It wasn't þroken then.' He covered his face with his hands. 'Why would someone do this? There's nothing here to steal.'

'Did you tell Phoebe about the camera, sir?' Karen asked.

He looked at her, aghast. 'You can't think . . . But she seemed so nice, and she's only a tiny thing. She hasn't got the strength.'

'You don't need much muscle,' Rick said, miming the action of a crowbar. 'It's all about leverage.'

Karen left Rick talking to the owner, and turned away, thinking. It was one thing for Phoebe to use a key to gain entry to the house she was about to buy, but forcing her way in and committing criminal damage was quite another matter. If Phoebe had done this, she must be desperate.

Something wasn't adding up. This case was one puzzle after another. How did they find a missing woman who didn't want to be found?

◆ ◆ ◆

Before Karen started the engine, her mobile rang. It was an unknown number.

'DS Karen Hart.'

'Oh, hello. Um, I need to talk to you. Can we meet?' a woman's voice said.

'Who is this?' Karen asked.

'Oh sorry. I should have said. It's Lou from CaP Diagnostics. I work for Cary and Phoebe. I'm their assistant.'

'Of course I can meet you. Where and when?'

'Well, not here,' Lou said hurriedly. 'Not at work. There's a coffee shop called 200 Degrees. Do you know it?'

'Yes, I know it. What time?'

'About half an hour.'

'That's fine. I'll be there,' Karen said.

Lou hung up.

'Well, that's interesting,' Karen said as she put the car into reverse and backed out of the drive. 'Lou from CaP Diagnostics wants to talk to me about something, but she doesn't want to talk at work.'

'Mmmhhm.' Rick stifled another yawn.

'Look, I'm going to drop you off at my house. If you can't sleep, you can lie on the sofa and watch Netflix, but you need some rest.'

'All right, Sarge,' Rick said, his eyelids drooping. He was in no fit state to argue.

'Do you want me to stay home tonight? I can get a takeaway.'

'No, I'll be fine. You're going out with Mike, and I'm better off on my own to be honest.'

'All right. If you're sure?'

'Yeah, I am. Thanks, Sarge.'

When they arrived at Karen's house in Branston, she went inside with Rick and gave him the spare key. 'The bedroom at the front is all made up. There are towels in the airing cupboard in the bathroom, and help yourself to anything you want in the fridge. You know how to work the coffee machine?'

Rick nodded. 'I'm sure I'll work it out.'

'All right. I'll leave you to it. Get some rest. Call me if you need anything.'

'Will do, Sarge. Thanks.'

When Karen got to the coffee shop it was late afternoon and fortunately not too busy. There was no sign of Lou, so Karen ordered an Americano and sat by the window in a spot that had a good view of the entrance.

The wood floor and rustic tables gave the coffee shop a warm, cosy atmosphere, and it was handily located right next to the walkway to the Central Car Park.

A few minutes later, Lou entered. She was wearing huge dark sunglasses. She didn't take the glasses off, and sat down opposite Karen looking incredibly self-conscious.

'I'm not really sure how all this works,' she said, looking around the café nervously.

'Do you want anything?' Karen offered.

'Oh, no thanks.' She put her elbows on the table and leaned forward. 'Is there a reward?'

'A reward,' Karen repeated.

'Yeah, for, uh, information that leads to Phoebe's whereabouts.'

'No, there's no reward. We just want to make sure she's safe.'

'Oh. Okay, I just thought I'd ask.' She shrugged. She lowered her dark glasses and peered over the top of them at Karen. 'There's something I thought you should know. Cary didn't tell you everything.'

'No? What did he miss out?'

'Well, the arguments for one thing. The huge rows they've been having recently. Massive bust-ups. On Friday evening, it was really tense when we went out.'

'What were they arguing about?'

'The direction of the business. Cary has always been a bit reticent about selling the company. He didn't want to rush into things, and Phoebe was the one who wanted Quentin's investment and later lined up a buyer. Eventually, Cary came around to the idea. Then Phoebe started talking about shopping around to get a better buyer. Cary didn't want to mess anything up. He thought that, as Quentin had lined up the deal, they'd be mad to drop out. But Phoebe thought they could get a better price and should keep their options open.' Lou exhaled and lowered her glasses a bit further. 'Cary warned her not to mess with Quentin. He said she didn't know who she was taking on.' Lou leaned forward to say the next part emphatically. 'He said Quentin wasn't the sort of man you let down. Phoebe just laughed.'

'She wasn't worried about Quentin Chapman?' Karen asked, pushing her coffee cup to one side.

'Didn't seem like it. Cary definitely was, though. He's been really down lately.'

'They're both about to come into a lot of money with this deal,' Karen said. 'Isn't it what they've been working towards for years? Why isn't he happy?'

Lou shook her head. She plucked a packet of sugar from the container in the centre of the table and began fiddling with it. 'I don't know. They don't talk to me about that sort of stuff. I just see emails or overhear them talking or having rows when they can't keep their voices down . . .' She smirked. 'Well, then I hear *everything*. That's how I know Phoebe suggested looking for a better price.'

'Do you think Phoebe might be hiding out somewhere because she doesn't want to do this deal with Quentin?'

Lou frowned. 'I don't know. It doesn't sound like Phoebe to me. She normally stands her ground, argues her point – and believe me, she can argue.'

'When you were with Phoebe on Friday night, do you remember seeing anyone watching her, or someone buying her drinks?'

'No. You already asked me that, and I still don't. It was just the three of us, and it was an awkward and tense evening. Cary was determined to pretend everything was fine, Phoebe was sulking, and I was in the middle trying to ignore them both, so I could make the most of the free drinks.'

'Right.' Karen pulled out her phone and opened a CCTV image of the curly-haired man, but this time with Vicky. 'What about him? Do you recognise him?'

It was slightly clearer than the image of him with Phoebe, but not by much, and the view focused on the top of his head thanks to the camera angle.

Lou looked at it. 'Sorry, no.'

'Okay. Well, thanks for your help, Lou. If you think of anything else let me know.'

'All right.' Lou sighed, pushed her glasses back up her nose and asked, 'There's definitely no reward?'

'No, I'm afraid not.'

After Lou left, Karen finished her coffee and then went outside. It was a gorgeous afternoon. A little girl was holding an ice cream and crying because it was melting too fast and dripping on the floor. Karen smiled as she overheard the child's exasperated mother trying to persuade her to eat the ice cream quickly, before it melted completely.

She turned to her right, and tensed when she saw one of the men who worked for Quentin Chapman. It was the slightly shorter one, with the ponytail.

He was staring at her with a cold smile. He wanted her to know he was watching.

Karen met his gaze, determined not to be intimidated. Even if Chapman wasn't involved in Phoebe's disappearance, he was up to *something*. This was a not-very-subtle warning that Karen should keep her nose out of Chapman's business.

She felt a pang of worry for Mike, for her family. Was history repeating itself? Was her job putting her family at risk again? She started to walk towards him, weaving through the people gathered near the restaurants.

His smile widened, then he turned and walked into a crowd of people outside the new cinema. By the time Karen got to the spot where he'd been standing, there was no sign of him.

Her mouth was dry, her palms sweaty. She looked up and around the square, but he was gone.

She pulled out her mobile and dialled her sister's number. 'Emma. It's Karen.'

'Oh, hi. Everything all right?'

'No, not exactly. Things are a bit complicated at work right now. There's an awkward case . . .' She fumbled for the right words. 'I just want you to be on your guard, and keep an eye on Mum and Dad for me, okay?'

'What? What are you talking about? Are we in danger?'

'I don't think so. I just want you to be careful.'

Emma gave an exasperated sigh. 'What is all this about?'

'It's a case I'm working on. A particularly nasty man. I noticed one of his henchmen watching me.'

'I don't believe this, Karen,' Emma said. 'I can't watch Mum and Dad every hour of the day. And what about Mallory? She's at school. If you've put her at risk, I'll never forgive you.'

'I haven't. I . . . I'm being extra careful,' Karen said. 'I just wanted . . .'

'What? You just wanted to *worry* me. Thanks a lot.'

Emma had made a very good point. What *had* Karen expected her sister to do?

Karen closed her eyes. 'I'm sure I'm overreacting, but I just want you all to be safe. So . . .'

'So what? I should what? Get a gun, a new house alarm?'

'No, sorry. I shouldn't have worried you,' Karen said, realising she'd done the wrong thing by calling her.

'It's not fair of you to do this,' Emma said, her voice cracking. 'It's not fair of you to put us at risk.' She hung up.

Karen slid her mobile back into her pocket, feeling wretched because her sister was right. It wasn't fair on them.

CHAPTER TWENTY

Karen slipped through the door just before the Operation Starling briefing was due to start. As there were no seats left, she wedged herself into a gap beside Sophie, who was leaning against the wall. DCI Simpson sat at the head of a very crowded table. DCI Churchill sat at the opposite end.

The large, rectangular whiteboard at the front of the room was covered with photographs. The faces of Operation Starling's known or suspected victims and the two images they had of the curly-haired man covered the left-hand side of the board.

On the other side was a list of names, complete with swooping long arrows between them. It looked like a hastily scribbled mess. Karen sensed Sophie practically buzzing with tension beside her. If Sophie had her way, she'd wipe the board clean and rewrite the names in neat, straight lines, complete with tidy arrows. It wouldn't be a bad idea. The list was barely readable.

Simpson kicked off proceedings, running through the basic tasks and giving everyone a chance to report their updates in turn. Finally, he focused on Karen.

'We believe the woman at Imporium on Friday night was Phoebe Woodrow, and thanks to DS Hart we have an ID on the man outside the club with Phoebe.'

DCI Simpson was old-school. There was no laser pointer for him. He'd found a long stick from somewhere and used it to prod a photograph on the board.

'We've identified this chap. He's Phoebe Woodrow's cousin, Simon Moore. He's thirty-two years old and lives alone, in Waddington. We believe Phoebe was driving his car on Saturday, and she hasn't yet returned it. So, locating this vehicle is a priority. The vehicle details are in your briefing notes.'

He looked at Rawlings.

'Absolutely, sir. We're on it.'

'Has it been located yet?'

'Not yet, but it will be soon. I'm confident of that,' Rawlings said.

DCI Simpson turned back to Karen. 'What did you make of Simon Moore? He's one of the last known people to see Phoebe. Should we expect to find her body in the boot of his car?'

All eyes focused on Karen. Churchill gave her a look that said *don't let me down.*

'He seemed genuinely concerned,' Karen said. 'I know it's impossible to say for sure, but my instinct tells me he's not our man.'

DCI Simpson nodded slowly.

'We need to find out where she went after seeing her cousin,' DCI Churchill said. 'That's a priority.'

'Well, of course it's a priority,' Simpson snapped back, then frowned. 'But I thought she visited her grandmother?'

'Unverified. The care home has no record of Phoebe's visit.' Churchill smiled, pleased to remember something about the case Simpson had forgotten.

Churchill was keen to earn some of the kudos from this case for his team, but DCI Simpson was determined to keep control of Operation Starling.

'Now, Rawlings,' Simpson said. 'The new victim, Vicky Cutler, was drugged at Imporium last night?'

'Yes,' Rawlings said. 'We got the drug panel back after requesting it be fast-tracked. She tested positive for Rohypnol. Like the other recent victims.'

'And she has support?'

Rawlings nodded. 'She's staying with a friend, and we have a liaison officer working with her.'

'Good. What about the identity of our main suspect?' Simpson asked, prodding the image of the curly-haired man. 'He's seen on the CCTV with Phoebe and Vicky.'

When no one volunteered any information, Simpson barked, 'Rawlings?'

'Uh, we've not made as much progress as we'd hoped,' Rawlings said, nervously staring at the sheets of paper in front of him, as though they might hold the answer. He cleared his throat. 'There's CCTV at the club but no cameras in the alley, which means we haven't been able to track his movements after he left the bar.'

'He may have picked Imporium for that reason. What about the other bars and clubs? Similar story?' Churchill asked.

Rawlings nodded. 'Yes, CCTV inside but no cameras pick him up when he leaves.'

'That's very unusual for a city centre. Do you think he has some inside knowledge?' Churchill asked. 'Maybe he knows where the cameras are? Or has he just got lucky?'

Rawlings didn't have an answer. He looked desperately at Simpson for help.

'It's something to bear in mind,' Simpson said.

'We also have the stalker who's been watching Phoebe Woodrow's flat,' Churchill said. 'That's a possible lead. The description doesn't match the man at Imporium, but it still needs to be followed up. Do you have the manpower to station a unit outside her flat?'

'I should be so lucky,' Simpson replied. 'I might be able to organise a local unit to drive by regularly, but in this climate of cutbacks, I don't have the staff budget to have officers sitting outside a building on the off-chance. Combing through local CCTV would be a better option.'

'I'm working on that,' Sophie said.

'Good.' Simpson turned back to Rawlings. 'What did you find at Phoebe's flat?'

'There was no sign of a struggle,' Rawlings said. 'But she left her mobile phone there along with her laptop. That's useful for us, of course, but it isn't a good sign. Who voluntarily leaves home these days without their phone?' He looked around the room. There were mutters of agreement and nodding heads.

'Anything from the laptop yet?' Simpson asked.

'Not yet,' Rawlings said. 'The emails and files are encrypted, but Harinder from tech is working on getting access.'

Simpson shuffled his papers and then pushed back his chair.

'What about the email tip-off?' Karen asked quickly, wanting to get her question in before he called an end to the briefing. 'Will Horsley. He was standing just feet away from that man on Friday night. It looked to me like they were part of the same group.'

'Says he doesn't know him,' Rawlings said.

'It might be worth talking to him again,' Karen suggested.

'He *said* he doesn't know him,' Rawlings said, slightly louder this time.

'He may have said that, but perhaps it was a friend, a work colleague. Maybe he didn't want to get him in trouble. I think you should talk to him again.'

'Oh, do you?' Rawlings said irritably, seeming to temporarily forget they were in the middle of a briefing with other officers.

Simpson intervened before Karen had a chance to reply. 'Actually, it's a good idea. Let's revisit Will Horsley. Are you happy to do that, Karen?'

Karen said she was, and Rawlings scowled, muttering to himself as he leaned over his notepad, furiously writing something down.

'Shouldn't we have more undercover officers working the bars?' Arnie said. 'I'd volunteer for that job.'

'Why doesn't that surprise me, Arnie?' Churchill asked drily.

Arnie flashed a grin and straightened his tie. 'I'd fit right in. I scrub up quite well in my going-out gear.'

Rawlings snorted. 'You're a bit old, pal.'

'You're only as old as you feel,' Arnie said pleasantly, not rising to the bait.

'Yes, we do need more officers undercover,' Simpson mused. 'We don't want to use the same faces too often. I'll put you on reserve, Arnie.' He smiled. 'Imporium seems like the hotspot now, but there are seven other locations where women had their drinks spiked and were later assaulted.'

It was a struggle to know where best to allocate resources. Karen was glad it wasn't her responsibility. The man responsible for the attacks followed a similar MO each time. After talking to his victims for a short while and finding out they lived alone, he added Rohypnol to their drink, and then, as the drug kicked in, he took them home. When they got there, he attacked, and when they awoke the next morning he was gone. It meant they had been able to gather plenty of evidence from the crime scenes, including DNA.

'I don't think he'll go back to Imporium,' Rawlings said. 'The heat will be on there. Surely he must realise we'll be watching.'

'I think he's got away with it so many times that he thinks he's untouchable,' Karen said.

'Well, if he thinks that, he's got a surprise coming,' Simpson replied gruffly.

Simpson tucked his folder under his arm and stood up. 'Everyone know what tasks they're assigned?'

There were a few mumbled affirmatives and some nodding heads in reply.

'Good. We'll meet again tomorrow.'

As Rawlings stood to leave, Karen approached him. 'How is Vicky doing now?' she asked.

He didn't look happy to talk, but replied, 'She's very shaken, but she's got friends and family she can rely on.'

'That's good,' Karen said. 'She's going to need them.'

He nodded and swept past her, heading for the door.

That night Karen had made time to have dinner with Mike at Olé Olé, a tapas restaurant in Lincoln. It was good to have the night off, but Karen couldn't help thinking about Rick. She hoped he'd been able to sleep. Tonight, they were staying at Mike's to give Rick some space.

They tended to stay at Karen's house because there was more room, and it was easier to park, but she kept some clothes and toiletries at Mike's. He had a large flat in one of the old houses surrounding the cathedral. His was one of a few that were privately owned.

The view from his kitchen window was timeless. It had hardly changed in hundreds of years. Karen looked down on the dark street as she waited for the kettle to boil. She could imagine monks and churchgoers bustling around the cobbled street.

Dinner had been delicious, and as usual Mike's company had helped her to forget the worries of work. Of course, at the restaurant she'd angled her chair so she could see the entrance, keeping a careful watch in case one of Chapman's henchmen was lurking nearby.

Karen had just started to undress for bed when her mobile rang. Both she and Mike started at the sound.

'That's late,' Mike said. 'Is it work?'

'It shouldn't be,' Karen said. She wasn't supposed to be on call tonight. 'It's one of the staff from Imporium,' she said and answered it quickly. 'Cassidy? Everything okay?'

'No, quick! You must come here right now. *Right now.*' Cassidy sounded hysterical.

'What's wrong? Where are you? At your flat? Is Vicky all right?'

'She's fine. Her sister's with her at my place, but I'm at Imporium. I'm at work, and he's here!'

'Who?'

'The guy that drugged Vicky.'

'Are you sure?'

'When he came to the bar, I took a picture of him on my phone and sent it to Vicky. She says it's *him.*'

'Okay. Don't panic. Try to keep an eye on him but keep your distance. I'm coming. I'm just around the corner. I'll be there soon.'

'Okay.'

'Call me again if it looks like he's leaving.'

'Okay,' Cassidy said again, her voice small and scared.

Karen reached for her shirt and tugged it back on.

'What's wrong?' Mike asked.

Karen was dialling a number. She held up her hand. 'Just a sec.'

When the call connected, Karen reported the incident, asking for the undercover officers to be directed to Imporium and for a local unit to assist.

When she ended the call, she turned to Mike. 'That was the bartender who works at Imporium. She thinks the man who's been spiking drinks is back.' She buttoned up her shirt.

'You're not going alone?' he asked incredulously.

'No, there are undercover officers in Lincoln tonight, so they're going to be called in, too.'

'Are they at Imporium now?'

'Apparently not, but they will be soon.'

Mike reached for his T-shirt and pulled it over his head.

'What are you doing?' Karen asked.

'Coming with you.'

'No you're not.'

'Be reasonable,' Mike said. 'You can't go out there on your own. It could be dangerous.'

Karen's heart was thumping. She was aware of the risks and didn't need *him* to explain them to her as though she were a helpless rookie.

'It's my job,' she snapped. 'And I know what I'm doing.'

'I don't care,' Mike said. 'I'm coming.'

'You're not!' Karen said, raising her voice. Now was not the time for Mike to become overprotective. 'I don't have time to argue, Mike. Don't interfere.' She left the room and headed to the front door. Sandy looked up from her basket, her head moving between the two of them. It wasn't often she heard them argue.

'Karen, wait!' Mike said.

'Just leave it, Mike. I'll call you when I can.' She grabbed her jacket from the peg and shut the door behind her.

She jogged along the cobblestone streets, breathing hard, her heart fluttering in her chest. When she saw the bright lights and pink sign for Imporium, her mouth grew dry.

There were people milling about on the street outside. The bar was busy.

Great. Just her luck.

Were the other officers there yet? She couldn't see them.

Karen headed straight to the bar, weaving her way through the crowd, and spotted Cassidy's pink hair. She waved Karen over.

The customers swarming around the bar were most put out. 'Hey, we were here first!'

Karen ignored them. She didn't want to flash her ID when it might spook the suspect.

Cassidy leaned over the bar. 'I think he's gone into the gents. It's down there,' she said, pointing towards the dark corridor beside the bar. 'I think he might have realised I spotted him. I was just trying to watch him, make sure he didn't disappear.'

'Is Dom here?'

'No, he's not in tonight.'

'Okay.' Karen left the bar and made her way through the bodies blocking her path to the toilets.

The corridor leading to the toilets was dimly lit. One bulb for the whole corridor – what appeared to be a ten-watt bulb at that.

There was a couple by the wall, heads close together, kissing, merging into one. They barely noticed her.

She passed the ladies' toilets. He could be in there. She'd check them too, but first . . . She stopped by the door to the gents and paused. The fire door at the end of the corridor was ajar, and yet the alarm hadn't been activated.

She dashed to the door and pushed it open. It led out on to a narrow alleyway. She looked around, but there was no one there. Nothing in the alley but three large bins.

No! She couldn't have lost him. She'd been so close.

She swore loudly.

She checked both sets of toilets, but he wasn't there. Karen clenched and unclenched her jaw, seething with frustration. Would they ever get a break on this case?

CHAPTER
TWENTY-ONE

Karen made a slow lap of the bar for completeness, though she knew he wasn't there. He was long gone.

Had he known the police were on the way? They should have caught him, but he'd left moments before she got to the bar. Had he noticed Cassidy taking the photograph? Had that spooked him?

Cassidy approached. 'Did you see him?' she asked.

Karen shook her head. 'No, looks like he left via the fire door. Do you know why the alarm didn't sound when the fire door was opened?'

Cassidy shook her head. 'Nothing to do with me. You'll have to ask Dom about that.'

Karen sighed and pinched the bridge of her nose. The heavy thump of music in the bar was giving her a headache. 'You're sure it was him?'

'Yeah,' Cassidy said. 'Vicky was positive.'

'Did he approach any of the women in the bar?' Karen asked.

Cassidy shook her head. 'No, I spotted him as soon as he came in and didn't let him out of my sight. As soon as I saw him, I knew it was him, even before I sent Vicky the photo. He didn't have time to spike any drinks.'

Karen would have liked to take Cassidy's word for it, but they would need to clear the bar and speak to everyone. It would take ages, but they couldn't afford a screw-up.

'We're going to have to look at the CCTV again.' Karen glanced up at the cameras. 'I can tell Dom hasn't adjusted the cameras yet, so we're probably not going to get great images from them. So I'm going to rely on your photograph. Can you send it to me?'

Cassidy nodded. 'I got a good shot.'

She was right. It was a good photograph and showed the man's face clearly, but Karen didn't recognise him.

Karen spent some time getting details from Cassidy, and then walked outside the bar, grateful to finally get away from the thud of the music.

Just outside the entrance, she spotted two uniformed officers talking to DC Cobb and DC Broadside, members of DCI Simpson's team.

Broadside nodded at Karen. She wore a cream leather jacket over jeans and a fitted black top. Her hair, normally tied back at work, fell past her shoulders.

Karen made her way towards them. 'I was too late. He was gone before I got here.'

Broadside cursed. 'Slippery sod!'

'We must have just missed him too,' Cobb said with irritation, raking a hand through his short brown hair. 'We left Imporium half an hour ago and went to the Waterwheel. We were planning to head back here at eleven.'

'It's so frustrating,' Karen said. 'He was *here*.'

'Yeah, we were so close,' Cobb said.

Karen was about to reply when she stopped and frowned. She saw someone standing on the other side of the road watching. Her jaw dropped.

'Are you all right?' Cobb asked.

'I'm fine. I'll just be a minute.' She stalked across the road.

Mike was standing there, bold as brass, hands shoved in his pockets, shoulders hunched, staring moodily at Imporium.

She was so furious she was shaking.

'Is everything all right?' he asked. 'You're trembling.' He reached out and touched the side of her arm, but she shrugged him off.

'I'm angry,' she snapped. 'I can't believe you came here when I asked you not to.'

'I couldn't just let you dash off,' he said.

'Yes. Yes, you could, because it's my *job*.'

Karen couldn't stop herself snapping at Mike. She felt vulnerable and outraged. It was one thing to have a relationship with him when he was at home, separate from all this, but to see him here, in the thick of it, just reminded her of how exposed they both were. Karen's husband and daughter had been targeted because of her job. The idea of that happening again to someone close to her made her feel sick.

Earlier today, Chapman's thugs had been watching her. What if they decided to target Mike to get at her? She couldn't handle it. Not again.

'Go home,' Karen said in a cold voice, calmer now but still fuming.

'You're being unreasonable,' Mike said. 'I just wanted to make sure you were all right.'

'Go *home*,' she said again.

She may have looked stony and emotionless on the surface, but inside, panic and adrenaline was coursing through her body.

'Fine,' he said, and turned and stalked away.

'Is everything all right, Karen?' one of the team called out.

'Yes, it's fine,' Karen said, taking a deep breath to clear her head as she walked back towards the bar. 'I'll go and ask Cassidy to turn the music off. We've got a lot of work to do.'

◆ ◆ ◆

Mike had already left the following morning when Karen woke up. They hadn't spoken since last night.

Her head was thumping, and she felt jittery, like she'd had too much coffee.

She stepped into Mike's bathroom and flinched at the sight of her face in the mirror. She looked shattered and had dark circles under her eyes, after tossing and turning last night. Every time she'd managed to drift off to sleep, she'd been haunted by dreams. She could only remember one of them: her sister, hands on her hips, standing over Mike's lifeless body saying, 'I told you so. It wasn't fair of you to put us at risk.'

Karen took a hot shower, which helped clear her head a little. She followed this with a strong espresso, which only brought back the butterflies in her stomach.

The flat seemed very quiet without Mike and Sandy.

Since she was in Lincoln city centre, she decided to talk to Will Horsley before going to the station. Will had to know more than he was letting on. He, or someone else he was with that night, must have noticed that curly-haired man.

Since she'd had such a rubbish night, Karen decided it was only right that she pick up a pain au chocolat from the deli for breakfast on her way to the council offices.

She locked up Mike's flat and then headed down the stairs. She stepped outside, closing the main door behind her, and then stopped abruptly. Leaning on the railings, only a few feet away, was one of Quentin Chapman's henchmen, the dark-haired one with the ponytail.

He was watching her.

'Morning,' he called out as she stalked towards him.

She saw red. How dare he? He'd been following her. And now he knew where Mike lived.

'What are you doing here?' she asked through gritted teeth.

'I came to Lincoln for breakfast.'

'Funny, it doesn't look like you're eating.'

'I just finished,' he said with a smug smile.

'Don't you have work to be getting on with?' Karen asked. 'Perhaps some little errands to run for Quentin Chapman.'

His smirk widened. 'Who says I'm not currently running an errand for Quentin Chapman?' This time his smile showed his teeth.

'What's your name?' she asked.

'Donald Duck.'

Karen rolled her eyes. 'Very amusing.'

'Your boyfriend didn't look too happy when he left earlier.'

Karen froze. 'Stay away from him.'

He grinned, pleased he was getting under her skin. 'Well, that's not very friendly.'

She walked past him, shutting the gate behind her, and then turned sharply, snapping a photograph of his face with her phone.

His smile disappeared and was replaced with a snarl.

'What are you doing?' he demanded, and tried to grab the phone. But she elbowed him hard in the gut.

'Don't even try it. Unless you want to be arrested for assaulting a police officer?'

He doubled over, clutching his stomach. 'You assaulted *me*, you crazy—'

'You really don't want to get on the wrong side of me,' Karen warned.

He muttered curses as she walked away.

Chapman's henchmen had to be following her for a reason. Maybe Morgan would have a better idea of how to handle all this, because confronting Chapman might not be the wisest move. Why did this have to happen now? Just when things had been going so well between her and Mike.

Her mobile rang. It was Rick.

'I heard about all the excitement last night,' he said. 'Sophie filled me in. I'm just heading into work. Do you need a lift?'

'That would be great,' Karen said. 'I'm going to speak to Will Horsley again. Do you want to meet me at the Greek2Me deli?'

'Give me ten minutes. I'll meet you there.'

◆　◆　◆

Will Horsley didn't look pleased to see Karen when he came down to reception, but he attempted a smile. 'Hello, Detective. I don't think I can help you. I've told you everything I know.'

'Let's go and get coffee again, Will,' Karen said. 'My treat.'

'Well, I'm quite busy. Could we do it another time perhaps?'

'No, Will. I need to speak to you now.'

'Oh, okay.'

He followed Karen out of the building. It was already another baking-hot day, even though it was still early in the morning.

They reached the deli just as it was opening. A woman was setting out chairs in front of the café. Karen smiled and ordered a coffee and a pain au chocolat. Will just ordered a coffee.

Karen kept a careful watch on people on both sides of the street, but there was no sign of the ponytailed thug.

She showed Will the photograph Cassidy had taken, pointing out their suspect.

'Do you know who this is?'

He looked at the image for a few seconds, then shook his head.

'I think you do know him, Will.'

Karen let those words hang in the air.

Will looked very uncomfortable, squirming in his seat. He wouldn't meet Karen's gaze.

He looked grateful when they were interrupted by the woman bringing their coffee.

'Sorry. I don't know him,' Will said, but he kept his eyes lowered.

Karen leaned forward and took the lid off her coffee, blowing across the top of it, taking her time, letting Will sweat.

'I don't know why you're protecting him. Are you close?'

'Um.' Will looked lost. He stared down at the table. 'Well, I'm not a hundred per cent sure,' he said, his gaze flickering up and then down again. 'But I suppose it does look a bit like a lad at work.'

Now they were getting somewhere, Karen thought, leaning forward and putting her coffee back on the table. 'Who?'

'I don't want to get anyone in any trouble,' Will said.

'I don't have time for this, Will. I need to speak to this man and rule him out of our enquiries. I don't need you wasting my time. This is the second time I've had to come and see you, Will. This isn't a game.'

Will's cheeks flushed pink. He looked thoroughly miserable. 'Sorry.'

'Don't tell me you're sorry. Just give me the answer I need, and stop wasting my time.'

It was at that moment that Rick turned up. 'All right, Sarge?' he said, pulling out a chair and sitting down.

Will looked at him, then at Karen, and shrank down further in his seat.

'Just in time, DC Cooper,' Karen said. 'Will was about to tell me who he thinks this curly-haired gentleman is.'

Will's mouth opened and shut, but nothing came out.

'Well, don't leave us in suspense,' Rick said. 'Who is it?'

'I . . . um . . . think it's a man called Todd Bartholomew,' Will said. 'He works in the council offices, on the admin side. He runs the booking system for appointments and assigns the jobs. He decides who gets the grotty ones.' He shrugged. 'It might be him. It might not. I don't know. I can't say for sure.'

But Karen was almost certain Will had given them the identity of the man they were looking for. They had finally caught a break.

CHAPTER
TWENTY-TWO

Karen and Rick walked back to the council offices with Will Horsley.

'Call him from reception and ask him to come down. But don't mention the police,' Karen said. 'We don't want to spook him.'

Will's shoulders slumped. 'But he's going to know it was me that identified him.'

'Are you scared of him? Has he threatened you?'

'No, but . . .'

'Then why are you protecting him, Will?'

'I'm not,' Will insisted, looking wretched. 'I just don't want to be involved.'

'Being a good person means doing the right thing, even when you don't want to,' Karen said.

He folded his arms over his chest and huffed. 'It's easy for you to say. You don't have to work with him.'

Karen rolled her eyes. 'Fine, I'll do it. I'll ask the receptionist to call him down.'

Will shot her a grateful look. 'Thank you. I'm not trying to be difficult. I'm new here. I don't want to be assigned all the bad jobs. And if Todd's being there could turn out to be a coincidence . . .'

Karen thought that unlikely. Todd's presence at Imporium and the way he'd grabbed both Phoebe and Vicky was damning evidence in her eyes.

But she didn't have the chance to put their plan in action.

As soon as they stepped through the council doors, Will stopped abruptly. His jaw dropped.

Karen looked over his shoulder and saw the reason why. A tall, slim, white man with curly light-brown hair stood by reception, shuffling through some paperwork.

'Is that him?' Karen whispered, though she was already sure it was.

Will managed to nod.

'Todd Bartholomew?' Karen said. 'We'd like a word.'

She pulled out her ID.

Todd turned around, his expression arranged in a confident smirk, but when he saw Karen's warrant card, his face changed.

The smirk was replaced by a look of panic. There was a slight hesitation, then he dropped the papers and darted past them.

Both Karen and Rick reached out to grab him, but they were too slow.

Todd was agile. He didn't pause for the steps, instead jumping down them, almost falling at the bottom. He crouched low, steadying himself with a touch of his fingers to the ground, before setting off again, racing along the pavement.

Both Karen and Rick chased after him. He was young and fit, and his legs were a lot longer than Karen's. She knew she wouldn't catch him.

Rick had a better chance. But on a day when he was sleep-deprived and grieving for his mother? Karen wasn't hopeful.

But Rick had a single focus as he streaked after Todd.

Karen kept running too, but she was falling back, despite her best efforts. She pressed a hand against her bag to stop it thrashing about as she ran. She was losing them, the distance between them growing greater and greater with every stride.

'Police,' Karen yelled. 'Stop!'

Of course that didn't work. But they had to announce who they were, or later in court, Todd could say he was running from them because he was scared and didn't know they were law enforcement.

Rick yelled, too, and pedestrians scattered to let them pass. Rick was gaining on Todd. He might just be able to catch him. It was so close.

They were almost level with the deli when Rick flung himself forward and grabbed Todd around the waist. They both fell hard on to the pavement, crashing into the tables and chairs outside the deli. Luckily, only one person was sitting outside. A young woman in office attire, who not only moved out of the way in the nick of time but also rescued her coffee.

By the time Karen reached the deli, Rick had Todd sitting in a chair and had read him his rights. Rick had shoved the chair back against the shopfront and stood right in front of it, so if Todd tried to make a run for it again, Rick would have time to grab him.

Karen nodded at Rick. 'Good job,' she said, and then apologised breathlessly to the café owner.

'I'll call it in,' she told Rick. 'Get a unit to pick him up.'

Todd scowled at her. There was a graze on his left cheek from where he'd hit the ground hard. His chest was still heaving.

'You all right?' Karen asked Rick.

'Never better,' he said. 'Nothing like a bit of morning exercise to get the blood pumping.'

Todd made a scoffing sound.

'You are Todd Bartholomew, correct?' Karen asked, but he just glared at her with hatred and didn't respond. 'Why did you run, Todd?' But again her question was met with silence.

'He's not very talkative today, is he, Sarge?'

'No, he isn't,' Karen said. 'Let's see if that changes when we get him to the station.'

The uniformed unit were quick to arrive. They cuffed Todd and put him in the back of their vehicle. Karen called ahead, letting Morgan know Todd Bartholomew was on the way to the station.

'I bet this goes down like a lead balloon with Rawlings,' Rick said with a grin, and Karen laughed.

'I think you might be right. I wouldn't mind being a fly on the wall when he hears you caught him. We'll need to show Todd's photograph to Vicky and the other victims, but I'm sure we've got our man. DNA will prove that.'

'Not a bad morning's work,' Rick said.

Back at the station, Rick parked in the shade of the birch trees, and as he was reversing into a spot, Karen noticed the black Range Rover.

'I don't believe the gall of that man,' Karen said.

'What is it?' Rick asked, turning off the engine.

'It's Quentin Chapman. He's involved in CaP Diagnostics, Phoebe Woodrow's company. From what I can work out, his investment seems above board, but that's probably the only thing in his portfolio that is. There are lots of whispers.' She paused and turned to Rick. 'And one of his heavies was hanging around outside Mike's place early this morning.'

'Really?' Rick leaned across Karen to get a better look at the Range Rover. 'He must be really rattled to order that.'

'Yes,' Karen agreed, 'but I don't know why. I'm going to have a word with him. You go in and talk to Morgan and update the rest of the team about Todd.'

'Don't you want me with you when you talk to Chapman?'

'No, I'll be fine,' Karen said, getting out of the car.

She didn't trust Chapman, but Rick had enough going on now without worrying about threats and targets on his back from a local gangster.

Chapman might call himself an investor, but in Karen's eyes he was a gangster moneyman, waist-deep in dodgy deals. The police just hadn't been able to gather enough evidence to prove it yet. Karen had looked into his background but couldn't work out where his money had originated from. There were rumours of drugs and illegal imports, but nothing concrete. Not yet anyway, and Chapman was obviously keen to keep it that way.

She left Rick and strode across to the Range Rover.

The driver's door opened. The skinhead got out, his face blank and stony. 'Mr Chapman would like to speak to you,' he grunted, and opened the back door.

As before, Chapman was sitting on the cream leather seat in air-conditioned comfort. Today he wore a light blue shirt, his greying hair carefully combed into place. He looked cool and refreshed. Quite the opposite of how Karen felt after chasing Todd Bartholomew.

'Detective,' he said, 'please join me for a moment, won't you?'

Karen slid into the seat. 'I'm glad you're here. I want a word with you.'

'Oh, really?'

'Yes. I don't appreciate you sending your men to follow me.' She nodded to Ponytail, who was sitting in the front passenger seat, staring straight ahead, pretending not to listen to the conversation, but Karen saw the tips of his ears turn pink.

'He was standing outside waiting for me this morning. If this is a threat to get me to back off, it's not going to work. Let's just make that clear up front, shall we, so we're on the same page?'

Quentin Chapman's face was the picture of innocence. 'Oh, you quite misunderstand me, Detective. I only want to know where Phoebe is.'

Karen frowned. 'So do I.'

'You haven't located her yet?' he asked softly. 'That's worrying. Our deal has to be signed off next week, and I confess I'm concerned.'

'About your deal or about Phoebe?'

'Both, of course, Detective.'

'Well, we haven't managed to find her yet.' Karen reached for the door handle.

He reached out and clasped Karen's arm. 'Someone *must* know where she is.' He sounded faintly exasperated. Was a crack appearing in his cool veneer?

She glared at his hand on her arm. He let it drop. 'My apologies.'

'We're working on it.'

She stared at him, and he returned her gaze steadily. There was no obvious tension in his face now, though Karen realised he must be about to lose a hefty sum if Phoebe didn't show her face soon.

'Do you think something's happened to her?' he asked.

'I don't know,' Karen said.

'It's your job to find out.'

'Thanks for reminding me,' she replied sarcastically. 'Look, I'm short on time, so if you don't have any fresh information, this conversation is over.' She opened the door.

'It's not that we have a short space of time, but that we waste much of it,' he murmured.

'Sorry?'

'Seneca said that.'

'Right. Fascinating. Right now, *you're* wasting *my* short space of time. Goodbye, Mr Chapman.'

CHAPTER TWENTY-THREE

There was a jubilant mood at the station after Todd Bartholomew had been brought in. DCI Simpson announced he would interview Todd personally.

Simpson told the officers working on Operation Starling that he was determined to build a case so watertight this monster could never wriggle out of it. He agreed to have DI Morgan partner him for the interview, after DCI Churchill's intervention.

The joyful mood didn't last long for Simpson and Morgan, though. For the first half an hour of the interview, Todd sat in silence, though his face betrayed his emotions.

He looked like he was enjoying himself.

The duty solicitor sat beside her client, passive and deceptively docile. There was no anger or outrage. For her, this was nothing new. It would take a great deal to shake her.

Todd even refused to confirm his name. After nearly an hour, he began to answer their questions with 'No comment'.

Morgan supposed that was progress.

'Where were you on Friday, the seventeenth of July?' Morgan asked.

'No comment,' Todd said with a wide grin. He was loving this.

His arrogance and apparent delight in his crimes made Morgan feel sick.

After the first hour was up, they paused the interview and took a break.

Outside in the corridor, Simpson said, 'He's our man. I know it.'

Morgan agreed.

Simpson gritted his teeth. 'He gets under my skin. He acts like he's proud of what he did.'

'I think he is. That's his weakness,' Morgan said. 'He's holding out for now, but he won't be able to resist boasting.'

'We need a confession.'

'Let's leave him to sweat for an hour or so,' Morgan said. 'Then regroup and go at him again.'

'But he's not giving us anything.'

'He will,' Morgan said. 'We just need time.'

The search was currently underway at Todd's home in Lincoln. There was a chance the search team would find evidence they could use in the interview. Matching Todd's DNA with the DNA found at the crime scenes would be the cherry on the cake, but that would take time. They needed something now.

DCI Simpson said, 'I don't think I've ever wanted to nail a criminal as much as I do this man. If it was up to me, he'd get sent down for life.'

◆ ◆ ◆

While the interview was underway, Karen left the station to go to Cassidy's flat and speak to Vicky. She'd brought a photograph of Todd, hoping for a positive ID.

Cassidy opened the door with the chain on. When she saw it was Karen, she removed the chain and let her in.

'Any news?' Cassidy asked.

'Yes,' she said. 'We've made an arrest. Is Vicky still here?'

Cassidy nodded. 'Yeah.'

Karen walked into the living area. Vicky was curled up on the sofa, hugging her knees.

She sat up when Karen walked into the room, her eyes wide and filled with apprehension.

Karen smiled and sat down on the other end of the sofa. 'Hi, Vicky. We've made an arrest and I've got a photograph to show you. Are you okay to take a look and tell me if it's the man who drugged you?'

Vicky shot a worried glance at Cassidy.

'It's all right. They've caught him,' Cassidy said.

'All right,' Vicky murmured.

When Karen handed her the printed image, Vicky inhaled sharply.

'That's him,' she said. 'Definitely. And you've caught him?'

'Yes, he's in custody now, being interviewed.'

'You're not going to let him out, are you? He might come after me.' She looked again at Cassidy.

Cassidy shook her head. 'He won't.'

'But he'll know I went to the police.'

'It's not just you, Vicky,' Karen said. 'Other women have told us about similar attacks.'

Karen didn't know if that information would make Vicky feel better, but at least she wouldn't think she was the only one who'd come forward.

Karen hoped they could put Todd Bartholomew away for a very long time, but she couldn't promise anything to Vicky. Arrests were one thing, convictions were another thing all together, and were sadly out of her control. The best she could do was build a strong case against him.

Cassidy offered to make coffee, and Karen spent some time chatting to them both, detailing how things might go in the next few days.

After she said goodbye to Vicky, Cassidy walked downstairs with her.

'She trusts you,' Karen said. 'You're really helping, you know.'

Cassidy sighed, trailing her hand along the banister.

'You're very passionate about this,' Karen commented as they reached the main door of the apartment block.

'We should all be passionate about it,' Cassidy said.

'Yes, we should. I just wondered if there was something personal in this for you?' Karen asked.

Cassidy stared at her for a few moments before replying. 'Yeah, I suppose it is personal.'

A moment passed, and Karen thought the conversation was over, but then Cassidy said in a quiet voice, 'My mum was attacked. He broke in at night, climbed through a window, raped her, and then tried to strangle her. He would have killed her if a neighbour hadn't rung the doorbell. They'd heard a disturbance and went to see if she was okay.'

'That's awful,' Karen said.

Cassidy looked away. 'Yes. That's one word for it.' She took a deep breath. 'And I'm the result of that attack.'

'Your father . . .' Karen whispered as Cassidy's words sunk in.

'Yes, my father was a rapist.' Cassidy's voice was hard and brittle. 'Try living with that knowledge and not being filled with rage every time you read a report about another woman's life being destroyed.' Her voice cracked. 'Try living with the guilt.'

'But you've got nothing to feel guilty for,' Karen said.

'I know that. Of course I know that. But knowing and feeling are two different things!'

'That makes sense. I'm sorry. It must have been incredibly difficult for you. Are you and your mum still close?'

Cassidy nodded. 'Yes. She married when I was seven, and my stepfather is great. I'm lucky to have them both.'

As Karen turned to leave, Cassidy put her hand on her arm. 'Karen?'

'Yes?'

'You're going to put him away and throw away the key, aren't you?'

Karen gave her a sad smile. 'There's nothing I'd like to do more,' she said.

◆ ◆ ◆

After leaving Cassidy, Karen went to Todd Bartholomew's apartment, where the search was underway.

She was greeted outside the apartment block by Tim Farthing, with the charming words 'Oh, it's you again.'

He was standing beside the SOCO van, dressed in a white hooded coverall. His face was red and sweaty.

'Yes, Tim. It's me. What have you got so far?' She smiled pleasantly.

'Quite a lot, actually,' Tim said, puffing out his chest. 'He wasn't exactly hiding his deeds. We found Rohypnol in the kitchen, and photos. A *lot* of photos. I don't think you're going to have any problem putting this guy away. His fingerprints are all over the photographs, so don't let him tell you they've been planted,' Tim said.

'He printed the photographs?'

'Yes, he has a fancy printer in there. Like I said, I don't think he worried much about being caught. Nothing was locked away.'

'Are they photographs of the victims?'

'More than likely,' Tim said. 'I've not seen the victims, but they're all women . . . young. They all look to be semi-conscious, arranged in . . . *positions*,' Tim said with distaste.

It was good news, but Karen couldn't feel happy about it. All those women had been abused by Todd, and even after his arrest it would haunt them. For them, this would never go away, not completely.

'There's probably more on his laptop.' Tim shook his head. 'I don't think you're dealing with a master criminal.'

'I think he was too confident,' Karen said. 'He believed he'd never be caught.'

'Overconfidence is a common downfall of criminals,' Tim said.

'And you're combing the place for any trace of Phoebe Woodrow?' Karen asked. 'She's still missing.'

'Yes, I heard she was still missing, but there's no sign of her so far. Of course, we'll study the trace evidence – hairs, fingerprints, DNA – when we get back to the lab.'

'Has every room been checked?' Karen asked.

She wondered whether Todd Bartholomew had been furious when Phoebe escaped his clutches and had gone back to get her. He might have taken her back to his place, angry at his failure. Maybe so angry that he'd commit murder.

'Yes, every room's been checked,' Tim said impatiently.

'The loft?'

'Of course the loft, DS Hart. I'm not stupid,' Tim said with a huff.

Karen raised an eyebrow but made no comment.

Tim bustled past her. 'Well, if that's all, I do have things to be getting on with. It's been lovely chatting, as always, DS Hart.'

Karen pulled out her mobile and called Morgan. He could certainly use the photographs while interviewing Todd. It might be the nudge that finally got him to talk.

An hour later, Morgan and Simpson went back in to interview Todd.

At first, just like before, he was cocky and sure of himself. But when Morgan slid a copy of the first photograph across the table, he seemed shaken.

He swallowed hard but said nothing.

Morgan pushed across another photograph.

'They're not mine,' Todd said.

'Funny, they were found at your house and they have your fingerprints all over them,' Morgan said.

Todd glared at him. 'I didn't give you permission to go inside my house.'

'I'm sure your solicitor can explain why a warrant means we don't need your permission,' Morgan said.

Todd turned to his solicitor and gave her a look full of hatred. 'You're supposed to be looking out for my interests.'

She tensed. 'You don't have to answer,' she said.

'What do you mean I don't have to answer? He's not asked me a question, you stupid cow. He's been in my house, poking through my stuff,' Todd yelled. 'Why did you let him do that?'

It wasn't true, Morgan hadn't been on the search, but he didn't feel the need to correct him. If the thought of Morgan going through his possessions got under Todd's skin, then that was good as far as Morgan was concerned. They needed to get under his skin. They needed to needle him until he couldn't hold out any longer.

'You're not going to squirm your way out of this one, Todd,' DCI Simpson said. 'The DNA results will be back soon.'

Todd retreated into silence, then turned to his solicitor and leaned close to mutter something in her ear.

She flinched. Morgan didn't blame her.

She shifted her chair a few inches from Todd and said, 'I'd like some time to talk to my client in private, please.'

'Of course,' Morgan said, allowing himself a small, satisfied smile when he caught the look of panic in Todd's eyes.

Todd had been so sure he was going to get away with it, but now the net was closing around him.

◆ ◆ ◆

When the interview resumed, Todd had regained some of his bluster. He was almost proud as he admitted to drugging the women in the photographs.

Todd smirked as they continued to question him.

Finally, Morgan pushed across a still image taken from Imporium's CCTV, showing Phoebe and Todd in close proximity. 'And this young woman?' Morgan prompted, pointing out Phoebe Woodrow.

Todd gave the image a bored glance. 'Never seen her before.'

'You're standing only inches apart.'

'So?'

'So, she's missing, and we think you know where she is.'

Todd shook his head slowly. 'Sorry, mate, can't help you there. No idea who this one is.' He pulled the printed image towards him, using a finger to slowly trace the outline of Phoebe's figure. 'She's pretty though.'

CHAPTER
TWENTY-FOUR

'What do you mean he didn't take Phoebe?' Karen demanded. 'He must be lying.'

Morgan watched Karen pace his small office.

'You don't believe him, do you?' she asked.

'Todd Bartholomew insists he had nothing to do with Phoebe's disappearance, and we don't have evidence that indicates otherwise,' Morgan said coolly.

'Well, he *would* say that, wouldn't he?' Karen raked a hand through her hair. She was hot. Hot and annoyed. 'He's holding her arm in the CCTV footage. Does he deny that, too?'

'No, he says he reached out when she stumbled against him.'

'Right, and I'm the tooth fairy.'

'Karen, we need to judge the facts at hand. Todd was caught on CCTV with Phoebe on Friday night, but we know she stayed at her cousin's that night. She didn't leave Imporium with Todd.'

Karen groaned, clenching her teeth as she walked back and forth across the carpet tiles.

Morgan interlaced his fingers behind his head and leaned back in his chair. He gazed up at the ceiling, thinking. That was the way he processed information: quiet contemplation. But Karen liked to talk things through, and she liked to keep moving. It kept her focus sharp.

She gave him a minute or two, but then couldn't hold back. 'We know Todd has been spiking women's drinks in Lincoln. Even if he denies having anything to do with Phoebe's disappearance, we have the photographs of his other victims. He can't deny those.'

'No, he's not denying those,' Morgan said.

'Only because we found the photographs in his home. He started out denying everything.'

'But we come back to the fact we know she left Imporium safely. We know she was with her cousin. We know she saw her grandmother on Saturday.'

'Her grandmother says so, but the care home says Phoebe wasn't there on Saturday,' Karen said, finally sitting down. 'Nothing adds up.'

'No, it doesn't.'

'It should be a slam dunk. Todd was there at Imporium with Phoebe. He grabbed her arm. It's all on CCTV.'

'I know,' Morgan said.

'Maybe,' Karen began tentatively, 'he drugged her at Imporium, but she managed to get away, met her cousin and went back to his house. Maybe the presence of her cousin scared Todd off? Then, after she visited her grandmother on Saturday, Todd came after her. He wanted the one that got away.'

'Possible,' Morgan said, 'but where did he take her? What did he do? We've got nothing.'

'Ask him again,' Karen said. 'He's still in custody?'

Morgan nodded. 'We have enough to charge him. The evidence from the other victims together with the photographs is more than enough. But we haven't got anything to help us pin Phoebe's disappearance on him.'

Karen nodded. 'Right. Then we need to find that evidence.'

A call came through, and Morgan picked up the phone.

While he was talking, Karen thought through the case again. They were so close. They had Todd Bartholomew in custody. He'd admitted his crimes against the other victims, so why deny his involvement in Phoebe's disappearance?

From what Morgan had said, Todd was almost proud of his crimes, crowing about them in the interview room, enjoying reliving each one.

So why wouldn't he admit what he'd done to Phoebe? Had he done something even worse to her? Murder would be a more serious charge. Perhaps he thought he could serve a few years in a minimum-security prison. But he didn't want to cop to a murder.

Karen hated the way her mind had accepted the fact that Phoebe was gone, but it was the most likely scenario.

If Todd had taken Phoebe, where would he have gone? His house would be the obvious choice. If she'd been there, they'd get DNA evidence. There would be a trace – blood spatter, a hair, skin cells, something to indicate she'd been in his home – and if they found that, then the next step would be looking for her body.

Members of Simpson's team were tracking Todd's recent movements. He had a satnav system in his car, and they'd be looking at that closely to see if he'd travelled anywhere that could be looked at as a potential dump site for Phoebe's body. They'd search the garden too, as killers often buried their victims very close to home.

Morgan put down the phone. 'Simon Moore's car has been located. It was left at an NCP car park in Lincoln. It's been towed away. No traffic cameras in the area, but it could have been there since Saturday.'

'That's near the train station,' Karen said.

'But we've looked at all the security footage from the station,' Morgan said. 'Phoebe hasn't been to the station.'

Karen sighed and stood up. 'I'm going to see how Rick and Sophie are getting on. I'll let them know about the vehicle.'

She left Morgan's office and went back to her own desk, deep in thought. Was Todd playing games with them? She wasn't yet willing to let go of the idea that he had something to do with Phoebe's disappearance, but they had to investigate other possibilities. If Todd wasn't behind Phoebe's disappearance, who or what was?

Karen looked out of the window, staring out at the open fields and farmland. Where was Phoebe? Was she even still alive?

◆ ◆ ◆

A short time later, Rick was sitting in his car outside Pinewood Care Home. He'd volunteered to speak with Phoebe Woodrow's grandmother again.

Now that Todd was insisting he had nothing to do with Phoebe's disappearance, they were trying to widen their net, work on alternative theories. Not that they had many to work on.

There was Phoebe's stalker. Then there was Phoebe's association with the alleged local mobster Quentin Chapman. He sounded like a nasty piece of work. If Phoebe had crossed him . . .

Rick was trying to focus desperately on the case to keep his mind off his grief. But his thoughts were a muddle. Confusing, perplexing and a challenge, the disappearance of Phoebe Woodrow was the type of case Rick loved to get his teeth into usually, but today he was finding it hard.

It was to be expected, he supposed. As much as he tried to push the thoughts of what had happened to his mum out of his head, he couldn't.

He'd told Karen and Morgan he needed to be at work, and he really did. At home, he'd kept replaying the events. Images of his mum lying on the pavement crowded his mind.

He felt strung out, worried the grief might send him mad. The guilt ate away at his insides. If he'd only remembered to switch on that alarm, it would have rung out when she opened the front door and he would have been able to stop her. She would never have got hit by that car.

He groaned, closed his eyes and rested his head against the steering wheel. He had to stop thinking about it. He had to get it out of his head. He had to focus. *Focus on work.*

There was a tap on the window. Rick sat up. A woman in a light lilac uniform was smiling at him.

'I thought I'd come and see if you were all right,' she said when Rick lowered his window.

He attempted a smile. He most definitely was not all right, but he pretended he was. 'I'm fine. I'm here to see Mrs Moore.' He pulled his ID from his pocket and held it out for her to see.

'Ah, okay. She'll be glad to see you. She's very worried about her granddaughter. Have you brought news?'

'I've got a few more questions for her.' He shut the window and got out of the car.

'Gorgeous day,' she said, looking up at the cloudless sky.

'Yes, lovely,' Rick said, not bothering to look.

'I'm Tara.'

'Rick.'

They walked together into the care home.

'I'd gone outside to enjoy the sunshine when I spotted you in the car. You looked really stressed. Are you sure you're okay?'

He nodded.

'Why don't I bring you a mug of tea? You look like you could use it.'

'That's very kind, thank you.'

He signed in and then followed Tara along the corridor to Mrs Moore's room.

'Is there any news?' Mrs Moore asked, recognising Rick straightaway.

'Not yet, I'm afraid, but we're using all of our resources to find Phoebe.'

She was sitting beside the patio doors as before. The sunlight streamed in. Though her face was in the shade, her body was bathed in a pool of warm light. She had a delicate oval face and bright hazel eyes.

A shadow passed over Mrs Moore. Rick blinked. He looked outside, but there was nothing to see apart from flowerbeds full of geraniums. He took a seat opposite her.

'Can you remember your conversation with Phoebe on Saturday? Any details at all? It might seem irrelevant now, but it could be a clue.'

Mrs Moore frowned. 'I'll try. I don't remember discussing anything in particular.'

Tara entered the room with a tray of tea and biscuits. 'I've brought you both a cup,' she said brightly, handing one to Rick and then putting the other cup on the coffee table for Mrs Moore. 'And I've brought your favourite custard creams and bourbons, Barbara.' She smiled at Rick. 'And there's some for you, too.'

'Thank you very much,' Rick said.

'I'll leave you to it,' she said cheerfully, and left the room.

Rick took a sip of his tea and then asked, 'Did she mention her job?'

'Oh, let me see. Yes, she did talk about her job. She was very excited. They're selling the company, but she said she'd still work there. I'm afraid I don't understand much about the business side of things.' She smiled apologetically. 'I love to hear what she's been up to, but some of it is over my head.'

'Probably mine, too,' Rick admitted. 'I don't know much about starting a business. I understand she did it all from scratch?'

'Yes. Well, of course, she has her business partner, Cary. They worked together, built it all up themselves. Very clever. They invented a new type of scanning machine to diagnose illnesses. I'm very proud of her.'

'Was she worried about anything at work? Perhaps the people she worked with?' Rick asked, knowing it was a leading question but desperate to get some answers.

'I don't think so. She's been very happy there. Cary occasionally gets on her nerves, but it isn't a big problem.'

'This will probably be quite hard to hear, but we know from Phoebe's neighbour that there was a man who used to sit outside her apartment, watching her.'

Mrs Moore's expression was grave. 'I didn't know anything about that . . . It's certainly disturbing to think that he could have hurt my granddaughter.'

'We don't have any evidence that's what happened,' Rick said hastily, trying to reassure her, 'but we do want to identify him.'

She nodded slowly. 'Did you ask her sister?'

'Yes, my colleague spoke to Lisa, but she didn't know anything about this man either.'

'No, I suppose she wouldn't. They're not very close these days, which is a shame.'

'Did they fall out?' Rick asked.

'No, nothing like that. They're just quite different people. They don't have much in common. It was different before I moved here. They all used to come to me for Sunday lunch.' She smiled at the memory, and her eyes skimmed her room.

It was a homely little room, but Rick imagined living at Pineview was quite different to having your own house. It must have been hard to go from a house to being stuck in one room all the time.

221

'Oh, don't get me wrong,' she said. 'I'm not complaining. It's lovely here. The staff are great. I just miss the time we used to spend as a family. Phoebe and Lisa's parents died in a car crash when the girls were in their early twenties. It was very sad, but we supported one another through it. It was nice to have those dinners together. It's the thing I miss most,' she said.

'It must be difficult.'

'Oh, I've got it much better than most,' she said. 'Gladys, in the next room' – she nodded at the wall behind Rick – 'has Alzheimer's. It's terrible. Her daughters come to visit her, but she doesn't remember them.'

Rick's chest tightened, but he forced himself to relax. 'That must be awful for them.'

Mrs Moore nodded and turned her gaze towards the gardens. She pushed forward in her chair. 'I think there's someone out there. I don't think he's a member of staff. Maybe a visitor?'

Rick stood and looked out. A young man dressed in a suit saw Rick and quickly moved back out of sight.

Rick opened the door and stepped out on to the patio. 'Who are you?'

The man looked flustered, like he'd been caught doing something he shouldn't. Was he a peeping Tom, getting kicks from spying on the elderly, or did he work here?

'I don't recognise him,' said Mrs Moore. 'He's not one of the gardeners.'

'Who are you?' Rick repeated.

'None of your business,' the man said, seeming to regain his composure.

'It's very much my business,' Rick said, pulling his ID out of his pocket and showing the man his warrant card.

The man looked horrified. 'Oh, I'm sorry. It's just a misunderstanding,' he said, quickly putting his hands up.

'What are you doing here? Do you have permission, or are you trespassing?'

'I . . . I . . .' The man raked a hand through his hair.

He looked to be late-twenties, good-looking, very smartly dressed. His suit looked expensive, although how he could wear a jacket in this heat was beyond Rick.

'I'm sorry,' he said again. 'I'm worried about Phoebe. I wanted to speak to her grandmother.'

'Then why didn't you sign in at reception?' Rick asked.

The man glanced around and stuttered. 'I . . . I just thought this would be easier.'

'Really?'

'Yes. I'm concerned about Phoebe.'

'You're concerned about Phoebe?' Rick repeated, his voice laced with scepticism.

'Yes.'

'Or were you worried about what her grandmother might be telling the police?'

The man's jaw dropped. 'No, no. Of course not. You've got it all wrong. I just wanted to ask Phoebe's grandmother if she knew where Phoebe might be.'

'I think it's time you told me your name.'

The man nodded. 'I've got nothing to hide. My name's Cary Swann. I work with Phoebe.'

Rick frowned. If he had nothing to hide, then why was he creeping around outside?

Cary looked at his watch. 'I didn't realise the time. I've got loads to do. Sorry, I didn't mean to trouble you.' He leaned past Rick to make eye contact with Mrs Moore. 'Very sorry.'

'Actually,' Rick said, stepping forward to block his path, 'I think it's time you came to the station for a chat.'

CHAPTER TWENTY-FIVE

Karen and Rick sat opposite Cary in interview room three.

'I'm afraid this has all been a misunderstanding,' Cary said. 'I was concerned for my colleague.'

'Why were you hassling Phoebe Woodrow's grandmother?' Rick asked.

'I wasn't.' He pressed a hand to his chest and leaned forward earnestly. 'I'm worried about Phoebe. I still haven't heard from her. We've got so much to organise for the deal, and she isn't here. She's always tended to leave most of the admin work to me, but I don't think even Phoebe would disappear for this long. CaP Diagnostics is just as important to her as it is to me.'

Karen found it hard to tell if Cary was being completely truthful. Turning up at the care home was suspicious behaviour, but his apparent openness suggested he was genuinely concerned for his business partner. He kept his voice level, his tone polite.

Cary showed none of the wariness Karen was used to dealing with when interviewing suspects. But he was young, handsome and probably used to applying charm to get his own way. He was nothing like Chapman or his thugs, but that didn't mean he was innocent.

'What is Phoebe's relationship with Quentin Chapman like?' Karen asked.

'Um, they have a business relationship.' Cary tugged at his collar. 'It's hot in here, isn't it?'

'Yes,' Karen said, pushing a bottle of water over the table to him. 'The air conditioning's not great in here.'

Cary looked up at the ceiling tiles. 'I think they get on okay. No, better than okay. He admires Phoebe, thinks a lot of her. That might have something to do with the fact she's young and female, though,' he said with a half-hearted smile. 'She flirts with him a bit.'

'Is there anything romantic between them?' Rick asked.

'Oh no, nothing like that,' Cary said. 'Phoebe just . . . Well, she has a kind of charisma, I suppose. People warm to her, want to work with her, want to please her.' He threw up his hands. 'I mean *I* did. I was thrilled when she agreed to go into business with me. I knew we'd make it, although I didn't think we'd have this much success.' He shook his head. 'That's why I can't understand why she'd just disappear. She was the one pushing for this deal.'

Nothing about Cary's behaviour suggested guilt to Karen, but he could simply be a very good liar. White-collar criminals were often adept at hiding their deceptions.

'Maybe she hasn't disappeared voluntarily,' Karen suggested.

Cary pushed his hands through his hair, seemingly upset by the suggestion. 'That's a horrible thought.'

'How often do you speak to Quentin Chapman?'

'At least once a week,' Cary said. 'We have a meeting with him. He usually comes to us.'

'And does Phoebe ever see him outside work?'

'I think so. She's been along to parties he's held. He's introduced her to some powerful people. He thinks she has a bright future ahead of her,' he said, making quote marks in the air.

'Are you invited to these parties?' Karen asked.

Cary smiled. 'Occasionally. Not very often.'

'Does that annoy you?' Rick asked.

'No, not really. They're not my sort of thing. Just a bunch of rich people with more money than sense, slapping each other on the back.'

Karen was surprised. In his sharp suits and with his carefully groomed appearance, she'd thought Cary would have fitted in with those rich people very well indeed.

'Have you been in touch with Quentin Chapman about Phoebe's disappearance?' Karen asked.

'Look, I don't understand why you're asking so many questions about Quentin Chapman. Do you think he's got something to do with Phoebe going missing?'

'What do you think?' Karen asked, turning the question back on him.

Cary spread his hands wide. 'I really have no idea. If I knew what had happened to her or where she was, I'd tell you.'

'So,' Karen said, '*have* you spoken to Quentin Chapman since Phoebe disappeared?'

'Yes, a couple of times.' He sighed and looked up at the ceiling again. 'More than a couple of times, to be honest. Quentin's getting jumpy about the deal. Understandable, really. He stands to lose a lot of money if this all falls through. So, you see, he can't have anything to do with her disappearance. Otherwise he'd know where she was. He wouldn't need to keep calling me to ask if there was any news, would he?' Cary said, though he didn't sound too sure of himself.

'Is there anything about this deal that's not above board?' Karen asked.

'Absolutely not,' Cary said emphatically. 'It's all legitimate. We've worked hard, built a strong company with an excellent product that will help a lot of people.'

'That's admirable,' Karen said, 'but you must know that Quentin Chapman is not known for his altruism. There's got to be something in it for him.'

'Well, there is,' Cary said. 'He's going to profit from it. His initial investment will more than double when we sell the company. The deal is such that he gets paid and gets shares in the purchasing company. He's going to make a lot of money out of it. So no, it's not altruistic, but there's nothing illegal about making money.'

Karen nodded slowly. In her experience, men like Quentin Chapman didn't acquire the bulk of their wealth legally. Though this investment could be a respectable front for his other dodgy dealings.

◆ ◆ ◆

After another half an hour of questioning, they let Cary go home. There wasn't the evidence to hold him any longer, and he'd cooperated and answered all their questions.

Sophie was hunched over her computer in the main office.

'How's Harinder getting on? Has he managed to access Phoebe's work emails?' Karen asked, wheeling a chair over to Sophie's desk.

'He's struggling,' Sophie admitted. 'They've been encrypted by an unusual program.'

'Something Phoebe didn't want anyone to see?'

'Or the encryption is a work requirement,' Sophie suggested. 'Perhaps the company is hot on security. Either way, her emails and files are very well protected. He's trying a lot of different programs. He'll crack it,' she said confidently. 'But it's going to take him a while.'

'I hope it doesn't take too long,' Karen said, 'because we're running out of solid leads.'

A short while later, Karen was sitting at her own desk when her mobile rang. It was Trisha.

'He's back. He's back!' Trisha said excitedly. 'He's here. Sitting on the bench. Right outside.'

'Okay, Trisha. We're coming. Keep back from the window, okay?'

'I will. I promise,' she said.

'Rick?' Karen said, standing up and grabbing her bag. 'You're with me.'

It took them less than ten minutes to get there. Karen spotted him straightaway. Medium height, slim build, dressed in a white shirt and light tan chinos. He wore frameless glasses and had a very narrow chin and broad forehead. He sat on the bench casually, his feet crossed at the ankles, and was staring up at the apartment building.

Karen pulled into a parking spot on the opposite side of the road. 'That's him. Can you see him?'

Rick released his seat belt. 'I can.'

They walked across the road slowly, not wanting to spook him.

When they were a few feet away, Rick pulled out his ID. 'Can we have a word, mate?' he asked.

The man lifted his slim, pointed face and blinked at them. His body tensed, and Karen knew he was about to run.

Sure enough, a second later, he jerked to his feet and took off in the other direction.

'Not again,' Karen groaned as they set off in pursuit.

This time he didn't have much of a head start, and he wasn't as athletic as Todd.

'Police. Stop!' Karen shouted in warning, in case the man hadn't got a good look at Rick's warrant card.

228

Rick was on the man within moments. He grabbed hold of his shirt, yanking the suspect back.

But the man wasn't about to give up easily. He turned and kneed Rick in the groin. A direct hit. All the air left Rick's lungs as he felt pain ricochet through his body. He bent double, but he didn't let go of the man's shirt.

Furious, red-hot anger flowed through Rick.

The guy was still wriggling, but Rick managed to keep hold. *Pin his arms*, Rick thought. *Immobilise him.*

But the man wasn't done. Twisting and turning, he tried to knee Rick again, and then threw a punch.

It wasn't a great punch. There wasn't much power behind it. It only grazed Rick's jaw, and the man didn't even clench his fist properly. It was a pathetic attempt at a punch really, but it triggered something in Rick.

Looking back later he wasn't sure how it happened, but suddenly Rick wasn't grappling with a suspect trying to run away. It was the driver who'd mown down his mother. The person responsible for his loss. The one responsible for the guilt he felt for forgetting to set the alarm, for everything that had gone wrong in his life.

He reacted with fury.

His right fist, clenched tight, connected with the man's jaw, smashing his teeth together. The man collapsed to the ground with a thud. There was no more resistance.

The red-hot anger was gone in an instant.

What had he done?

He'd lashed out. A single blow could kill. He'd seen it before. Lives ruined by one punch.

Rick reached for the man, tapping him gently on the side of his face. 'Are you all right? Are you still with me?'

The man was bleeding from the corner of his mouth. He might have bitten his tongue. 'Are you all right?' Rick said again.

The man blinked and gazed up at him, eyes unfocused. 'You hit me!' He sounded astounded.

'You were resisting arrest.'

Rick heard Karen's voice behind him and straightened up. The man sat up, groggily holding his jaw.

◆ ◆ ◆

Karen crouched beside them. 'Can you get to your feet, sir?' she asked him. 'What's your name?'

'Gavin Griffin,' he said thickly, wiping the blood away from his lip with the back of his hand and looking at it in horror. 'I'm bleeding.'

'Just a bit,' Karen said. 'I think you bit your tongue when you fell.'

'When he hit me, you mean?' he said, glaring at Rick.

Karen said nothing. She saw what Gavin had done, but they had strict rules to follow for good reason.

Rick shouldn't have hit him. They would have to report it. Rick could lose his job.

They helped Gavin to his feet, and as Karen looked up at the apartment building, she saw Trisha standing at her kitchen window holding her phone, likely filming everything.

She cursed.

They called it in. Karen wanted another officer on the scene to oversee the arrest and get Gavin taken in. They spent an awkward ten minutes waiting for the squad car to arrive. Karen wanted Gavin as far away from Rick as possible.

Once the other police officers arrived and Gavin had been taken to the station to be processed, Karen and Rick went back to the car.

'I'm so sorry, Sarge,' Rick said. 'I don't know what came over me.'

'I know,' Karen said. 'I need you to stay in the car. Keep the door open if it's too hot. I'm going to go and have a quick word with Trisha.'

She didn't mention she suspected Trisha had been recording the incident. Rick already looked devastated.

Upstairs, she knocked on the door of Trisha's apartment. 'We've got him,' she said when Phoebe's neighbour opened the door.

'I know. I saw. I was watching,' Trisha said, beaming. 'Got it all on video. Can I post it to social media?'

'I'd prefer it if you didn't,' Karen said.

'Oh, really? It was awesome. Do you want to see?' She held out her phone.

Karen hesitated. She wanted to get rid of the recording for Rick's sake. But it was the wrong thing to do. As police officers they had to be accountable. They dealt with awful criminals but had to hold themselves to a higher standard.

Karen winced at the sight of Rick raising his arm.

'Pow!' Trisha said with glee as Rick's fist connected with Gavin's jaw.

She glanced up and noticed the expression on Karen's face. 'I could watch that over and over again. If you ask me, he deserved it. In fact, he deserved more than that, the creep.'

'Maybe so,' Karen said, 'but as police officers we're not supposed to . . .' She gestured to the phone.

Officers were not allowed to go around hitting people. No matter how tempting criminals made it sometimes. And it wasn't Rick's fault. He shouldn't have been out here. He shouldn't have been doing this today. He was too emotional. It was Karen's fault. She had let him down. Her judgement had been way off. What had she been thinking?

It was one thing for Rick to be behind a desk, keeping himself busy by wading through paperwork, but taking him out like this had been a serious lack of judgement on her part.

'Anyway, you don't have to worry,' Trisha said. 'I'll delete it.' She swiped the screen. 'See, I've got rid of it. I never saw a thing.' She tapped the side of her nose. 'It'll be our little secret.'

Karen felt sick. This was not her. She prided herself on acting with integrity. The video was evidence.

But how could she let Rick suffer?

If she was working by the book, she should ask for a copy of the video, report it to her senior officers and then there'd be an enquiry. Rick would be suspended, possibly lose his job.

He was a good officer. Should he suffer because Karen had screwed up?

Trisha looked at Karen quizzically. 'You okay? You look a bit pale. I suppose that would have shaken me up too. I bet that sort of thing happens all the time though, doesn't it? You'll let me know as soon as there's any news about Phoebe, won't you?'

Karen nodded and thanked her for her help.

She walked down the stairs feeling numb. What had she done? Watching Trisha get rid of that video and doing nothing to stop her had been wrong. It was everything she'd stood against. Everything she hated.

She rubbed the back of her neck to ease the tension building there, and exited the building. Rick was slumped in the passenger seat, looking thoroughly miserable. She might have done the wrong thing by letting Trisha delete the video, but she'd done it for him.

She got into the driver's side. 'All right?'

He nodded. 'I'm *so* sorry, Sarge.'

Karen looked across the road at the now-empty bench. 'We'll talk about it later.'

CHAPTER TWENTY-SIX

They had no problem getting Gavin Griffin to talk. In fact, they had trouble stopping him talking.

Karen and Sophie sat opposite Gavin in interview room two, the smallest of the interview rooms. The confined space made the heat seem worse than in the rest of the station.

The air conditioning unit on the wall must have failed, though it was making rumbling and gurgling noises in its attempt to pump out cooler air. Maintenance hadn't been in a hurry to fix it. Probably because if the English weather followed its typical pattern, by the time they repaired the unit, it would be too cold to use it.

Gavin had refused the services of the duty solicitor.

'I have no idea where Phoebe is,' Gavin insisted. 'I haven't seen her for a few days.'

'Do you sit outside her apartment every day?' Sophie asked, trying and failing to keep the incredulity out of her voice.

'Most days. If I'm not otherwise occupied.'

'You don't have a job?' Sophie asked.

'I do! I'm an inventor. It requires a lot of quiet time to think, to be creative. And I can do that just as well sitting outside Phoebe's place.'

Karen was starting to think Gavin was suffering from delusions. According to her research before the interview, Gavin was unemployed.

Gavin's head bobbed as he talked, as though his long, narrow neck wasn't strong enough to fully support it. His wide forehead and narrow chin gave him the appearance of a boffin. He'd fiddled with his frameless glasses throughout the interview, taking them off, polishing them on his shirt and then putting them back on. It was distracting.

Karen was struggling to focus. She was so worried about Rick. She'd left him upstairs in the office. Soon, she would have to talk to DCI Churchill and report the incident.

'I've got nothing to hide,' Gavin Griffin said for the umpteenth time, spreading his hands and shrugging. 'Nothing at all. I'll answer all your questions.'

A bruise was blooming along his jawline, and he kept touching it with his fingertips.

'Can you tell us why you were outside Phoebe Woodrow's apartment?'

'Can you tell me why I shouldn't have been?' Gavin said, smiling as though he'd gained the upper hand. 'I haven't broken any laws. I was just sitting on a bench, minding my own business.'

'Why did you run and resist arrest?'

'I . . .' He paused. 'You took me by surprise. I've never been arrested before. I panicked.' He touched his jaw again and winced.

'Are you sure you don't want to see a medic?' Karen asked.

'No, I'm fine,' he said. 'I shouldn't have hit a police officer. I apologise. He was just defending himself. It all happened so fast.'

'It was a tense arrest. You have the right to lodge a complaint.'

Karen felt Sophie stiffen beside her.

Gavin shook his head. 'I don't want to do that.'

'You're sure?'

'Yes. I'm normally law-abiding. I don't know what happened. I just . . . wasn't expecting to be approached by the police.'

He was a white male with no criminal record. Not a demographic who would usually have good cause to be fearful of the police. His behaviour during the arrest suggested he was quick to lose his temper.

Karen pushed a photograph of Phoebe across the table. 'Do you know who this is?'

'Of course. Phoebe Woodrow.'

'And you admit you were sitting outside her apartment building.'

'Yes,' he said, as though it was a perfectly normal thing to do.

'Why have you been stalking her?'

'What? I haven't been stalking her.'

'You've been sitting outside her apartment, watching her come and go. What else would you call it?' Karen asked.

'I was *shaming* her,' he said.

'Shaming her?'

'Yes. They stole my idea. CaP Diagnostics. The scanner was all my idea. They could never have built it without me.'

Karen eyed him sceptically. 'So why didn't you go through legal channels? Why were you sitting outside her apartment?'

'Because I can't afford legal channels,' he said, pushing his glasses up the bridge of his nose. 'I wanted her to know I hadn't forgotten, and I wouldn't just let it go. They stole my idea and expected to get away with it.'

'So why didn't you talk to Cary, or sit outside his home?'

'It wouldn't have done any good,' Gavin scoffed. 'He's a capitalist through and through. He dreams about money. I thought that Phoebe might have a conscience.'

It didn't add up. If CaP Diagnostics had stolen his idea for the scanner, did he really think the best way to handle the situation was to sit outside the home of a single female? Didn't he understand how threatening that appeared?

He had no record. No criminal charges. But that didn't mean Gavin wasn't unhealthily obsessed with Phoebe. It was not normal to sit outside someone's home, watching them. And why target Phoebe and not Cary? Because Gavin thought she was the weaker of the two? Was he hoping for a pay-off?

'How did they get hold of your idea for the scanner?' Karen asked.

'I . . . did a presentation a couple of years ago on the theory. They used my ideas, my intellectual property, and turned it into their scanner.'

'Do you have a copy of this presentation?' Karen asked.

'S . . . somewhere,' he said. 'Probably.'

'Any witnesses who heard it? Apart from Phoebe and Cary.'

Gavin hesitated. 'I suppose, but I can't remember who was there offhand.'

He swallowed and gave a nervous smile.

He was lying.

Was he a grifter chancing his arm, putting pressure on Phoebe because she was coming into money? Did he hope she'd send some his way if he made a nuisance of himself? If she'd refused, maybe laughed at him, could the situation have turned violent?

According to her neighbour, Trisha, Phoebe certainly hadn't taken Gavin Griffin seriously.

'Have you ever visited Imporium?' Karen asked.

'Where?'

'It's a bar, in Lincoln.'

'Oh no, bars aren't really my scene.'

Even if he wasn't behind Phoebe's disappearance, Karen hoped he'd seen something while sitting outside her home. She slid a photograph of Todd Bartholomew across the desk. 'Have you ever seen this man? Perhaps with Phoebe or near her apartment?'

Gavin glanced at the image and shrugged. 'I've never seen him near Phoebe's apartment or anywhere else.'

Karen glanced at Sophie, who was taking notes, her mouth closed in a prim line. She disapproved of Gavin Griffin's antics.

'We'll take a break here, Mr Griffin,' Karen said. 'Would you like a drink?'

'Yes, I'll have another cup of tea, thanks,' he said, and leaned casually back in his chair.

◆ ◆ ◆

When they left the interview room, Karen headed upstairs to talk to Rick. She found him sitting at his desk where she'd left him. His computer was off and he was fiddling with a pen, even though there were no papers in front of him.

She sat down. 'I'm going to talk to Churchill now.'

He looked startled. 'I suppose you have to tell him what happened?'

'Yes, I do.'

'I'm sorry, Sarge,' he said again. 'I don't know what came over me.'

'Gavin has said he's not interested in lodging a complaint. He said you were defending yourself. So, let's see what Churchill has to say, okay?' She put a hand on his shoulder. 'Hang in there. When we're finished with Gavin, I'll give you a lift back to my place, all right?'

He nodded. 'All right.'

As expected, Churchill was furious. Karen sat on the other side of Churchill's large desk, fumbling for the right words. There weren't any. Rick had reacted due to the stress he was under, and it was Karen's fault. He should not have been dealing with the public.

'Why was he working?' Churchill demanded. 'You said he was on compassionate leave.'

'Yes, he was, but he wanted to keep busy,' Karen said.

'Then he should have been behind a desk doing paperwork,' Churchill snapped.

Karen knew he was right. There was nothing she could say.

'So, what's the likelihood of this man pressing charges?'

'I don't think he will. But there's something else you should be aware of. Phoebe's neighbour, Trisha, was recording the incident.'

'Oh, great,' Churchill said, covering his face with his hands. 'Exactly what we don't need. Can you imagine the optics? This is going to look terrible, Karen.'

'She deleted the video, but I thought you should be aware.'

Churchill met her gaze. His eyes narrowed. 'Did you ask her to delete it?'

'No! Of course not.'

'That's something, I suppose.'

'Do you want to speak to Rick?'

Churchill shook his head. 'No, not now. I despair of you both. I'm seriously disappointed.'

He went on for another few minutes, making sure Karen was aware just how disappointed he was. She didn't try to put forward any excuses. This time she deserved the lecture.

'Send him home, pending an investigation,' Churchill said.

Karen nodded. She'd expected as much. 'He's downstairs now. I'm going to take him back to my place.'

'Why your place?' Churchill asked.

'He's having trouble sleeping at home after what happened.'

'I see,' Churchill said with a nod. 'Let's hope the fact Gavin Griffin hasn't lodged a complaint means we don't have to take this much further, but it's still going on his record, Karen.'

'I understand, sir,' Karen said. She might not like it, but she understood.

After she left Churchill's office, Karen called Tim Farthing. She knew Tim wouldn't appreciate it but chasing for results worked. It didn't hurt to underline how important the lab's findings could be to the investigation.

'Tim,' Karen said, forcing her voice to sound bright and cheerful when he answered. 'Sorry to bother you. I know you're incredibly busy, but I hoped you'd have good news for me regarding the evidence from Todd Bartholomew's house.'

She paused on the stairs and bit her lip. *Please let him say they've found something belonging to Phoebe at the scene.*

That would be the evidence they needed to turn the focus back on Todd Bartholomew.

She heard Tim sigh. 'I work miracles, Karen, but I can't just magic up evidence. It takes time.'

'I know,' Karen said. 'But we need something to tie Phoebe to Todd. The CCTV isn't enough, because we know they went their separate ways on Friday night. So, I *need* something from the scene, Tim.'

He sighed again. 'Everybody does. Everybody's chasing me.'

'Well, that's because you're the man to come to when you need a result,' Karen said, through gritted teeth. She needed to butter him up, but it was grating to pile on the flattery when he could be so prickly and difficult.

'Well, the DNA swabs won't be back for a week,' Tim said.

'A week! You can't be serious? We can't wait that long.'

'Fast-track it then,' Tim said.

'We can't. The budget is tight as it is. I doubt Simpson will—'

'That's not my problem, Karen,' Tim said and hung up, leaving Karen staring furiously at her phone.

◆ ◆ ◆

Morgan took over the Gavin Griffin interview so Karen could take Rick home. After she'd dropped him off, she headed back into Lincoln and parked in Lucy Tower Street.

She hurried along the Brayford Wharf, crossed the bridge, and headed to the tall glass building of CaP Diagnostics.

This time, instead of Cary coming down to greet her, it was Lou. She hurried towards Karen.

'You've not said anything, have you?' she asked in a hushed whisper.

Karen shook her head. 'No, I've just come to speak to you and Cary again.'

'Oh, right. Okay. Um, I don't really want to talk with Cary in earshot. Come with me,' Lou said and ushered Karen to the lift. She pressed the button for the penthouse, but when they got out, instead of heading to the offices she walked along the corridor to the maintenance staircase and led Karen up to the roof.

'Does everyone come up here?' Karen asked, stepping out into the sunshine.

'Most of the people who work in the building. It's nice to get some fresh air,' Lou said. 'It's a great view, and on a day like today, it seems a shame to be inside. Anyway, what is it you wanted to ask? Remember you promised not to tell Cary what I told you. It would make my life impossible, and I'd probably lose my job.'

'I didn't promise. I said I'd do my best.'

'But—'

Karen lifted a hand. 'I haven't told him anything. I've got a question to ask you about a man called Gavin Griffin. Do you know him?'

'Gavin. Oh, yeah,' Lou said, pulling a face.

'Tell me about him,' Karen said.

'Well, there's not much to say. He's a bit of a geek,' Lou said. 'I only know him through Cary and Phoebe. He did a master's with them, I think. The same course. Anyway, he got a bee in his bonnet last year. He claimed he'd invented the scanner, which was ridiculous. Absolute rubbish.'

'Are you sure?'

'Yes, one hundred per cent,' Lou said. 'He got chucked out of university for trying similar scams on two different start-up companies. He's not even that bright. He passed his degree, but there were rumours he paid for someone else to do his coursework. Trust me. He's a serial liar.'

'I see.' Karen's instincts had told her as much, but it was good to have it confirmed. She would need to investigate these previous cases. Lou gave her the names and details.

Karen leaned against the guard rail, putting up a hand to shield her eyes from the sun. 'We arrested Gavin outside Phoebe's place. He'd been sitting outside, watching her apartment.'

Lou pulled a disgusted face. 'That's *creepy*,' she said. 'What a weirdo. He used to come here loads, but then we got security and he wasn't allowed in the building anymore. I imagine he took to sitting outside Phoebe's place after that. He doesn't give up easily, I'll give him that.'

'Do you think Gavin could be violent?'

Lou thought for a minute, then said, 'No, I don't think so. There was a bit of a scuffle with security once as they dragged him out, but I don't think he ever instigated violence. There were no physical threats.'

'Do you believe he could have hurt Phoebe?'

Lou's expression grew serious. 'I don't honestly know,' she said. 'I wouldn't have thought so, although you never *really* know, do you?'

No, thought Karen, *you don't*.

After a moment's silence, Lou asked, 'What do you think has happened to her?'

Karen didn't have an answer.

All she knew was that Phoebe was still missing, every suspect was a dead end, and as the days passed, the chances of finding Phoebe alive grew slimmer and slimmer.

CHAPTER
TWENTY-SEVEN

Karen and Lou went down to the penthouse level so Karen could speak to Cary. Lou rapped on his office door and then made herself scarce.

Karen entered Cary's glass office, which gave Karen the unnerving impression of being inside a goldfish bowl.

Cary angled his screen so she couldn't see what was on it. Then he looked up and gestured for her to sit down. He looked tired.

'Any news on Phoebe?' he asked.

'We haven't found her yet.'

His face fell. 'That's not good news.'

'What can you tell me about Gavin Griffin?'

Cary snorted out a laugh. 'Oh, that waste of space has been a thorn in our side since we started CaP Diagnostics.'

'In what way?' Karen asked.

'He claims our scanner was his idea. Which it wasn't,' Cary said. 'He wants us to pay him off. Give him money to shut him up.' His expression hardened. 'But we're not falling for it. Phoebe and I are both in agreement on that front. We tried to humour him, but it soon became clear he's deluded. Ask him a few basic engineering questions and he looks like a rabbit caught in headlights. He's not got a clue. He's a complete phony.' Cary folded his arms. 'We've employed security now. He doesn't get in the building.'

'I never noticed the security,' Karen said.

'You wouldn't. They're discreet.'

'Does your security have anything to do with Quentin Chapman?'

Karen watched his response closely.

He gave a thin-lipped smile. 'He put us in touch with a team we could rely on.'

'Did Phoebe ever feel uncomfortable around Gavin Griffin?'

'Uncomfortable? I don't think so. I'd say angry. Annoyed, at first, and then more recently she used to laugh at him. I think once we'd worked out that he was trying to play us, we didn't give him attention. Phoebe said it was best to treat him like the joke he is.'

Had that made him angry? Had Phoebe and Cary not taking him seriously caused Gavin to lash out? Karen had seen the anger he was capable of when Rick took him down. He knew they were police, and yet he'd still lashed out. That wasn't the action of a passive man, even if he had been taken by surprise. They'd announced they were police. He could have come quietly.

After asking a few more questions about Gavin Griffin, Karen asked, 'You seem stressed, Cary. Are you worried about the sale?'

He sighed, running a hand over his face. 'I'm worried about everything,' he said. 'The stress of getting ready for the sale. The fact that nobody's seen Phoebe for days.'

'When's the sale meant to complete?' Karen asked.

'Next week,' Cary said. 'We've not finalised the date yet.'

'Will it fall through without Phoebe?' Karen asked.

'That's not going to happen,' Cary said with a firm shake of his head. 'I think she'll probably waltz in at the last minute. She's always had a sense of the dramatic.'

Karen studied him carefully. Did he really believe that? That Phoebe was biding her time, getting ready to make a big entrance?

No, she thought, noting the circles under his eyes and the tense way he held his shoulders. He didn't believe that. He was worried. Very worried.

◆ ◆ ◆

Back at the station, Sophie approached Karen's desk with good news.

'Harinder's cracked it,' she said proudly.

'The emails?'

Sophie nodded. 'Yes, I told you he'd do it.'

They headed down to the tech lab, where Harinder was sitting in front of multiple computer screens.

He smiled widely as they walked in. 'I thought you'd want to be the first to see these.'

'I'm hoping they give us a way forward,' Karen said. 'We really need all the help we can get. What can you tell me?'

'Well, I've only just managed to get into the files, but I can tell you there are a *lot* of emails, and her account was last accessed on Friday.'

Karen digested the information. That meant Phoebe either hadn't had the desire or hadn't had the opportunity to look at her emails.

'There is a lot of information to go through,' Harinder said. 'Absolutely tons.'

'Okay, we'll need to divide the emails and work our way through, looking at the most recent first,' Karen said. 'Let's see if there are any emails from Gavin Griffin.'

'Do you think he's responsible, Sarge?' Sophie asked.

'I don't know,' Karen said. 'He's been trying to bully Phoebe into giving him money, and money can bring out the worst in people, so let's not rule him out. Also look for anything about Quentin Chapman. Any reference to him at all.' She turned to Sophie. 'That reminds me. Have we got the warrant to search CaP Diagnostics yet?'

Sophie grimaced and shook her head. 'It was denied.'

'What?'

'We couldn't get it signed off.'

'That doesn't make sense,' Karen muttered, 'unless . . . Was it Chapman's influence?'

I wouldn't put it past him, she thought. Maybe he'd applied some political pressure.

'What did Simpson say?' Karen asked.

'Not much,' Sophie said. 'He just looked confused.'

'Let's get some of Simpson's team to look through the emails as well, if he can spare anyone.'

'I'll organise that,' Sophie said.

'Right. I'll divvy them up now,' Harinder said. 'And make copies.'

'Great,' Karen said with a smile. 'Now, what about Phoebe Woodrow's phone?'

'Yep, I got into that,' Harinder said. 'Made a copy.' He opened a file on his computer. 'But she'd deleted her messages.'

'Maybe Phoebe didn't delete them,' Sophie said. 'Someone else could have done it. Someone who wanted to remove incriminating messages.'

'That's a very good point,' Karen said.

They spent hours on the emails, gradually putting things together. Many contained technical details about the scanner that completely went over Karen's head. There were long email chains between Phoebe and Cary relating to problems and troubleshooting.

There was little of interest from Quentin Chapman. A few updates here and there. Most of Chapman's responses to the updates were single-word replies: *thanks*.

Karen pushed away from her desk. She still hadn't spoken to Mike. He hadn't replied to her text messages, and Karen couldn't stop thinking about Chapman's thugs watching him.

She was going to have to confront Chapman. She'd warned him off once, but he hadn't taken her seriously. Maybe it was time to turn the tables.

◆ ◆ ◆

Karen pulled onto the long gravel driveway leading to Chapman's house: a large property on the outskirts of Burton Waters.

There was a huge fountain in front of the house. It wasn't a tasteful, delicate water feature but a full-on fountain – at least twelve feet wide, with statues in the centre, water cascading over their outstretched arms. Karen shook her head at the sight of it. Who had a *fountain* in their driveway? It must have cost a fortune.

It was seven thirty, still light and still warm. There were lots of cars parked near the house – including two Ferraris, a Bentley and even a McLaren F1. Karen didn't know a huge amount about cars, but she knew that was rare. Rare and expensive.

Surely they couldn't all belong to Chapman.

When she got out of the car, she heard music coming from the house. He was having a party.

Karen smiled, imagining Quentin Chapman's reaction at her gate-crashing his function, embarrassing him in front of his guests.

It would be good to make a note of some of his guests, too, Karen thought. Helpful to know who his associates were.

Chapman would hate her turning up unannounced like this, which was Karen's plan. He thought there was nothing wrong with ordering his men to invade her privacy, follow her and lurk outside her partner's flat. Now she'd get to see how he reacted when the shoe was on the other foot.

She checked her phone again, but Mike still hadn't replied. She started to walk towards the front door and then stopped when her phone rang. It was Erica.

'Erica, sorry I haven't been in touch. I—'

'Not at all,' Erica said quickly. 'It's me who should be apologizing to you. You're very busy. You don't have time to chase after an old friend of mine.'

'I meant to update you, but things have been hectic. We've not located Phoebe, but we're still looking for her,' Karen said. 'I'll let you know when I have more information.'

'You don't need to. Like I said on Monday, Phoebe often goes away without telling anyone. I'm sure she's fine. I overreacted. Please, don't worry about it.'

Karen frowned. That was a sudden turnaround. Erica had been very concerned about Phoebe on Monday when she'd told Karen that Phoebe was missing.

'It's gone beyond me now,' Karen said. 'It's an official investigation.'

'Is it?' Erica's voice sounded strained. 'I didn't realise it had gone that far.'

'I'll let you know as soon as I've got news.'

'Okay.'

'I'm sorry, Erica, I've got to go. I'm just about to go into someone's house.'

'No problem. Sorry to bother you,' Erica said quickly and then hung up.

Well, that was odd, Karen thought. Maybe she should pop in and see Erica tomorrow, make sure she was okay.

The music grew louder as Karen walked towards the house. A party was definitely underway.

Two bay trees stood in stone pots each side of the large grey front door. Now she was closer, Karen could see it was a new-build designed to look older than it really was, with Georgian-style sash windows, white pillars and a portico around the front door.

It was huge, at least three times as big as Karen's own house. The front flowerbeds were impeccably tended, but Karen guessed Quentin probably didn't do the job himself. She couldn't quite picture him in gardening gloves, holding secateurs.

Karen heard peals of laughter coming from inside and lifted her hand to knock.

CHAPTER
TWENTY-EIGHT

Karen had been expecting the door to be opened by one of Quentin Chapman's henchmen. But instead she was greeted by a young woman wearing what looked to be a black and white server's uniform.

'Can I help you?'

'I'm here to see Quentin Chapman.' Karen walked past the woman and entered a vast hallway that was as big as the entire downstairs of Karen's house. The floor was covered with light marble, and a sweeping staircase led upstairs. A huge crystal chandelier hung from the ceiling.

'Were you invited to the party?' the woman asked, looking over her shoulder nervously.

Karen was disappointed. She couldn't see Chapman's goons anywhere. After looking them up, she now had their names and addresses, but still thought of them as Ponytail and Skinhead. Ponytail had previously been arrested on an assault charge, though sadly the charge hadn't stuck.

'My invitation,' Karen said, holding up her warrant card.

The woman's mouth formed a small soundless o, and the general chatter around them died down as people turned to see what was causing the disturbance.

'Is Quentin home?' Karen walked further into the hall, and the woman didn't try to stop her. 'Where is he?' Karen asked, raising her voice above the sound of the music.

It was some party. He'd hired caterers. There were several people in white and black uniforms, holding trays of drinks.

One of them offered her a flute of champagne as she approached. 'No thanks. I'm still on duty,' she said, drawing concerned looks from some of the guests.

'He's in the kitchen. I'll take you to him,' the woman said, rushing ahead of Karen.

She followed the woman into the kitchen, where Chapman was holding court, surrounded by his adoring associates. He looked in his element as he laughed with them. Dressed in a well-cut suit, his grey hair neatly styled, he looked like a perfectly respectable rich grandad.

The granite islands were covered with trays of food – pastries, olives, various types of cured meats and cheeses. Huge bifold doors that ran the length of the kitchen had been opened, and other guests gathered outside on the patio, mingling among the fairy lights.

It took him a few seconds to notice Karen's presence. Finally, Quentin sensed the weight of her stare and turned around.

His eyes narrowed almost imperceptibly, and he graciously excused himself from his guests. 'So sorry. I'll be back with you shortly,' he said, bowing out.

'Hello, Quentin,' Karen said. 'I'm perfectly happy to talk here if you are.'

He gave her a tight smile. 'Let's go to my office.' He led the way through the kitchen and into a smaller room with two tan-leather chesterfield sofas, dark wood panelling, and a large desk with a plush leather chair behind it. The polished wood floor was covered with a huge Persian rug. The only light was from a small lamp on the desk.

He didn't sit down, and instead opened a wooden box on the desk and pulled out a cigar. 'Do you smoke?'

Karen shook her head.

'Good. It's a terrible habit,' he said, and lit up. 'So, DS Hart. What an unexpected pleasure. Is there a reason you've dropped in unannounced? I'm sure you wouldn't usually be so rude.'

Rude. He was one to talk. 'Oh, I didn't think you'd mind,' Karen said. 'After all, you know where I live *and* where my partner lives. You feel comfortable enough to have your *staff* follow me around Lincoln.'

His smile grew slowly, and then he chuckled and raised the cigar to his lips.

There were pictures on his desk. Karen pointed to one in an ornate silver frame. 'Is that your wife?'

He nodded. 'Yes. My second wife.' He reached over and straightened the photograph.

'Kids?' Karen asked.

His expression hardened, then he shook his head. 'No. You?'

Karen shook her head, and then felt a bite of betrayal. She could leave it there, skim over it, but she was done hiding. She wasn't going to let Quentin use her history to pressure her in any way.

'I had a daughter,' she said. 'But I lost her when she was five.'

His face fell. 'I'm sorry,' he said. 'No one should have to suffer the loss of a child.'

His face was reflected in the dark glass of the window. He looked genuinely sympathetic, which Karen hadn't expected.

He moved to a small drinks cabinet beside the desk. 'Would you like one?' he asked, lifting a cut-crystal decanter. 'It's port.'

'No, thank you.'

'It's two hundred pounds a bottle. Are you sure you can't be tempted?'

Karen shook her head. 'No, thanks. Not when I'm on duty.'

'Take a seat, Detective,' he said, waving a hand at the nearest sofa. 'You're making me nervous standing there like that.'

'I wonder why?' she muttered as she sunk down into the chesterfield. It was surprisingly comfortable.

'Are you going to tell me why you're visiting me at home? Do you have some news on our mutual friend?'

Karen tilted her head to one side, studying him as he poured himself a glass of port.

She was going to ask the questions, not him. 'Where were you last Friday and Saturday night?'

'So direct and to the point,' he said, smiling as he took a sip from his glass and closed his eyes as though relishing the taste.

'There's no point in being otherwise.'

'I was at home,' Quentin said.

'Alone?'

He shrugged. 'I'm sure I could provide an alibi if needed.'

He was taunting her, but she'd expected nothing less.

'What happens to your deal if Phoebe doesn't come back?' Karen asked.

His face hardened again. He lifted his glass and took another sip. 'I hope it won't come to that, and surely with you on the case, she'll be found quickly.'

'Are you pressuring Phoebe into the sale?' Karen asked.

'Of course not. You do think badly of me, Detective.'

'I'd like something from you, Mr Chapman.'

'Please, call me Quentin,' he said.

'I'd like you to keep your thugs away from me and my family.'

She kept her voice steady, determined not to betray any nerves. She didn't want to show any signs of vulnerability.

He said nothing, but selected a leather-bound book from the shelves behind his desk. He turned it over in his hands before lifting it up to show Karen the cover. 'Marcus Aurelius, Roman emperor. He said, *You have power over your mind, not outside events. Realise this and you will find your strength.*'

What was he implying?

'I don't need self-help advice from you or a long-dead Roman emperor, thanks all the same,' Karen said. 'I just need your men to stop following me.'

'My apologies. Of course, you're right,' he said, putting the book on his desk. 'I thought the quote would resonate with you.'

'Why?'

'You suffer from the torments of the mind.'

'I have no idea what you're talking about.'

'You think you hide it well, but you're transparent.'

Karen looked around the room as though the conversation bored her. He was playing mind games. He'd had her followed, so likely already knew about Josh and Tilly. He probably knew she attended counselling, too, so it didn't take a genius to guess Karen had struggles with her mental health. It was nothing to do with her being transparent and everything to do with Chapman using the information he'd gathered against her.

'I'm interested in you,' he said when Karen didn't rise to his bait.

'Why?'

'Because you are interested in *me*.'

'You're worried I'll find something, aren't you? What do you have to hide? If you're an innocent man, you shouldn't have anything to worry about.'

He ducked his head and smirked. 'You really are braver than you look. Out here alone with me and my associates.' He looked her up and down. 'Yes, brave, or perhaps a little out of your depth.'

Karen tensed. 'Everyone knows I'm here. If anything were to happen to me, the weight of the Lincolnshire constabulary would be on your back.'

He lifted his eyebrows. 'You really do think badly of me.'

He was mocking her. She'd had enough of him leading the conversation. 'Can you tell me why the warrant to search CaP Diagnostics has been blocked?'

Chapman shrugged. 'I have no idea. I don't know the ins and outs of police procedure. I also don't know why you would want to search the company. What do you hope to find?'

Karen didn't answer his question. 'You'll find your life is much easier if you cooperate, Mr Chapman.'

'Of course, because right is on your side. Is that not so?' he asked.

She nodded. 'Yes, it is.'

'So then how could I have any influence on your warrant?'

'I don't know yet, but I'll find out.'

He no longer looked amused. He picked up the photograph of his wife again and studied it for a long moment in silence, then put it back in the same position.

'You have drive and tenacity. I've humoured you so far, Detective, but don't push me.' He pressed a button under his desk, and a second later the door opened and a tall slim man with a narrow, pinched face appeared.

'DS Hart is just leaving,' Chapman said. 'See her out.'

The man nodded and jerked his thumb at Karen.

She got to her feet and let herself be escorted outside. Now she was more certain than ever that Chapman was crooked, but she still had no idea if he was behind Phoebe's disappearance.

She called Morgan to let him know how her chat with Chapman had gone. He wasn't best pleased she'd gone alone. *Reckless* and *foolhardy* were some of the words he peppered their conversation with.

'Why didn't you tell me you were going? I could have come with you,' he said.

She wanted to explain that it was personal. That the visit was about proving to herself that, even though she was scared of Chapman, she could still do her job. But she couldn't find the words.

'I just wanted to unnerve him a bit,' Karen replied. 'He's far too confident.'

'Do you think he's got anything to do with Phoebe's disappearance?'

'That I don't know, but he's definitely a nasty character, someone we should keep our eye on.'

'The force has been keeping their eye on him for a while. Sadly, nothing's been pinned on him.' He sighed. 'Get an early night. We'll come at it fresh in the morning.'

After Karen hung up, she sat in the car, watching Chapman's house. She didn't want to go back to Mike's apartment. He was away with Sandy on the training course, and he still hadn't returned her calls.

He was hurt and angry, which was understandable, but he'd crossed a line. Somehow, they were going to have to tackle it and talk it through if their relationship was worth saving.

She sent Rick a text to see if he wanted to share a pizza. He replied with a yes and three exclamation marks. She told him she'd be there in about an hour.

First, she wanted to call in on Erica. She'd been through a tough time and her concern for Phoebe had been vindicated, despite being unhelpfully dismissed as hysterical by the officer she'd first reported her concerns to.

Erica buzzed Karen into the block, but it took her a while to open the apartment door.

'Is everything okay?' she asked.

'Yes. I'm sorry it's late,' Karen said. 'I just wanted to check in. I feel like I've been neglecting you.'

'It's fine. I've just been watching TV.' She glanced over her shoulder.

'Are you okay?' Karen asked, wondering if Erica's anxiety was returning. It could be a tumultuous journey. Anxiety didn't have an off switch. 'I thought you might need to talk. You sounded a bit off on the phone.'

'Oh, I'm sorry,' Erica said. 'Come in. I'm fine, really. Just had a busy week at work. Is there any news?' she asked.

'Not much, unfortunately,' Karen said as she followed Erica inside. 'But I am concerned.'

After they both sat down, Tommy strolled into the living area, barely giving Karen a glance, and jumped on to Erica's lap.

'He seems to have settled in well,' Karen commented.

Erica smiled as she stroked the cat. 'Yes, I'm growing quite fond of him.'

'I don't know how familiar you are with Phoebe's business, but she's involved with an investor called Quentin Chapman, and I'm not sure he's above board.'

'That doesn't sound good,' Erica said.

'Did she ever mention him?'

Erica shook her head. 'No, I've never heard his name before.'

'We know that Phoebe was okay on Saturday morning. She was at her cousin's house. He let her borrow his car. Her grandmother said she visited on Saturday, but then she disappeared. We found the car abandoned near the wharf.' Karen lifted her hands. 'We've drawn a blank after that.'

'Perhaps she went away for a couple of days?'

'She hasn't used her bank cards. She didn't take her phone. We're not sure she had any transport because she abandoned the car, and she hasn't been captured by CCTV at the train or bus stations.'

'Very strange,' Erica said.

Karen had decided not to mention Todd, or the druggings at Imporium. They had no proof that Todd Bartholomew had harmed Phoebe – despite his connection to the recent assaults – and it would only worry Erica if she said anything.

'I think she'll probably turn up,' Erica said as Tommy purred in her lap. 'Anyway, tell me how you've been getting on.'

Karen was surprised at the quick change in topic. 'Oh, not too bad. Busy at work.'

'And how are things with you and Mike?'

'Not great,' Karen admitted. 'We had a bit of a bust-up and I've not heard from him today.' She sighed. 'I got a call-out for work, and he followed me. I'd asked him not to, and he did anyway. He didn't listen.'

'Why not?'

Karen smiled. She knew what Erica was doing. It was a technique they used in their counselling sessions. A way to use simple questions to push people to see the problem in a different way. Here Erica was trying to get her to see things from Mike's point of view.

'He came because he was worried about me,' Karen said.

'And that caused the argument? It was because he was concerned?'

'No, we argued because I'd asked him not to come, and he ignored me. There's a chance my job will put him at risk. And when he turned up like that . . . to a potential *crime scene*, it reminded me again of how much I stand to lose if something were to happen to him.'

'Have you come to any conclusions about what to do next?'

Karen shook her head.

'You were considering stepping down from your role in the police service, or doing something else?'

'I was,' Karen said, 'but I'm not sure.'

How could she give up her job? She couldn't even consider that now. She needed to find Phoebe.

But there would always be another Phoebe, another case, another person needing justice. Was she supposed to sacrifice her own happiness for her job? Why couldn't she have both?

'Maybe you can have both,' Erica said, seeming to read Karen's mind. 'But you need to talk to Mike about it.'

'I know,' Karen said, before yawning and stretching. 'Sorry.'

'Have you eaten?' Erica asked.

Karen checked the time. 'I haven't, but I promised a friend I'd pick up pizza, so I'd better make a move. I just wanted to check in on you and make sure you're all right. But it seems like you've played the agony-aunt role for me instead.'

Erica smiled. 'I'm always happy to do that for you, Karen. That's what friends are for.'

CHAPTER
TWENTY-NINE

Karen let herself in holding two pizza boxes.

'Hey, Rick. Dinner is served,' she called out.

He appeared at the top of the stairs, smothering a yawn.

'Did you manage to get any sleep?' Karen asked as he came down the stairs.

'A little.' He took the boxes from her as she slipped off her shoes.

'How are you feeling?'

'Not too bad,' he said. 'I just can't believe in the space of a couple of days my life has completely turned upside down.'

He carried the pizza into the kitchen, and Karen followed.

'It's my fault. You should never have been out there.'

'It's not your fault,' Rick said. 'I wanted to work.'

'And I should have said no,' Karen said, grabbing a couple of drinks from the fridge. She handed one to Rick. 'Have you heard from your sister?'

'Yes, she's coming back tomorrow.'

They sat down at the table to eat the pizzas.

They ate in silence for a while.

Finally, Karen said, 'You know that you're going to have to be off work while all this gets sorted.'

Rick nodded but didn't say anything.

'The fact that Gavin Griffin hasn't put in a complaint is a good sign, though. Best-case scenario, you'll be back in a few weeks. You'll have it on your record, though. There's no way around that.'

'I understand,' Rick said, polishing off a second slice of pepperoni.

'Well, it's good to see you haven't lost your appetite,' Karen teased, as he reached for another helping.

He smiled. 'I didn't realise how hungry I was. I appreciate this, Sarge. I'll be out of your hair soon. Promise.'

'You're fine,' she said. 'Mike's away tonight, so I thought I'd stay here if that's all right with you.'

'Of course it is. It's your house,' Rick said.

'Yes, but you might not want company.'

'I don't know what I want at the moment,' he said, shaking his head. 'My mind is all over the place.'

Karen's phone rang. She reached for it hoping to see Mike's name flashing on the screen, but it was Morgan.

'Karen, can you get to Lincoln?'

'Sure,' she said. 'What's happened?'

'It's Cary Swann. He's dead.'

The pizza suddenly felt heavy and greasy in Karen's stomach. 'I'm on my way.'

◆ ◆ ◆

A light drizzle was falling when she arrived at the scene. For the first time in days, she felt cold.

The road had been cordoned off and police vehicles lined the kerb. A white tent had been set up at the base of the tall glass building, presumably to protect Cary's body from the elements and interested members of the public.

Karen stared up at the glass office block, which seemed even taller than she remembered.

Cary had taken her up to the roof. They'd stood side by side. He'd said he liked it up there. It had made him feel *free*. Had she missed something in their conversation? Had he been implying he otherwise felt trapped? But by who? Quentin Chapman? There hadn't been anything in his behaviour indicating he was suicidal.

Still staring upwards, she wondered, would he have jumped? When she'd seen him earlier, he'd appeared stressed, under a lot of pressure, but she hadn't suspected he'd do this.

She turned her focus back to street level and spotted Morgan near the white tent.

He saw her at the same time and raised a hand.

His hair was wet from the rain. When she got closer, she saw his jaw was tight, fists clenched.

She said, 'It's a bad one?'

'Yes, a real mess.' He took a deep breath. 'The crime scene officers are already on the roof.' He nodded towards the white tent. 'And Raj is in there with him now.'

'It was lucky he didn't hit any pedestrians.'

Morgan nodded. The wharf wasn't as busy as in the city centre with the pubs and bars, but there were usually some people milling around at this time. A few onlookers had gathered by the cordons, craning their necks, trying to see what was going on.

'You really think he jumped?' Karen asked.

'It looks that way,' Morgan said. 'Although we'll have to wait for Raj's verdict, and for the crime scene to be processed. Apparently, the railings around the edge of the roof are pretty low.'

'They're about waist-height,' Karen said. 'On you, anyway. On me they're a bit higher.'

'So, on Cary they would have been at waist level too?'

She nodded. 'Not difficult to bypass if he was determined to jump.'

Morgan rubbed his chin thoughtfully.

'So, what's our working theory?' Karen asked. 'Quentin Chapman was forcing him to go along with this deal and it all got too much? Or do you think he was behind Phoebe's disappearance? Maybe he thought he was about to get caught?'

'If that's the case, let's hope there's a suicide note, because that will make our job a lot easier.'

'Cary told me he liked going up to the roof at night when he was working late. He liked the view. He'd go up there to smoke.'

'I doubt that was permitted.'

'No,' Karen said. 'But it wasn't unusual for him to be on the roof. When I was up there, he sat on the guard rail. It didn't look safe.'

Morgan grimaced. 'You think he could have slipped?'

'I suppose it's possible.'

'Is the roof easy to get to?' Morgan asked.

'Yes, there's maintenance access from the penthouse office.'

Karen saw Tim Farthing scurrying towards the SOCO van carrying evidence bags.

'I'm going to talk to him,' she said, and darted across the street to meet him at the van.

'Tim?'

'Oh,' he said, not sounding in the least bit glad to see her. 'This is one of your cases, is it?'

She nodded. 'Yes. The victim worked with Phoebe Woodrow. What do you think happened?'

'I'm not the detective,' Tim said. 'That's your job.'

'I know, but I'm asking for your take. I value your opinion, Tim.'

He narrowed his eyes, studying her. 'Sometimes I can't work out if you're teasing me or not.'

Karen gave him a look that she hoped conveyed *would I do that?*

He shrugged. 'There were scuff marks on the edge of the roof where we think he went over. And a packet of cigarettes nearby. Maybe he'd gone out for a smoke.'

'Do the scuff marks indicate signs of a struggle?'

'Far too early to say,' Tim said. 'You're thinking murder rather than suicide then?'

'I don't know,' Karen said. 'I just want to understand what happened.'

'Don't we all,' Tim said. 'Anyway, if you don't mind, I do have a lot to be getting on with.' He brushed past her, and Karen turned to walk back to Morgan, who was now speaking with Raj.

She smiled at the pathologist. 'Good to see you, Raj.'

It sounded odd to say that since they always met under such tragic circumstances.

'Hello, Karen,' he said, and continued with his explanation to Morgan. 'When he reached the ground, he hit the back of his head first. So it's possible he went over backwards. Death would have been instantaneous.'

'Were there any defensive wounds? Injuries perhaps not caused by the fall?' Morgan asked.

'None that I could see, but the body is in a bad way. I've got no definite answer for you yet. I'll know more after the PM. I'll check his hands before we move him.'

Morgan nodded. 'Thanks, Raj.'

Karen looked up at the roof again and ran a hand through her wet hair. Was it suicide or murder? Did Cary know what had happened to Phoebe? Had guilt caused him to jump?

Or had he been too deeply involved with Chapman? Perhaps Chapman had decided to dispose of Phoebe *and* Cary to get rid of any witnesses to his crimes.

But she had no proof Quentin had done anything wrong.

A thought struck her. Earlier, when she'd gone to Chapman's house, there had been no sign of his henchmen. Was that because they'd been performing another job for Chapman tonight? Had they been getting rid of Cary?

Karen had an idea. She pulled out her phone and scrolled through her notes. Ponytail lived in St Giles, but Skinhead lived just around the corner. It would take only minutes to walk there.

'I'm going to see Henry Mortimer,' Karen said, using Skinhead's real name. 'He lives close by. He's one of Quentin Chapman's thugs. Maybe he paid Cary a visit this evening.'

Morgan nodded. 'Good idea. Do you want me to come?'

'No, you stay here. I'll get a uniform to accompany me.'

He knew as well as Karen did that getting to a perpetrator quickly, soon after they'd committed a crime, meant a better chance of catching them out. The earlier the better. Getting to them while the adrenaline was still coursing through their system and clouding their mind was ideal.

She put her hands in her pockets, hunched her shoulders against the rain and walked to Victoria Street with PC Jim Willson. They stopped at number eighty-four and pressed the doorbell.

The door was opened by a red-haired woman. She gave Karen a puzzled smile. 'Can I help you?'

Karen showed her warrant card and introduced herself.

The woman's face hardened. 'You'd better come in.'

Karen turned to PC Willson. 'Jim, can you wait out here? I'll just be a few minutes.'

He nodded and stepped back under the shelter of the porch.

The woman led Karen into the kitchen. 'Morty,' she called. 'It's the police, for you.'

There was a small hatch in the kitchen wall that looked through into the living/dining area. Karen saw Henry Mortimer on his hands and knees, playing with a toddler beside the table. He got up with a groan, heaving his big frame from the floor.

He didn't look happy to see Karen. His usually stony, blank expression held more emotion than usual.

'What are you doing here?' he hissed.

He didn't like her intruding on his private life. He wasn't keen on his work bringing trouble home to his wife and child.

'Not much fun, is it, *Morty*?' Karen asked. 'It's not nice when people invade your personal space uninvited.'

'What are you doing here?' he asked again. 'In my kitchen. In my home. It's not right.'

'Oh, I see. You want a private life. You don't like being followed?'

He scowled heavily. 'This isn't funny. It's not a joke.'

'I'm not laughing, Morty,' she said. 'Where have you been this evening?'

'I've been here,' he said.

'Really? All night?'

'Since six o'clock when I got home,' he said. 'My wife, she can verify.'

His wife nodded. 'It's true. He came home at six. We had dinner, and he bathed our son, and they've been playing since then. He's not been out.'

If she was telling the truth, and he'd been home for the past three hours, then he wasn't involved in Cary's fall from the roof.

She left Henry Mortimer, saying she'd be in touch, which he viewed more as a threat than a promise. He stood on the doorstep scowling after her as she and PC Willson walked away.

When she returned to the crime scene, Morgan waved her over. 'They've found something very interesting. Tim is busting a gut. He's desperate to tell you himself.'

'Why?'

'He wants to impress you,' Morgan said.

'I doubt that,' Karen said. 'He can't stand me. It's probably because he wants to prove how amazing he is.'

Morgan raised his voice. 'Tim!'

Tim strode over in his white coverall. 'Ah, DS Hart. About time. Where did you disappear to?'

'I had to see someone—'

But Tim wasn't interested in her answer. 'We've found something. When we were getting ready to move the body, we noticed his fists were closed.' Tim mimed the action of a clenched fist. 'And wrapped around the fingers of his right hand was a strand of long, dark hair.' He held up an evidence bag to show Karen. 'So maybe he grabbed an assailant's hair before he went over the railing.'

'So, there *was* a struggle,' Karen said, 'with someone with long, dark hair.'

'Exactly,' Tim said with a broad smile. 'Thought you'd like to hear that. And yes, before you ask, we'll get it processed and run DNA.'

'Excellent job,' Karen said.

'I know.' He turned on his heel and headed back to the crime scene van.

Modest as ever, Karen thought.

Tim turned and looked over his shoulder. 'I hope this gets a mention in your report. I do feel we get overlooked at times. Everyone wants results from crime scene officers, but we don't often get the glory. All the praise goes to the detectives.'

But Karen wasn't listening to Tim's grumbles. She was thinking of a suspect who'd just jumped to the top of her list. Chapman's dark-haired, ponytailed henchman, Jamie Goode.

CHAPTER THIRTY

After a long night at the crime scene, Karen only managed to snatch a couple of hours' sleep before she returned to the station. They had some good news. Todd Bartholomew had been charged with multiple counts of sexual assault. The case against him was strong. With any luck, he'd be sent away for years.

Sadly, things weren't going quite so well in other areas.

The black hair found wrapped around Cary's fingers was a vital clue that could prove that Jamie Goode had interacted with Cary last night before he died. Karen thought it was good evidence they'd had an altercation. One that had ended in Cary's death.

The crime scene evidence could reveal more, but analysis would take time. What she needed now was solid CCTV footage that put Jamie Goode at the scene, or at least in the vicinity.

There were cameras at the front of the building and three others along the street.

It should have been easy.

It wasn't.

She ran her hands through her hair in frustration.

'Not having much luck?' Arnie asked, strolling by Karen's desk.

'That's an understatement,' Karen said. 'I don't understand it.'

'What don't you understand?' He pulled up a chair and sat down.

'I'm looking for Chapman's henchman, Jamie Goode, on the security footage. If he was there last night, then he should be on this video.' Karen pointed to the recording playing on her computer screen. 'But he's not.'

'Is there another entrance into the building?' Arnie asked, stating the obvious question.

Karen had thought of that. There was another entrance, but you couldn't enter without a pass. And why would Jamie Goode have one of those? Could he have stolen one?

'There's an entrance at the back of the building,' Karen said. 'But it was locked, and you need a swipe card to enter.'

'Is there a camera around the back?' Arnie asked.

Karen shook her head.

'Typical!' Arnie grunted. 'Cameras everywhere these days, except in the one place you need them.'

There was a car park near the rear of the building that would have council cameras. She would have to investigate those.

She'd hoped to have the CCTV footage before she brought Jamie Goode in for questioning. She wanted to show him recorded evidence, so he couldn't deny it. But that wasn't going to happen now.

When Tim Farthing came back with the DNA results, that would be enough to nail Goode even without the CCTV.

'Come on then, Arnie,' Karen said. 'You're with me. Let's go and bring him in.'

Arnie reached for his jacket. It was still raining and hadn't stopped since last night.

'That's the British summer over,' Arnie commented as they did their best to avoid the puddles in the car park.

He was probably right, Karen thought, looking up at the grey sky. It had turned from one extreme to the other. The wind had picked up, too, buffeting against them as they headed to the car.

'So, where does he live?' Arnie asked as he got into the passenger side.

'Not far,' Karen said. 'Just outside Lincoln. It won't take long.'

And it didn't. They were there within ten minutes. Karen managed to find a parking spot, and they walked along a row of terraced houses to number seventy-nine.

There was a collection of rubbish lying on the patchy lawn in the tiny front garden. A rusted child's bike lay on its side next to a wheelbarrow, and a crumbling low brick wall separated the garden from the pavement. The windows were filthy, as were the bedraggled net curtains that hung inside.

Karen pressed the doorbell.

'I don't think it's working,' Arnie said, leaning over her to rap on the door.

A man, wearing pyjama bottoms and no top, eventually opened the door, scratching his chest. His hair stood on end, and it was clear he'd just woken up.

'Yeah?' he said, bleary-eyed.

'We're looking for Jamie Goode,' Karen said.

'He's not here,' the man replied, and began to close the door.

Arnie put his foot out to prevent him. 'Hang on a minute, lad. We need to speak to him, officially.' He held out his warrant card.

The young man was suddenly alert. He swore under his breath.

'So, where is he?' Karen asked.

'I don't know.'

'Will he be back soon? When did he leave?'

'He left months ago,' the man said. 'He doesn't live here anymore. He was the previous tenant. I keep getting letters addressed to him.'

Karen clenched her fists in frustration.

'Do you have a forwarding address?' Arnie asked.

'No, sorry,' he said. 'Maybe you could ask the letting agency.'

'Who are?' Karen prompted.

'Silverton Smith,' he said. 'At least, that's who I let the place through, so I guess he was with them, too.'

'Right. Thanks for your time,' Karen said.

'No problem.' He yawned as he shut the door.

'Great,' Karen said. 'Just what we don't need. A morning wasted chasing estate agents.'

'Tell you what,' Arnie said. 'Let me do it. I'll get the address. You can go back to the station.'

'Are you sure?' Karen asked.

'Of course. I'll walk. It's not far from here. I know the letting agency. It's at the Carlton Centre.'

Karen nodded. 'All right, Arnie. Thanks. I appreciate that. We really need to get hold of him soon.' She checked her watch. 'Although I know where he works, or rather who he works for.'

'Quentin Chapman?'

'Yes. If I track him down, Jamie Goode is likely to be with him.'

Arnie considered that, then said, 'It might be quicker. I'll try to find his current address, and you try to locate Chapman.'

Quentin Chapman wasn't home. Karen had expected a member of staff to open the door, but it seemed the house was deserted.

She gazed up at the mock-Georgian building, muttered a curse and then turned to march back across the gravel to her car.

If they didn't find him soon, they'd have to put out an all-ports alert. She wouldn't put it past Chapman to whisk Goode out of the country, so he couldn't do a deal and turn against his boss.

When Karen got back to the station, she found Sophie kneeling on the floor of the open-plan office, piles of papers arranged around her.

'What's going on?' Karen asked.

Sophie looked up; her cheeks were flushed. 'I'm working on something,' she said. 'Trying to work out a timeline.'

Karen peered over her shoulder. 'For what?'

'We've been going through the emails. Me, Harinder, Rawlings and a couple of other officers from Simpson's team, and we've all found the same thing. There are communications between Cary and Phoebe, detailing things about the scanner. Worrying things.'

'Worrying how?'

'Well, it seems this scanner isn't all it's cracked up to be. It's having problems. It's unreliable when run at certain temperatures.' She waved her hand. 'Due to some scientific reason I don't fully understand yet. But the gist is that the scanner doesn't always work. And the software crashes constantly unless it's run on a computer with massive processing power.' She looked up at Karen. 'You know what this means?'

'What?'

'It means it's not ready. There are major faults, and Phoebe and Cary were worried, but as far as I can tell, they haven't disclosed those faults to the potential buyer, which is very underhand. I don't know whether Chapman knows. I can't say for sure. That's what I'm looking for now. Any message from Phoebe or Cary to Chapman to let him know the state of the scanner.'

Karen glanced at the papers on the floor. 'I don't think you're going to find anything,' she said. 'Chapman's too smart for that. I bet he told them only to send routine emails. Everything else they would have discussed in person.'

'Maybe, but the emails were encrypted. They might have believed no one else could access them.'

Karen shook her head. 'Chapman's old-school,' she said. 'He would have been careful. There's no way he would have let them put anything sensitive that mentioned him in an email.'

'If that's true, we won't be able to prove that he knew the scanner didn't work.'

'I think we're going to need some experts to look at all this.'

Sophie nodded. 'Yes, we're going to need a scientist who can tell us exactly what the problem is with the scanner.'

Karen considered this for a moment, then said, 'Perhaps Cary and Phoebe wanted to come clean. Maybe they weren't comfortable going ahead with the sale knowing there was a problem with the scanner and . . .'

Sophie finished her sentence. 'And maybe Chapman wanted the deal to go ahead, and he was prepared to kill them to make sure it did.'

Karen nodded slowly. 'It's possible.'

Her phone beeped. It was Mike.

'I've got to go to lunch,' she said. 'I wouldn't usually as we're so busy, but I need to talk to Mike. I won't be long.'

'No problem. I'll just keep going through these.' Sophie picked up another printed email and began to read.

◆ ◆ ◆

Karen met Mike in a pub in Lincoln. He was already sitting at the table when she entered.

She smiled, and was relieved when he smiled back. 'Where's Sandy?'

'I left her at the training centre,' he said.

'Right.' She sat down, and someone immediately came over to take their order. Karen asked for an orange juice and a chicken salad. Mike opted for the burger.

When they were alone, Karen leaned on the table and took a deep breath. 'I'm sorry,' she said. 'You didn't deserve that reaction.'

Mike looked at her steadily. 'I can't even say I regret it, because if it happened again, I'd still go.'

Karen frowned but reached for his hand. 'I need you to understand I'm struggling with this. There's a clash between my job and my life with you. I don't have evidence of any specific threat, but you know what it's like out there. There are some really nasty people I have to deal with, and the thought of something happening to you, because of me . . .'

'It won't,' he said.

'You can't know that. And the thought of it happening again, I just can't get it out of my head. But I need to, if I want us to work. If I want to keep my job as well as you, then I need to find a way to deal with it.'

'Well, one way is to talk about it,' he said.

'Right,' Karen agreed. 'Which we are. So, we're already winning.'

He grinned. 'I guess we are.'

Mike leaned back in his chair and sighed. 'I need to compromise, too. Your job is dangerous, and it might go against all my instincts, but you're right. It is your job, and you can handle it. I need to respect that. I was a bit hurt, I suppose. Wounded pride.'

The server turned up with their drinks. After she'd gone, Karen asked, 'So, how did Sandy get on at the training course?'

'She was amazing,' Mike said. 'She showed all the other dogs up.'

Karen laughed. 'She's a treasure.'

'It was a great course. We saw huge progress in the other dogs and handlers, considering it was only held over two days.'

'Do you think you'll hold more courses?' Karen asked.

'I think so. It really helps to be on site because everyone keeps their focus. It feels good to be doing something useful.'

Mike had come so far since Karen had first met him. He'd been working as an estate hand, a moody, solitary figure. Despite the odds against them, they'd managed to bond, helped by the fact that he too had suffered the loss of a child, and it had affected him greatly.

Somehow they'd found each other, and helped each other heal. For Karen, it had been unexpected. She'd thought she'd never be able to move on after losing Josh and Tilly, but she had. And Mike had played a big part in that.

She knew their relationship was far from perfect, but was anything ever really perfect?

'So,' Mike said as they finished up their lunch. 'You got the guy who was drugging women in Lincoln?'

'We did.'

Mike smiled. 'I should have known you would.'

CHAPTER
THIRTY-ONE

When Karen returned to work, she felt like a weight had been lifted. Things were better with Mike. Not perfect, but they were working at it. Each understood where the other was coming from, which was a start.

As soon as she entered the open-plan office and took a seat at her desk, the heavy weight of Phoebe's disappearance and Cary's death settled back on her shoulders.

Arnie had come back from the letting agency, delivering the bad news that they had no forwarding address. The DMV still had Jamie Goode's old address registered, and so they were at a loss. Quentin Chapman's business addresses were all empty, which was suspicious. It looked very much like they were non-operational and only used to lend legitimacy to his criminal operation.

Karen leafed through Todd Bartholomew's interview notes and thought back to the beginning of the case, when she and Sophie had first spoken to Will Horsley. He'd told them about the woman at the club, who had turned out to be Phoebe Woodrow.

He'd believed she'd been drugged. But they'd caught Todd Bartholomew, who had confessed to drugging many women at that location but denied spiking Phoebe's drink.

And because Cary was dead, they'd taken the pressure off Todd, investigating other reasons behind Phoebe's disappearance. Had they taken their eye off the ball? Were they letting Todd off too easily? Todd was an evil sexual predator who had showed no remorse in his interview. A man like Todd would only tell the truth when it served him. He'd get a kick out of derailing the investigation.

Karen had assumed Todd was a misdirection in the case. But the longer she thought about it, the more she was sure they were missing something. Will Horsley had said Phoebe looked as though she'd been drugged, and Todd *had* grabbed her arm. There had been an interaction, as much as Todd wanted to deny it.

Karen walked to Morgan's office.

He looked up. 'I know that face. What's wrong?'

'We need to talk to Todd Bartholomew again. I think he drugged Phoebe.'

'Do we have any further evidence linking him to Phoebe? Did Farthing uncover more from Todd's house?'

Karen shook her head. 'Not yet, but I think we need to apply more pressure.'

'We've got him for all those other women,' Morgan said. 'All those photographs, but there's nothing of Phoebe.'

'But what if he drugged her and she got away?'

'Possible, though he denies it.'

'He denied the other charges until he was confronted with indisputable evidence.'

'True,' Morgan said. 'Okay, say he did drug her. We know she got away. She stayed at her cousin's house and then saw her grandmother the following day.'

'Let's ask him about Phoebe again,' Karen said. 'I'm sure he knows more than he's letting on.'

Morgan thought for a moment, then nodded. 'Fair enough.'

◆ ◆ ◆

Karen and Morgan sat opposite Todd Bartholomew in interview room three.

Todd slumped back in his chair, looking sulky and peevish. He refused to look at either of them. They'd asked him multiple questions, but he remained unwilling to cooperate.

'If you're lying, it won't go well for you in court. You won't appear repentant if you don't come clean for *all* your crimes,' Morgan said. 'Tell us about Phoebe.'

'I don't even know who you're talking about,' Todd said, rolling his eyes.

Karen pushed the still CCTV shot of Phoebe Woodrow at Imporium across the table. In the image, she was standing close to Todd. 'Maybe this will jog your memory?'

He scowled at Karen. 'I told you. She just walked into me. Must've been drunk,' he said.

'I don't think she was drunk, Todd. I think she'd been drugged, and I think you spiked her drink.'

He gave her a nasty smile. 'Prove it then.'

They went round and round in circles for a while until finally Morgan said, 'She got away from you, didn't she? Outsmarted you?'

'What?' Todd snapped.

'You spiked her drink,' Morgan said. 'You were waiting for it to kick in, but she left before it did. Isn't that right?'

Todd's cheeks flushed.

Karen wondered if Todd was telling them everything. They had no evidence he was holding back. But still, she had to try and get more from him. They had no other suspects, and they needed to wrap this up.

Karen took over the questioning, determined to push Todd. 'You'd done it so many times before, but this time Phoebe got the better of you, didn't she?'

The duty solicitor shot Karen a warning look.

'Todd, your solicitor will try to get you a lesser sentence. But it won't work if you're not sorry for what you did. It won't look good if you've held back the truth.'

Todd muttered something to his solicitor, who nodded reassuringly.

'So what if I did,' Todd said, turning back to look at Karen and Morgan. 'I didn't touch her afterwards.'

'You spiked her drink?' Karen asked to clarify.

He shrugged. 'Yeah, but she didn't drink it all.'

Karen felt her skin crawl as she looked into his cold, flinty eyes. He wasn't repentant at all.

'You put the Rohypnol in her drink,' Morgan said. 'She drank some of it, and then what happened?'

'She got up and walked away. Told me she was going to find her friends, but they were long gone.' He shrugged again. 'I went back to my mates, and then we saw her walk past ten minutes later. She might not have drunk much of it, but she was only a tiny thing.' He smiled, showing his teeth. 'So, it already had an effect. She was all wobbly. She walked into me.' His eyes were glazed and his smile widened. He was seemingly lost in a sick memory. 'Then she wandered past, and I grabbed her arm.' Todd pointed at the image and then looked up, taking in the disgust on Karen's face.

He bit his lower lip, enjoying her discomfort. He was feeding off it, but Karen couldn't help showing emotion.

She broke eye contact and looked down at her notes, trying to gather her thoughts.

'Then I followed her outside,' he said in a low voice, almost a whisper. 'But she was talking to some other guy.' He shrugged. 'I decided to cut my losses.'

He spoke casually, like it was an everyday occurrence. As though he'd done nothing wrong.

Karen swallowed. Her throat felt dry. It was too hot in the small interview room.

She met Morgan's gaze, and he understood without her having to say a word.

'Let's take a break,' Morgan said and paused the tape.

Outside in the corridor, Karen leaned against the wall. 'He's sick,' she said. 'He's enjoying it.'

'I know. Do you want me to get Arnie in as a replacement?'

'I can handle it,' Karen said.

'I know you can. I don't doubt that. But I think he's getting off on the fact that you're female.'

'It's not pleasant to sit at a table with an abuser like that, but we got him to talk. Now we know he *did* drug Phoebe.'

'Right, but she got away, so where did she go on Saturday after seeing her grandmother? If Todd came after her, we should have found evidence. There was nothing at his house or her flat.'

They started to walk back to the office.

'If Todd isn't responsible for her disappearance, then who is?' Karen asked.

'Maybe she decided to get away. The incident with Todd could have shaken her. Perhaps she needed some time on her own, somewhere she felt safe,' Morgan suggested.

'But Phoebe had a big deal on the table. Would she really walk away from that?'

Morgan looked thoughtful. 'If she knew the scanner wasn't all they hoped it would be, it's possible her conscience wouldn't allow her to do the deal.'

Karen nodded slowly. 'Or maybe Quentin Chapman was putting pressure on her to do the deal anyway. So, we come back to the same story. We still don't know what happened to Phoebe, and now Cary is dead.'

They stopped beside the coffee machine, and Karen pressed the button for a black coffee.

'Who inherits the company?' Morgan asked. 'If Phoebe's not on the scene and Cary is dead, then . . .'

She shrugged and handed Morgan the first coffee before getting another for herself. 'I suppose it depends if Phoebe is alive. If she's not, and she died before Cary, then it would go to his beneficiaries. He told me he'd made a will.'

'It's something to check,' Morgan said, and then sipped his coffee.

'But it doesn't make sense. Why would Quentin Chapman want them out of the way? He needed at least one of them alive for the deal to go through. Unless . . .' Karen trailed off.

'What?' Morgan asked.

Karen frowned. There was something there, but she couldn't quite fit it together. 'Phoebe left her cat with Erica on Friday night. Erica's kind, trustworthy. Phoebe would have known she'd look after her pet if she didn't return.'

'So you're saying Phoebe anticipated whatever happened to her.'

Karen said, 'I can't say for sure, but maybe she knew she wasn't coming back.'

Back in the open-plan office with a second cup of coffee, Karen reached for the phone.

'Tim,' she said, trying to infuse a lightness she didn't feel into her tone. 'Have you got any results back from the scene?'

'Which scene?' he huffed. 'I'm dealing with quite a few, Karen.'

Karen gritted her teeth. He always managed to make her mood worse. 'Sorry, I should have been clearer. I meant the scene from last night. Cary Swann.'

'Give me a chance,' he said. 'It happened less than twenty-four hours ago.'

'No DNA?'

'The DNA queue is backlogged. We've got tests coming out of our ears. I can't make the process go any faster.'

'It's so important, Tim. We really need this.'

He hesitated, then sighed. 'Fine, I'll see if the lab can bump it up the queue.'

Karen smiled. 'Thanks, that would be very helpful.'

Maybe he wasn't so bad after all.

But then he said, 'Karen . . .'

'Yes?'

'You owe me.' And he hung up.

She put her phone on her desk and stood up. She paced slowly in the small space between the cubicles. They still had a few minutes until they had to go back downstairs to continue questioning Todd Bartholomew, and Karen was using that time to think. To try to make connections. To try to put her finger on what she was missing.

Morgan came out of his office. 'You're making me nervous,' he said, nodding at Karen, who was now striding back and forth as she continued to sort the evidence in her head.

Arnie leaned back in his chair. 'I'm glad it's not just me. It's off-putting. I'm trying to pick my numbers,' he said, scrolling through his phone.

'What numbers?' Karen asked.

'Lottery ticket,' he said. 'Big rollover this week.'

'Oh, silly me,' Karen said. 'I thought you might be working.'

Arnie ignored the jibe.

'I've got an idea,' she said, speaking to everyone. 'Let's focus on what Sophie and the others found in Phoebe's emails. We know she was nervous. They both were. News that the scanner could be less than perfect would scupper their deal. They were going to lose out on millions. So maybe Phoebe decides to lie low.' Karen paused when she saw confusion on their faces.

'It doesn't make sense,' Arnie said.

'Why not?'

'Well, for one thing, if she's lying low, where's she been? Where is she now? And for another thing, what's lying low going to do? It's only going to delay the inevitable. She's still not going to get the deal, is she?'

Arnie was incredibly annoying. Annoying, but in this case, right.

'Maybe she's avoiding Quentin. Or maybe . . . This might sound odd, but we know she'd been arguing with Cary. Their assistant, Lou, told me they'd been having big bust-ups. We can see their disagreements in their emails. Phoebe suspected she'd been drugged, but she didn't know about Todd Bartholomew. She didn't know about the other women. She might have believed it was personal. Maybe she thought it was Quentin coming after her, or even Cary. They'd been fighting. Maybe she thought he wanted her out of the way.'

Morgan was the first to see the connection. 'So that means Cary . . .'

Karen nodded. 'Right. They don't trust each other. From their emails we can see that. Maybe they met on the roof last night, and there was a struggle, resulting in Cary falling to his death.'

'Hang on a minute,' Arnie said. 'You thought Quentin Chapman's henchman was responsible for that. The one with the long, dark hair. Jamie Goode. That's the one I've been trying to track down.'

'Yes, but Phoebe also has long, dark hair,' Karen said. 'That hair wrapped around Cary's fingers could have been hers.'

Arnie's face screwed up. 'I don't believe it. Phoebe is tiny. How would she have had the strength to do that?'

Karen thought back to the time she'd spent with Cary on the roof. She remembered how he'd sat precariously perched on the safety rail. She recalled how he'd seemed amused by her concern, laughing it off as perfectly safe. But if he'd been sitting on the guard rail last night, it wouldn't have taken much to unbalance him. One firm shove would have been enough.

'She wouldn't need much strength if she caught him off guard,' Karen said. 'If he'd been sitting on the guard rail like I'd seen him do before.'

'I don't know,' Arnie said, leaning back and folding his arms. 'It still doesn't explain where she is now. And we didn't see her on the CCTV.'

'I don't know where she is now,' Karen admitted. 'She would have had her pass, so it's possible she entered at the back of the building.'

Arnie still looked sceptical, and Morgan didn't seem convinced either.

'My money's still on Jamie Goode,' Arnie said. 'Once a thug, always a thug.'

'It's just a theory,' Karen said.

'A wacky one, if you don't mind me saying so,' Arnie said. 'Not that I have anything against wacky theories. I've been a detective too long to rule anything out.' He let out a low whistle. 'Our missing young woman could actually be a killer . . . Didn't see that one coming.'

When he said it like that, it did seem far-fetched.

'I'm not suggesting we drop other possibilities. I don't trust Quentin Chapman. I'd bet he knew this scanner was dodgy, but wanted to go ahead with the deal anyway.'

Morgan had been quiet until now, thinking through the idea. He said, 'I think the theory has promise. We need DNA from that strand of hair.'

Karen nodded. 'I've asked Tim Farthing to rush it through.'

'Did he agree?'

'He said he'd bump it up the queue.'

Morgan's eyebrows lifted. 'I told you he likes you. All that prickly sarcasm hides a soft interior. You're practically best buddies now.'

Karen grimaced.

'I'll remember that when I need a little lab work fast-tracked,' Arnie said with a chuckle.

The phone on Karen's desk rang. It was Tim. 'I've done as you asked. Front of the queue. We'll have results in a couple of hours.'

CHAPTER THIRTY-TWO

Over the next couple of hours, Karen, Sophie and Morgan went through emails and CCTV footage.

Karen rubbed her eyes as the playback finished. Someone had been on the roof with Cary last night. The strand of dark hair had to have come from somewhere. But after an exhaustive search of the security feeds, she was sure whoever had been on the roof with Cary hadn't entered by the main door.

The only other way into the building was at the rear, but unfortunately the swipe cards weren't logged, so there was no telling when the back door had been opened. It was one dead end after another.

DS Rawlings had volunteered to help Arnie track down Jamie Goode. He'd been eager enough to take the search from Karen, probably because he thought it would be a feather in his cap and an easy one to bring home. But it hadn't turned out that way.

They were no closer to finding him now than they had been two hours ago.

When Karen's mobile rang, she glanced at the screen and then hurriedly answered. It was Tim.

'What have you got for us?' she asked, then held her breath, hoping for good news.

'We've got a match,' he said, then waited, drawing it out to lengthen the suspense.

'To whom?' Karen asked.

'The hair around Cary's fingers was a match for Phoebe Woodrow.'

Phoebe. Karen paused, letting it sink in. Perhaps her wacky theory wasn't so crazy after all. 'So, she's still alive?'

'Unless Cary managed to get hold of her hair and wrap it around his fingers before jumping off the building, I'd say yes.'

Karen exhaled a long breath, ignoring Tim's sarcasm. 'This doesn't add up.'

'No,' Tim said. 'Thankfully, it's not my job to unravel the threads of your case. I've done my part.'

'Yes, you have. I appreciate it, Tim. Thanks for getting that fast-tracked.'

'You're welcome,' he said, and Karen didn't need to see his smug smile to know it was there.

◆ ◆ ◆

On hearing the news, Simpson called a briefing. This new evidence really did change everything. They'd been searching for Phoebe, assuming her to have been drugged and possibly abducted and murdered. Now, after just a few hours, Phoebe had changed from a victim to a potential killer.

'We now believe Phoebe Woodrow is alive,' Simpson said, standing at the front of the briefing room. He spoke gruffly, taking the lead firmly, but he looked as confused as Karen felt. 'So, where is she?' Simpson asked. 'Where has she been hiding out? As far as we know, she hasn't had access to a vehicle. She hasn't rented a car, and the Honda Jazz she borrowed from her cousin was left in the city centre. So, has she borrowed another car? Is there something we're missing?' He looked around the room as though one of the officers might have the answer. 'Any ideas?'

Karen spoke up. 'There's a chance Phoebe was staying at the property she was about to buy, the house in Burton Waters. When we went there and met the current owner, we found a back window had been jimmied open.'

Simpson blinked.

Rawlings grunted. 'Unbelievable. You knew that, and let me waste all day chasing after Jamie Goode.'

'You knew it too,' Sophie said primly, twirling a pen. 'Or you would have done if you were following the case notes in Operation Starling's database, like you're supposed to.'

Rawlings's eyes bulged, and his face flushed red. He looked like he might explode. Karen made a mental note to give Sophie some gentle advice about diplomacy after the meeting.

'We still need to eliminate Goode from our enquiries,' Simpson said, putting a hand up to indicate Rawlings should calm down. 'It's not a wasted day. But even if she was at the house in Burton Waters, we know she's not there now. She wasn't there when you went to speak to the owner.'

'No,' Karen admitted. 'That's true. Sophie has been checking in with the owner daily. She must be hiding out somewhere else now.'

'Right, but where?' Simpson said, sounding desperate. 'Come on, people, I need ideas.' He looked around the briefing room.

DCI Churchill hadn't come down for the meeting, but everyone else from Operation Starling was crowded around the large table, some sitting, most standing. Unfortunately, no one seemed to have any bright ideas.

'Right,' Simpson said eventually. 'Then the obvious thing to do is speak to the family again. Someone must know something.

Phoebe hasn't left the city via the main train or bus stations, and we believe she hasn't had access to another vehicle, so chances are she's still in Lincoln.'

Simpson began doling out tasks, giving his team instructions.

'What about her grandmother?' he asked Karen. 'Do you think she's worth another visit?'

'Possibly,' Karen said. 'They are close. It seems likely that Phoebe knew she was going to be out of contact for a while and wanted to see her grandmother beforehand. Hence the visit to the care home on Saturday. I'd wondered why she didn't sign in at the entrance, but now it makes sense. She was hiding.'

'But who was she hiding from?'

Karen shrugged. 'Possibly Cary. We know there was bad feeling between them, and that may have spilled over last night, leading to Cary's horrific fall.'

Rawlings made a huffing sound. 'The fact he took a handful of her hair clutched in his fist, and plummeted sixteen storeys to the pavement, makes me think it was *probably* murder.'

Karen didn't answer. He could be right, but they didn't know how it had happened yet. There could have been a struggle. Perhaps Cary had attacked Phoebe, and then somehow lost his balance. She pictured how Cary had looked when she'd seen him on the roof.

Phoebe was slightly built, but a well-timed shove would have caused Cary to lose his balance if he'd been sitting on the guard rail.

'Right,' Simpson said, clapping his hands. 'That's it for now. We need to find Phoebe. Let's get as many people as we can watching CCTV, and let's speak to her family and friends again.'

'Can I ask you a question, sir?' Rawlings said as people around him began to stand.

'Yes, go ahead.'

'Do we still believe Phoebe is in danger, or are we treating her as a murder suspect?'

'For now,' Simpson said, 'both.'

'She could have been hiding from Quentin Chapman,' Morgan commented as he stood to leave. 'She might still be.'

'Yes,' Simpson said, sucking in a breath. 'We've had a harassment complaint from Mr Chapman.'

'You're kidding,' Karen said. 'Against me?'

'It was very vaguely worded,' Simpson said. 'Not an official complaint. A warning shot.'

'Well, we can't stop looking into him,' Karen said. 'I know he's crooked.'

'It's one thing knowing, another thing proving,' Simpson barked. 'Anyway, you know what you've got to do. Get on with it.'

And with that, the meeting was over.

Karen walked back to the open-plan office with Morgan.

'I really thought we were going to find Phoebe's body,' Morgan said.

'Me too,' Karen said. 'I'd have bet on Quentin Chapman getting rid of both Cary and Phoebe if he could profit from it.'

Karen returned to her desk and took out her mobile, scrolling through her messages. But she was only skimming them. Her mind was still puzzling over what must have happened last night on the roof of CaP Diagnostics.

Phoebe was alive, and the evidence strongly suggested she'd been on the roof with Cary and there'd been an altercation.

But where was she now? She'd probably stayed for a while at the house in Burton Waters, but as the owner checked the property every day now, it wasn't a place she could stay.

So, if that wasn't a long-term option, where else would she have gone? She'd go to a place she felt safe, with someone she could trust.

Karen frowned and flipped to the messages from Erica. There was nothing untoward there, but she thought back to when she'd called in to see Erica last night.

Erica had seemed on edge, and Karen had put that down to anxiety after a busy day. But what if it was more than that?

And what had Erica said on the phone yesterday? She'd apologised for wasting Karen's time. She'd said she was sure Phoebe was fine.

That was a complete turnaround.

That wasn't the same Erica who'd been concerned for her friend's safety. Erica had been trying to tell Karen to leave it alone, that she didn't want it investigated anymore.

And there was only one good reason for that.

Karen grabbed her bag, shoved her phone inside and told Morgan she was heading out to speak to Erica Bright.

CHAPTER
THIRTY-THREE

The sky was thick with dark grey clouds when Karen parked in front of the apartment block. The wind had whipped up again, blowing her hair into her eyes. She pushed it back, vowing to book a hairdresser's appointment for the weekend. Heavy spots of rain began to fall as Karen hurried over to the building.

Erica's car was in its usual parking spot, but it took a long time for her to answer the buzzer at the main entrance. Karen had to press the button three times.

Eventually the door released.

She stepped into the foyer and made her way up to Erica's apartment. Again, Erica took her time answering the door. When she did, she looked flustered.

'Karen, I wasn't expecting to see you again so soon. There's not a problem, is there? Is it about Phoebe?'

'Can I come in?' Karen asked.

'Of course. It's my day off,' Erica said, self-consciously looking over her shoulder. 'Can I get you a drink?'

'No, I'm fine. I noticed last night you were a little out of sorts. I thought there might be something you wanted to tell me.'

'Tell you?' Erica gave a puzzled smile, and then shrugged. 'No, I don't think so.'

'Nothing you want to talk about?' Karen suggested.

'I think we do enough talking at our counselling sessions, don't you?' She laughed. Then she looked out of the large windows. 'The weather has certainly turned, hasn't it?' She nodded at the grey, stormy clouds.

Karen spotted Tommy. The cat was meowing and nudging the edge of a closed door at the end of the hallway.

'He's determined to get in,' Karen said.

Erica looked alarmed. 'Tommy, stop that! He's always up to something. I . . . er . . . I shut the door because I don't want him getting hair on the bed.'

Karen walked along the hallway towards Tommy.

Erica froze.

'I think there must be something in the room that he wants to see. Don't you?' Karen put her hand out and grasped the door handle.

'No, don't!' Erica said.

Karen half turned. 'Oh, Erica. I didn't want to believe it. You're hiding her. Why?'

Erica looked down at the floor miserably.

Karen opened the bedroom door to see a pair of boots sticking out from under the bed before they disappeared underneath.

'It's not going to work, Phoebe,' Karen said. 'You may as well come out now.'

Phoebe shuffled backwards and then got to her feet. Her gaze darted about the room, as though looking for an escape route.

There wasn't one.

'It's over,' Karen said. 'No more running. No more hiding.'

'I didn't mean for this to happen,' Phoebe said. 'And don't blame Erica. It wasn't her fault.'

Karen gestured for her to leave the bedroom, and they returned to the main living area of the apartment.

'I didn't intend to lie to you,' Erica said, clasping her hands. 'I felt terrible, but I was so worried. Phoebe *was* missing. I wasn't lying about that, but then she showed up here on Wednesday. You must listen to her, Karen. She's scared. The men she's been doing business with have been trying to shut her up. They want this deal to go through at any cost. They tried to *drug* her. I wanted to tell you, but Phoebe said it was too dangerous. That they'd find out where she was.'

Karen took a deep breath. 'Let's sit down at the table, and then you can explain.' She looked at Phoebe, who nodded meekly.

She looked even more petite in person. Karen weighed her up. Could she have pushed Cary over the edge? Or had Phoebe been defending herself from Cary when she fell?

They took seats around Erica's table. Karen had handcuffs in her bag but Phoebe was cooperating, and she didn't yet know if Phoebe was a killer or a victim. Phoebe sat with her arms crossed and head down, though Karen caught a defiant look in her eye.

Erica looked crumpled and thoroughly miserable.

'So, what happened?' Karen asked.

'He tried to drug her on Friday night,' said Erica.

'Phoebe?' Karen prompted.

She nodded. 'Cary, my work partner. On Friday night he put something in my drink. Luckily I found my cousin and went home with him and managed to sleep it off. But I was violently ill. He wanted me gone. He wanted to kill me. You see, if I was out of the way, Cary got all my money.'

'And the other way around?' Karen said.

Phoebe paused. 'What do you mean?'

'If Cary died, you got his stake in the company?'

'Well, yes, but—'

'Which is why you killed him?' Karen suggested.

Silence.

Phoebe froze. But she didn't immediately deny it. Her eyes searched Karen's face. She was trying to work out how much Karen knew, planning her next move.

Erica's jaw dropped open. 'What?'

'You've got it wrong. I haven't done anything,' Phoebe said, but the defiant look was replaced with uncertainty.

'Cary fell from the roof of CaP Diagnostics last night. He's dead, Phoebe, but I think you already knew that.'

Phoebe looked down at the table, refusing to meet Karen's gaze. 'I didn't know. That's awful.' She rubbed her eyes, but there were no tears. 'He'd been very down lately. Depression, I think. I told him to see someone about it, but he wouldn't. Perhaps the guilt of what he tried to do to me drove him to jump.'

'I don't think he jumped.'

Phoebe bristled. 'I'm just saying he might have been depressed. I don't know what happened. I wasn't there.'

'You *do* know because you were at the scene.'

'That's ridiculous!'

'We have evidence.'

Phoebe was quiet then, desperately calculating her options. After a moment, she said, 'Whoever saw me must have been mistaken.'

'Your hair was found at the scene,' Karen said, wondering how Phoebe was going to try and worm her way out of that. It didn't take long for her to come up with an excuse.

She gave a confident smile. 'Well, that's just because I've been up to the roof loads of times.'

'Except your hair was wrapped around Cary's fingers, likely from where he reached out and tried to grab you as he fell.'

Phoebe flinched.

'What was he doing, Phoebe? Was he sitting on the guard rail? Was the opportunity too tempting to pass up? One quick shove, and he was out of your way once and for all? The whole company would be yours then.'

Karen had come to Erica's with an open mind. There had been a chance Phoebe's hair had been wrapped around Cary's fingers because she'd been defending herself during an altercation, but Karen didn't believe that now. She kept returning to the things people had said or implied during the course of the investigation: Phoebe put herself first. Phoebe was selfish. But could she really be a cold-blooded killer?

Phoebe looked flustered. 'It's nonsense,' she said, turning to Erica. 'You *know* me. I'd never do that.'

'It's not nonsense, Phoebe, and you need to start telling the truth, otherwise things are going to get a lot worse for you.'

'No, wait. You must understand. I didn't mean for it to happen. It was an accident,' she said. 'I knew he'd tried to drug me, so I went to talk to him. I had a rape alarm and a spray in my pocket. If he tried anything, I was ready for him. So I went to talk things through. He had cold feet about the deal. I wanted us to sell, so we could go our separate ways. I knew I could never trust him again. But he refused. He was going to throw it all down the drain, everything we'd worked for.'

'So you wanted to do the deal? What about the problems with the scanner?'

'Problems?' Phoebe narrowed her eyes. 'Cary told you about that, did he? They were minor issues. Nothing to worry about. But

Cary was a wimp. He said he didn't think it was ethical if we went ahead with the sale now. He was so pathetic. I just wanted to get rid of the company and start up again on my own, without him pulling me down.'

Phoebe jerked forward, glaring at Karen. 'Don't look at me like that! I had good reason to want to get away from him. He drugged me on Friday night. I think he wanted me incapacitated so he could kill me. So, what I did . . . it was self-defence.'

Karen stared at her. 'What happened last night on the roof?'

Phoebe continued to talk. 'I told him I knew he'd tried to drug me, and he just laughed at me. I was so angry. I slapped him, and he grabbed my arm, laughing all the time, like it was the funniest thing in the world. He was sitting on the rail, the way he always did. Confident, cocky, laughing at me. So, I pushed him away from me, and he fell.' She shrugged. 'He just fell. It was an accident.'

Erica inhaled sharply. 'When you turned up here, you said you were scared, that they were out to get you, but *you* killed *him*.'

Phoebe shook her head stubbornly. 'No, I was defending myself.'

'You didn't tell me what you'd done.' Erica sounded close to tears.

'I imagine there's a lot she didn't tell you,' Karen said. 'So it was Cary who wanted to hold back the deal. He wanted the problems with the scanner to be ironed out before the sale went ahead. And I suppose you and Quentin Chapman wanted to push on regardless.'

'I didn't mention Quentin Chapman. Who told you that?' For the first time, Phoebe looked genuinely scared.

'Your emails,' Karen said.

Phoebe paled as Karen got up from the table and reached for her phone to call it in.

As they waited for the squad car to arrive, Erica got Phoebe a glass of water. Her hand was shaking as she put it down on the table.

'I'm sorry, Erica,' Phoebe said. 'I know you're shocked, but honestly it was self-defence. He drugged me. He *poisoned* me. He would have killed me if he had the chance. I know it.'

'Actually, Cary didn't drug you,' Karen said.

'What are you talking about? I think I'd know if I was drugged. I was violently sick, completely out of it, and I'd only had two drinks. I know my own body,' Phoebe said.

Karen nodded. 'I don't doubt you were drugged, Phoebe. In fact, I'm certain you were, but the man who did it wasn't Cary. It was a man called Todd Bartholomew, who has been charged with multiple counts of assaulting women after spiking their drinks in bars.'

Confusion passed over Phoebe's face.

Karen continued: 'Running into your cousin meant you had an extremely lucky getaway on Friday. But you didn't escape from Cary, as you thought. You escaped from Todd Bartholomew, a predator.'

'You mean . . . Cary was telling the truth when he said he didn't know what I was talking about?'

'Yes, the fact you were drugged had nothing to do with him.'

Phoebe's breathing got faster. Beads of sweat appeared on her forehead. 'But he shouldn't have laughed at me. Why did he laugh at me?'

'Did Quentin Chapman know where you were all this time?' Karen asked.

Phoebe shook her head. She took a deep breath and pressed a hand to her chest. The news Cary hadn't drugged her had come as a harsh shock. Her hand trembled as she reached for the water. Karen almost pitied her. Phoebe had believed Cary was a threat, and perhaps thought that would add weight to her self-defence argument with a sympathetic jury. But now that plan had fallen apart.

'So, where did you stay after you disappeared?' Karen asked.

'I stayed at my cousin's place on Friday night. On Saturday morning, I went home to change and then visited my grandma, but I decided not to go into work or back to my apartment. I was scared of Cary. I left my phone at home so he couldn't trace me. I really thought he intended to kill me.'

'Why didn't you go to the police?' Erica asked.

When Phoebe didn't reply, Karen said, 'She didn't go to the police because then the problems with the scanner would be revealed, and it would ruin her deal. She would lose out on a huge payday, as would Quentin Chapman.'

Phoebe rested her face in her hands. 'I just thought I should lie low until it was time to sign the deal. Then I could turn up. I thought Quentin would persuade Cary to sign, and once the deal was done, I never had to see Cary again. I stayed at a property I'm in the process of buying.'

'You broke in,' Karen said. 'It isn't your house.'

'I hardly think it's the worst crime in the world. Besides, I'll be living there soon,' Phoebe said coolly.

Karen noted how quickly Phoebe recovered her composure. It gave her an uneasy feeling that Phoebe was playing a role rather than displaying any kind of genuine emotion.

'I don't think you'll be living there for a while,' Karen said.

Phoebe tossed her hair. It wasn't just self-confidence she exuded. There was an arrogance about her. Did she really think she'd get away with causing Cary's death?

'I'll lawyer up,' she said. 'Trial might be tough, but Quentin Chapman will see I'm well represented.'

'Why would he do that?'

'Because without me the deal falls through. I'm indispensable to him now that Cary's dead.'

She spoke bluntly. She didn't care that Cary, a man she'd worked with for years, had died – that she had *killed* him. Phoebe only cared about the money. She and Chapman had a lot in common.

CHAPTER
THIRTY-FOUR

Suddenly Phoebe's demeanour changed. Tears trickled from her eyes, but Karen wasn't fooled. There was no genuine emotion there, just crocodile tears. Because she'd been caught. Because she'd realised it was what she would be expected to do.

'I'm sorry, Erica,' Phoebe said, turning and reaching out. 'I thought he tried to kill me. It was self-defence.'

Erica pulled away, unmoved. 'No, it wasn't. You lied. Cary wasn't trying to hurt you. He didn't drug you.'

'I didn't lie. I really thought . . .' Phoebe broke off and started to cry again.

Ignoring the waterworks, Karen pressed on. 'Did Quentin Chapman have anything to do with Cary's death?'

Phoebe sniffed and wiped away the tears with the back of her hand. 'No, why would he?'

'But he knew the scanner had faults and wanted to proceed with the deal anyway.'

'The faults were minor. It was only Cary being pathetic as usual. Worrying about things that didn't need to be worried about.'

Karen had heard enough. 'Phoebe Woodrow, I'm arresting you for the murder of Cary Swann. You—' But she didn't get to finish her sentence.

Phoebe jumped up, knocking her chair to the floor, and bolted.

The only way out was the front door, so Karen covered the path to the exit, but Phoebe went straight to the kitchen area.

Karen followed, but by the time she got there, Phoebe had grabbed a sharp knife from the rack beside the microwave. She turned, holding it in front of her.

'Stand back,' Phoebe shouted, brandishing the weapon.

Karen raised her hands. The way Phoebe held the knife told Karen she was no expert, but it didn't take an expert to deliver a deadly blow.

Should she try to grab her wrist and break her hold on the knife, or was that too much of a risk?

Speaking calmly and slowly, Karen said, 'Phoebe, you don't want to do this. Even Quentin Chapman's lawyers won't be able to help you if you attack me. Resisting arrest is not a good move if you want to walk away from your trial a free woman.'

'What are you doing, Phoebe? Have you lost your mind? Just stop it. Put it back,' Erica pleaded, walking forward, her arms outstretched towards Phoebe.

Karen saw the danger immediately. 'No, Erica. Stand back. Don't get too close!'

But it was too late. Phoebe grabbed Erica, putting the point of the knife against her neck.

Erica's eyes were wide and panicked. Her terrified gaze met Karen's.

'Phoebe, calm down. This has escalated too far. Don't do something you'll regret. Just think about it. You told me Cary was an accident. No one's going to believe that if you hurt me or Erica.'

'No one's going to believe me anyway. Like you said, I'm not going to be living in my new house. I'm not going to be able to do my deal. All that hard work, and it's all wasted.' She backed out of the kitchen using Erica as a shield.

Erica whimpered and stumbled as she was forced backwards.

Karen could only watch, berating herself for not slapping handcuffs on Phoebe the moment she'd crawled out from under the bed.

But she'd thought there was a chance Phoebe was a victim in all this. She'd stupidly given her the benefit of the doubt, given her time to explain. Backup would be here soon. She needed to talk Phoebe down before they got here, before the situation got way out of hand.

But it was Erica who took the initiative. In one swift movement, she pushed the knife away and then elbowed Phoebe hard in the stomach.

Phoebe made an *oof* sound as the breath left her lungs. Then, clutching a hand to her stomach, she ran, heading for the front door. Karen gave chase.

In the corridor, Phoebe shot around the corner, before slamming open the doors to the fire escape and charging up the stairs.

Karen was determined to keep up, but she had a horrible feeling she knew where this was going. They were heading up to the roof. Surely Erica's apartment didn't have a roof accessible to residents? Why weren't the doors locked? What had happened to health and safety? Did nobody care about that sort of thing anymore?

Phoebe burst on to the roof through a fire door, setting off a peeling alarm, and Karen followed.

The wind had picked up and it made Phoebe's long hair wave around her head madly. She still held the knife. 'Don't come any closer,' she warned, backing up.

'Phoebe, there's nowhere to go. You're on the roof,' Karen said. 'We can talk it through.'

'No,' Phoebe said. 'We won't talk it through. You'll twist my words. Nobody will believe it was a mistake.'

It was true. Karen didn't believe Cary's fall was a mistake. She did believe there had been mistakes along the way – Phoebe thinking Cary had drugged her, for one. But the push? Shoving Cary to his death? She didn't think that had been a mistake at all.

'What are you going to do?' Karen said. 'Put the knife down.'

But Phoebe ignored her, stepping back until she was at the edge of the roof.

Not again.

There was nothing below but shrubs and trees.

'Phoebe, no!'

There was no guard rail this time, just a raised stone lip. Phoebe climbed on to it and stood up, her shirt billowing out in the wind. Rain started to fall again in big, fat drops.

The storm was close.

Phoebe opened her arms, closed her eyes and took a shuffling step backwards.

'Phoebe, don't do this. You're upset, but it won't seem so bad if you just step down and talk about it,' Karen said.

Phoebe shook her head. 'I'm not going to prison.'

And then she turned and jumped.

CHAPTER
THIRTY-FIVE

The next few weeks were busy. They had a case to build, but some of the enthusiasm and energy of the investigation had been lost.

They had answers now, but who would have justice? Not Cary, certainly. He'd wanted to do the right thing, and that had got him killed.

Phoebe had chosen death over prison, and the guilt of that ate away at Karen. If she'd cuffed her as soon as she'd arrived, if she hadn't implied Phoebe wouldn't get to live in her new property, if she'd forced her to give up the knife in the kitchen . . . There were so many things she could have done differently.

And they had nothing on Quentin Chapman.

The one positive thing on the horizon was Todd Bartholomew's trial. The case against him looked strong.

Karen knocked on the door of Morgan's office. 'Fancy a coffee?' she asked, holding up a mug.

'You read my mind,' he said. 'How's it going?'

'Slowly,' she said, 'although Simpson's team is doing a lot of the form-filling and admin. I wouldn't mind doing all cases like this. I'm happy to let DS Rawlings handle my paperwork.' She grinned.

'I bet that's gone down like a lead balloon.'

Karen smiled. 'Yes. He's about as happy as you might expect.'

'Have you heard from Rick?'

'I saw him yesterday,' Karen said.

'How's he doing?'

'All right. I hope he'll be back at work as soon as the enquiry is over.'

'I was shocked when I heard what had happened,' Morgan said. 'It didn't seem like Rick.'

'It wouldn't have happened if he hadn't been under such pressure. It was my fault for taking him out with me. It's his mum's funeral tomorrow. He's been talking about going on holiday soon, taking a trip to Italy. That's where his grandparents were from.'

'That should do him good,' Morgan said. 'He could do with a break.'

'Yes, and Sophie's been helping him with all the paperwork and admin stuff.'

'I suppose that's Sophie's strong point,' Morgan said with a smile.

Karen shook her head. 'I sometimes worry about her. It's not natural to get so much enjoyment from filling out forms.'

Morgan chuckled. 'I've never known anyone to enjoy paperwork quite as much as Sophie.' He grabbed the empty mug from his desk and they walked to the coffee machine. 'What happens with CaP Diagnostics now that Cary and Phoebe are both dead?' Morgan asked.

'Well, Lou is still running the place. She was their assistant,' Karen said, 'but she's not doing much other than answering phones, fielding queries, and just keeping the office going. I think it works out that, because Phoebe died after Cary, her sister will inherit the company, though I'm not a hundred per cent sure. I know there are lawyers involved, as there always are when there's a lot of money at stake.'

Morgan frowned. 'Doesn't seem right if Phoebe killed Cary. Why should her family benefit? What about Chapman?'

'I've not spoken to him yet,' Karen said, putting her mug on the coffee machine. 'But I intend to.'

◆ ◆ ◆

An hour later, Karen was back at her desk when she heard a familiar voice.

'Hi, Sarge.' Rick smiled. He'd lost weight, but the circles under his eyes had gone.

'What are you doing back? You're not supposed to be back for another week at least.'

'I'm not. Officially you haven't seen me.' He winked. 'But I left something in my desk drawer and wanted to pick it up.' He held up a copy of *Meditations* by Marcus Aurelius.

'Have you been reading it?' Karen asked.

'Not really. Dipping in and out.'

'Me too. How have you been doing?'

'Not bad,' he said. 'I'm getting there.'

'Sleeping any better?'

'Yes. The house is still full of memories, but I've had a word with my sister and we're going to clear out some things at the weekend. I called the district nurses last week, and they arranged to have all the hospital equipment picked up. Mum's room looks so empty now. It's not all her belongings I want to clear out, just the things that remind me of when she was so ill.'

'I can understand that,' Karen said. 'I'm glad you're doing better.'

'We'll probably sell the house. I'll have to look for somewhere else to live.'

'You don't have to do that now though, do you?'

Rick shook his head. 'No, not straightaway.'

Sophie entered the open-plan office and spotted Rick. 'Oh, I'm glad you're here. I've got some more forms for you.'

'I had no idea there was so much paperwork involved with handling an estate,' Rick said. 'I'm the executor, and I'm doing it on my own rather than getting a solicitor.' Then he gestured to Sophie. 'When I say *on my own*, I mean Sophie's doing most of it.'

Sophie smiled. 'I don't mind. It's a pleasure to help.'

'Thanks, I don't know what I'd have done without you.'

'Probably filled all the forms in wrong,' Sophie teased.

Karen's phone rang. She picked it up.

'Hello, Detective. This is Quentin Chapman.'

'Hello, Quentin.'

'I'm outside. If you would be good enough to come down, we can have a chat.'

Karen rolled her eyes. 'You could always come in to the station?' *Like a normal person.*

'Oh, no. I don't think so. I don't feel comfortable in police stations.'

What a surprise. 'All right. I'll be down in a minute.'

She hated dancing to his tune, but she needed to speak to him.

As usual, he had his two heavies with him, Ponytail and Skinhead. Skinhead stayed behind the wheel while Ponytail got out and opened the door for her, smirking.

Karen sat in the back of the Range Rover, next to Quentin, on the buttery-soft, cream leather seats.

'We really do have to stop meeting like this,' she said.

He smiled. 'I apologise, but police stations are not my natural habitat.'

'You've heard what happened to Phoebe and Cary?'

He nodded. 'Yes. Such a shame. Phoebe had great promise. Cary, he was a nice guy, but he didn't have the same drive as Phoebe. You need nerves of steel to succeed in the business world.'

Or the morals of a sewer rat, Karen thought.

'But things have a way of working out,' he said cheerfully.

'What do you mean?' Karen asked. 'Two people are dead, and your investment is sunk now, isn't it? The only person left at CaP Diagnostics is Lou and—'

'No, my investment still stands,' Quentin said. 'And I've recently contacted Phoebe's sister. A very nice woman, Lisa Woodrow. Have you ever had the pleasure of meeting her?'

'I have,' Karen said, narrowing her eyes as she realised what he intended to do. He was sneaky and as slippery as a snake.

'I've offered my assistance. With help from an excellent legal team, she'll inherit the whole company, and our deal will be back on.'

'But Lisa doesn't know the first thing about the scanner. She's an artist,' Karen said.

'It really doesn't matter. It's not *what* you're selling so much as *how* you sell it. We've already got a buyer. There's just been a slight delay.'

Karen gritted her teeth. After everything, Quentin Chapman was about to come out on top. How was that fair?

'We've looked through the company emails. There were communications between Phoebe and Cary suggesting the scanner had problems. Were you aware of those problems?'

He chuckled. 'I have no idea what you're talking about, Detective.' But he gave a slow smile that suggested otherwise.

'So, Phoebe and Cary die, and you profit. Is that how it works?'

Quentin shrugged.

'You don't seem very upset,' Karen said.

'If you'd indulge an old man, I'd like to offer you another quote,' he said. '*The first rule is to keep an untroubled spirit. The second is to look things in the face and know them for what they are.*'

Karen stared at him. She knew exactly what he was. A man desperate to succeed no matter the human cost. He was putting himself first, saving his own skin. Getting ready to manipulate Lisa Woodrow just as he had Phoebe and Cary.

Karen reached for the door. 'Very interesting,' she said. 'I picked up a copy of *Meditations*.'

'You did? Splendid.'

'Yes, and my favourite quote so far is: *The best revenge is to not be like your enemy.*'

He gave a low chuckle. 'Very good, DS Hart. No doubt we'll see each other again at some point in the future.'

'No doubt,' Karen said as she got out of the car and slammed the door.

CHAPTER
THIRTY-SIX

On her way back from lunch, Karen called in on Cassidy. She opened the door with her bright pink hair in a ponytail, wearing a baggy grey sweatshirt and purple leggings. She was holding a duster in one hand and a can of Mr Sheen in the other.

'I thought I'd come around and give you a quick update,' Karen said, 'if you've got time.'

'Sure, come in. I was just cleaning the flat.'

'How is Vicky doing? Is she still staying with you?'

'No, she's back at home now. She's doing well. She ended up telling her mum what happened, and she's stronger than she thinks.'

'What about you?' Karen asked as they went inside. 'Are you back at work?'

'I put my notice in at Imporium. Dom knew it was only a temporary job for me,' she said. 'I'm starting uni in September, down in London. So it'll be a fresh start.' She looked around her small flat. 'I can't wait.'

'I'm pleased for you,' Karen said. 'What are you going to be studying?'

'Social work,' she said. 'I want a career where I can make a difference.'

'I think that's a really good idea.'

'Did you want a coffee?' she offered.

'Thanks.'

Cassidy switched the kettle on to boil and asked, 'Is he going away for a long time? Todd Bartholomew, I mean?'

Karen nodded. 'It looks like it. The CPS thinks the case against him is very strong.'

After Cassidy had finished making the coffee, Karen said, 'What does your mum think of your new uni course?'

Cassidy smiled. 'She's pleased.'

'I bet she's proud of you.'

This time, Cassidy grinned. 'I guess, although she's not too keen on my pink hair at the moment.' Her grin widened. 'But I quite like it.'

'Me too,' Karen said.

◆ ◆ ◆

Two days later, Karen sat on an uncomfortable wooden bench in the park.

The weather was warm, although cloudy and humid, and thrips kept landing on her white shirt.

It made her think of Gavin Griffin, the man who'd sat on the bench outside Phoebe's place. What a waste of time that had been. Although they'd given him a firm warning about his tendencies to make bogus claims, Karen wasn't sure he'd paid any attention.

She shifted nervously, clutching the folder on her lap. Karen had never done this sort of thing before, and with good reason. She was about to risk her job and a whole lot more than that if anyone ever found out.

She stared down at the folder and took a deep breath. Yes, it was a risk, but it was one she had to take.

A woman approached. The breeze had no effect on her helmet-like, straight blonde bob.

She sat beside Karen and said, 'Is that for me?'

Karen nodded and handed her the folder.

'Is it all here?' the woman asked. 'Everything I need?'

'I think so.'

Cindy Connor smiled, bright pink lips stretching over her white teeth. 'Good. Very pleasant doing business with you, Detective,' she said. 'Isn't it nice when we cooperate?'

'Don't get used to it,' Karen said.

She'd had run-ins with Cindy Connor before – a local journalist who'd run hit pieces on bent counsellors and businessmen, including Chapman. She often wrote harshly critical articles on the police, too, which was the reason Karen wasn't particularly fond of her.

But now she needed Cindy.

Cindy flipped through the pages in the folder, then stood to leave.

Karen said, 'I'm trusting you to do the right thing.'

Cindy turned and gave her another smile. 'I'm honoured.'

And then she walked away, holding the folder full of information about CaP Diagnostics' scanner and the potential for Quentin Chapman's dodgy deal.

It was a big risk. Huge. Quentin could strike back.

If he found out Karen was behind the story, he would be vengeful. She'd be stupid if she wasn't scared, but she had to do the right thing.

She'd spent the last few weeks looking over her shoulder, worried her job might cause a criminal to retaliate and attack her family or her, but now she had to face that fear.

If she was going to keep her job, she needed to somehow deal with that anxiety, and this was her method of doing it. This was her way of proving that, even when she was frightened, she could do her job just as well as she ever had.

And bringing Chapman's deal down around his ears was the right thing to do.

She was sure of it.

◆ ◆ ◆

The story was published with the headline *Local Businessman's Scam Falls Apart.*

Cindy had, of course, asked the pharma company who were due to buy out CaP Diagnostics for comment, and they did their own digging. More thorough due diligence unearthed the problems with the scanner, and the deal fell through.

Karen hadn't shared any police files or documentation from CaP Diagnostics. All she'd given Cindy was her own account of what she believed was happening.

Cindy, despite her faults, was a decent investigative journalist, and she'd turned over every stone to get to the truth.

The article was well researched, and it created enough buzz that any other potential buyers would think twice.

Phoebe's sister, Lisa Woodrow, would lose out on quite a payday, but the upside was she would hopefully avoid any interactions with Chapman from now on. She could continue her painting and live a peaceful life without a thug like Chapman intruding.

Despite Erica harbouring Phoebe, it was likely she'd avoid any charges. She hadn't known Phoebe had committed a crime and had just been trying to help a friend she believed was in danger.

Karen's relationship with Erica would never be quite the same. They still saw each other in the counselling group, but maintaining their friendship was a challenge. Erica tended to rush away when the meeting was finished. Sometimes Karen caught Erica staring at her, an accusatory look in her eyes. She held her responsible for Phoebe's death. Erica hadn't seen how events had unfolded on the roof, and though she tried unsuccessfully to hide it, Karen knew she blamed her.

Karen missed their chats and hoped that, given time, Erica could forgive her for not handling things differently.

◆ ◆ ◆

The team finished work for the day and headed off for drinks at The Plough. The sun was warm again, as the remnants of the British summer edged their way back, determined not to give over to autumn just yet.

As they walked towards the pretty frontage of The Plough, Morgan asked, 'How are things going with you and Mike now?'

'Good. I think we've turned a corner,' Karen said. 'The worry will never go away, but I think we've found a way to deal with it.'

'Why don't you invite him to join us?' Morgan suggested as he pushed open the door.

'I think I will,' Karen said, and she pulled out her mobile and sent Mike a quick text.

They enjoyed their drinks, toasting the success of Operation Starling. Even Rawlings made an appearance, though he chose the seat furthest from Karen.

Arnie was munching on his second plate of chicken wings when Mike arrived.

Karen stood up and waved him over. 'Good day?'

'Yeah, great,' he said. 'I'll get the drinks in.'

'I'll get yours,' Morgan said. 'I've just got a round in. What are you having?'

'Pint of Landlord, please,' Mike said and sat down beside Karen.

Arnie began to describe his precise method of rating chicken wings. 'It's not just about flavour,' he said earnestly to Mike.

Rick was sitting on Karen's other side, and next to him was Sophie.

Rick was clearly making a real effort. He still looked sad, and somewhat distracted, but he had their support. He had the team around him. If he needed them, they wouldn't let him down.

'You see,' Sophie was saying, 'I've already made an Excel spreadsheet of the tasks required regarding the house sale. It's all in order of priority.'

'Of course,' Rick and Karen said in unison.

'It's very straightforward,' Sophie said, 'and as you can see here, I've added the projected numbers to the spreadsheet.'

As Sophie continued to talk, Rick's gaze met Karen's, and he grinned and mouthed, *Help me.*

Karen snorted into her drink. Mike and Arnie looked around, bemused.

'What was that?' Sophie said, looking up.

'Maybe we could do this later, Soph,' Rick said. 'I really appreciate all your help. It's just, you know, we're supposed to be unwinding.'

'Oh yes, sorry,' Sophie said, smiling apologetically, dimples appearing in her cheeks. 'I wasn't thinking. I got a bit carried away. I do like organising.'

'Oh, we know,' Rick said. He put an arm around her shoulders and squeezed. 'And we love you for it. Don't ever change, Sophie. Don't ever change.'

ACKNOWLEDGEMENTS

A huge thank you to my fabulous editor, Leodora Darlington, and the team at Amazon Publishing. It's been a pleasure to work with such a talented group of people.

Special thanks to Russel McLean for his help and invaluable attention to detail over the series.

To my family, thank you for everything. To Chris, thank you for being my first reader. I couldn't ask for a better one.

And finally, most importantly, thank you to the readers who have read and recommended my books. Your kind words and encouragement mean the world to me.

ABOUT THE AUTHOR

 Born in Kent, D. S. Butler grew up as an avid reader with a love for crime fiction and mysteries. She has worked as a scientific officer in a hospital pathology laboratory and as a research scientist. After obtaining a PhD in biochemistry, she worked at the University of Oxford for four years before moving to the Middle East. While living in Bahrain, she wrote her first novel and hasn't stopped writing since. She now lives in Lincolnshire with her husband.

Follow the Author on Amazon

If you enjoyed this book, follow D. S. Butler on Amazon to be notified when the author releases a new book!
To do this, please follow these instructions:

Desktop:

1) Search for the author's name on Amazon or in the Amazon App.
2) Click on the author's name to arrive on their Amazon page.
3) Click the 'Follow' button.

Mobile and Tablet:

1) Search for the author's name on Amazon or in the Amazon App.
2) Click on one of the author's books.
3) Click on the author's name to arrive on their Amazon page.

4) Click the 'Follow' button.

Kindle eReader and Kindle App:
If you enjoyed this book on a Kindle eReader or in the Kindle App, you will find the author 'Follow' button after the last page.